A PHILOSOPHICAL INVESTIGATION

Philip Kerr was bon in Edinburgh in 1956, and lives in London. He is the author of *March Violets*, *The Pale Criminal*, *A German Requiem*, *A Philosophical Investigation*, *Dead Meat* – which was shown on television as *Grushko* – and *Gridiron*. He has also edited two anthologies. His new novel, *Esau*, is published by Chatto & Windus.

BY PHILIP KERR

Philip Kerr

A PHILOSOPHICAL INVESTIGATION

V

VINTAGE

First published in Great Britain by
Chatto & Windus Ltd, 1992

Vintage
Random House, 20 Vauxhall Bridge Road,
London SW1V 2SA

Random House Australia (Pty) Limited
20 Alfred Street, Milsons Point, Sydney
New South Wales 2061, Australia

Random House New Zealand Limited
18 Poland Road, Glenfield,
Auckland 10, New Zealand

Random House South Africa (Pty) Limited
Endulini, 5A Jubilee Road, Parktown 2193, South Africa

Random House UK Limited Reg. No. 954009

A CIP catalogue record for this book
is available from the British Library

ISBN 0 09 976061 4

Papers used by Random House UK Ltd are natural, recyclable products made from wood grown in sustainable forests. The manufacturing processes conform to the environmental regulations of the country of origin

Printed and bound in Great Britain by
Cox & Wyman, Reading, Berkshire

For Jane

The best that I could write would never be more than philosophical remarks; my thoughts were soon crippled if I tried to force them on in any single direction against their natural inclination. – And this was, of course, connected with the very nature of the investigation. For this compels us to travel over a wide field of throught crisscross in every direction.

Ludwig Wittgenstein: *Philosophical Investigations*

There will be time to murder and create,
And time for all the works and days of hands
That lift and drop a question on your plate;

T. S. Eliot: *The Love Song of J. Alfred Prufrock*

1

'The unfortunate victim, twenty-five-year-old Mary Woolnoth, was found naked in the basement of the offices of the Mylae Shipping Company in Jermyn Street, where she had worked for three years as a receptionist, her face beaten in with a claw hammer.

'So severe was the beating that her lower jaw was broken in six places, and almost all of her porcelain-capped teeth pounded loose. Disintegrated fragments of the woman's skull and brain tissue were scattered in the neighbourhood to an extent that was consistent with their newly-acquired momentum. Having recovered the murder weapon it is possible to construct an equation which gives us the kinetic energy of the blow: this is found by multiplying the mass of the weapon by the square of the velocity and dividing the result by two. Using the kinetic energy of each hammer blow, the cranial depth of each fracture, and the angle of depression, the computer has calculated that the killer stands 1.82 metres tall and weighs approximately 85.72 kilograms.

'The poor woman's red silk suspender belt was tied tight around her neck although by this stage she was already dead. A Simpson's store carrier bag was later pulled over the victim's head covering her ruined features from view. Possibly this took place prior to intercourse.

'Using a Christian Dior Crimson Lake lipstick from the victim's handbag, the killer wrote some four-letter abuse onto her bare thighs and stomach. Immediately above the pubic line was written the word "FUCK", while on the underside of her thighs and buttocks was written the word "SHIT". Across each breast was written the word "TIT". Last of all the killer drew a happy smiling face onto the white plastic carrier. I say "last", because there was evidence of the lipstick having crumbled more during this drawing.

'The unhappy victim's vagina contained traces of a latex-based spermicidal compound consistent with the killer wearing a condom prior to intercourse. He was no doubt mindful of the need to avoid DNA profiling. The said spermicidal compound is of a type most used by the RIMFLY brand of prophylactic, commonly used by homosexuals because of its greater strength. In past years we have also found that this is also the average rapist's favourite condom for the same reason.'

Jake opened the file on the table in front of her to examine the photographs. Before looking at them she took a deep breath that she did her best to conceal from the four men, three of whom were detectives, seated around the conference table with her. Her small sham of equanimity was unnecessary, as one of the other detectives did not bother to examine his file of photographs at all. Jake thought this was unjust. A man could always say something about how it was too close to lunch to spoil a good appetite and nobody would mind. There were, however, no such easy excuses for her. Jake felt quite certain that if she didn't look at the photographs now they would say it was because she was a woman. No matter that she had already seen the body when first it had been found. With the exception of the detective who declined to look at the pictures, they had all seen the body.

The fourth man at the table, a scenes-of-crime officer whose name was Dalglish, continued with his oddly sympathetic exposition.

'You will note the poor girl's right leg folded underneath the left leg, the handbag placed carefully by the right elbow, and the spectacles laid a short way distant from the body.'

Jake glanced briefly at each one of the numerically-arranged photographs, a series of white bodies on the low damp ground. The curious arrangement of the legs put her in mind of a Tarot card: the hanged man.

'The contents of the carrier bag were laid carefully on the ground. These included a silk-rayon-mix skirt and a bottle of synthetic perfume, both purchased in the store; and a copy of a novel by Agatha Christie, purchased from the Mystery Bookshop in Sackville Street, Piccadilly, and still in its paper bag. The title of the book was *The Murder of Roger Ackroyd*. But we won't hold that against her.'

'Who? Mary Woolnoth or Agatha Christie?'

Dalglish looked up from his notes and glanced around the table. Unable to determine who it was who had spoken he pursed his lips and shook his head slowly.

'Right then,' he said finally. 'Who'll open the bidding?'

After a short silence, the detective seated on Jake's right, the one who had made the remark, raised a grimy forefinger.

'I'd like to claim this one,' he said tentatively. 'For a start there's the killer's M.O. – ' He shrugged as if nothing else needed to be said about it.

Dalglish started typing onto his laptop computer. 'You're the – ?'

'Hackney Hammerer,' said the owner of the grimy forefinger.

'All right,' said Dalglish thoughtfully. 'That's one for the Hackney Hammerer.' But a second detective was already shaking his head.

'You can't be serious,' he said to the first detective. 'Look, Jermyn Street is well off your man's patch. Miles away. No, this is one of mine, I'm quite sure of it. This woman was a receptionist, right? Well we all know that the Motorcycle Messenger has already killed several receptionists and I don't think that there can be any reasonable doubt that this Mary Woolnoth is his latest victim.'

Dalglish typed again. 'So,' he said, 'you're claiming her as well then.'

3

'You bet I am.'

The first detective was pulling a face.

'I don't know why you're claiming her, really I don't. The Messenger always uses a blade. That's his M.O. So why should he suddenly start using a hammer? That's what I'd like to know.'

The second detective shrugged and looked out of the window. The wind gusted violently against the glass and for once Jake felt glad to be in a meeting at New Scotland Yard.

'Yes well why should the Hammerer suddenly decide to move up west? Just answer me that.'

'Because he probably knows we've got the whole of Hackney under surveillance. If he so much as bangs his own thumb over there we'll have him.'

Jake decided that it was time for her to speak.

'You're both wrong,' she said firmly.

'I suppose you're going to claim this as one of yours,' said the second detective.

'Well of course I am,' she said. 'It ought to be obvious to an idiot that this is the work of the Lipstick Man. We know he preys on girls who wear red lipstick. We know he uses their lipsticks to write abuse on their bodies. We know that for whatever reason, he's careful always to put the handbag by the right elbow, and that he uses RIMFLY condoms. Of course I'm claiming Mary Woolnoth.' She shook her head with irritation. 'I just can't believe the way you're fighting over this girl, like she was some kind of prize. Jesus, you should hear yourselves, really you should.'

The first detective looked up from trying to thumbnail some of the dirt off his forefinger and shook his head back at her. 'When did the Lipstick Man ever use a hammer to kill his victims? When did he ever put a bag over their heads? Never. That's my man's M.O.'

'And when has this Hammerer ever so much as indicated that he even knows how to write – let alone with a lipstick?'

'Maybe he read about it in the papers?'

'Oh come on,' said Jake. 'You know better than that. All special features of a killer's *modus operandi* are held back from the papers for precisely that reason.'

Anticipating some further argument from the second detective, Jake turned to face him, and added, 'The fact that this girl happened also to be a receptionist is purely coincidental.'

'It may be convenient for you to look at it that way, Chief Inspector Jakowicz,' he said. 'But if you'll think about it for just a minute longer you'll remember what you're so often telling the rest of us. Multiples tend to pre-select a type of victim to murder and then stick with it. Whereas the M.O. can vary a great deal, depending on the killer's level of confidence, which is itself a factor of how many people he's killed.'

'I don't think you can ever properly define a type of victim by profession,' argued Jake. 'Her age and physical appearance are what count most of all. And for what it's worth, I've never been all that convinced by your theory that the Messenger is predisposed to kill only receptionists. As I recall, one of his early victims was an office cleaner. Moreover he has never attempted to penetrate any of them, with or without a condom.'

Jake felt herself flush with anger. She made a fist and tried to hold on to her temper. The fact that Mary Woolnoth had once been a beautiful young woman with her whole future in front of her seemed to have escaped her two colleagues. She stared balefully at the third detective, the one who had declined to examine Mary Woolnoth's forensic photographs and who, until now, had remained silent.

'What about you?' she snapped. 'Are you in the game or not? You'd better put up now, or keep out.' It was indeed, she considered, like some ghastly game of poker.

The man raised his hands in surrender.

'No, not mine, this one,' he said. Looking around the table he added, 'But for what it's worth, I agree with the

Chief Inspector. This looks to me like the work of the Lipstick Man.'

'I must say, I agree,' said Dalglish.

The first detective pulled another face.

'Come off it, George,' said Dalglish. 'Look, I know you're desperate for a lead, but this isn't it, I'm certain. Your Hammerer's never once murdered outside of Hackney.'

The second detective remained resolutely unconvinced.

'Receptionists, typists, cleaners,' he said moodily. 'Fact is, they all work in an office. We know that's the way the Messenger selects his victims. He kills them while he's making a delivery.' He paused for a moment and then added, 'Look I'd still like Mary Woolnoth as a possible.'

Dalglish glanced at Jake who shrugged back at him.

'Provided my man gets the first credit for this kill, I've no objections,' she said. 'And if there are any developments, I'll be sure to let you know.'

Dalglish returned to his computer. 'All right then, we're agreed,' he said. 'That's number – ?'

'– six,' said Jake.

'Number six for the Lipstick Man.'

After the meeting Jake stopped the detective who had supported her claim, to thank him.

'That's all right, ma'am,' he said.

'Detective Inspector Stanley, isn't it?'

He nodded.

'Forgive me,' she said, 'but as Head of Gynocide, I'm supposed to know all the cases of multiple murders involving females – '

Stanley lowered his voice and glanced over his shoulder. 'Actually, I'm Homicide, ma'am,' he said. 'Really I shouldn't have been there at all, only there was a bit of a mix-up. Somehow we received information that it was a man, not a girl who had been found. I'm looking for a multiple who's killed seven men. Well, I didn't want to say anything in case I looked stupid.'

Jake nodded. That explained why he hadn't bothered to examine the photographs.

'As it happens,' Stanley added, 'I found it quite fascinating. Are these meetings always like this?'

'You mean, do we always squabble about whether a body belongs to this or that investigation? No, not often. Usually, things are a little more clear cut than today.'

As she spoke, Jake thought of the pictures of Mary Woolnoth and of what the pathologist's scalpel had done to her. You couldn't get more clear cut than that, she reflected. For a moment something started to rise in her throat. No murder was ever quite as brutal as what took place on the autopsy slab. A clear cut, from chin to pelvis, the skeleton and the organs hauled out of the flesh, like a suitcase ransacked by customs at the airport. She choked back her emotions with another question.

'A multiple who preys on men. That's quite unusual, isn't it?'

Detective Inspector Stanley agreed that it was.

'I presume that this would be the Lombroso Killer that we're referring to?'

He nodded.

'I thought Detective Chief Superintendent Challis was in charge of that investigation.'

'He is,' said Stanley. 'It was him who sent me along to this meeting. Just to check that it wasn't one of ours.'

'What's his M.O.?'

'Who, the Lombroso Killer? Oh, nothing particularly unusual. He always shoots them in the back of the head. Six times. Mafia-style. Why do you ask?'

Jake shook her head. 'No reason. Just curious I suppose.' She looked at her watch. 'Well I must be going. I have a plane to catch. Not to mention my own multiple.'

I always shoot them in the head, and it's not just because I want to make sure of the job. I think it's because the head, theirs and mine, is where all the trouble started: theirs and mine.

I don't think they can feel very much. Of course it's hard for me to say, only they rarely make a sound. That much I can be sure of because the gun is so quiet. Six bullets in six seconds, with no more report than a short fit of coughing. Actually, that's not precisely true since there is also the distinctive sharp crack of the successful head shot, which is very different from the sound of a bullet piercing an ear. I imagine that this is the sort of thing you would just not notice if you were using a conventional gun, which makes a lot more noise.

While working I tend to concentrate my fire at the back of the head. If you know anything about the brain and its topography you will be aware that cortical vents are so widely dispersed that, short of using something like a steam-roller, no brain injury can destroy them entirely. There is however a great deal of medical evidence to show that people survive frontal brain damage more often than any damage to the rear of the brain. Witness the number of boxers who die, not from a hard blow to the forehead, but when they hit the backs of their heads on the canvas. Believe me it's true, I've read a lot about it, as you might perhaps expect under the circumstances. Seen something of it too.

The human brain may be compared to a chess board, with the pawns to the forefront and the knights, bishops, rooks, king and queen, the so-called pieces on the eighth rank at the back of the board. Thus it may be said that

I more or less ignore the pawns and try to eliminate as many pieces as possible. This strategy seems to work very well. Even so, one of my victims, I believe it may have been the third, survived in a coma for several days before he finally died. There's no accounting for cerebral asymmetries.

Most often, I perform these executions at night, or when working hours permit. This follows a short period of surveillance when I establish the victim's identity and his habits. Possession of a comfortable vehicle with music and microwave minimises any inconvenience that might be occasioned by such an operation.

You would be surprised how regular are the comings and goings of most people's lives. And so, usually, it's only a matter of following my target a distance away from his place of domicile and, at a suitable place, killing him.

I am avoiding the use of words like crime, assassination and murder for the obvious reasons. Words can have different significations. Language disguises thought, to the extent that sometimes it is not possible to determine the mental action which inspired it. So for now I will simply say that these are executions. It is true that they are not given the official sanction of law in any socially-contractual sense. All the same, this word 'execution' goes a long way to avoiding any tendency to pejorate what is after all my life's work.

When I got closer to him I realised that he was a little taller than I had thought. Almost two metres. For the evening he wore yet another change of clothing. But it was more than that somehow. He seemed to embrace so many different fashions during the course of one day that one could have been forgiven for thinking that he had a brother or two. His walk was distinctive, however. Too distinctive to mistake him for someone else. He moved partly on tiptoe which lent him a nefarious air, as if he were hurrying from the scene of some dreadful deed.

More like hurrying to commit one, I thought at the

9

time. It's only a matter of time before neuronal connectivity makes itself apparent, for him just as for me. Freedom consists in the impossibility of knowing actions that still lie in the future. But neither one of us was truly subordinate to his will. And the fact that all I could wish for is happening now can only be a favour granted by fate, so to speak. If I can alter something, I can alter only the limits of the world.

By removing him from it.

He turned into the High Street and for a brief moment I lost sight of him. What would he have seen if, like Tam O'Shanter, he looked back? No, that's much too prosaic. It's not that I meant to scare him, or to drag him down to hell. This is something that has to be done without malice. This merely corresponds with logic. Even God cannot do anything that would be contrary to the laws of logic. But one takes a certain pleasure in a logical method, for this endows meaning.

I caught him up as he tripped off to the right, down a long cobbled alleyway that led to the pub where normally he would drink several litres of the brew he considered to be palatable. Only this time it led to the moment which would not be an event in his life and which he was never meant to experience.

The gas-gun felt big and powerful in my hand as I pointed it at the back of his head. I do not understand this weapon's kinetic properties except to say that they are formidable in something that is freely available over the counter, no licence required. Nothing like the air-gun I owned as a small boy.

Two of the shots were fired even before his knees had started to buckle. I waited until he hit the ground before emptying the rest of the clip into him at rather closer range. Not much blood, but it was immediately clear to me that the man, whose Lombrosogiven identity was Charles Dickens, was dead. Then I holstered my weapon underneath my leather jacket and walked quickly away.

I never cared all that much for Dickens. The real

Dickens that is, the English language's greatest novelist. Give me Balzac, Stendhal, Flaubert any day of the 168-hour week. But mostly I avoid novels altogether and prefer to read about the essence of the world, about the relative unimportance of and yet the possibilities for the individual case, of that which exists between the empirical and the formal, of the clarification of propositions. And there's not much of that in Charles Dickens.

There's not much of anything except the deaths of Little Nell and Nancy and Dora Copperfield, and both Pip's and Oliver's mothers. Not very safe being one of Dickens's women. Not much I can do about that now. But at least now that the other Charles Dickens is dead, perhaps things will be that little bit safer for women everywhere. Of course, they'll never know this. That's unfortunate. But what we cannot speak about we must pass over in silence.

2

THE THIRD EUROPEAN COMMUNITY SYMPOSIUM ON TECHNIQUES OF LAW ENFORCEMENT AND CRIMINAL INVESTIGATION, HERBERT MARCUSE CENTRE, FRANKFURT, GREATER GERMAN REICH, 13.00 HOURS, 13 FEBRUARY 2013. SPEAKER: DETECTIVE CHIEF INSPECTOR ISADORA JAKOWICZ, M.SC, LONDON. METROPOLITAN POLICE FORCE. MEMBER COUNTRY: UK. TITLE OF TEXT: INCREASE OF THE HOLLYWOOD MURDER.

It is Saturday evening, towards the beginning of the millennium. The wife is in bed. There are no children. You switch on the Nicamvision, settle your spectacles on your nose and select a videodisc. A Chinese takeaway and a few bottles of Japanese lager have put you in just the right mood. Your nicotine-free cigarettes are by your side, the futon cushions are soft beneath you, the central heating is on, and the air is warm and pleasantly deionised. In these blissful circumstances what kind of disc is it that you want to watch? Naturally it's one about a murder. But what kind of murder?

Sixty years ago, George Orwell described what would be, from an English newspaper's point of view, 'the perfect murder'. 'The murderer,' he wrote, 'should be a little man of the professional class. He should go astray through cherishing a guilty passion for his secretary or the wife of a rival professional man, and should only bring himself to the point of murder after long and terrible wrestles with his conscience. Having decided on murder, he should plan it with all the utmost cunning and slip up over some tiny unforeseen detail. The means chosen should, of course, be poison.'

Arguing the decline of this, the archetypal English murder, Orwell pointed to the case of Karl Hulten, an American Army deserter who, inspired by the false values of American cinema, wantonly murdered a taxi-driver for the sum of eight pounds sterling – about EC$3.

That the most-talked about murder of the last years of the Second World War was this, the so-called Cleft Chin Murder, and that it should have been committed by an American, was a cause of some regret to the curiously patriotic Orwell. For him, Hulten's 'meaningless' crime could not begin to compare with the typically English murder which was 'the product of a stable society where the all-prevailing hypocrisy did at least ensure that crimes as serious as murder should have strong emotions behind them.'

Today, however, crimes like Hulten's, pitiful, sordid and without much emotion behind them, are relatively commonplace. 'Good murders', of the kind that might have entertained the *News of the World* reader of Orwell's day, are still committed. But these are of little interest to the public at large in comparison with the apparently motiveless kind of murder that has become the norm.

Nowadays, people are routinely murdered, often for no obvious reason. Just over half a century after Orwell's death, society finds itself subject to a virtual epidemic of recreational murder, which is the work of a breed of killer even more purposeless than the comparatively innocent Karl Hulten. Indeed, were Hulten's case to occur today, his crimes would rate no more than a couple of paragraphs in the local newspaper. It might seem incomprehensible to us in the year 2013 that the case of the Cleft Chin Murder should have been, as Orwell tells us, 'the principal *cause célèbre* of the war years'.

With all this in mind, one can construct, as Orwell does, what would be, from the modern *News of the World* reader's point of view, today's 'good murder'. He might refer us to the videodisc he had been watching that

Saturday night. The murderer would be a young and maladjusted man living somewhere in the suburbs, surrounded by his unwitting potential victims. Our chosen killer should have gone astray through some fault of his mother, thus firmly attaching the real blame for the murders to a woman. Having decided on murder the killer should not restrict himself to the one homicide, but should dispatch as many victims as possible. The means chosen should be extremely violent and sadistic, preferably with some sexual, ritualistic, or possibly even anthropophagous aspect. Those killed should most often be young attractive women and their deaths should occur while they are undressing, taking a shower, masturbating, or having intercourse. Only with this kind of background, the Hollywood style of background, can a murder have the dramatic and even tragic qualities which will make it memorable in the present day.

It's no accident that a significant percentage of the murders committed in modern Europe have an element of this Hollywood atmosphere.

One of the traditional motifs of the Hollywood murder, and what brings me to the point of my speech, is the male-bonding which frequently occurs between male law-enforcement personnel and their homicidal quarry. Since this conference is taking place here in Frankfurt, in the Herbert Marcuse Centre, it's worth reminding ourselves of what the Frankfurt School of Social Science and Marcuse himself had to say about this kind of behaviour.

For Marcuse, the one-dimensional patriarchal society was characterised by examples of what he called 'the unification of opposites': a unification which served to deter social change at an intellectual level by enclosing consciousness in a masculine and, therefore, one-dimensional way. The historical domination of law-enforcement agencies by men is merely one aspect of this monolithic and homogeneous view. Until comparatively recently the average murder inquiry placed little or no reliance on the specifically feminine qualities.

The behaviourists and psychologists tell us that hormones undoubtedly play a major part in organising male and female characteristics in the brain. Whereas, for instance, men tend to think spatially in terms of distances and measurement, women on the other hand tend to think in terms of signs and landmarks. Women are much better than men at focusing on their immediate surroundings, which may actually make them superior to men in the matter of the observation of fine detail. Thus the usefulness of women to any criminal investigation, especially an inquiry where there exists a wealth of forensic detail such as the Hollywood-style murder, should be obvious. Other specifically feminine qualities such as non-violence, emotional capacity and receptivity may also be mentioned as having investigative utility.

During the early 1990s, computer analysis of the twentieth century's inquiries into multiple-killings enabled British statistical criminologists to determine that those inquiries which included a woman among their senior personnel had a much higher rate of success in apprehending the culprit than those inquiry teams which did not include a female police officer.

As a result of this study, a Home Office Select Committee made a number of recommendations to the Metropolitan Police Commissioner, Sir MacDonald McDuff, which sought to increase the representation of female police officers in all serious crime investigations, but with particular regard to the Hollywood style of gynocide. Five years ago these recommendations were adopted, with the result that a female of at least Detective Sergeant rank must now be included in any investigation where a recreational killer may be responsible, thereby ensuring an improved, more two-dimensional approach to the inquiry.

The results speak for themselves. During the 1980s, when there existed no such sex-representation guideline

15

and women accounted for less than 2 per cent of the senior personnel investigating the Hollywood-style gynocide, there was an arrest made in only 46 per cent of cases. During the late 1990s and the first decade of the twenty-first century, where there existed such a gender guideline and women accounted for 44 per cent of senior police personnel in this type of gynocide, an arrest was made in 73 per cent of all cases.

Of course the last ten years have also seen some substantial improvements in law-enforcement and forensic detection technology which has partly helped to explain this dramatic increase in the performance of British murder inquiries. Not the least of these has been the adoption, throughout the EC, of identity cards with barcodes and genetic fingerprints. However even when developments such as these are statistically discounted, it seems probable that the British experiment with sex guidelines for police investigations has achieved an overall increase in successful arrests of at least 20 per cent.

No doubt you are comparing the gender guideline with that figure of only 44 per cent of senior police personnel being women. Perhaps you are saying 'why not 100 per cent?' Well the new two-dimensional approach has been hindered by the small numbers of women who are in positions of relative seniority within the force. However, I am pleased to be able to report that all this is now changing with the advent of recruitment drives among British women, new pay scales, crèche facilities, and improved career structures. So it is hoped that before very long, a policewoman of the rank of Detective Sergeant or above will be included in every inquiry relating to a Hollywood-style gynocide.

That represents the view from the bridge. My own experience has been largely on deck. George Orwell mentioned nine cases of murder which he considered to have stood the test of time. Coincidentally I myself have been involved in nine investigations of murder. I doubt that any of them will stand something as mythologising as a test of time. I certainly hope that they do not. But there is one case which I do propose to describe to you as an example of the investigative two-dimensionality I've been referring to.

On the face of it we were presented with a fairly typical case of Hollywood gynocide. A maniac was terrorising the women of a university town in southern England, killing eight women within as many months. His *modus operandi* was to beat his victim unconscious, drag her to some quiet, secluded spot where he would strangle her, and then gratify himself in her lifeless mouth. Perhaps the strangest feature of the case, and what partly distinguished it from the more usual kind of recreational killing, was that when he had finished he would insert two batteries into the dead woman's vagina.

Male colleagues working on the case adopted a typical phallocentric view of this last item of behaviour, as was clear from the nickname they soon gave to the killer: the Everready Man. Familiar as they were with the kind of pornography in which foreign objects are routinely inserted into a woman *ab vaginam* as penis substitutes, these male police officers saw little that was particularly significant about two dry-cell alkaline batteries. And beyond making a few enquiries among the town's electrical retailers, these police officers made no real attempt to try and comprehend this, the most unusual feature of the murderer's working method. There was even a tacit assumption among them all that the batteries were dead – the sub-text of this being the thought that nobody would waste a good battery on something like a dead woman's vagina.

It was female police personnel working on the case who first thought of establishing whether or not these were new batteries. In fact, we later discovered that they were purchased specially for the murders. It was also our theory, also verified after the killer was in custody, that there was nothing at all phallic about the insertion of batteries into the woman's vagina; and that having rendered the woman lifeless for his sexual purposes, the killer then sought to bring her back to life, to re-energise her with a fresh source of power, like a portable disc player.

Yet another unusual feature of the case, and what once again illustrates the two-dimensionality of including women in all serial gynocide investigations, was the significance of the times when all the victims were killed. It was always between 10.30 and 11.30 at night.

I'll return to this fact in just a moment. But first let me go back to the beginning of the investigation when, as a matter of routine, the names of all sex offenders in the area during the previous twelve months were called up on the computer. Police constables questioned these men with a view to establishing their alibis. (I should also add here that this case took place prior to the inclusion of the genetic fingerprint on identity cards.) One man in particular, a twenty-nine-year-old male who had tried to rape a woman in a park where subsequently one of the murder victims was found, drew the interest of the male officer leading the inquiry. Meanwhile, I and another officer continued to make enquiries among the area's previous sex-offenders.

It was while questioning a forty-two-year-old single man called David Boysfield, convicted of exposing himself in a local department store, that I noticed several copies of one particular issue of a woman's magazine. Perhaps it is significant that my male colleague did not notice this. Not that there is anything wrong with a man reading a woman's magazine. But all the same it made me curious to find out just a little more about Boysfield. And when I looked up the facts of his case it appeared that he had been in the store's electrical department when the indecent exposure took place. What was even more interesting was the evidence of one witness which seemed to indicate that Boysfield had not exposed himself in the direction of the female members of staff, but to a number of television screens.

By now I was really curious and checking back through the television company's broadcast sheets of the day of the offence, I discovered that a programme featuring a well-known television newsreader, Anna Kreisler, had been broadcast around the time that Boysfield was in the store. Indeed the programme was devoted to raising money for charity and at one stage Anna Kreisler had stripped naked for a telephonic pledge of one million EC dollars. It was Anna Kreisler who had also appeared on the front cover of the magazines I had seen in Boysfield's apartment. More checking now revealed that she had been reading the ten o'clock news on every night when the killer had struck.

Obtaining a search warrant for the suspect's home I found a number of pornographic magazines in which cut-outs of Ms Kreisler's head had been glued onto other naked female torsos. I also found a personal televideodisc which Boysfield had used to watch his own custom-made pornographic movies using intercut footage of Ms Kreisler reading the news. And a masturbatory sex-mannequin, with Ms Kreisler's voice, recorded off television, and a battery-powered suction-operated vagina. Both the videodisc player and the mannequin were found to be fitted with the same brand of batteries that had been found inside all eight murder victims. It appeared that, for want of a better term, Boysfield was a gadget freak. His apartment was full of electrical appliances of every conceivable kind. Everything from an electric bottle opener, to an electric clothes-brush, and an electric fish-filleter. It was quite clear that in Boysfield's gadget-run world, women had been reduced to the status of mere domestic electrical appliances.

A forensic DNA profile subsequently confirmed that Boysfield had restriction fragment length polymorphisms that were identical with the killer's. He later confessed that he had killed all eight women after watching Anna Kreisler read the TV news. Obsessed with her, he had for a long time satisfied himself by exposing himself to

Kreisler's head as it appeared on his own high definition television screen. He fantasised about having oral sex with her, and so when after a while he could contain himself no longer and he started to attack women, he sought to ejaculate within the mouths of his victims. Boysfield was able to escape a sentence of punitive coma by virtue of the fact that his insertion of the batteries into the vaginas of his victims was deemed to have proved that he could not have had an intention permanently to deprive them of life. Boysfield is now detained indefinitely in an asylum for the criminally insane.

Of course, two-dimensionality works two ways. Just in case any of you were under the impression that I don't think too highly of my male colleagues, I should like to say this: only a few weeks ago, in a situation that I myself had completely misjudged, it was only the quick-thinking of a male colleague which prevented me from being killed or seriously injured. Incidentally this was the same colleague who accompanied me to Boysfield's apartment and failed to notice the women's magazines there.

Earlier on I described the incidence of the Hollywood-style gynocide as a virtual epidemic. I did not exaggerate. European Bureau of Investigation statistics show that serial sex-killings in the EC have increased dramatically, by over 700 per cent, since 1950. Last year there were an estimated 4,000 such murders in the Community, comprising over 20 per cent of all Europe's homicides for the year. Not only that, but the EBI estimates that even now there are at the very least 25 and possibly as many as 90 active killers of this type roaming the EC.

People still talk about Peter Sutcliffe, the so-called Yorkshire Ripper, who killed thirteen women during the 1970s, and Jack the Ripper, who killed six. But there are people out there now killing twenty or thirty people, or more. And while the victims continue predominantly to be female, it behoves women everywhere not to leave it to men to try and put a stop to it.

Of the other seventeen Community members, only

Denmark, Sweden, Holland and Germany show any signs of adopting the British model of the two-dimensional gynocidal inquiry. To those other member countries whose police forces remain resolutely patriarchal, not to say macho, I say this: unless you wish forever to categorise women as potential victims, you must permit them to abandon whatever submissive role you have historically kept them in, so that they may become joint custodians of our society's future health. Thank you.

The audience applauded politely as Jake finished her speech and having acknowledged the applause for no longer than seemed modest, she stepped down from the rostrum and returned to her seat. The conference chairman, a fat German bureaucrat with an expensively-cut pink suit that did a great deal to disguise his bulk, came back to the microphone.

'Thank you, Chief Inspector,' he said in English. Some of the women in the audience, enthusiastic for Jake's brand of feminism, continued clapping for another minute which obliged the chairman to pause before adding, 'That was most informative.'

'Yes indeed it was,' said Mark Woodford, as Jake found her seat beside him. 'A little strident in some parts, but I suppose that's only to be expected considering the subject matter.' He glanced around the auditorium uncertainly and chuckled. 'Even welcomed.'

'I'm sorry?'

Woodford's smooth English features took on a devious aspect as he folded his arms and stared up at the vaulted mosaic ceiling, reminiscent of some early-Christian basilica, except that the scene depicted was a modern one reflecting Frankfurt's history: Charlemagne, Goethe, the Rothschilds, and Marcuse all meeting up in one uneasy group against a sky-blue background, as if they had been waiting for God to put in an appearance and offer judgment.

Jake regarded Woodford's aquiline, inbred-looking and horizontal profile. Was there not some resemblance there to the King? she asked herself.

'It's always nice to show the French, the Italians, and the Spaniards lagging behind us in something or other,' he murmured. ' "Patriarchal, not to say macho." Yes, I liked that.' His head dropped forward again as he caught sight of his Minister out of the bottom of his eye.

'Ah now it's the Minister's turn. This should be good, don't you think?' He pointed to the title of the lecture as it appeared in the program resting on his thigh. ' "Retribution: the theme for a new century." That should get 'em going.'

Jake nodded but stayed silent. She didn't much care for the Minister's Old Testament view of crime and punishment. No more than she cared for the Minister's private secretary.

Woodford glanced at the empty seat beside him as the Minister, a tall handsome black woman wearing a well-tailored lilac suit, joined the German at the microphone. In their expensive, pastel-coloured outfits they looked like two exotic cage birds.

'Gilmour's going to miss this,' remarked Woodford. 'If he's not careful.'

Jake leaned forwards on her chair to look across Woodford's negligible stomach. Until now she had not noticed that Gilmour was absent from his seat.

'Where is he?' she asked.

'File a message on his portable computer and see if you can find out what's keeping him.'

Jake retrieved her shoulder bag from the floor and took out her own PC. She unfolded the envelope-sized screen and tapped out Gilmour's name and number on the miniature keyboard. After only a few seconds the word 'responding' appeared on the grey-green glass.

'Woodford wants to know what's keeping you,' Jake typed. 'Minister's about to start speech. Sure you wouldn't want to miss it.'

'Indeed not,' came the silent and, Jake suspected, sarcastic reply. 'But looks as if another man from the Lombroso Program been murdered. Need to make some calls.'

Mark Woodford, reading over Jake's shoulder, sighed and shook his head. 'She's not going to like this,' he said quietly as the Minister cleared her throat and took hold of the lectern. 'Better tell your APC to set up a pictophone conference with the UK. I want the officer in charge of the case on the satellite as soon as possible.'

Jake typed out what the Minister's secretary had said and, motivated exclusively by a desire to escape what was coming, added her own offer of help. She sent the message and watched the blinking cursor expectantly.

'No thanks,' came Gilmour's reply. 'You stay and enjoy Mrs Miles's lecture.'

Out of the corner of her eye Jake checked to see that Woodford was not looking over her shoulder. But all his thoughts were for his Minister now, with a face that was as proud and attentive as a parent at a school nativity play. Jake wrote, 'Lucky old me', sent the message and then returned the PC to her bag.

Jake had the impression that Grace Miles MP didn't much care for her. The Junior Home Office Minister seemed to be one of those women who preferred only male colleagues and, since there were eight male bureaucrats in the Police Department responsible for scrutinising the activities of 45,000 employees at the Yard, on matters of law enforcement at least, any such preference would have been easily accommodated.

Gilmour's decision to choose Jake to accompany him to the conference had, she suspected, been as much inspired by a desire to irritate Mrs Miles as by the wish to demonstrate the equal opportunities of the Metropolitan Police Force. He had warned Jake it would be difficult. Now she knew why. Gilmour had told Jake that it had been the Minister's own wish that Jake's speech should precede her own, in the disappointed expectation that she would make a mess of it, leaving Mrs Miles to provide a comparatively expert demonstration of how to handle a conference.

In the event the Minister's account of the failure of deterrence as a suitable basis for a modern theory of law enforcement did not meet with the enthusiastic response she had expected, leaving everyone with the distinct impression that she had been upstaged by a mere police officer. And so Jake was not deceived by Mrs Miles's appreciation of her efforts when they saw each other again at the meeting which Gilmour had convened at Woodford's instruction.

'A very good effort, Chief Inspector,' said Mrs Miles as she took her place at the head of the table. 'Sounds to me as if you must have been on one of these public-speaking courses for beginners.'

'You flatter me, ma'am,' said Jake, adroitly, knowing that had not been her intention.

Mrs Miles smiled vaguely in the hope that the ambiguity of her remark might linger with Jake a little. But Jake, seating herself beside the Assistant Police Commissioner, ignored it.

Mark Woodford nodded at Jake and Gilmour, then introduced the man who had followed him into the room, and was now closing the door behind him.

'I'm sure we all know Professor Waring,' he said. 'I've asked him to join us because of his keen interest in all aspects of the Lombroso Program.'

That was understating it, thought Jake. Waring was Professor of Forensic Psychiatry at Cambridge University and the Government's principal advisor on crime prevention strategies. It had been Waring who had chaired the committee which produced the report recommending the Lombroso Program's implementation.

'Yes, of course,' said Gilmour. 'I should have thought to invite you.'

Waring shook his head at the APC as if to say that these smaller etiquettes were of no consequence to him.

Woodford consulted his wristwatch and nodded at the empty flickering screen of the pictophone. 'What time are we expecting the call?' he asked Gilmour.

The APC checked his own watch. 'About two minutes from now,' he said. 'Detective Superintendent Colin Bowles of the Birmingham City Police will be making the report.'

'Birmingham?' Mrs Miles said tersely. 'Did you say Birmingham?'

'That's right, ma'am.'

'Exactly where in Birmingham was the body found?' she demanded impatiently.

'Well until I've heard Bowles's report . . .' Gilmour shrugged.

'The Minister's constituency is in Birmingham,' explained Woodford.

The pictophone buzzed loudly. Gilmour, holding the remote control, pressed a button and a bald man, aged about fifty and still straightening his tie, came onto the screen. The small camera lens on top of the set in Frankfurt began to turn as it automatically focused on a wide shot of everyone seated round the table.

'Make your report, Superintendent,' said Gilmour.

Bowles's eyes flicked between the sheet of paper in his hands and the camera lens on top of his own pictophone set. When he started to speak there was hardly any sound.

Mrs Miles groaned. 'The bloody idiot's still got the secrecy button switched on.'

Bowles coloured. The Minister might not have heard him, but he had certainly heard her. He picked up his own remote control and pressed a button. 'Sorry about that,' he said. Then he cleared his throat and started to read again.

'At approximately ten o'clock last night, the body of a thirty-five-year-old male Caucasian was found lying in an alley in Selly Oak Village.'

The Minister swore. Jake, who was aware that the Minister's constituency was Selly Oak, cheered inside herself. Superintendent Bowles, faltering, glanced back at the camera uncertainly.

'It's all right,' Woodford said smoothly. 'Proceed with your report.'

'Sir. The man had been shot six times in the back of the head between the hours of nine and nine-thirty. Following an examination of the body and the immediate vicinity by scenes-of-crime officers, the body was taken away for forensic examination. The pathologist subsequently removed six .44 calibre conical-conoidal air bullets, each weighing approximately forty grams and fired from a high-powered gas-gun at a range of less than ten metres. Death was more or less instantaneous.

'The man was later identified as Sean Andrew Hill of Selly Oak Road, Birmingham. When the deceased's particulars were entered onto the police computer at Kidlington HQ, the Lombroso computer automatically indicated that this was a person who had tested VMN-negative, codenamed Charles Dickens. This, and the killer's *modus operandi*, leads us now to suppose that Hill was another victim of the same person who murdered Henry Lam, Craig Edward Brownlow, Richard Graham Swanson, Joseph Arthur Middlemass . . .'

'Thank you, Superintendent,' Gilmour interrupted. 'There's no need to read the whole list.'

'Superintendent,' said Woodford. 'Have your scenes-of-crime people found anything?' He pursed his lips and shook his head as if trying to find something to prompt Bowles. 'Clues?'

'Clues?' Bowles looked pained at the very mention of the word. 'No, sir, we haven't found any of those.'

'And what about witnesses?' he continued. 'Did anyone see or hear anything?'

Bowles smiled nervously as if suddenly aware that he was speaking to someone who had only the vaguest idea of what he was asking. 'Unlikely they'll have heard anything, sir,' he said. 'As I said before, the killer used a gas-gun to murder his victim. It's totally silent.' He nodded slowly. 'But it's early days and we're still making our enquiries.'

'Yes, of course.' Woodford glanced around the table. 'Anyone else?'

'Perhaps the Detective Chief Inspector,' the Minister said helpfully. 'This is your field of expertise, isn't it? What was that curiously tabloid phrase you employed in your lecture? "The Hollywood-style murder", wasn't it?'

Jake sat up in her chair. 'With respect, ma'am, that refers exclusively to the recreational murder of women.'

'But this is a case of recreational murder,' Mrs Miles insisted. 'I can't see that it matters much whether it's a man or a woman. Surely there must be some common denominators?'

'I have no questions for the Superintendent,' Jake said firmly.

'Thank you, Superintendent, that will be all for the moment.'

Gilmour's thumb ended the satellite link and for a moment the room was silent.

Jake appraised her surroundings. It was the kind of all too common meeting-room in which comfort had yielded to colour, geometry and functionality. The kind of room that made her feel like a plastic toy in some architect's model. She wouldn't have been at all surprised to have looked out of a window and seen tree-foliage that was made of foam rubber.

'How many is it now, Mr Gilmour?' asked Mrs Miles.

'This makes the eighth killing, in as many months.'

'I'm sure I don't have to remind you of just how sensitive a matter this could become.'

'No indeed, Minister.'

'The Lombroso Program has cost millions of dollars,' she continued. 'True, it's just part of the increased spending on law enforcement and crime prevention to which, time and again, this Government has committed itself.

But it is perhaps the flagship of that general policy. It would be unfortunate if the Program had to be interrupted or even scrapped because of this maniac.'

'Quite so, Minister.'

'I cannot sufficiently underline just how electorally damaging it might be if the press were to make this thing public,' she said. 'The fact that the Lombroso Program itself is the only common factor in eight murders. You can see that, can't you?'

Gilmour nodded.

'But we can only keep the press off it for so long. Journalists have a nasty habit of going up against Government on this kind of thing. Even if it is something that's covered by the Secrecy and Information Act.'

She glanced at Professor Waring who was occupied in the creation of an elaborate doodle on the triangular-shaped blotter in front of him.

'And what do your inkblots tell us this time, Norman?' she said crisply.

Waring continued with his doodle for a few seconds. He spoke slowly.

'We've gone a little way past using the perception of unstructured forms as a diagnostic tool,' he said punctiliously, adding a wry smile to the remark.

'I want some ideas, Norman,' she said. 'If this psycho stops the Program your research might find it never recovers from the shock. If you receive my meaning.'

Waring shrugged with frustration. 'With all due respect, Minister, we don't yet know that he is a psycho.' He looked meaningfully at Gilmour. 'No more than the police know how to catch him. I've spoken about this matter with Professor Gleitmann on many occasions and he still has no idea how such a breach of security might have occurred. I myself am unable to imagine how such a thing might even be possible.'

'Nevertheless,' the Minister insisted, 'it has happened.'

There followed another uncomfortable silence. This time it was Jake who ended it.

'If I might make a suggestion – '

'Yes, well that's why we're all here, Chief Inspector.'

'Surely the fact remains that somehow a breach of the Lombroso Program's security has occurred, whether one likes it or not. As I see it, the priority must be to establish whether that breach occurred from within or from without. Only when that question has been answered can an investigation properly proceed.'

Professor Waring returned to his doodle. 'Chief Inspector,' he said. 'How much do you know about the Program?'

Jake shrugged. 'Only what I've read in the newspapers, and seen on television.'

Waring began to score aggressively at the centre of his drawing. 'Then have you any idea what it is that you are suggesting? The Lombroso computer system is highly sophisticated. To suggest, as blithely as you do, that it might be possible to breach the system's security is almost as nonsensical as the idea that one of Gleitmann's own staff could have something to do with this whole dreadful business.'

'Nonsensical or not, sir, those are the only two logical possibilities.'

Waring snorted and shook his head impatiently. The doodle was starting to look more like an engraving.

'What would you do, Chief Inspector Jakowicz?' asked Mark Woodford. 'If it was you who was in charge of this particular investigation?'

Jake ran through a few ideas in her head. Then she said: 'Well, sir, the first thing I would do would be to have the Yard's Computer Crime Unit assign me their best man. I'd have him take a look at the Lombroso computer and try to find out what happened. What I would also do – ' Jake hesitated for a moment as she wondered how best to approach her next suggestion.

Woodford was typing her ideas onto his PC. He looked up expectantly. 'Yes?'

It seemed to Jake that there was no other way but to

be direct. ' – is polygraph all the staff working on the Lombroso Program.'

Waring tossed his pen onto the table. As it bounced it left a little line of ink droplets on the polished walnut table. 'I don't believe I'm hearing this,' he snarled. 'Chief Inspector, you cannot seriously think that one of Professor Gleitmann's staff could be lying.'

He fixed her with a sharply-pointed stare which Jake did her hard-eyed best to blunt. 'Either one of his staff, or Professor Gleitmann himself,' she offered provocatively.

Waring let out a burst of indignant air which the Minister and her secretary seemed to find amusing. But Jake hadn't finished.

'With respect, sir,' she said to Woodford, 'it is the only logical course for any investigation while there continues to be an absence of any – ' She found herself half-smiling as she prepared to utter what was for her an infrequently used word. ' – clues.' The word prompted a picture of herself winding in a ball of thread to find her way out of a maze. 'We must start from the inside and work out,' she added. 'The Program itself holds the key to establishing some kind of a pattern to these killings. But while we persist in trying to address only the exterior facts of each case, there will be no progress.'

To Jake's surprise she found the Minister agreeing with her. 'That's the most sensible thing I've heard all day,' said Mrs Miles.

'Minister – '

She turned her handsome profile to Waring and silenced him with a wave of her heavily-ringed hand. Jake noticed a manicure that looked less than Ministerial. Mrs Miles had fingernails that were the shape and colour of pieces of orange peel.

'No, Norman, the Chief Inspector's correct. Perhaps that's what this investigation really needs – a woman's perspective, just as the Chief Inspector was telling us in her lecture this morning. After all, we don't seem to have got very far with a man in charge of it, do we?' Mrs

Miles ignored Professor Waring's attempt to interrupt her again. 'Perhaps some of that attention to fine detail for which women are so distinguished is just what has been lacking until now.' She smiled as she added, 'And a little less phallocentrism around here certainly wouldn't do any harm.' She turned to the Assistant Police Commissioner.

'John,' she said. 'I want you to make sure that Chief Inspector Jakowicz is assigned to take charge of this investigation. Is that clear?'

Gilmour nodded uncomfortably. He hated being told how to handle an inquiry by anyone, least of all a politician, and more especially, the Minister herself. But at the same time Gilmour had the feeling that what Jake had said was right and that she was indeed the right person for the job.

'Is that all right with you, Chief Inspector?' said Mrs Miles.

Jake, who was slightly taken aback at the speed of the Minister's decision and the imperious way in which it had been communicated to herself and Gilmour, shrugged uncertainly. She thought of the enormous case-load waiting for her back at the Yard and of the consternation her new assignment would cause her superior, Chief Superintendent Challis. She thought of the pleasure that Challis's consternation at being removed from the case would afford her and found herself nodding. 'Fine by me, ma'am,' she said. 'However, I would like to keep my finger on the pulse of one particular investigation I've been handling.' Jake was thinking of the lipstick on Mary Woolnoth's body, her face battered to a pulp, and how much she'd like to catch the man who had killed her. 'In fact, I should insist on it.'

Mrs Miles smiled broadly, revealing a row of perfect white teeth. It was a good smile. The sort of smile that won votes. The sort of smile that had helped Mrs Miles capitalise on her athletic career as a 100- and 200-metre

Olympic Gold medallist and put her into the House of Commons at the early age of twenty-nine.

'I have no problems with that,' she said. 'Good. That's settled then. Mark?'

'Minister?'

'I want you to call Professor Gleitmann and tell him that he's to extend the Chief Inspector and her team whatever cooperation she deems appropriate. You too, Norman? You got that?'

Waring nodded sullenly.

Mrs Miles stood up and walked like a big strong cat to the impossibly tall door, attended by her secretary. Waring followed at an embittered distance. On her way out, the Minister turned on her high heel, tightening the material of her already tight skirt against the curve of her muscular buttock and her pantie-line.

'Oh and Chief Inspector?'

'Yes?' said Jake.

'Please don't disappoint me. I want results. And I want them quickly. I'm sure I don't have to tell you that I usually get my way. But when I don't I'm apt to be rather vindictive. Do you understand me?'

'I think so, Minister,' said Jake. She didn't doubt that Grace Miles would make sure Jake's career was effectively blocked and re-directed into one dead-end or another.

'Well,' said the APC when he and Jake were alone. 'You walked right into that one.'

She smiled wryly. 'Looks like it, sir.'

'Oh I don't doubt that you may have the right idea about this investigation and exactly how it should proceed. But I would hate to lose one of my best detectives merely because of the whim of a Junior Minister with a nettle down her panties. She doesn't seem to like you very much. She might like to see you fall flat on your face with this particular inquiry.'

'Maybe.' Jake shrugged.

'You know, I could always have a word with Sir Mac-

Donald when we get back to London. Have him persuade Mrs Miles that he would rather someone else handled this.' He rubbed the back of his neck. 'What am I talking about? Someone else is handling this.'

'Challis.'

'Yes.'

'I'd like to get this collar, sir,' she said. 'If I can.'

'She affected you that much eh? The bitch. Well, if you're sure you want to. I'll back you all the way. But what am I going to tell Challis?'

'How about telling him you want me to take charge of the day-to-day enquiries?' Jake suggested. 'That you think a fresh viewpoint is required. That you think he's too important to get involved in the inquiry itself. Perhaps he could continue to exercise some kind of executive role.'

Gilmour grunted. 'Doesn't sound all that convincing,' he said. 'Never mind. I'll think of something.' He picked up his briefcase and placed it on his lap, before rummaging in its contents and withdrawing a box of computer disks. He thumbed one out and handed it to Jake.

'Here,' he said. 'This'll tell you everything you need to know about the Lombroso Program.'

For me, the realisation that I am a freak was not the result of a childhood's accumulation of unkind remarks about my appearance. Nor, for that matter, was it the consequence of an inadvertently-placed mirror, a job-offer in a circus sideshow, a horrified plastic surgeon, or a callously disinterested schoolgirl. Rather the dawning was the outcome of an esoterically designed medical test for which I volunteered following a severe attack of the law and orders. One minute I was, to all intents and purposes, normal. Fifteen minutes later I was a medical curiosity occurring in only three cases in a hundred thousand.

The order of the number series is not governed by an external relation but by an internal relation.

Yes, indeed, internal. The essence of my freakishness cannot be perceived by the sense-data of others any more than I can perceive it myself. But of course it has been established empirically and therefore, from a phenom-enological point of view, my freakish state is not a matter of simple apriorism, even if it has had the existential result of revealing my true situation in the world.

Of course, I always knew I was different. Nothing so ordinary as somatype – I am in fact the classic ecto-morph. Were you to see me naked, you would be con-fronted with a thin, male body, of delicate build, and lightly muscled. It is possible that this may have been a contributing factor. According to Sheldon's hypothesis, the dimensions of my ectomorphic, sand-kicked-in-my-face physique make me temperamentally inclined to the cerebrotonial personality type, which is characterised by self-consciousness, overreactiveness, and a preference for privacy. But then I also exhibit a few of the character-istics of the average somatotonial personality type, which is characterised by a desire for power and dominance, and which Sheldon associates with the more muscular, mesomorphic physical type. So let's forget about any-thing so crude as my physical characteristics. Let's agree that it has nothing to do with the kind of guy I am. This sort of thing really only works in Shakespeare.

Knowledge of my difference was quite naturally tem-pered with an awareness of what the philosophers tell us is simply solipsism – the theory that nothing exists except me and my mental states. So I have no real evidence to support the perception that I was different in that I considered my mental states to be unusual. Anyone else reading this account would doubtless be quickly able to judge whether or not my thought processes make me different. But since the essential nature of what I am writing is introspective then that's really not much help either. Really, all I have to go on is the existence of an altogether separate psychopathological syndrome and a novel by Keith Waterhouse.

With Tourette's Syndrome there exists such a disorgan-isation of thinking that the individual finds himself shout-ing out obscenities wherever he may be. Billy Liar describes the adventures of a young man who, strictly speaking, is not a liar at all, but merely suffers from an unfettered imagination which constantly causes him to construct elaborate fantasies – to alternate upon reality, as George Steiner has described this.

Consider then a combination of these two: Tourette's and an uncontrolled fantasy world. Consider me.

A trip to the macromarket is a walk on the wild side. Mentally armed with a selection of military hardware I maim, rape and murder my way along the High Street. A dog tied to a lamp-post and barking for its master makes an easy target for my Magnum .47. An old lady dragging her shopping-trolley behind her like a miniature chariot and impeding my self-important path is blasted aside with the hand-held rocket launcher. A grenade dropped into a busker's guitar-case makes mincemeat of him and his instrument: the neck of the guitar, flying through the air, crashes through a car windscreen and then the head of the driver who has had the temerity to sound his horn at me. A child's balloon is easily burst with a dab of my cigarette. A woman in a short, tight skirt is bent over the macromarket's checkout desk, her underwear ripped off her quivering backside and then raped mercilessly from behind. A black man, dropping a handful of litter onto the pavement, is toasted with a short burst of my flame-thrower.

A series of pictures which Goya might have painted, or Michael Winner might have filmed.

A picture is a model of reality. A picture is a fact. It is impossible to tell from the picture alone whether it is true or false. All right then, I can compare it with reality. But there are no pictures which are true a priori. Whatever it is you happen to be thinking about.

To look at me of course you would think that I was probably a well-adjusted sort of person. Well we're not talking Mr Edward Hyde here, let's face it. Catch me trampling over some innocent child's body to leave her screaming on the road? No way. I am courteous and well-mannered, opening doors for ladies and helping young mothers with their push-chairs on the escalators. The usual stuff. And though I say so myself, not bad looking, if a trifle thoughtful.

In Victorian times, Cesare Lombroso, the Italian criminologist, thought that criminality could be explained anatomically, using ethesiometer and craniometer to weigh and measure the skull. Not enough forehead or too much lower jaw were the visible indicators that you might be a wrong 'un. He was the first criminal anthropologist.

Nonsense of course. But while Lombroso was misled in attempting to explain criminality in relation to things like the size of a man's nose, mouth and ears, subsequent neurological research has demonstrated that he wasn't so very wide of the mark. When he laid open the skull of an Italian version of Jack the Ripper and perceived, on the internal occipital crest, a small hollow – a hollow which related to a still greater anomaly in the cerebellum (the hypertrophy of the vermis) and to which he later ascribed the propensity to degenerate criminality, he was onto more than even he could have realised.

Of course, Lombroso had still not grasped that the real pointer towards a man's criminal tendencies lay not on the surface of the skull, but on the surface of the brain. What a pity he got sidetracked with all that nonsense about the habitual criminal's earlobes.

As it happens my own earlobes are large and Lombroso (the first one) would very possibly have classed me as the criminal type. It's perhaps just as well that no one can tell what's going on inside your head. That is no one except the second Lombroso. And this is a kind of tautology.

3

Jake's hotel, at least the exterior, reminded her of a detention centre she had once visited in Los Angeles. Outside, there was only a doorman and a taxi-rank to remind you that it was a hotel at all. She would not have been surprised to see a machine-gun nest on top of the knot of the bowtie-shaped building.

She went into the bar and sat up at the counter, ordering a whisky sour and twenty Nicofree, and munching a handful of pistachio nuts while the pale-faced barman unwrapped the cigarettes for her. He lit her silently and then set about mixing her drink.

Jake glanced over her shoulder and checked the room, careful not to make eye-contact with any of the lonely-hearts business travellers who, seeing an attractive single woman, might think they could get lucky with her.

Like the interior of an expensive German car, the hotel bar had a relentless, almost Spartan modernity about it. Charcoal-grey carpet covered the floor and the walls up to the sills of the toughened tinted windows. The black leather seats might have met with a chiropractor's approval but were hardly relaxing to sit in. The handsome, polished walnut counter displayed a variety of small screens informing guests, at the flick of a cue-button, of everything from the bar-tariff to the evening's programme of films on cable in the hotel bedrooms.

Jake turned back to face the sharpshooter's array of bottles behind the bar and fetched her drink off the counter, trying to ignore the hopeful who was already standing next to her in his smooth Italian suit.

'Is anyone sitting here?' he asked, in halting German.

'Nobody but the Lord,' she replied with greater

fluency. She fixed the man with a smug beatific smile of the kind she had seen deployed by the most sickly sweet televangelists.

'Tell me, friend,' she asked him quickly. 'Are you saved?'

The man hesitated, his confidence fading fast in the face of this apparent display of religious zeal.

'Er, no . . .'

Jake smiled to herself as she reviewed his likely thought processes. How lucky could a man get with a woman who seemed interested only in the state of his immortal soul?

'Some other time perhaps,' said the man, retreating.

'There's always time for Jesus,' Jake remarked, her eyes widening like a madwoman's. But he was gone.

Jake sipped her drink and laughed. The missionary routine: it never failed. She was an old hand at drinking alone in bars. Unwanted male approaches (and for Jake, all male approaches were unwelcome) seemed no more of an irritation than mosquitoes for some hardened South American explorer: easily swatted and, after a while, you got used to them. She knew that she could have avoided them altogether if she had only frequented lesbian bars. If only things had been that simple.

'Can I buy you a drink?' He was an American and naturally assumed that the whole world could speak English.

Jake, who spoke good German, flirted with the idea of pretending to speak not a word of English and then rejected it: she knew that when a man wanted to get into a girl's pants, conversation could count for very little.

'I don't know whether you can or you can't,' she said dully.

'What?' said the man, wincing.

Jake took a square look at him. Short-haired, fresh-faced, he seemed to be not much older than his collar-size. If he had appeared a little more intelligent, she told herself, she might have fucked him.

'Yes, it is hot.'

The young American smiled bitterly. 'What is your problem?'

'Right now it's that aftershave, sonny.' Jake shifted on her stool. 'Run along before it affects my contact lenses.'

The American's face took on a nasty look. His lips pursed several times before he thought of something to say back to her.

'Ball breaker,' he snarled and then stalked away.

Jake snorted with contempt, although she knew that was what she was: that and a bit more. She could almost have been lesbian except that she hadn't much liked it when she tried it. Faith, a lesbian friend at Cambridge, had once told her that Jake's sexuality reminded her of something Jeremy Bentham had said about John Stuart Mill: he rather hated the ruling few than loved the suffering many. It wasn't, Faith had said, that Jake loved women but that she hated men.

Her hatred of men was every bit as intense as aversions to heights, open spaces, and spiders were for other people; and it had been learned in much the same way as a rat is conditioned to press a lever in order to avoid an electric shock.

The instrument of her own aversive conditioning, a term with which she became familiar when she studied natural sciences at Cambridge, was less direct than electricity, and left no visible scar tissue; but the particular stimulus produced an effect that was just as painful as anything that might have been inflicted with a couple of strategically-placed electrodes; and while the injuries may have been invisible, they felt just as permanent as if they had been burnt into her naked flesh.

An ungrateful child was no match for the venom in the cerebro-spinal needle of a father's hatred.

She finished her drink and ordered another. The barman mixed it quickly as if he had learned his trade in the pits at the Indianapolis 500. But there was nothing wrong with the way it tasted and Jake nodded appreciatively at him.

She glanced at her wristwatch. Before she went to bed she ought to read the information file Gilmour had given to her. There wasn't much to stay in the bar for. Easy to see why Frankfurt was host to so many international trade fairs and conferences, she thought. It was the kind of city with absolutely no distractions: no nightlife, no scenery to speak of, no historical buildings, no theatres, no decent cinemas. About the most interesting place she had seen was Frankfurt airport. She finished her drink, signed the bill and then went out to the lobby.

The lift arrived in a rush of air and Jake stepped in. She told the computer the floor number and watched the doors close. They were not quite quick enough to prevent the young American who had talked to her at the bar from squeezing his way into Jake's lift at the last second.

'You should be more friendly,' he said, and touched her breast.

Jake smiled, the better to catch him off his guard. She was still smiling as she raked his shin with the side of her shoe. The man yelled and clutched instinctively at his injured leg. Which left him leaning nicely into the smart uppercut that was already rising like a piston towards the point of his chin. It was all over in a few seconds. The lift door was opening at Jake's floor and she was rubbing her knuckles and stepping over the American's supine body.

'Ground floor,' she said to the computer and walked onto the landing, the lift doors closing silently behind her. The hotel corridor was as long as an autobahn. She hoped to be back in her room before the man recovered himself and made it back up from the lobby. Outside the door of her room she stopped and fumbled in her bag for her key. Then she remembered there was no key. The door was voice-print activated.

'Jakowicz,' she said, and the door sprang open.

Halogen light escaping from the four enormous glass

parapets which dominated the top of the hotel's two wings poured through the embrasure-sized window like a cinema projection. Jake lit a cigarette, nicotine free, but the smoke felt good in her lungs, and picked up her PC and inserted Gilmour's information disk.

PROPERTY OF METROPOLITAN POLICE INFORMATION DEPARTMENT.
DISK LMP/2000/LOMBROSO PROGRAM/GENERAL FILE.
MENU   1. WHAT IS LOMBROSO?
           2. BACKGROUND TO LOMBROSO:
              a. FAILURE OF PREVENTION STRATEGIES FOR VIOLENT CRIME.
              b. SOCIAL AND PHILOSOPHICAL BACKGROUND.
           3. SOMATOGENIC DETERMINANTS OF VIOLENT CRIME.
           4. IMPLEMENTATION.
           5. TREATMENT AND INTEGRATION.
PRESS 'RETURN' TO RUN INFORMATION BRIEF IN NUMERICAL ORDER.

When she had read the menu she pressed the 'Return' key as instructed.

1. WHAT IS LOMBROSO?

L.O.M.B.R.O.S.O. stands for Localisation of Medullar Brain Resonations Obliging Social Orthopraxy. A machine based on the old Proton Emission Tomographer, and developed by Professor Burgess Phelan of the Nuffield Science Institute at Cambridge University, is able to determine those males whose brains lack a Ventro Medial Nucleus (VMN) which acts as an inhibitor to the Sexually Dimorphic Nucleus (SDN), a preoptic area of the male human brain which is the repository of male aggressive response. A computerised national survey of British males was started in 2010 with the aim of offering therapy, and/or counselling, to those who have been tested VMN-negative. While the Lombroso computer's program first decretal protects with a codename the identity of those who have tested VMN-negative, the computer is, however, linked with the central police computer at Kidlington: should the name of a suspect fed into the police computer within the course of an inquiry into a violent crime be that of a male who has tested VMN-negative, the Lombroso computer will inform the CPC of this fact. The very fact of being VMN-negative is, however, not admissible in criminal evidence. During the 2 years that the Lombroso Program has been in operation, over 4 million men have been scanned and of these, 0.003 per cent have been discovered to be VMN-negative. Of these, only 30 per cent were in prison or had some kind of a criminal record. At the time of writing, the Lombroso Program has been instrumental in the apprehension of 10 murderers.

Jake read this first section of the information program, yawned and then went to the window of her hotel room. In the distance she could see the Main River which was the same washed-out colour of grey as the sky. A barge the size of a high street hooted as it made its slow, smooth way across the riverscape. She didn't care for Frankfurt anymore than she cared to spend her evening reading about crime prevention strategies. The truth was that Jake had little faith in any of these. She saw it all as a great waste of money when criminal investigation was still comparatively under-resourced.

Thoroughly distracted now, she turned the Nicam-video set on and flicked through the 42 cable-channels. Her German was good but there were no programmes that seemed to make it worth the trouble of listening. Briefly she found herself detained with a sex film in which a couple were taking a bath together. The girl reminded her of Grace Miles: a strong, athletic-looking black woman with large breasts and a behind like a well-stuffed haversack. But when she started to suck the man's cock with all the languorous concentration of a child eating an ice-cream, Jake wrinkled her lip with distaste and turned the set off.

Could they actually imagine that a woman enjoyed doing that kind of thing? She shrugged. Perhaps they just didn't care.

She lit another Nicofree and returned reluctantly to her PC to read the rest of the information disk.

2. BACKGROUND TO LOMBROSO:
a. FAILURE OF PREVENTION STRATEGIES FOR VIOLENT CRIME.

During the last two decades of the twentieth century, British society sought to control whole groups, populations and environments. The emphasis was not so much on community control as on control of communities. Technology and resources were directed towards surveillance, prevention and control, rather than 'tracking' the individual adjudicated offender. The thinking was to manipulate the external environment to prevent the initial infraction. The community continued to be involved but the reality was rather less comfortable. Fortress-living, armed guards patrolling schools and airports were simultaneously solutions and problems: problems in that they were helping to create the urban nightmares which caused people to revolt against their physical environments.

With the failure of schemes which aimed to ameliorate the environment, the accent returned to tracking the individual offender. The adoption in 1997, following mass-immigration to the EC of Hong Kong Chinese refugees, of an EC national identity card scheme enjoyed considerable success. This was made even more effective when the ID card was able to include DNA-Profiling. As a result, and for the first time ever, the machinery was now in place which enabled Government to track the individual before he offended at all.

b. SOCIAL AND PHILOSOPHICAL BACKGROUND.

The 1990s witnessed the discrediting of socially and economically fatalistic theories of why people commit violent crime. Attending only to the exterior causes of crime diminished any sense of personal responsibility. Today society no longer takes exclusive blame for how a person became a criminal any more than the individual himself: a combination of social and individual factors is seen as a better way to account for every kind of criminal behaviour.

Determinism is not considered to constitute a menace to freedom in the new century. A pragmatic assumption of order made for the sake of advancing scientific enquiry can hardly be questioned. This reverses an earlier trend in the social sciences which mistakenly sought to protect freedoms by confining determinism to the physical world, thus effectively 'outlawing' all attempts at establishing some kind of 'biological determinism'.

Modern social science does not consider predictability and generalisation to be dangerous. Indeed, any advance in social science without first establishing certain notions about human behaviour would not have been possible. To claim infinite adaptability for human behaviour is no longer valid. Thus the concept that violent criminality has no real roots in us, being an external socially-produced phenomenon, is now wholly discredited.

3. SOMATOGENIC DETERMINANTS OF VIOLENT CRIME.

The last ten years has seen enormous advances made in the science of somatogenics, and in particular the aetiology of most mental disorders (with the exception of conversion disorders, such as neurosis). It is now accepted that most mental illness has some organic cause. There has occurred a similar revolution in what is known about organic pathology and its relation to violent crime.

Neurological research has centred on sexual dimorphism, that is, the difference between male and female brains. Leading this field was Professor Burgess Phelan of the Department of Anatomy and Cell Biology in the University of Cambridge, and director of the Laboratory of Neuro-Endocrinology at the London Brain Research Institute.

Phelan's work followed the discovery, by a UCLA scientist, in the preoptic area of the male rat, of what became known as the Sexually Dimorphic Nucleus (SDN). This area, which helped direct sexual behaviour, was five times larger in male rats than in females. Yet another area of the rat brain that showed difference in size according to sex was the Ventro Medial Nucleus (VMN), associated with both eating and aggression. It was discovered that amputation or even a small lesion of a rat's VMN made the male rat extraordinarily aggressive. But a similar lesion in the VMN of the female rat did not affect it at all.

Using surgical brain atlases and the brains of volunteer male convicts, Burgess Phelan discovered an SDN and a VMN in the human brain. That like rats, the human male's SDN was several times larger than a female's. He also discovered that in human males, the VMN acted as an inhibitor to male aggression; that if the SDN was removed, the man was not aggressive at all; but that otherwise the absence or amputation of the VMN made the male, like the rat, more aggressive. Equally, aggression in human females, with smaller SDNs, was not affected by the absence or amputation of the VMN.

The results of Phelan's research were taken up by Professor David Gleitmann, of the Department of Forensic Neuro-endocrinology at the London Brain Research Institute. He discovered that some violent criminals had no VMN at all; that they were VMN-negative.

Originally this important discovery was made surgically. However, a breakthrough in the technology of Proton Emission Tomography, the so-called PET scan, enabled Gleitmann to take detailed colour photographs of the brain inside living human skulls. With these pictures Gleitmann was able to establish, within a matter of a few minutes, the presence or absence of a VMN and, as a corollary, latent criminality.

Professor Gleitmann's research has so far revealed that violent criminality in the VMN-negative subject may always remain merely latent. Current scientific investigation centres on the possibility that many men who are VMN-negative somehow manage to stabilise their own levels of aggression by producing an increased quantity of oestrogen.

4. IMPLEMENTATION.

In 2005, the average cost in the EC of a murder investigation was an EC$ 750,000. The same year there were some 3500 homicides, representing an investigative cost to the

Community of EC$ 2.6 billion. In an attempt to try and reduce this staggering cost it was decided by the Europarliament to adopt Professor Gleitmann's research within the context of an experimental program to be undertaken in one member country. Because of its higher than average record of violent crime, the UK was chosen and in 2011 the experiment began in the shape of the Lombroso Program.

Using a specially designed computer and a number of scanning centres in London, Birmingham, Manchester, Newcastle, and Glasgow, men submit themselves to an examination. Those few who are discovered to be VMN-negative are guaranteed confidentiality in that only the computer is aware of their real identities. Codenames are issued by the computer, prior to the men being invited to attend a personal counselling session where the implications of the result are explained by a fully-qualified therapist. The accent is on help. Treatment is offered in the form of somatic therapies (most commonly oestrogen and/or psychiatric drugs). It is explained that the VMN-negative's confidentiality will only be broken by the Lombroso computer if the respondent's name occurs within the course of a police investigation into a violent crime.

So far over 4 million men have been scanned. Of these 0.003 per cent (120 men) have been revealed as VMN-negative. Of these, 30 per cent (36 men) were in prison or had some kind of a criminal record. At the time of writing, the Program has been instrumental in the apprehension of 10 violent criminals.

While the test is not mandatory, a number of factors have helped to persuade many men to take a test. In the first year of the Program there were small cash incentives which operated in the same way as giving blood. The Central Office of Information ran a series of television commercials to encourage men to be 'good citizens' and have themselves tested: these helped to dispel some of the myths and negative images which inevitably became attached to the Program. It wasn't long, however, before employers in the public sector began to insist on tests for all their employees. And these were swiftly followed by health and insurance companies. It is generally held that the only barrier to testing more men has been the limited capacity of the Program facilities themselves.

5. TREATMENT AND INTEGRATION.

Hereditary diathesis is only the immediate cause of any aggressive disorder and it is important for the counsellor to remind the subject that a number of other factors, for example USS (Unemployment Stress Syndrome), ESS (Environmental Stress Syndrome), SEFSS (Socio-Economic and Familial Stress Syndrome), may be needed to trigger the pathological process in persons with the initial diathesis. These may be very remote and thus the VMN-negative subject may be perfectly able to function reasonably well in the ordinary world.

There should be, it is stressed, no imputation of mental illness. To this effect, subjects are usually reminded of the standard work on structural personality tests. These reveal that the Psychopathic Deviance (PD) scale of the old MMPI (Minnesota Multiphasic Personality Inventory) shows that high PD scorers tend to be aggressive; but also that high PD scores are characteristic of professional actors and others who show a significantly above-average level of creativity.

Subjects who persist in regarding themselves as in any way mentally defective are encouraged to assess their condition from the perspective of R. D. Laing, i.e. as a voyage of self-discovery.

Elsewhere it may be considered that society itself may have reason to be glad of these men since one of them may yet turn out to be a Gauguin or a Beethoven. This is not to say that society endorses the acts of people which may have unlooked-for artistic by-products. But at the same time, moral values must be treated not as unquestionably supreme, but only as one value among others.

INFORMATION ENDS.

For Jake it did not make agreeable reading. It was full of phrases which seemed almost to indicate a certain sympathy for these men who had the potential to become violent killers. A sympathy which as a law-enforcement officer she found irritating, and which as a woman and potential victim of violent crime she found outrageous.

When she had finished with the information disk, Jake

hauled it out of her PC and, finding that the bedside table, which looked as if it had been constructed from three of Harry Lauder's walking sticks, was too small for anything other than the baton-shaped lamp resting on it, she threw them both onto the bed with a snort of contempt.

She sat down in front of the window.

So what, if someone decided to kill a few potential psychos? It would save her the time and trouble of catching them. Not to mention the lives of all the innocent women they might eventually kill. Women like Mary Woolnoth. Jake could just picture herself facing the mother of one such victim and saying that her daughter's murderer was only assessing his condition from what the information disk had referred to as R. D. Laing's perspective — as a 'voyage of self-discovery'.

'Well that's all right then, Chief Inspector Jakowicz. For a moment there I was really worried that my girl was raped and murdered for no good reason.'

She laughed out loud. It made, she thought, quite a change for someone to concentrate on killing men. Jake was struck by the irony of what she, the expert on serial gynocide, was expected to do. Briefly she entertained herself with visions of the stupid scared bastards accompanying each other home at night. Perhaps she might even issue a warning for men to stay indoors after dark. That would certainly put a severe dent in the well-polished bodywork of the collective male ego. Despite the Minister's implied threat to her, something told Jake that she might actually enjoy this case.

At first I was a little shocked.

I wandered out of the Brain Research Institute in Victoria Street, having swallowed the two Valium which the counsellor had given me, as well as having agreed to the course of oestrogen tablets and psychotherapy that he had recommended, and went into the Chestnut Tree Café across the road. There I numbly took stock of my new situation in the world.

I remember being so dazed at what had happened that I completely forgot to imagine myself carrying out any mindless acts of violence against the other people in the café. Instead I drank several cups of coffee, ate a plate of cholesterol-free bacon-sandwiches and toyed glumly with the novelty of my new Lombroso-given name.

Situations can be described but not given names. Names are like points; propositions like arrows – they have sense. Maybe we'll come back to the name. Let's deal with the situation first.

I left the café and telephoned my own analyst to make an appointment for the next day. When I was back in my flat in Docklands, I stood beside the window for a while, as I often do, and watched the progress of the Thames down Greenwich Reach, past the Isle of Dogs. Reality often disappoints and, under the brown fog of a winter noon, the city seemed somehow much less real than of old. And had done so for some time now.

What on earth did people do before there was Reality Approximation? What was there for those who found no substitute for sense to seize and clutch and penetrate? It was only my RA exoskeleton that enabled me to enjoy a world of colour and sensation – a world that resembles the real world, and more. This is the normal way in which I relax after a hard day. It's no more addictive or a waste of time than television. I can occupy myself with an approximately real experience, often of my own devising, for hours at a time. Usually, I am climbing into the RA equipment the minute I come through the door, but on this occasion I didn't feel like it at all. It was as much as I could do not to go into the bathroom and slash my wrists.

Can you blame me? From good citizen to social pariah in the space of a single afternoon? I ought to have seen the funny side, I suppose: me, the right-winger, always banging on about law and order, forever raising my voice against the abolitionists who would punish a murderer with nothing worse than a couple of years in a nice warm prison. Me, suddenly catapulted onto the other side of the jurisprudential fence. What a supreme irony. The sheer injustice of it. After all, I voted for them specifically because of their law-enforcement programme. I thought that something like this Lombroso Program would be a good idea. And look what happens: I get given the mark of Cain; on a computer file anyway.

Until that moment I had never given much thought as to which of my personal details appeared on what computers. I dare say I was aware that my bank, my employer, my building societies, my doctor, my dentist, my analyst, and possibly even the police (there was that old parking-ticket) all had information about me. But it never seemed to matter very much. I certainly wasn't one of those who bleated on about civil liberties and Big Brother when the EC made the carrying of ID cards compulsory. Not even when they added a bar-code containing things like your genetic fingerprint. I have never even read 1984. What's the point? It's long past its sell-by-date.

They were reprising an old television series called 'The Prisoner' the other night. Very popular with the more disaffected sections of society. 'I'm not a number, I'm a free man,' exclaims the granite-jawed hero. Well now I know what he was so upset about. Russell said that there were simple relations between different numbers of things (individuals). But between what numbers? And how is this supposed to be decided? By experience? There is no pre-eminent number. Not number six. And certainly not number one.

The more I thought about it, the more I wanted to erase my name and number from those files. I was not persuaded by all the guarantees of confidentiality that had seemed so irrelevant before taking the test. I felt like someone who had been persuaded to give a half-litre of blood in the expectation that it would be used to save a life, only to discover that it was to be fed to a colony of vampire bats in a zoo. Bats, what is more, who might well come and attack me while I was asleep. Because there is no telling what can become of information these days. Any database can become the target of unauthorised entry. Electronic vandalism is rife.

Suppose, I thought, that someone managed to break into the Lombroso Program's database and, having got hold of the identities of those people who had tested VMN-negative, sold them to the News of the World? I could just envisage the headlines: WE NAME THE HUMAN TIME-BOMBS IN OUR COMMUNITIES/ TOMORROW'S RIPPERS?/ SEEKING OUT THE PSYCHOS/ POSITIVE STEPS NEEDED TO CANCEL OUT THESE NEGATIVES ...

I had read enough about the activities of the Cologne Chaos Computer Club to know that for the really determined electronic burglar, even the most sophisticated system of data-security is vulnerable.

Probably it was the effect of the sedatives, only it took me several more minutes to realise that if someone else could break into the Lombroso database and steal personal information about me, then so could I. Not only was I possessed of all the equipment for such a task – PC, modem, the telephone company's Jupiter computer *information system, digital protocol analyser – I suddenly recalled the most important fact of all, which was the basic information for entering and using the system.*

I have always been interested in all kinds of electrical equipment, an interest which originally was encouraged by my grandfather, who owned a chain of electrical retailers. There was nothing electrical which he and, after a while I, couldn't fix. So when I was back there in the waiting room at the Brain Research Institute, confidently anticipating my PET scan, it had been quite natural for me to start trying to adjust the television set they had in there when I saw that it was on the blink.

The problem was a simple one – a channel improperly tuned – and I had just started to rectify this when I noticed that the set, which was rather an old one, was picking up electromagnetic radiation from one of the computer installations in the building. Somewhere in the Institute, a VDU was radiating out harmonics on the same frequency as the television set. There was something almost readable on the television screen and by adjusting the direction of the desktop antenna I found that I was able to see that it was an image of information that someone was feeding into the Lombroso computer. It's roughly the same principle that used to enable the old television detector vans to see if you were using an unlicensed set, when there were still such things as TV licences. It wasn't a particularly clear image, just black letters on a white background, and the picture had a tendency to swim, but it was easy enough to recognise a basic entry code, an individual operator's personal 'key' word, and the Lombroso system's password for the day.

The image of the computer-hacker spending many hours in front of a screen trying to break into a system is a false one. He is more often to be found scavenging in a company's refuse bins in an attempt to find a piece of information that will provide a clue as to the computer system's password. In other words, I had already achieved what is ordinarily the most difficult part of any hacker's task.

I cannot say that at the time I consciously committed this information to memory. There was no reason for me to have done so, believing as I did then that I would pass the PET scan without a problem. Perhaps fate plays a hand in these things, for later on I found that I was able to visualise the various numbers and codewords on that anonymous operator's VDU as easily as if I had been sitting in front of it myself.

Of course, all a password does is to get you into the system. Then you have to find out which set of rules or protocol the target system is using so that you can interface with it and speak the same computer language. That's where the protocol analyser comes in handy. It has got some ingenious software that examines the other system's entry port to see which of the many data communication protocols is in use.

But I'm getting ahead of myself, because I encountered my first major difficulty the minute I buttoned the Brain Research Institute's telephone number. They weren't even on the public switched telephone network. They were using a private leased line – the newly installed ECDN, the European Community Data Network. This included records for all member governments and their various departments on one exclusive network.

I was still not thinking properly, and it was at least another minute before I recalled that the computer system at work was on the ECDN. All employers in the public sector, Police, Inland Revenue, Customs and Excise, Medical, Information, Employment, Women, Conservation were on it.

I tapped my head with the flat of my hand. It was obvious that if I really was going to do this and use the computer system at work, I was also going to need some juice. So the first thing I did before unplugging the analyser and going out to the van was to find my cognitive enhancement pills.

Nobody at work was surprised to see me. I'm often working late at night, catching up on the administrative paperwork for which there's little time during the course of an average, underpaid and over-working day. Anyway, I switched on the computer, and while it was warming up and coming on line, I started swallowing. Dilantin for sustained periods of concentration. Hydergine for a general intelligence increase through the drug's creation of extra synapses. And Vasopressin, a neural hormone which helps to improve the memory. To be honest, I've been using a combination of cognitive enhancers for a while now, so I was just topping up the dose. The effect on the human brain, while we're in the way of talking about computers, is that of upgrading a machine from say 40 to about 50 terabytes. But to really get myself warmed up, I finished this cocktail of drugs I had swallowed with some cocaine.

Have you ever shot coke in the vein? It hits that medullar brain centre like electro-convulsive therapy and switches you on like the Christmas lights on New Oxford Street. For about fifteen minutes you're in the seat of an F26 with all your cannons blazing, your laser-guidance keeping you locked onto the tail of some enemy plane. As an aid to pure concentration it's terrific. No wonder Sherlock Holmes found it an aid to investigation. You feel as if there's a new intelligence working within you. If you were to inject some into the computer's software port you would not be surprised if the machine were literally jolted into life itself, like something dreamt up by Mary Shelley. Normally I'll use about .20 of a gram, however I had the suspicion that I was going to need a longer flight than normal if I was to be able to run where I wanted within the Lombroso system. So I made a solution that was twice my normal percentage and pushed the needle into the skin.

Using the ECDN, and with a legitimate identity, I was interfacing with the BRI in less than a minute. They must have anticipated having to deal with unauthorised entrants to the system, because the very first thing that happened was that a nude Marilyn Monroe graphic appeared on my screen and, with a wiggle of her lifelike bottom, asked me if I felt lucky.

'Because if you can answer just three little old questions you and your reality approximation software get to fuck my brains out.'

Marilyn was referring to the software which controlled the computer's optional body attachments and which enabled one to enjoy an approximate physical sensation of whatever kind of reality was being created. This kind of Reality Approximation program was very popular in the amusement arcades. Like I said before, I own an RA machine and body suit myself.

'Well?' pouted Marilyn. 'Cat got your tongue?'

Even though I did not have my own RA suit with me, I wasn't about to fall for this. The point of Marilyn was to trap the unwary schoolkid hackers into wasting their time and not progressing any further within the system. I knew the chances were that if you did manage to answer Marilyn's questions correctly and got to fuck her, then you were liable to discover that your own computer software had been infected with a very nasty, possibly terminal virus.

Marilyn dropped a hand between her legs and rubbed herself provocatively.

'What's the matter sugar?' she cooed. 'You one of them, or something?' And, right on cue, Marilyn was immediately joined on screen by James Dean, wearing nothing else but the kind of gladiator-style outfit that would have looked very fetching in the heavy leather bars of Earls Court or Chiswick.

Before Jimmy could try and tempt me with his own particular brand of sexual allure, I typed 'goodbye' and then the Lombroso system's password for the day which, according to my watch was due to expire in less than fifty minutes.

Marilyn and Jimmy disappeared as the password

transported me into the basic operating system. Now I had to find the root directory with all the system files stored on it, and the easiest way of doing that was to reboot the system, to shut it down completely. So I pressed the right keys simultaneously and watched the screen clear itself of everything but a flashing 'root' prompt which told me that I was getting closer.

Next I told the computer to list all the sub-directories which were contained in the root. First up was the directory containing Lombroso personnel, and then several others which dealt with things like accounts, payroll, counselling procedures, PET scan operating procedures; last of all came the two subs I was particularly interested in accessing, which contained the super operating system and the VMN-negative database.

My optimistic attempt to immediately view the sub containing the VMN database was, as I had expected it would be, firmly denied with a reminder of the system's first decretal, which was the confidentiality of this particular information. It seemed logical to assume that if I was going to be able to roam freely through the system as I wished, I would have to do it from the privileged access point of the so-called super operative – which in any system is usually the person who created it. So I accessed the super-op sub, and set about the creation of a trap door. I hadn't been in there very long when I met Cerberus.

It's difficult to say exactly how I triggered him. It could have been the very fact of my using an outside keyboard. Or it could have been the fact of my attempting to create a trapdoor from the super-operating sub into the VMN database, but suddenly there he was on-screen, a three-headed black dog graphic with blood-chilling sound effects, and guarding the system from anyone like me who sought to circumvent its first decretal. From the size and number of his teeth I was very glad I had not been wearing my Reality Approximation body suit. It was *clear that I wasn't going any further until I had dealt with him.*

My intoxicated mind was already racing through a number of classically-inspired solutions. Could I drag the monster away, like Hercules, and release it outside of the Lombroso system, somewhere within the BRI's ordinary administrative program files? Or, like Orpheus, could I lull the brute to sleep with the playing of my cithara or my lyre?

Well, I have always liked music and, quickly exiting the Lombroso system program, I set about the creation of a simple tune which I hoped might, in Congreve's phrase, soothe the savage beast.

Re-typing the day's password I faced Cerberus once more and played him my little melody, but to my surprise and irritation he shook each of his three heads, and growled, 'I don't like music, and what's more Eurydice isn't here. There are no women allowed in this particular nether world.'

Exiting the system once more I tried to remember how dead Greeks and Romans had been able to pass into Pluto's kingdom without molestation. And wasn't I forgetting Aeneas and the Sybil who had guided him through the Inferno? What was it that she had given Cerberus? A bone? No, that was not it. Some meat? No. It was a sop: a cake seasoned with poppies and honey with which she drugged the dog. And this was how the Greeks and the Romans had managed it too. A cake placed into the hands of the deceased. The only question was, what sort of cake might seem appetising to a computer-generated guard dog?

Cerberus was programmed to eat up anyone who attempted to disobey Lombroso's first decretal which was to protect the confidentiality of its information. Thus the trick would be to create a cake that would enable Cerberus to fulfil a standard legitimate routine, specifically to eat someone or something, but which would hide a piece of unorthodox active instruction, specifically to fall asleep.

This took rather longer than I thought it would and by the time the cake was baked, so to speak, I could feel the effect of the cocaine beginning to wear off. Even so, I was working at a furious pace and I don't think that I could remember the exact lines of operating system code that I used in my programming recipe. However, the general effect was similar to a computer virus, except that the basic premise was to limit the action of the binary mechanism to Cerberus himself.

Back in the super-op sub-directory, I offered the shiny black beast the cake and, to my delight, he snapped it up greedily. He even licked his chops. For several seconds I waited to see if the 'drug' inside the cake would take effect. Then, almost as quickly as he had appeared, Cerberus fell to the bottom of the screen with a very audible computer SFX thud, and remained motionless.

With the system-guardian out of the way I returned to the trapdoor I had partially created. It seemed there were no other safeguards for halting unauthorised entry and so all I had to do was locate a set of partially accessible pages of data on how the VMN database was constructed, and then to progress from there. Think of it as like an architect knowing which walls were there to support a ceiling and which were not, and which walls might hide a ventilation shaft, or an inspection tunnel, through which a burglar might be able to pass.

Once the trapdoor was completed, I simply dropped through into the VMN database and, like some ghastly nouveau riche in an expensive restaurant ordering the waiters around as if he came there every night of the week, I told the computer to go and search for my file. Thus, in only a matter of a few seconds I had it and, in a few seconds more, had deleted it.

As with reference libraries, most major computer systems have a horror of missing material, and it's normally one of the cardinal rules of electronic burglary that one leaves the database in the same condition as when one logged in. And so I accompanied my own heretical instruction to delete my file with a command that the computer make a hard copy of the whole VMN-negative database, in order that I should placate the system into permitting this one excision.

I don't know that I meant to keep the hard copy I made on disk. As I say, at first it had been my intention merely to delete my own file. But then you don't get to visit the underworld every day of the week. The more I thought about it, the greater was the temptation to do precisely what I had imagined some other unauthorised user doing, and retain the hard copy I had made of all the other VMN-negatives which Lombroso had recorded. Perhaps it was the drug which overcame whatever scruples I might have had about doing such a thing, but in the end the temptation was too great and I kept it.

It would be wrong to say that I knew what I was going to do with the list. I had certainly no intention of selling it to the News of the World. Money means little to me. Apart from that I had no more idea of what to do with it than I had of ethics or morals. It was something done on impulse, for which I made no apology since I firmly believe that one should be a creature of impulse. Principles and such things seem to me to be nonsense, unless of course they are principles of mathematics.

All the same, I feel that I must honestly record the fact that not only did I try to cover my tracks within the program itself, but also that I left in place a logic bomb for anyone who would attempt to uncover them. In logic nothing is accidental. Therefore I must believe that subconsciously at least, the real purpose of copying Lombroso's list of VMN-negatives was already known to me. If at that stage my purpose, in a manner of speaking, could not be consciously imagined, nevertheless it must still have had something in common with the real world.

One hour later, when I was back in my own apartment, watching a film on the Nicamvision, a new state *of affairs began to make itself obvious. To what extent the film itself was responsible, I have no idea, but my own situation seemed somehow to fit a thing that could already exist entirely on its own. Perhaps I had better describe the film. It was one of those old-style vigilante movies, a dystopian tale of the 1970s with a man taking a rough and ready concept of Justice straight through the chests and stomachs of evildoers. Stalking the streets and riding the New York subway at night, this terrible simplifier made himself the bait for unwitting muggers and murderers who, revealing their criminal hands, were themselves gunned down. This was a potent image for one such as myself. Because if things can occur in states of affairs, this possibility must be in them from the beginning.*

Even if one discounts the depression I was feeling in the wake of my cocaine-use, the proposition which presented itself then still strikes me now as logical. As the only logical extension of the Lombroso Program.

But here am I reminiscing – I'd quite forgotten that I am supposed to be planning another execution.

4

'How was Frankfurt?'

Detective Inspector Ed Crawshaw closed the door of Jake's office at New Scotland Yard and sat down.

'That's what I want to talk to you about, Ed,' she said. 'You've probably heard about this multiple who's killing men?'

He nodded. 'Something about it, yes. To do with the Lombroso Program, isn't it?'

'That's right. While I was at the conference, the APC asked me to take over the investigation. I'll still be leading our own inquiry into the Lipstick killings, but there's pressure from the Home Office to get this other one solved, so I'll be spending more time on doing just that. It'll mean that I have to leave you on your own a lot more. You'll have to make your own initiatives and follow up your own ideas. Just keep me informed of what's going on. And if you need to come and pick my brains about something, don't hesitate to walk right in here. I want this bastard caught, Ed, and caught soon.'

Crawshaw nodded slowly.

'Did you put Mary Woolnoth's details through the computer?'

'Yes,' he said. 'There was something that came up. Victim number five, Jessie Weston, liked reading murder-mysteries, same as Mary. Her briefcase contained a copy of *Burn Marks* by Sara Paretsky. I was wondering if she might have bought it at the same shop where Mary bought her Agatha Christie. The Mystery Bookshop in Sackville Street.'

'No reason why not,' said Jake. 'She worked in Bond Street. That's not far from Sackville Street. If you're right it could be that he's not just interested in reading about murder . . .

'. . . he's also interested in doing it too. It's a thought, isn't it? Want me to get a man in there, undercover?'

'Like I said, you'll have to make your own initiatives, Ed,' said Jake. 'But I think you'd do a lot better if you tried to find a few women police constables to volunteer for book-browsing duty.'

'A stake-out.'

Jake winced. 'I've never much liked that term,' she said. 'It always seems to imply that whatever is staked out gets devoured. When I was back in the European Bureau of Investigation's Behavioural Science Unit, we always used to call that kind of operation a golden apple. Psychologically, it's a lot more encouraging for the volunteer.'

Jake glanced at her watch and stood up. 'I have to be downstairs,' she said and then added: 'And, Ed. Make sure they wear lots of red lipstick. I think our man could turn out to have a chromatic trigger for his aggression. I wouldn't want to lose catching this son-of-a-bitch because some little fashion-conscious WPC prefers a different shade of lipstick that suits her skin a lot better. It's got to be the colour of blood or nothing.'

The Police Computer Crime Unit occupied an air-conditioned section of the basement at New Scotland Yard. Semi-transparent sliding doors succeeded in hiding the mess, which was that of an electrical repair-shop, without stopping the light.

Jake picked her way through a large room that was home to a miniature city of redundant monitors, discarded keyboards, and stocking-snagging laser-printers. She cursed loudly at the discovery of this last fact, but continued on to the end of the room where a brightly coloured open iron stairway led straight up to a short gallery of offices. Jake knocked at the crinkled fibreglass that was the door of one of these and went in. She was supposed to meet the head of the CCU there and be introduced to the expert assigned to her investigating team: the best man in the CCU, as had been requested.

The best man in the CCU, according to its own Chief Inspector, was Detective Sergeant Yat Chung.

Jake found herself repeating the name with some surprise. 'Kind of a name is that?'

Chief Inspector Cormack shrugged. 'Yat,' he said again, nodding. 'He's a Chink.'

Jake smiled thinly. 'Yes, well I didn't figure he was the Prince of Wales.'

'He's God as far as I'm concerned,' Cormack stated. 'There's nothing he doesn't know about artificial intelligence. And quite a lot he could guess at that hasn't even been invented yet. Gilmour says I'm supposed to lend you my best man. But you people worry me. There's a psycho involved here, isn't there? Normally the most dangerous thing Yat has to deal with is a short circuit. So I'll tell you frankly that if there's the slightest chance of any physical harm coming to him from your investigation, I'd prefer to tell you to sod off and risk the disciplinary hearing.'

'Relax,' Jake told him. 'I won't so much as let him floss his teeth in case he makes his gums bleed. All I want him to do is a scenes-of-crime on a computer, not talk a gun out of a killer's hand.'

Cormack nodded. He was a tall, gruff Scot with a prophet's beard and a scruffy, unworldly air about him, as if he had grown up on a Petri dish. Behind smudged glasses Cormack's eyes stared. They followed the ladder in Jake's black stocking up to her thigh and under the hem of her short skirt. Even though he himself knew he was too long in the tooth for such things, he still found himself breathing heavily like an infatuated sixth-former at the vision of womanhood sitting opposite him. Tall, severely feminine with a knuckle-rapping voice and the kind of stare that could crack a man's glasses and frost his beard. He had a taste for women like Jake: handsome rather than pretty, athletic as opposed to elegant, intelligent rather than charming. Women who looked as though they knew one end of a soldering-iron from the other. But most of all Cormack liked them to be hard bitches, the type he had often seen in magazines wearing leather and wielding whips.

'What kind of a computer?' he said swallowing a couple of litres of oxygen.

'A Paradigm Five,' she answered.

'And the operating system?'

'The European Community Data Network.'

He sighed and shook his head. 'Shit,' he said wearily. 'They've not long finished installing it. Where's the breach?'

'The Brain Research Institute. The Lombroso computer.'

'Yes, I thought I did hear something about that.'

'Yeah, well keep it under your toupee. The Home Office is pretty touchy about the whole thing. I want your man to tell me whether the breach came from the inside or the outside.'

'Who's their bod?'

Jake spread the PC open on her lap and consulted the file.

'Doctor Stephen St Pierre,' she said. 'Know him?'

Cormack grunted. 'St Pierre was formerly the head of computer security in the British Army,' he said.

'And?'

Cormack rocked his head from side to side as if deliberating which side to come down on. At the same time Jake crossed her legs. After a few seconds of vacuuming the sight of Jake's underwear onto his retinas, Cormack pursed his lips and said, 'Basically he's all right. If he does have a fault it's that he's too literal. Tends to sound as if he writes computer manuals in his spare time. Trouble is that most computer crime these days is committed by people with rather more imagination than you could find evidence for in any system manual.'

'Army security, eh?' Jake typed a note onto the file. 'How long?'

'Five years. Went into the army straight from Cambridge.'

'College?'

'I believe it was Trinity. He read classics.'

'So where does the interest in grey goods come from?'

'Computers? Oh, his father worked for IBM.' Cormack smiled. 'That's something we have in common.'

'Your father too?'

'No. Me actually. I used to design business software. Accounts packages, that kind of thing.'

'Interesting,' said Jake.

'Not really. That's why I joined the Met. To catch electronic burglars.'

'The Lombroso people were pretty stiff about the suggestion that anyone could have broken into their system. But they were just as stiff about the idea of an inside job. What do you think? Is it possible, from the outside?'

'Twenty years ago, when the UK Government installed the Government Data Network specification on all departmental computers, they thought it was impregnable. But within five years, the system was revealed to have more holes than a Russian condom. You see, systems are designed by people, and people are sometimes fallible, and sometimes corrupt. If you could eliminate the human element of the equation altogether then you could probably make a system that was completely secure.' He shrugged. 'The most probable case-scenario here? Someone was careless. Probably they change the password every day at this Brain Research Institute. Well that's a double-edged sword. On one level it makes it difficult for someone to work out what the password could be by process of elimination. But it also makes it difficult for the people who work there to remember.

Maybe someone writes the word down. Maybe he asks someone else to remind him. In this way an unauthorised person might catch sight of or overhear the password. And then he's in. It could be that simple.'

Cormack lit a small cigar. Smoking was forbidden anywhere in the building, but with the door shut, nobody was likely to make a fuss about it except Jake herself and Cormack knew that so long as she was asking favours from his department she would not object to it.

'Of course, having got into the system he then has to understand its language. He'd need a protocol analyser.'

'What's that?'

'A protocol is a set of rules. An analyser is a portable device with its own miniature screen and keyboard. Looks much like that computer on your lap. Bigger maybe. This examines the target system's telephone line or the port itself and carries out tests to see which of the hundreds of datacomm protocols are in use. A good one, fully digital, will handle asynchronous or synchronous transmissions. Some of them even have dedicated hacker's software to make the whole process even easier.'

Jake was relieved when the intercom on Cormack's desk buzzed noisily. Technical explanations like this one left her feeling short of air. Cormack stabbed the answer button as if it was a midge which had been irritating him.

'Detective Sergeant Chung, sir,' said a voice. 'You said to buzz you.'

'Yat, I want you to come up to my office,' he said, so loudly that he hardly seemed to require an intercom at all. 'Someone I want you to meet.'

Cormack released the button and pointed the same finger at Jake.

'Just a word or two about Yat,' he said, frowning. 'He's a bit of a grumpy bastard. Like most Hong Kong Chinese, he's had a pretty rough time of it. Came here when he was a kid, when the colony folded. But – well you know what I'm talking about.'

Jake who still remembered watching the whole tragic affair on television knew very well what Cormack was talking about. The return of the colony to Communist China had been achieved with a spectacular degree of inefficiency and injustice. At the same time, Jake hated the idea of having to persuade people to do what they were supposed to do anyway. She didn't much care to tiptoe round the feelings of people who thought that their sex or race gave them special privileges. New Scotland Yard was full of that kind of bullshit.

'I'm sure we'll get on just fine,' she said coolly. 'Just as long as he gives me his best work.'

It never seemed to rain anymore, thought Jake as the police car taking her and Yat Chung to the Brain Research Institute crawled slowly along the dusty streets. Here it was, the middle of winter and the previous summer's water-rationing was still in force. In some parts of southern England they had been taking their water from stand-pipes for over five years now. She wondered what the slight little man sitting beside her thought about it. He lived near Reading, in the centre of the main drought area. After living in Hong Kong, he was possibly used to taking water from a communal tap. She wondered if he would have laughed at the suggestion. Considering the matter a second time she thought it seemed unlikely that he would have laughed at all. Cormack had not exaggerated about Yat Chung's temperament. He seemed to possess a temper that was the equal of any of three killers Jake had helped send into punitive coma.

'I don't believe this fucking country,' he snarled as once more the car came to a halt. It had taken them fifteen minutes to drive fifty metres.

'What don't you believe about it?'

'Fucking traffic for one thing,' he said, hardly looking at her.

'Yeah, well we'd have walked but for all your computer equipment. It's not like this place is very far away.'

'Fucking people for another.'

Furious at something, he jerked his head in the direction of an enormous crowd of people who were waiting to get on a bus.

'Look at them all. Why doesn't someone do something?'

'It wasn't always this bad,' Jake said drily. 'I remember a time when life in this city was really quite tolerable.'

'Yeah? When was that then?'

'Before 1997.'

'And then all us fucking lot turned up, eh?' He grinned quite unexpectedly. 'You're one fucking funny lady.'

Jake smiled back. She disliked being called a lady almost as much as she disliked being called a fucking funny one.

'Don't think I don't appreciate the compliment,' she said. 'But I'd rather you watched your fucking language a little more when you're with me, please.'

'My language wasn't always this bad,' said Yat. 'Before 1997, it was really quite tolerable.'

He laughed so heartily at his own joke that for a moment Jake found herself wondering if he could be quite as expertly familiar with computers as Cormack had said: there was a crude aspect to him that seemed to be quite at odds with the very idea of something as precise as a computer.

Out of the corner of her eye she toyed with the complexity of trying to describe him, supposing, for whatever reason, a police description had been required. Slim, medium height, aged about thirty-five, wearing an expensive-looking navy blue tracksuit with the sleeves rolled up his bony forearms. Then what? His face was young, almost childlike. The skin enviably smooth and soft-looking. Pretty much like any other young man from Hong Kong. It made her think about what it was to try and construct a description. Of how much more it was in the eye of the beholder, an internal as opposed to an external thing. Any description of another human being could reveal as much about the person who was constructing it as the person being described.

At last they pulled up outside a building of gold-hued plate-glass, reflecting the afternoon sky as if it were really some kind of meteorological centre. A jet moved from one side of the refractive edifice to the other, followed closely by a flight of silent pigeons and the disturbing speed of a bank of cloud. Coming up beside her, Yat followed the line of Jake's gaze.

'Does heaven always move like this for you?' he asked.

She bit her lip and started purposefully towards the main, camera-controlled door. But Yat, insensitive to the rhythm and volume of Jake's high heels which spoke volumes of her irritation, easily kept pace with her despite his several bags of equipment.

'When you want the earth to move for you, just speak to me, right?' He grinned suggestively.

Jake made the door first and held it open for him. As he passed through, she said, 'Cormack tells me that you're a bloody genius with computers. You'd better start proving it, Yat boy.' She followed him up to the security desk and added, 'I've got nothing personal against your kind. But I could make an exception in your case, Sergeant. Understand?'

He sneered back at her. 'Trouble with you whiteys, you got no sense of humour.'

The Brain Research Institute was located in an intelligent building, with its own central computer controlling the lighting, security, temperature and telephone system. The building did more or less everything itself, from locating a fire and calling the fire brigade, to acting as the Institute's receptionist. While Chung put the bags through the X-ray machine, Jake typed out their details onto the screen of the reception computer, which then told them to wait until someone could collect them. After a minute or so a thermal printer produced a couple of security passes which they affixed to their jackets. At the same time, a lift door opened and an immensely tall man wearing a white coat and a poorly-shaven face advanced to greet them, his outstretched hand extending from a shirt cuff that barely concealed what looked like a combination suit of body hair.

Jake almost gagged with disgust. Hirsuteness was the thing she found most physically repellent in men.

'David Gleitmann,' declared the lugubriously-faced man. 'I'm Professor of Neuro-endocrinology here. I run the Research Institute and the Program.'

Jake introduced herself and Sergeant Chung who grunted and pointedly looked in the opposite direction. She had known him for less than an hour and already she felt like coshing him to a pulp.

The lift carried them to the top floor.

Womb-like: that was Jake's thought as she followed Gleitmann into his office. The walls were the same shade of beige as the floor and the ceiling, and but for the expensive hardwood furniture, you could have turned the room upside down or sideways and inhabited it just as easily. What at first impression looked like windows were flat, rectangular-shaped lights. And although it was equally modern in its origin, the furniture had a slightly classical air about it, all plinths, cross-beams and arches, as if having once belonged to some mediaeval Greek philosopher, an effect which was enhanced by some enormous leather-bound books which lay on the floor like a pile of paving slabs. A free-standing bookcase that was the size and shape of a pagan family shrine occupied each of the room's seven corners. Another man was already seated at the refectory-sized table. He stood up as they came into the office and Gleitmann introduced him as Doctor Stephen St Pierre. The computer man, Jake said to herself, noting only that he seemed nervous.

Gleitmann offered them coffee. Yat Chung announced that he would prefer tea and then avoided his superior's eye as she tried to glare balefully at him.

They seated themselves at Gleitmann's table, with Yat Chung several places away from the other three, almost as if he didn't wish to be part of the meeting. But Jake noticed his renewed interest in being there when Gleitmann's secretary, a beautiful Chinese, arrived bearing a tray of refreshments, which included Yat's tea. She watched the sergeant's eyes following the girl out of the door and approved of his taste. The girl was worth the look.

'I've been told by the Home Office people that I'm to extend you every facility,' Gleitmann stated with apparent discomfort.

'If you wouldn't mind,' Jake said politely. Whether you mind or not, she said to herself.

Gleitmann stretched his lower lip against a perfect row of teeth and then bit it. 'Mark Woodford mentioned something about everyone having to take a polygraph.'

'That's right. Detective Sergeant Jones from my investigating team will be handling that part of the inquiry. But I'd like him to carry out the tests as quickly as possible.' She opened her bag, took out a packet of sweeteners and then added one to her coffee. 'When can I tell him to bring his equipment?'

She saw Gleitmann exchange a brief look with St Pierre, who shook his head and then shrugged.

'Whenever you like, Chief Inspector,' Gleitmann sighed. 'If you think it's really necessary.'

'I do,' Jake said firmly. 'Tell me something, Professor: are you still carrying out testing within the context of the Lombroso Program?'

'I've certainly had no instructions to say that I should stop.' He tapped the ends of his long fingers together as if waiting to be contradicted. Jake said nothing. 'That is correct, isn't it? There has been no order from the Home Office telling us to stop.'

Jake noticed the way a singular had been transformed into a plural. This was an obvious sign of weakness and she decided to take advantage of it.

'It's hardly a question of needing an order, surely,' she said. 'Under the circumstances I should have thought that you yourself might wish to call a halt to the Program. At least until Detective Sergeant Chung has had a chance to determine the origin of the security breach.'

'I can't see how that would help.' This was Doctor St Pierre. 'I think we have to assume that the killer is already possessed of all the information he or she requires.'

'In my experience, it's safer not to assume anything with this type of killer,' said Jake, glancing negligently at her fingernails. 'But if there are any assumptions to be made, Doctor, I'll make them, if you don't mind.'

'But surely, Chief Inspector, stopping the Program now would be a case of shutting the stable door — '

Chung frowned, uncomprehending, as Gleitmann neglected to complete the saying.

'Your assumption is that the killer's familiarity with the Lombroso Program data is not current. I don't think that it's valid to decide that he, or she (although I believe that we are dealing with a man), no longer has access to the system, albeit unauthorised access. Until we know how system security was broken I would suggest that by continuing to make tests, you could be putting even more men at risk.'

Gleitmann stirred his coffee thoughtfully. 'I'm afraid I can't agree with you there,' he said flatly. 'If you want to put a halt to the Program, I think you'll have to take it up with the Home Office.'

Jake shrugged. 'Very well then.'

The professor's long dark face took on an exasperated sort of look.

'Chief Inspector,' he said pompously. 'I don't think you can have considered the substantial investment that a project like this represents. There are other ramifications beside the rather more manifest one of individual security. Need I remind you that this is a private facility? Any governmental association here results from a purely contractual obligation. I have a duty to my shareholders as well as to the patients. The financial, not to say political, implications of what you're proposing – '

Jake brought him to a halt with the only traffic signal she could still remember from her Hendon training. Several gold bangles shifted noisily on her strong, slim wrist like a tiny tambourine.

'I have considered these factors,' she said. 'And I say to hell with them.'

Doctor St Pierre leaned forward across the table and clasped his wrestler-strangling hands. Jake considered that he was not the obvious army type. A bulky strong man, he wore his dark hair cropped labour-camp short and his beard Karl Marx bushy. Rimless glasses enhanced an appearance of some intellectuality. He looked like a well-read Hell's Angel. She wondered if such an obviously masculine personal image might not mean that St Pierre was gay. He smiled and when he spoke it was with a slight defect, as if his moustache was interfering with the manipulation of his lips.

'Will that be in your memorandum to the Minister?' he asked.

Gleitmann butted in before Jake could reply. 'Your brief, as I understand it, Chief Inspector, is merely to determine the source of our security breach. Is that not so?' He wasn't looking for an answer. 'That hardly seems to cover something as important as the continued operation of the Program. I suggest that you stay within your original brief. Naturally we shall afford Detective Sergeant Chung here all the help we can. We're as anxious as you are to clear this thing up. But anything more than that – ' He shrugged eloquently. 'I'm sorry, no.'

'As you prefer,' said Jake. 'However I would like to speak to each of your counsellors.'

'May I ask why?'

'So as not to waste any time I'd like to work on the assumption that the security breach occurred externally. Moreover that it was somebody who had himself been tested VMN-negative who was responsible. Let me explain. As I understand it, the Lombroso Program determines those men who may eventually suffer from a serious aggressive disorder. At least for the moment I'd like my investigation to proceed on the basis that one such VMN-negative male has done just that – developed a serious aggressive disorder – and that it is directed against those others like himself. It may be that one of your counsellors can recall an individual who may have exhibited a significant level of hostility towards the Program and its participants.'

'You do appreciate that all men testing VMN-negative are given codenames by the computer,' said St Pierre. 'Even if one of our counsellors could remember such an individual as you describe, it would only be by that codename. I can't see how that would help you.'

'Nevertheless I should still like to question them. Or do you have objections to that as well?'

St Pierre combed his beard with both sets of fingers and then cleared his throat. 'No objections at all, Chief Inspector. I'm just trying to save you some work, that's all.' He glanced at his wristwatch. 'Perhaps I could show Sergeant Chung the Paradigm Five now.'

Jake nodded at Yat who drained his tea cup and stood up. While he and St Pierre were on their way out of the room Jake stared at the smudged red-crescent her lipstick had left on her own cup and wondered how Crawshaw would be getting on. This was going to be harder than she had imagined. Gleitmann and his people didn't look like they were going to be much help. She already had troubles back at the Yard with her superior because of his having been removed from the case. Except for the ban on smoking in all office buildings she would have had a cigarette. Probably two. Then Gleitmann said something to her.

'I'm sorry?' she said.

'I said, let's hope your man can sort this out.'

'Yes, let's,' Jake agreed. She helped herself to more of

the coffee. 'We were discussing your counsellors,' she said.

'Yes. Doctor Cleobury is head of psychiatry here at the Institute. She's responsible for all the counsellors. Would you like me to ask her to join us?'

Jake shook her head. 'No that won't be necessary at this stage. We'll start here in London and then question the counsellors in Birmingham, Manchester, Newcastle and Glasgow.'

'All of them?'

'All of them. Oh, and I'd appreciate it if you could provide me with an office with a pictophone and a computer, from where I can conduct my enquiries.'

'Of course. I'll have my secretary arrange it. But please speak to the computer if you need anything else. This is an intelligent building, after all. Meanwhile I'll have Doctor Cleobury make all the counsellors available to you.'

'Thank you.'

She watched him make the call and then turned her attention to his library. Quite a few of the books were familiar to her from her days as a forensic psychologist with the European Bureau of Investigation; and quite a few had been written by Gleitmann himself, some of them collected in bulk as if he had been running a bookshop. On one shelf alone she counted fifty copies of *The Social Implications of Human Sexual Dimorphism*. He was proud of his work, that much was clear. She pulled a copy down and started to read.

'I'd like to borrow this,' she told him when he had finished on the pictophone.

Gleitmann smiled sheepishly. 'Help yourself.'

When she returned home Jake ate the remains of a tuna salad she had made the night before. Then she sat down at her electronic piano. She selected a disc from the many she had collected and slid it into the piano's software-port. It was the Schubert piano trio in B flat, or at least the recordings of the cello and violin parts, with the score for the piano appearing on the keyboard's integrated LCD screen.

Jake, who had been an accomplished pianist as a teenager, played with precision, although she lacked the skill of the two string players on the recording to add the expression that made the piece such a masterpiece of youthful optimism. She particularly relished playing the scherzo with its extended staccato crotchets and quavers and its artful counterpoint. If there was one piece of music that was almost guaranteed to put her in a good humour it was this Opus 99 scherzo. And when the gypsy-like rondo of the fourth and last movement had brought her playing to its charging, bouncing climax, she collapsed into an armchair and sighed with pleasure.

The memory of the music lingered on her finger ends and in her invigorated senses for several minutes afterwards; and later on, she was even equal to the task of reading Gleitmann's book.

It was, she considered, not a bad book at all. She liked it better than she had expected. It was true, a lot of it was guesswork, but it was intelligent plausible guesswork.

Jake was reminded of her own work in the field of male sexual psychology with the EBI, before a career at Scotland Yard had beckoned. Sometimes she was asked why she had joined such a male-dominated institution as the Yard, especially when men were so obnoxious to her. For Jake the answer was simple: with so many women falling victim to male criminals it did not seem politic to entrust the protection of women exclusively to men. Women had the responsibility to help protect themselves.

When at last she put Gleitmann's book down, having read almost half of it, she was amused to discover that he had previously signed it.

That, she told herself, was just men all over.

Be patient. I'll describe the next execution in just a minute. In Cold Blood, as Truman Capote would say. First, let me quickly mention the last factor in my life's new gestalt.

After my night on the computer and my idea about those other men who tested VMN-negative, I kept the appointment I had made before the test with my analyst, Doctor Wrathall.

You will ask why I was already seeing a psychoanalyst. Actually, I'm a bit of a neurotic and I've been having a weekly session for almost two years now. My relationship with Doctor Wrathall has really helped me a lot. (This is all so imprecise, but it can't be helped.) Much of what he and I discuss relates to my own feelings of personal dissatisfaction.

The world is independent of my will, at least in so far as my will is essentially the subject of ethical attributes, and of interest as a phenomenon only to people like Doctor Wrathall. So it is easy to see that by discussing the phenomenon of my will in this way, I was attempting to determine the limits of my world and how these might be altered.

So straightaway I asked Doctor Wrathall if a man who suddenly perceived his real duty in life should risk everything to achieve it. I was not referring to the kind of duty one owes one's fellow motorists. Nor the kind of duty one has to honour one's father and mother. No. I was of course referring to the greatest duty one can ever owe, which is the duty one has to oneself, to the 'creative demon'.

Doctor Wrathall hummed and hawed and finally said

that by and large he was himself of the opinion that in life it was good to take a few risks now and again. A sense of mission and purpose was what made it worth living.

It would be wrong to add a structure to what was said. Doctor Wrathall is a simple soul and, like most analysts, he is not able to articulate much that is of any real consequence. Usually it is quite enough for me that he has listened, albeit uncomprehending. And so this question was a comparatively rare phenomenon, occasioning an even rarer response. Indeed, Doctor Wrathall was moved to ask a question or two himself, as to the nature of this 'creative demon'. By the tramline-thinking of his profession he even made the predictable enquiry as to why I thought I had used the words 'duty' and 'demon'. I lost the poor devil when, by way of an answer, I asserted that the issue was metaphysical rather than empirical. What untidy minds some people have!

By the time I reached home again I was convinced not merely that I should follow my impulses with regard to my brother VMNs, but that I had a moral obligation to do so. Look at Paul Gauguin for instance: he threw up everything – wife, home, children, job, security – because he had a passionate, profound, intense desire to paint pictures. That's the sort of man to be.

Perhaps you will say that killing isn't much of a vocation compared with painting. But I ask you to look beyond the conventional moralities and consider the phenomenology of the matter. I blush to use a word like 'existentialism'; however, that is the essence of what I am describing. Think of the character of Meursault in L'Etranger and you have it. Only the prospect of death – one's own, or of others, it makes no difference – makes life real. Death is the one true certainty. When we die the world does not alter, but comes to an end. Death is not an event in life. But killing . . . killing is.

Consider then the concept of killing: the assertion of one's own being by the denial of another's. Self-creation by annihilation. And how much more self-creating where those others who must be destroyed are themselves a danger to society in general. Where the killing is done with a very real purpose. Thus, the taint of nihilism is avoided. The authentic act of pure decision is no longer committed at random with scant regard to meaning. All this provides the key to the problem, how much truth there is in solipsism.

My next victim, codename Bertrand Russell, was an art lover. In all else he was unpredictable. So unlike his illustrious namesake with his mathematical logic. Russell left for work at different times of the morning and returned home at different times of the evening. I imagine he was on flexi-time or whatever it is they call it. He was employed in an office on the Albert Embankment in some minor sales and marketing role for the company that makes a brand of caffeine-plus beverage called Brio: 'Coffee's never been so full of beans'.

But every lunchtime at precisely 12.45, Russell would cross over Vauxhall Bridge and walk up Millbank to the Tate Gallery, where he would eat a sandwich in the café downstairs (I don't think I ever saw him drink any coffee), and then spend approximately thirty minutes looking at the pictures.

He was an odd-looking fellow, although he seemed to blend in well with all the art-students that the place attracts. There was something gnomic about his features: the ears too large and too prominent, the chin too recessive, the nose too bulbous, the eyes too small, and the head too large for his scrawny neck. You could have used him as the cover illustration for any gothic fantasy novel. This effect was enhanced by the long, grey coat he was wearing which seemed a couple of sizes too big for him and which put me in mind of Dopey in Snow White and the Seven Dwarfs. And yet there was nothing benign about this peculiar creature. Russell's was a wicked face of the kind that guest-star in children's nightmares. If ever a man looked like a potential killer it was Bertrand Russell.

Following him around the gallery (he seemed to be particularly fond of the Pre-Raphaelites, which, in itself, is a good reason to shoot anyone) I wondered how much he knew about the Cambridge philosopher whose Lombroso-given name he bore. When you think about it, I ought to have introduced myself. I could have made some caustic remark about the Principia Mathematica, or even disputed the value of his attempt to arrive at atomic propositions. Not that it really matters. We never really got on, he and I. I always thought that he was a bit of an old fraud.

Of course none of this crossed my mind as I trailed after him, awaiting my opportunity to grant him the temporal immortality of the human soul, that is to say, its eternal survival after death, assuming that such a thing exists. I must confess that I was just a little nervous about (and contrary to my usual practice) the prospect of killing in a public place, in broad daylight. So I said nothing at all. Just watched.

Did he sense something perhaps? Was there, in the ether between us, a picture of a deadly thought that slowly transferred itself from my mind to his? Because there was one moment – I think it must have been while he was bending over a glass case to inspect some watercolours painted by William Blake – when he looked up and, catching my eye, smiled at me. I cannot say what I might have looked like. Nevertheless, I have the impression that I must have appeared comic somehow, or perhaps my jaw dropped dramatically, because he laughed. He laughed as if I had been a small child saying something impossibly cute.

At this I felt real anger towards him for the very first time and, in the same second, realising that that part of the gallery which houses a woefully inadequate number of the works of the greatest Englishman who ever lived was empty, I drew my gun from my shoulder-holster and fired at the very centre of his under-resourced forehead.

Russell collapsed onto the floor, catching his chin on the edge of the cabinet as he fell. For a brief second one hand pressed at the hole my first shot had made as the blood started down the bridge of his nose, while the other held on to the cloth cover that protects the drawings and watercolours from the damaging sunlight. I almost thought that he would tear it, but then it was through his fingers and I was striding round the cabinet to stand over him and let go with the rest of the clip. My second and third shots silently blasted away two of his fingers. And there was more blood than perhaps I am used to — another reason why working in daylight is more difficult. Some of his gore even splashed onto the toe of my shoe. For all these reasons I could not recall if I heard the sound that denotes a successful headshot or not.

It was then I became aware that I had shot him in the front and not the back of the head, which is of course my usual practice. So, as I strode nonchalantly away from Russell's body, I was possessed only of the probability that I had succeeded in killing him. And we only use probability in default of certainty.

5

Jake paused in front of one of the pictures. She liked William Blake. Always had done. There were two prints of his paintings on the wall of her bathroom. Blake was not everyone's taste, she knew. Some people found him too mystical, especially for a bathroom. But Jake had a soft spot for all kinds of mysticism and her best investigative thinking was often done in the smallest room. While her thinking was more temporal than terrestrial, nevertheless Blake's pictures inspired her with an insight as to the darker side of man which, as a detective, she found useful.

She turned her attention to the large bloodstain on the floor which was now being photographed from every conceivable angle, as if its shape contained some symbolic significance. The scenes-of-crime officer, whose name was Bruce, squatted down beside her.

'What have we got, Sergeant?' she asked him.

'Well, it's not Jerusalem, ma'am,' he said. 'I'll tell you that much.'

'I will not cease from mental fight, Sergeant Bruce,' she returned. 'Nor shall my sword sleep in my hand. But I'd be grateful if you would kindly stop stating the obvious, albeit poetically.'

'Yes, ma'am,' said Bruce, quickly flipping open his PC. 'Oliver John Mayhew, of 137 Landor Road, SW9. Shot six times in the head, fairly close range, at around 1.20 this afternoon. The security guard found him. Says he didn't see or hear anything.'

'Dead?'

'Not quite. Been taken to Westminster Hospital, ma'am. I've sent a constable with him just in case he has time for a last soliloquy. What's the Yard's interest in this case?'

'I'm not at liberty to tell you, Sergeant,' she said, disliking herself for this reticence.

Jake hated keeping any investigating officer in the dark, but with the Home Office taking such a particular interest in keeping the lid on the Lombroso connection, she had little choice in the matter. She was as surprised to find herself there, staring at the bloodstain on the floor of the Tate Gallery, as the sergeant. Less than half an hour before she had been at the Brain Research Institute when a call came in from the Yard. Even while she had been standing next to the Paradigm Five as Yat Chung tried to trace the origin of the Lombroso system burglar, the machine had tracked the name Oliver John Mayhew as appearing, albeit as a victim, within the context of a violent crime inquiry on the police computer at Kidlington, and alerted the other computer to Mayhew's status as a VMN-negative.

'Let's just say that I'm investigating a similar case,' she told Bruce. 'Any of the art lovers see anything?'

'Doesn't look like it so far. If any of them did, they probably thought it was some kind of performance art.'

'Broad daylight. Don't tell me, all the goddamned doors were locked as well. I don't think I feel like playing Sergeant Cuff this afternoon. No witnesses at all? Jesus Christ.'

'Speaking of whom, the director of the gallery is over there, ma'am. Perhaps, as the senior investigating officer, you wouldn't mind speaking to him. Mr Spencer.'

It was the sergeant's revenge for her not telling him anything. Jake smiled wryly. She'd have done the same thing herself. Looking over her shoulder to the edge of the room which housed the Blakes, she caught sight of a tall, distinguished man wearing a grey suit. He stood, with his arms folded, barely able to contain his impatience.

Jake went over to him, introduced herself and then let

him complain about how intolerable it was that no one, himself included, should have been permitted to leave the gallery. Jake waved Sergeant Bruce towards her.

'Have your men finished checking ID cards yet, Sergeant?'

'Yes ma'am.'

She turned to address the director. 'Well, Mr Spencer. Everyone can leave now. Yourself included.'

But Spencer had not yet finished with his complaints about the high-handedness of the Metropolitan Police.

'Mister Spencer,' said Jake after a couple of minutes of patient listening. 'You know, this isn't much of a room for England's greatest artist. Don't you think it's on the small side for a man with as big a vision as Blake?'

Spencer's frown deepened. 'Don't tell me how to run an art gallery, Chief Inspector,' he growled.

'Well then, please don't tell me how to run a police investigation,' Jake returned.

Just at that moment, Spencer wailed and pointed frustratedly at one of Bruce's team who was cutting out the bloodstained area where Mayhew's body had been found, with a lino-knife.

'Oh really,' he said. 'This is too much. What about that? What about my carpet?'

'Don't worry sir,' said Jake. 'We'll return it to you just as soon as we've finished all our tests. Who knows, with a nice frame, you could try exhibiting it.'

Spencer's mouth opened and closed, and hearing nothing emerge from its mephitic pinkness, Jake wished him a good afternoon and then left.

Mayhew's company medical scheme meant that he was taken to a private clinic attached to the Westminster Hospital. The clinic itself looked like an expensive hotel. Thick pile carpets, leather furniture, big modern paintings, and bonsai trees. There was even a small fountain trickling along with the Muzak in the reception hall. The smell of disinfectant and the occasional white uniform seemed oddly out of place, as if some kind of accident had happened to disturb the atmosphere of quiet luxury.

Detective Inspector Stanley was waiting for her in a silent corridor outside the operating theatre. When, on taking charge of the investigation, Jake recalled the circumstances of their first meeting, she had asked herself if she should keep him on the case: if a police officer investigating a homicide who could attend a scenes-of-crime report on the gynocide could be anything but a liability. Ed Crawshaw, who knew Stanley from Hendon, said he was a good copper, reliable if also rather literal. Jake was inclined to accept this criticism as a point in Stanley's favour. Trusting herself to make the imaginative leaps necessary to solving a case, she preferred working above all with people whom she could trust to do only what they were told. Jake's opinion of the majority of her colleagues at the Yard was that imagination was usually an indication of corruption.

Stanley was a tall, fit-looking man with long hair and the pallor of goat's cheese. He swayed a little on his feet as he started to make his report.

'Shit, what's the matter with you?'

'Hospitals,' he said biliously. 'They always set me off. It's the smell.'

'Well, don't pass out in here. You couldn't afford it.' Jake searched inside her shoulder bag and found a small bottle of smelling salts she had carried since she was a beat copper. 'Here,' she said. 'Snort on this a bit.'

Stanley held the bottle underneath his flaring nostrils. He sniffed a few times and then nodded gratefully. 'Thanks,' he said weakly.

'You'd better hang on to it,' she said. 'Feeling up to filling me in?'

He nodded. 'They're operating on Mayhew right now. But it looks pretty hopeless. The front of his head has got more holes in it than a bowling ball. And he's lost a great deal of blood. But he did come round very briefly while the constable was with him in the ambulance.'

Stanley beckoned to the armed policeman who was standing a short distance away. The man walked towards the two senior officers, his boots squealing on the expensive rubber flooring like a pair of small furry animals.

'Constable, tell the Chief Inspector what Mayhew said to you in the ambulance.'

The constable pushed his machine pistol out of the way, unbuttoned the breast pocket on his flak-jacket and took out his computer. 'He said, "Those bastards. They lied. They lied. I should have known, they always meant to kill me. They lied. Brain. Brain".' He shook his head. 'He wasn't very audible, I'm afraid.'

'You're sure of all that?' said Jake. 'That was exactly as he said it?'

'As exactly as I was able to judge, ma'am. He was more or less delirious.' The constable returned the computer to his pocket and swung the machine pistol back across his chest.

'And he only spoke the one time?'

The constable nodded. 'By the time we got here he'd stopped breathing. I believe they managed to revive him in the operating theatre. The nurse has promised to keep an ear on anything else he might say while he's in there.'

'Thank you,' said Jake. 'If he says anything else, no matter how trivial, I want to know about it. Understand?'

'Ma'am.'

Jake and Inspector Stanley were half way along the corridor leading to the front door when they heard a shout behind them. They turned and saw the constable wave them back. Beside him stood a man in a green overall.

'I'm sorry,' said the surgeon, when they reached him. 'But your man never regained consciousness.'

Lester French, a firearms expert in the Forensic

Pathologist's Office at the Yard, stood up from his collection of microscopes and cameras and dropped a bullet into Jake's outstretched palm.

'That's what killed Mayhew,' he said. 'That, and five others like it. Your killer's no fool, I'll tell you that much. There's quite a lot of stopping power in that little beauty.'

'And this is the same kind of bullet that killed all the others?'

French nodded firmly.

'How does it work?'

'The cartridges themselves are masterpieces of precision engineering,' he said with real admiration. 'A machined brass cartridge case with a self-contained high pressure air reservoir. A simple and effective valve system.' He picked up a small gas cylinder from the laboratory's work bench. 'You charge your cartridges up with this.'

'Are you saying that this killer has been manufacturing his own ammunition?' Jake asked uncertainly, confused by the expert's enthusiasm for his special field.

'No, no. As I said, it involves precision engineering. This particular shell is made by a Birmingham gunsmith. You buy the cartridges from any gun shop. But you stick whatever bullet you like on the end of it. To that extent, your man has been manufacturing his own. And it's pretty heavy stuff too. Hollow-nosed, conical-conoidal, pointed and streamlined.'

'But it is a gas-gun,' Jake said, in search of further elucidation. 'Is that like an air-gun?'

'In the firing of the weapon, yes. But with regard to what comes out of the barrel, no.' He lifted the piece of misshapen metal from Jake's palm and held it up to the light. 'I mean, a conventional air-pellet bears no more resemblance to this than a bloody pea. Whatever you hit with this, stays hit.'

'What does the gun look like?' said Stanley.

French led them through a door at the back of the laboratory to a small firing range. On a trestle table lay what looked like a long-barrelled .44 calibre revolver. He picked the weapon up and handed it to Jake. 'That's the sort of thing,' he said.

'It looks like a normal gun,' she said.

French pursed his lips. 'It does everything that a normal gun is supposed to do.' He nodded in the direction of one of the targets. 'Try it. It's loaded.'

Jake thumbed back the hammer. It felt lighter than a conventional revolver.

'That's it,' said French. 'Now push the safety off and you're ready to fire.'

She levelled the barrel at the target, aimed and then squeezed the trigger. The gun hardly moved in her fist as it fired, with no more sound than a hand slapping a desk top.

'Smooth, eh?'

French led them down to the target.

'This plywood's two centimetres thick, so it ought to give you a pretty good idea of what a good-sized gas-gun will do to a man.'

Jake's bullet had hit the human-shaped target in the centre of the groin.

'Nice shot,' said French. He pulled a pen from his top pocket and probed the hole. 'Clean through. Impressive, eh?'

'It certainly is,' murmured Stanley.

'You can even buy a silencer for this weapon if you still think it's too noisy. But the most remarkable thing about it is that no firearms certificate is required. Anyone over the age of seventeen can walk into a shop and buy one today, no questions asked.'

Jake shook her head. 'How come?'

French shrugged. 'With all the legislative attention focused on conventional firearms, nobody noticed that air-guns were becoming more and more sophisticated. Mind you, you'd have to pay over five hundred dollars for a piece like the one you're holding, Chief Inspector. Twice that for a rifle.'

'You mean to say that there are rifles like this too?' said Stanley.

'Oh yes. Some of them with laser-guided nightsights if it's a bit of poaching you fancy. And, with mercury or glycerine exploding bullets, a gas-rifle would be just the thing for your amateur Lee Harvey Oswald.'

'Presumably the rifles are even more powerful,' Jake observed.

'With the right sort of ammunition, a good gas-rifle could drop a decent-sized stag. Of course, some of those weapons are regulated.' French grinned fiercely. 'Let's hope your man hasn't got hold of one of those. There's no telling what he'd do. Still, it's not like he hasn't been busy already, eh? To shoot a man in the Tate Gallery, in broad daylight. The newspapers are going to love that.'

Later that afternoon Jake had an appointment with her psychotherapist, Doctor Blackwell. The clinic was a smart, three-storey house in Chelsea, just off the King's Road, and Jake had been seeing Doctor Blackwell for almost a year.

Blackwell belonged to the Neo-Existential school of psychotherapy. This avoided the more mechanistic aspects of classical Freudian analysis and encouraged the patient to take charge of her own life. The key element in the relationship between existential therapist and patient was the encounter, wherein the patient's problems were discussed and the therapist tried to direct the patient to the life-enhancing, authentic solutions that were to be discovered through the exercise of free choice. According to Doctor Blackwell the experience derived from these encounters was ultimately transferred to the way in which the patient saw herself and others.

The receptionist smiled as Jake came into the clinic and stood up from behind the desk.

'You're to go straight in,' she said, 'as soon as you've undressed.' She led the way to the changing cubicles.

In common with other Neo-Existential therapists, Doctor Blackwell required that her patients should make the encounter in a state of total nudity, to encourage a sense of greater personal openness. Jake entered the cubicle and drew the curtain behind her. She took off her jacket and laid it on the chair for a moment. Next she unzipped her skirt and hooked it on a hanger to which she then added the jacket. While she was unbuttoning her blouse she heard the familiar rustle of Doctor Blackwell's skirt as she approached the other side of the curtain.

'Just come through when you're ready, Jake,' said the doctor.

It was a small, well-spoken voice that bordered on the edge of being reverent, as if Doctor Blackwell were the Mother Superior of a quiet and very devout order of nuns. The kind of voice that reminded Jake of the headmistress at her own convent school. Perhaps that was one reason why she consulted Doctor Blackwell and not someone else: because she was like someone who had once been kind to her and understanding, and at a time when, thanks to her father, she most needed it.

'All right,' said Jake, stepping quickly out of her pants and unclipping her brassiere. There was a full-length mirror on the wall of the cubicle and briefly Jake regarded her own naked body with criticism. Her breasts were too big, but apart from that everything still looked about the same as when she left Cambridge. Not bad for a woman of thirty-seven. Some of Jake's friends who had had families now looked more like her own mother. There was no doubt, it was having children that really aged a woman.

A red cotton dressing gown that seemed to Jake to be rather masculine was hanging from the clothes peg. Jake put it on, tied the sash and then pulled the curtain back.

Doctor Blackwell's room was big and airy with a deep-pile blue carpet that was specially designed to feel relaxing under barefoot. She was sitting at a large grey leather-topped desk that faced the wall and on which was hanging a copy of a painting by Francis Bacon. Behind her shoulder were two arched windows that were each the size of a telephone box. As Jake came into the room she looked up from Jake's case-notes and smiled sweetly.

'And how have you been?'

'Fine,' said Jake. 'Well, I mean, about the same really. No different.'

Doctor Blackwell nodded. She was a largish woman of about fifty with big, farmer's wife hands and an incongruously doll-like face. Her hair was expensively cut, curving neatly in under each side of her lower jaw, and she wore a short white bouclé dress which showed the tan of her arms and seemed only remotely clinical.

'Is it warm enough for you in here?'

Jake said that it was.

'All right then. Close your eyes and try to relax. That's it. Breathe in, breathe out. Now when I tell you to, I want you to slip off your gown and at the same time I want you to imagine that you're throwing off all your inhibitions, that you're uncovering not just your body, but all your innermost feelings as well.' She paused for a second. 'Now take it off.'

Jake shrugged the gown onto the carpet and stood silently at attention. She felt no sense of shame or embarrassment, only a sense of complete liberation.

'Open your eyes,' Doctor Blackwell said cheerily. 'And lie down.'

In the centre of the room was a black leather couch, and beside it a chair. Jake lay down and stared at the expensive light fitting that helped to heat the room. Then she heard the chair creak as Doctor Blackwell sat down.

'Any more nightmares?' she asked.

'Not lately.'

'Seeing anyone at the moment?'

'You mean am I sleeping with anyone, don't you?'

'If you like.'

'No, I'm not sleeping with anyone.'

'How long has it been since you made love?'

Jake shook her head and remained silent. Then she said: 'I don't know that I've ever done that.'

She heard Doctor Blackwell write something on her notepad.

'And do you still experience feelings of acute hostility to men?'

'Yes.'

'Tell me about the most recent one.'

'There was a man in a hotel in Frankfurt. He tried to pick me up and I was rude to him. Later on, when I saw him in the lift, he assaulted me.'

'How did he assault you?'

'He touched my breast.'

'Did you think he meant to rape you?'

'No, I don't think so. He was just a bit drunk, I think.'

'So what happened then?'

Jake smiled uncomfortably. 'What do you think happened? I decked him.'

'And how did that make you feel?'

'For a while I felt just fine about it,' she said. 'But later on, I wished I hadn't. At least I wished I hadn't hit him quite so hard. Like I said, I wasn't in any danger. I don't know why I did it.'

'Ultimately we are what we choose to do.'

'Well that's why I come here,' said Jake. 'To feel better about the choices I do make.'

'I'm not sure I can help you feel better about assaulting someone,' said Doctor Blackwell. 'But tell me how you feel in general when you discover that some of the choices you've made have been wrong ones. As with this man you hit.'

Jake sighed. 'I feel as if my life has no real meaning.'

'What about your father: how do you feel about him these days?'

'I suppose I hate him even more now that he's dead.'

'Even so, your father was just one man – not every man.'

'A father is every man when you're a child.'

'If your father hadn't been the monster you tell me he was, Jake . . .'

She snorted loudly.

. . . Sometimes she thought it might just have been easier to have told Doctor Blackwell that she had been sexually abused by her father, because the reality of what she had experienced was so much more difficult to explain. Incest between father and daughter and the traumatising effect it could have on a girl was so much more tangible, so much easier to understand than what Jake had been through. It didn't seem quite enough to say that throughout her adolescence Jake had been verbally abused and reviled by her father; that he never missed an opportunity to belittle her in front of other people; that he displayed absolutely no affection for her at all.

She might have been able to have forgiven her father all of that. What she could never have forgiven was his hatred of her mother.

Jake's mother had been a timid, long-suffering sort of woman, apparently able to ignore or to excuse each and every manifestation of her husband's vile behaviour: his crippling sarcasm; his angers; his sulks; his many infidelities; his lies; and his violence. She never found the courage to leave him. Life may have been unspeakable with him, she had said to Jake, but it would have been unthinkable without him. Until finally the day came when that unspeakable existence had suddenly become unbearable and she had killed herself.

It had been the seventeen-year-old Jake who found her lying on the floor of the garden shed, with a kitchen knife in her chest. Naturally she had assumed that her mother had been murdered by her father. Perhaps that was how she had meant it to look. But the police had discovered that a vice on her father's work-bench was adjusted to the width of the knife handle. They had concluded that she had fixed the knife in the vice and then deliberately impaled herself upon it, in the manner of a Roman general. For a long time Jake had held the belief that the police had been wrong and that her father had indeed murdered her mother. It was only after she herself joined the police that she was finally able to accept the truth of their conclusion.

Discovering her own mother's suicide left Jake with an abiding horror of suicide. Not to mention a fully focused hatred for her father; and by the time he himself died of a brain tumour some three years afterwards, which at least explained his appalling behaviour, Jake's hatred for the most important man in her life had become something altogether more generic . . .

'. . . do you think it's possible you might not have hated men in general?'

Jake paused for a moment. 'Yes,' she said, 'it's possible.'

'And in theory, do you think it's possible that you might have experienced a satisfactory relationship with a man?'

'That's a hard question. If you were in my line of work and you saw some of the things that men, and only men, are capable of . . . Jesus.'

She thought of Mary Woolnoth's dead body, and the abuse lipsticked on it.

'Well in theory, yes, I suppose it's possible. But look, I'm not here because I think there's something wrong with my sexual make-up.'

'Yes, I know, you're here because you think your life has no meaning.'

'That's right.'

'All the same, your life has no meaning because of your own ontological insecurity, Jake. Because you're divided against yourself. The division in you manifests itself in these pathological displays of hostility to men.

You're an intelligent woman. You don't need me to tell you that.'

Jake sat up and covered her bare breasts with her hands. She sighed deeply and swung her legs off the couch. Doctor Blackwell stood up and walked back to her desk where she sat down again, and made a note on Jake's file.

'You know, we've made real progress today,' she said with equanimity. 'This is the first occasion when you've admitted that but for your father things might have been different for you.'

Jake got off the couch, picked the gown off the carpet where she had dropped it, and slipped it on.

'So what does that prove?' she said.

'Oh I don't know that it proves anything. Proof is not something that's accorded particular importance in Neo-Existential therapy. But it's obviously something that's of fundamental importance in your life.'

'Of course it is. I'm a cop, for Christ's sake . . .'

'That's just fine. Only I question its validity as the sole criterion for determining your personal life as well. The violence and hostility are merely reinforcement techniques for what it is that you're trying to prove to yourself. And what you're trying to repress. Perhaps when you have accepted the veracity of the choices you do have, proof will seem to be of less importance to you. But you know, before anything improves, I think you have to discover at least one man you can wholeheartedly admire, in the same way that you once admired your father. Maybe then you'll start to feel authentic again.'

Jake nodded sullenly. 'Maybe,' she said.

Doctor Blackwell smiled. 'That's what choice is all about.'

Jake, who was in her mid-thirties, lived alone in Battersea, close by the Royal Academy of Dancing. She remembered a time when she wanted to be a ballet dancer, only her father had told her she was too tall and for once, he had been right.

Her flat was on the top floor of an old-style modern building and, from a small concrete terrace which hosted an unlikely profusion of greenery, it commanded a fine view of the river. Jake loved her flat and her garden terrace and if it had a disadvantage it was that it was too close to the Westland Heliport. White-bodied helicopters had a tendency to circle noisily above her terrace, like giant seagulls, especially when she was sunbathing.

For a brief period Jake had tried sharing her home with a lodger, a girl called Merion, whose mother was a friend of Jake's mother. At first she and Merion had got along well enough. Jake had not even minded when Merion started bringing her hairy boyfriend Jono back to the flat, to make noisy love in Jake's bathtub. She had not even objected that they did not clean it particularly well afterwards. But when, in an unforgivable state of total sobriety, Jono had made a very determined pass at Jake and Jake had responded by punching him out cold, Merion took exception to Jake's forthright manner and left soon afterwards.

There followed a period of intense promiscuity in which Jake engaged as much to celebrate the return of her privacy as it was born of any real appetite, and which matched an equally intense, equally protracted and equally unsatisfactory period of promiscuity during her twenties. After that she had a brief and inevitably stormy relationship with an actor who lived in Muswell Hill and who maintained a fashionable hostility to South London and the police, with Jake an occasional and simultaneous exception.

Since then two years had passed, during which Jake had remained more or less celibate. The more when a man she had been questioning kicked her in the crotch and left her having to take four weeks off work; and the less the previous New Year's Eve, at a party with an equally callous man who worked for the BBC.

When Jake arrived home she watered her plants and then cooked herself a microwave dinner. Then she turned on the television and picked up the evening paper.

French had been right. The shooting had made the final edition of the *Evening Standard*, and although there was no mention of the Lombroso Program, the writer was still able to say that the police were working on the assumption that the attack on Mayhew was connected with a number of other recent and unsolved killings.

Jake took an extra interest in the report, knowing that it contained an important piece of misinformation. At her own order, the Press Office at New Scotland Yard had concealed the fact of Mayhew's death. Instead they had fed the newspapers the story that a policeman was remaining beside Mayhew's bed night and day in the hope that he might recover consciousness and offer a description of his assailant. It was Jake's vague hope that the killer might be moved to try and finish the job. She knew it wasn't much of a plan, but it was worth a try. If the killer did show his face at the Westminster Hospital, he would find the Tactical Firearms Squad waiting there for him.

Fat chance, she thought. That sort of thing only ever happened in the movies. Which was why she was at home and not at the hospital, and thinking about a bath and an early night. Professor Gleitmann's book was on her bedside table and looked like providing her with an effective soporific. But first she turned on the Nicamvision to see if there was anything about Mayhew.

The TV news didn't even bother to report it. It was only a shooting after all, and nothing to compare with the stories of war, famine, and human disaster which constituted the greater part of the bulletin. After the news there was a programme which devoted itself to the pros and cons of punitive coma. This was timely, because an IRA terrorist, Declan Fingal, was to have his sentence of irreversible coma carried out at Wandsworth Gaol the following evening.

Tony Bedford, MP, the opposition spokesman on Crime and Punishment, had joined a number of demonstrators outside the prison to protest against the sentence, and told the cameras of his repugnance at what was being done in the name of the law. He was his usual windy self and while Jake was generally in sympathy with most of what he said about punitive coma, she was left with the impression that if Bedford had been Home Secretary he would have sent Fingal back to Ireland with nothing worse than a stiff lecture.

There followed a studio interview with Grace Miles. Looking more relaxed than she had been in Frankfurt, Mrs Miles wore a black dress with jewelled buttons that were the size and shape of Viking brooches, and which was cut low on her well-bosomed chest. She looked more glamorous than a rockful of sirens. The camera cut to a wide shot of the Minister sitting in her chair and almost as if she had heard a cue, Mrs Miles crossed her legs to reveal just a fraction too much thigh, and, Jake could hardly believe it, a stocking top. That was one for the tabloids, she found herself thinking. Mrs Miles was the only woman in the Government who could, and did, trade on her own sex appeal.

While there was no doubt in Jake's mind that Mrs Miles was an attractive woman, there wasn't much that was attractive about what Mrs Miles had to say to her interviewer about punishment. And the voice was too hectoring and insistent to make for easy listening. Jake didn't like to remind herself that she had voted for this woman's stiff-necked punitive policies. But being a police officer, she reflected, sometimes played havoc with your political inclinations.

A pictophone-call at three in the morning is not usually a source of much pleasure for a police officer. The best that Jake could normally have hoped for would have been an obscene caller, exposing his genitals to the camera in the hope of outraging some helpless spinster. Blindly thumping the headboard that controlled the lights and the speaking clock – 'The time is 3 a.m.' – Jake shook her head clear of sleep and reached out for the remote control handset that worked the pictophone. For a brief moment she thought that it might be the hospital and that the stakeout might have worked. But when she had thumbed one of the buttons to take the call, it was Sergeant Chung's face that appeared on the small screen on her bedside table.

'I hope I didn't wake you up,' he said with delighted insincerity.

Jake sneered sleepily. 'Do you know what time it is?'

'Do I know what time it is? Of course I know what fucking time it is. Listen, I've just had my wife on the box to tell me the fucking time. Wanting to know why I'm still here at the Brain Research Institute instead of at home, fucking her.'

'Yes, well I bet she's missing that,' said Jake, adjusting the colour on the screen, turning up the yellow until Chung's head looked like a large lemon.

'You're fucking right she is,' said Chung, oblivious to Jake's irony.

Jake reached for her cigarettes and lit one. 'Look, Sergeant,' she said, 'if you've got something to report . . .'

'I didn't call just so as I could see you without your make-up,' he snarled. 'Or who you're sleeping with.'

'Sleeping with?' Jake murmured. 'Why the sudden coyness?'

'Eh?'

'Forget it. Look just tell me what you've got so I can get back to sleep, you little yellow bastard.'

'You want to watch it, you know. I could report you to the Racial Harassment Unit for a remark like that. I've solved your problem, white lady.'

Jake sat up in bed. 'You mean you can explain the breach of security?'

'Not bad,' said Chung, grinning at the sight of Jake's suddenly exposed breasts. 'Not bad at all. Tell you what: give me a quick flash of the rest and we'll call it quits about the racism, okay?'

Jake gathered up her sheet and held it up to her neck. She wanted to tell Chung to fuck himself, to put him on a charge. At the same time she didn't want to risk him becoming even more uncooperative than he was already. She knew him well enough to realise that he was capable of any amount of obstruction. So she gritted her teeth, ignored his sexist remark, and asked him to explain what it was that he had discovered.

'If I were you, I'd get my white arse down here,' he said. 'Right now. See, it's not something that's easy to explain on the pic and I won't be here if you come looking for me in the morning. I've been working solid on this thing for over twenty hours and as soon as I've explained things to you, I'm off home to get some fucking sleep.'

'This had better be worth it,' Jake growled, and hit the remote to end the call.

Naturally I was just a little concerned when I saw the evening paper. It only goes to prove what I was saying about encephalisation of function. I knew it was a mistake to shoot him in the anterior as opposed to the posterior of the brain. That's what you get for being impatient.

Mind you I didn't doubt that, at the very least, I would have left Russell visually impaired, the optic nerve and septal and pre-optic areas all being located around that part of the brain. (Come to think of it, I might have also damaged his all-important hypothalamus, which is of course, where his, and my trouble started.) So the chances of his being able to identify anything more than the inside of his own eyelids were slim, despite what was written in the Evening Standard. You see how it doesn't do to believe everything you read in the Evening Standard? All the same, in future I would have to be more careful and always aim for the cerebellum and cortex.

It's a fascinating area, brain function. Anyone who doubts me should try and think exactly which part of his brain is doing the thinking at that precise moment. Try it: close your eyes and concentrate on a picture of your own brain. Easier if you have a Reality Approximation machine to help you, but if you don't, let me try and describe it.

Viewed from the top, your brain most resembles something from Dante's Inferno, a pit to which lost souls have been consigned, their fleshy bodies coiled together with hardly a space to separate their desperate agonies of damnation. It is a sight such as might have greeted the liberators of Auschwitz as they stared into the mass piles of naked, unburied corpses. A ghastly, pressed jelly of humanity, this pâté de foie gras of thought.

Seen from the side, your brain is a dancer, or an acrobat, impossibly muscled – will you look at those biceps and those pectorals – bent into a foetal position, the arm (temporal lobe) wrapped around the leg, the head (cerebellum) resting on the shins (medulla oblongata).

From underneath, your brain is something obscenely hermaphrodite. There are the frontal lobes meeting like the labia of a human vagina. And beneath them, the pons and the medulla oblongata that reminds you of a semi-erect penis.

Dissected, sectioned coronally from ear to ear, the imperfect symmetry of your brain is like a Rorschach inkblot, that diagnostic tool of unstructured personality tests once favoured by psychologists.

But where, you say, among all these lobes and hemispheres, stalks and tracts, fissures and bulbs – where are the thoughts, these logical pictures of facts? The plain fact is that we must think on an even smaller scale if we are to find their origin. We must come down to a measurement of one thousandth of a millimetre, to the simplest element of nervous action, the neuron.

Now can you picture them? So quick in their synaptic jumps from one to the other that you could be forgiven for missing it the first ten thousand times. And listen, can you hear the electrical energy that is generated as these synapses take place? You can? Congratulations. You're thinking.

So now think of this: if you could lump all the true thoughts together, namely the logical pictures of facts, what you would have would be a picture of the whole world.

We cannot think what we cannot think; so what we cannot think we cannot say either.

6

Sergeant Chung was seated on a triangular stool at a grey perspex table in the main computer room at the Institute. Along one section of the circular table's circumference was a keypad and, in the centre, a holographic projection of the data he was currently using. In the partly darkened room the machine had the appearance, to Jake's eyes, of some ancient oracle.

'Holy Priest,' she said, on seeing Chung, 'ask it if we will think it worthwhile to have been turfed out of our beds at three o'clock in the morning.'

'You can afford to lose a bit of beauty sleep,' Chung growled over the lip of his coffee cup.

'Coming from you, Yat, that sounds suspiciously like a compliment.'

'Yeah, well I'm tired,' he said, and yawning, rubbed his eyes. 'It's these holograms. I can't stand them. It's like hallucinating. I prefer a proper screen myself.'

Jake drew up another stool and sat down next to him at the operator table. The bulk of the Lombroso computer was underneath their feet, with the information fed through the table legs and onto the projector. Closer to him now, she sensed his smell, which was none too good.

Chung caught the prickle in her nostrils and snorted derisively.

'If I stink, it's because I've been sitting here for the best part of three days.'

Jake decided that it was an opportune moment to smooth and flatter Chung.

'And don't think I haven't appreciated it,' she said. 'I know how hard you've worked. I couldn't have asked for more. Believe me, Yat, if you've got a lead which opens this case I'll see the APC gets to hear about it.'

Chung's narrow eyes became even narrower.

'All right, all right,' he chuckled. 'I get the picture. No need to go over the top. To be honest, I don't give a fuck what you tell anyone.'

But at the same time, Jake could see that he was pleased.

'Please, Yat,' she said, affecting a sort of girlishness. 'I'm dying to know what you've found out.' She hammered her fists on both knees and uttered a little squeal of excitement.

Chung smiled coolly and then stroked a keypad on the table.

'I'll try to keep it simple.'

'Please.'

'First of all, this was an outside job. When you log onto the system the main frame underneath this table records the transaction with a number and identifies which terminal was being used. Of course there are hundreds of such transactions every day, from any one of thirty-nine terminals in this building and the other four Lombroso facilities in Birmingham, Manchester, Newcastle and Glasgow.' He pointed at the hologram in front of them. 'This is one of today's transactions: number 280213 – that's the date; then the transaction number – 718393422; TRINITY – that's yesterday's password; and lastly 09 – that's the terminal number. This one, as a matter of fact.

'Now this was the laborious part: I programmed the computer to check back over all the system's transactions for the last twelve months, to see if there were any made from an unspecified terminal. That is a terminal without an identifying number, and therefore outside any one of the five institute facilities. And what do you know? I found one, dated 221112.'

Jake nodded. 'So you're saying someone broke into the system on November 22nd last year.'

'That's right. Now this system is part of the ECDN, the European Community Data Network. It means that only someone with access to the ECDN could have broken into Lombroso. In other words, he could only have done it from any one of a dozen systems in the public sector. There's no other way of doing it. ECDN is a private leased telecommunications line to which the public has no access.'

'Then our suspect is quite probably a public sector employee.'

Chung nodded. 'But here's where he starts to get clever. The very fact that he was using a terminal outside the institute facilities was enough to trigger the system's back-up security device. This is designed to stop the unauthorised person from going any further.'

'Unauthorised?' Jake frowned. 'Didn't he have an operator code and the day's password?'

Chung pressed another key on the flat glass of the table, to reveal a list of transaction numbers. Jake could see one that was short of a couple of digits.

'Yes, he did. The password he used was CHANDLER. But don't ask me how he got it, I don't know. Not yet anyway. No, he was unauthorised simply by virtue of his terminal lacking an identifying number on the system.'

Jake nodded. 'Okay.'

'The security device was a holographic of a three-headed dog.'

'Cerberus,' said Jake.

'You know the program?'

'No, but I know my classical literature.'

'Yeah, well so did our burglar. That's the trouble with these computer security people. They assume everyone is as ignorant as they are.'

'Does that go for Doctor St Pierre as well?'

'It goes especially for Doctor St Pierre,' said Chung. 'We had a lot of his kind in Hong Kong. Bloody stiffneck. Can only think down a straight line.'

'I guess I'm to take it that our burglar managed to evade Cerberus, right?'

'Evade?' He grinned happily and quickly typed out a series of instructions.

The numbers disappeared from the air to be replaced by a lifesize graphic of a sleeping three-headed dog. From the look of the brute, Jake was glad it was asleep, hologram or not.

'He drugged it,' said Chung.

'Drugged a computer-generated dog?' Jake said incredulously. 'How does one do that?'

'Take too long to explain, but it's a technique which goes under the generic name of Trojan Horse. There are lots of different sorts, but you get the general idea.'

'Beware of Greeks bearing gifts, huh? Clever.'

Chung shook his head. 'The really clever bit is still to come. You remember you questioned all the psychiatric counsellors? You asked if they might remember the codenames of some of the men who tested VMN-negative and who might have exhibited a greater amount of hostility to the program than others?'

'Yes. There was a list. But it was just codenames. St Pierre said that the computer's first decretal was to protect the confidentiality of their identities. He was adamant that the computer would not release their names and addresses.'

'Even though the burglar managed to get it to do just that.'

Jake lit a cigarette. It was too early in the morning for anyone to concern themselves with a no-smoking ban. 'I was going to get you to try and do the same thing when you'd finished tracking the breach,' she said.

'Then I'm already ahead of you,' he said and then added, 'Mind where you're blowing that smoke. It interferes with the hologram.'

Jake held the cigarette behind her at arm's length.

'There is a separate list of all the codenames kept on another system which is not subject to Lombroso's first decretal. Unfortunately it's the codenames, and nothing else. Anyway, what I did was to take that list and use it to ask Lombroso a question.'

'And that was?'

'Well, you see, I kept thinking to myself, suppose it was my name in the Lombroso system files. Would I trust the system's security? No way. So I'd want to try and erase my name and address pretty damn smartish. All I did was to confirm each name on my list of codenames as belonging to the primary file, in the suspicion that our man has already erased his identity.'

'All right,' Jake said expectantly.

'One by one, that's exactly what I did. And finally I found what I was looking for. Or didn't find it, if you see what I mean. I typed in a codename which I knew for certain had been issued, and asked for a confirmation, only to be told that as far as the Lombroso system was concerned, no such codename existed.' He paused for a moment, and then shrugged apologetically. 'That's when it happened.'

'When what happened?'

'Fucking logic bomb. Bastard left a booby trap which I triggered when I tried to confirm his codename.'

Jake frowned. 'What the hell's a logic bomb?'

'It's a fuck of a lot of money, that's what it is. You see, it's a program, with a delayed effect.' He bit his lip. 'With a delayed destructive effect.'

'Oh Christ,' breathed Jake. 'You're not telling me that this logic bomb, or whatever you call it, has trashed the whole system?'

'Not exactly, no. I tried all my own special software. But by the time I found the right one and stopped the program replicating itself, one particular area of the system was badly damaged.'

'Which particular area of the system?'

'The VMN database.'

'Shit.'

'Not the whole thing. Just a percentage.'

'How big a percentage?'

Chung shrugged. 'Hard to say exactly. Maybe 30 to 40 per cent.'

'What am I going to tell Gleitmann?'

'It was bound to go off sooner or later,' said Chung, with an uncomfortable sort of laugh. 'The logic bomb was just sitting there, in the root memory, waiting for the trigger. Had it been anyone else who tripped it, the bomb would have trashed the whole disk. Lucky for them that I had the right software with me: a program I wrote myself, as a matter of fact. Sort of a vaccine if you like. It works against about 200 different types of virus.' He nodded with some satisfaction. 'Too right, lady. But for me the whole Lombroso Program would be forensic history. Think about that for a minute.'

'I'll do my best.'

'Look on the bright side,' he instructed her. 'You know the date on which our burglar broke into the system. You know he must work in the public sector. You know he's a smart boy where computers are concerned: maybe even got a record for other unauthorised system entries. You got his codename. You even got a counsellor who remembers him.'

'Yes, just what was that codename?'

Chung consulted a sheet of paper. 'Wittgenstein,' he said. 'Ludwig Wittgen-stein.' He pronounced the surname with the accent on the second syllable and shook his head, grimacing. 'If they gave me a codename like that I wouldn't be surprised if I wanted to kill a few people myself.'

Jake wondered if Chung could be anti-Semitic and looked forward to the possibility of reminding him that she herself was Jewish. Not that it meant all that much to her, but she felt it might be fun to accuse him of racism.

'And what's wrong with it?' she asked.

Chung looked away, trying to hide his grin. He seemed about to say one thing but then apparently changed his mind, laughed and said another: 'Bit of a bloody mouthful, that's all.'

So that was it, she thought. He had never heard of Ludwig Wittgenstein. He was embarrassed at his own ignorance. Not that she knew much about him herself, beyond a few basic items of biographical information of the kind that counts as good general knowledge. But she had a feeling that before this case was ended she was going to know a great deal more.

Is the classification of things into names always truly arbitrary? Or is there not some meaning to how something is named? While a name itself is a primitive sign and cannot be dissected any further by means of a definition, at the same time there are names which, when given, seem to be replete with mystical significance.

Names have power. The name of Jehovah, considered too sacred even to utter. Or Macbeth, never mentioned by superstitious, luvvy-duvvy theatre folk. At the name of Jesus, every knee shall bow. The name of the slough was Despond. Keats's name was writ in water.

And some are written in blood.

Names have numerological significance, too. Readers of Tolstoy's War and Peace *will recall that Pierre Bezukhov, under the influence of his brother Freemasons, manages to turn the name of l'empereur Napoleon into numbers, the sum of which equals 666. The name of the Beast, or the number of his name. Oh! breathe not his name, let it sleep in the shade where cold and unhonour'd his relics are laid.*

Never ever tell anyone a baby's Christian name until after it is christened, or the pixies may hear it and charm the child away. There are names to conjure with. Names that liveth for evermore. And the naming of cats is a difficult matter.

Some names must be blotted out of the book, and others cannot be cured. My name is Legion, for we are many.

I am become a name.

Tell me honestly, do you like your name? Are you not bored with it? As a child didn't you hanker to be called something else, a name with more of a ring to it — a name with more dash, more spirit? You wondered how ever your dim-witted parents could have been so lacking in imagination as to have named you as they named you. To say nothing of the surname they, or at least one of them, inherited. They fuck you up, your mum and dad. But Philip Larkin (a good name) omits to mention in his poem, the most crucial aspect of that parental act of sabotage which is, of course, your name. It's not just misery that man hands on to man, but a name. That's what really fucks you up.

You wear your name like a hidden shirt. But once it is revealed to someone, it can never again be properly hidden. That person can never then forget that you are wearing it. Having explained to your friends that you are 'x' they will for ever after think of you in terms that may simply be expressed as 'x'. It is a pure sign of you, of who, and why, and what you are and where you come from. The Sign of Four.

A name means an object. The object is its meaning. I can only speak about names. I cannot put them into words. But to live your whole life with a meaning that is not of your own choosing would seem to me to be quite unbearable.

'My name is for my friends,' says T.E. in the film Lawrence of Arabia. How right, how very right. Once given out, your name may be used against you. But there is power in the unspoken name, in The Man with No Name. The Outsider. L'Etranger. He rides into town, shoots a few people and then rides away again. Anonymous. The best name of all. If I could have taken my own name, if I did not now have my Lombroso-given name, I would take that name: Anonymous. Think of all the quotations, the poems, the stories that could now be attributed to you.

In truth, this is more of a tract than a story, more of a journal than a piece of prose. I leave this manuscript,

I do not know for whom; I no longer know what it is about: stat rosa pristina nomine, nomina nuda tenemus.

7

When Jake had finished making her report to the Assistant Police Commissioner, Gilmour chewed his finger absently for a few seconds before uttering a profound sigh.

'Does Professor Gleitmann know about this yet?' he said wearily.

'Yes, sir.'

Gilmour's bushy eyebrows moved in to ask a silent question.

'He wasn't very pleased, sir,' said Jake.

'I can imagine. But you're satisfied that it wasn't Sergeant Chung's fault, this logic bomb?'

'Wholly satisfied, sir. Chung's boss from the Computer Crime Unit has been over to the Institute to investigate exactly what happened. He has already confirmed Sergeant Chung's account.'

'Good. The last thing we want is the Home Office trying to post the blame for this one through our door.'

Gilmour leaned back in his chair and swivelled around to stare out of the window of his New Scotland Yard office. They were only a kilometre away from the Tate Gallery, the site of the last Lombroso murder. Somewhere overhead could be heard the sound of a police helicopter as it constantly patrolled the rooftops around the Home Office and the Houses of Parliament, looking out for terrorists or lone crackpots. Jake knew that aboard it were cameras powerful enough to have photographed the comb in her hair and quite possibly the string on her tampon, not to mention the sophisticated eavesdropping equipment the helicopter carried. The temptation to use this equipment was obvious and sometimes the Police

Airborne Surveillance teams went too far. The newspapers were still full of the political scandal that had been the result of one airborne team having recorded the compromising conversation of two homosexual Members of Parliament as they sat eating their sandwiches in Parliament Square.

'So what's next?' asked Gilmour.

'Well, sir, Sergeant Chung tells me that with the computer system the BRI have been using, it is sometimes possible to recover material that has been accidentally deleted. It's called an electronic spike. I've told him to make that his first priority.'

Gilmour shook his bald head and proceeded to stroke his Mexican-style grey moustache nervously. 'I don't understand these blasted computer people,' he said irritably, transferring his attention to the buttons on his well-pressed uniform. 'Either something has been deleted or it hasn't.' Anger made his light northern burr become more noticeably Glaswegian.

'That's what I said,' Jake reported. 'But Chung says that sometimes artificial intelligence will find a way of erasing something from a file directory and yet keep it hidden safely, somewhere within the main memory.'

'Any other bright ideas, Jake? Mayhew's last words. What about that?'

Jake shrugged. 'It could be he thought that the Lombroso people set him up to be killed. It could be he was even right. Could be he was just paranoid.'

'Yes, well I know just how he must have felt.'

'Sergeant Chung has had one other idea, sir. He thinks he's got a way of breaking into what's left of the Lombroso database. You'll recall that the Lombroso computer is connected to our own at Kidlington? And that their system is supposed to alert us if a name which we have entered into our computer, in the course of a violent crime investigation, should be on the Lombroso list of VMN-negatives?'

Gilmour grunted an affirmative.

'Well, Chung wants to take the entire UK telephone subscribers-list, which exists on a series of discs, and feed all the names and numbers at random into the police computer within the context of a fictitious murder investigation. It might take a while, but the idea is that one by one, Lombroso will be forced to release all the names and numbers of those men classed as VMN-negative. Or at least the ones it has left since the killer's logic bomb went off. That way we can at least keep some of them under surveillance.'

Gilmour held his head weakly. 'Spare me the technical explanations, Jake. Do it, if you think it's a good idea.'

'I've also prepared a letter addressed to each VMN-negative person who has elected to receive psychotherapy. There are about twenty of them. Professor Gleitmann has agreed that Lombroso counsellors will give these letters to their patients. The letter asks each man, for the sake of his own safety, to contact me in total confidence. The only trouble is that these men aren't much disposed to trust the police. They think it's part of some grand plan that at some stage we're going to round them all up and put them in a special prison hospital. But I still think it's worth a try. I'd also like to take out some advertisements in the newspapers. Just a list of codenames, nothing else. But warning them to get in contact with a number.'

'I think I'd have to clear that with the Home Office,' said Gilmour.

'We've got to try and warn all of these men,' said Jake. 'Surely – '

'I'll see what I can do, Jake. But I can't promise anything.'

Jake felt herself frown.

'Was there something else?'

'Perhaps now is not the best time,' she said defensively. 'It's a bit wild.'

'No, I'd rather hear it, Jake. No matter how fantastic.'

She led Gilmour up to it gradually, telling him how

she already had a team of officers checking the sales of gas-guns and combing the police files for those who had a record for unauthorised computer entry. Finally she described how one of the counsellors at the Brain Research Institute remembered having talked to the man, codenamed Wittgenstein, now assumed to have committed the murders.

'At least, he can remember the codename and not much more,' she explained. 'So what I want to do is hypnotise him to see if his subconscious can make a better job of a description.'

Gilmour pulled a face and Jake wondered how much longer he had before retirement. Not very long, she imagined. But he nodded.

'If you think that it's necessary.'

'I do, sir.'

The nod turned into a shrug of resignation.

'There's something else, sir. I'm convinced that our man believes that what he's doing is in the public interest.'

'How do you mean?'

'Killing men who have tested VMN-negative. Men who are potentially killers themselves. I'm sure that – our man . . .' She still couldn't bring herself to refer to the killer by his codename. It seemed too absurd that a homicidal maniac should be named after one of the twentieth century's greatest philosophers. 'Well, he might just have worked out some sort of justification for his actions, sir. I'd like to draw his fire a little. Try and engage him in some sort of dialogue.'

'How would you manage that?'

'I'd like to arrange a press conference, sir. To talk about these murders. Naturally I won't refer to the Program itself. But I would like to try and provoke him a little. Talk about the complete innocence of the victims, how these murders were committed without reason, the work of a lunatic, that sort of thing. If I'm right, he won't like that much.'

'And suppose you only succeed in provoking him to go to the newspapers to explain what he thinks he's up to? We're just about keeping the lid on this as things stand. But if this lunatic were to go to the newspapers with a story, that would be it, I'm afraid.'

'No, sir, I'm certain he wouldn't do that. He wouldn't want to alarm all the other VMN-negatives he's got on his list. It would make his job a lot harder if they were all scared shitless and looking out for him as a result of reading his story in the newspapers. No, sir, my guess is that he'd try to contact us, to try and put the record straight.'

'And if you do manage to get him to contact you, then what?'

'Depending on how he chooses to make contact, there's a lot of valuable profiling data we might be able to obtain: handwriting analysis, linguistic analysis, personality assessment – all of this would be invaluable in tracking him down. I'm sure I don't have to remind you, sir, that this is notoriously the most difficult kind of killer to catch. It may look as if we're grasping at a few straws here but frankly, sir, it's only these small fragments of data that will enable us to build up a complete picture of our man.'

Jake paused to see if Gilmour was with her. He wasn't, she knew, a sophisticated kind of man. He was one of the old school of policing: left school at sixteen to join the force and then up through the ranks. The Scot knew as much about forensic psychiatry and criminal profiling as Jake knew about Robert Burns. But seeing that his eyes hadn't yet glazed over, she kept on going.

'I'm talking about systematic composite profiling,' she said. 'We're trying to establish the type of man responsible, as distinct from the individual. The Yard's own Behavioural Science Unit has already compiled in-depth psychological studies of everyone from the Yorkshire Ripper to David Boysfield. We'll be using their body of work as a comparison in an attempt to identify the type of offender that we're looking for. But I can't make bricks without straw. I need some data. Contact with the killer would give us something.'

Gilmour nodded gravely. 'What kind of man do you think we're looking for, Jake?'

'My guess?' Jake shrugged. 'Well, this is no disorganised asocial we're dealing with, I can tell you that much. He's a cunning, methodical, calculating killer for whom homicide is an end in itself. That is, on its own, highly unusual. Most serial killing is driven by lust. But this man is inspired by nothing other than his own sense of mission. It means he has no obvious weakness, and that makes him very dangerous.'

Gilmour sighed. 'All right, Jake, you've made your point. You'll get your press conference, if I have to go down on my knees to that bitch.'

'Thank you, sir.'

'One more question, Jake.'

'Sir?'

'Exactly who was this fellow, Wittgenstein?'

The psychiatrist who remembered counselling a VMN-negative codenamed Wittgenstein was Doctor Tony Chen. Like Sergeant Chung, he was another immigrant from Hong Kong, only a little older and better-mannered. He seemed pleased to cooperate with Jake's inquiry, even one which involved raiding his own subconscious mind.

'I don't remember too much about the guy,' he admitted. 'I've counselled quite a few VMNs since then. After a while, it's difficult to separate them. Especially the ones who don't come back for regular counselling. Wittgenstein didn't; that much I can remember.' He rolled up his sleeve. 'All right, let's do it.'

Doctor Carrie Cleobury, the Lombroso Program's Head of Psychiatry, took charge of her colleague's hypnosis in her office at the Institute, accompanied by Professor Gleitmann and Jake. Having injected Chen with a drug to help him to relax, she told him that she would induce trance with the aid of both stroboscopic light and a metronome.

'This has the advantage of combining auditory and visual fixation,' she said to Jake. 'I find it the most effective technique.'

Jake, who herself held an M.Sc in Psychology, was already well aware of this, but she remained silent on the subject, reasoning that she preferred having Doctor Cleobury working for her rather than against her.

Chen sat in an armchair facing the light, and waiting for the drug to take effect. After a minute or two he nodded at Doctor Cleobury who switched on the light machine and set the metronome in motion, adjusting the speed until it matched the flashing of the light. Then she began her induction talk. She had a pleasant voice, calm and self-assured, with just the trace of an Irish accent.

'Keep looking into the light and think of nothing but the light ... In a little while your eyelids will begin to feel heavy and you will feel drowsy ... and relaxed, as your eyelids become heavier and heavier ...'

Light and shadow flickered on Chen's broad Oriental face like the wings of a great moth, and as the minutes passed, his breathing grew more regular and profound.

'... you will want to close your eyes soon, because they are becoming so heavy and you feel so drowsy ...'

Chen's small nostrils flared, his mouth slackened a little as his eyes grew so narrow that it was soon impossible to tell whether they were open or closed.

'... and now, as your eyelids close, you will relax, deeper and deeper ... and your head will fall forward ... and you will be pleasantly, comfortably relaxed ...'

His head swayed and then dipped inexorably towards his chest. Cleobury continued with a series of suggestions, gradually narrowing Chen's conscious mind and removing any distractions that might have inhibited the impact of what she was saying. She turned off the light, but her voice kept the same even reassuring tone, as if she was coaxing a cat to come to her.

'And with every breath you take, you will become still more deeply relaxed . . . deeper and still deeper . . .'

Jake noticed a slight quivering of Chen's eyelids and a twitching around his mouth. As his respiratory movement slowed it was clear he was entering a light trance.

'Pay attention to my voice. Nothing else seems to matter, just the sound of my voice. There's nothing else to disturb you now. There is only my voice.'

The first part of Doctor Cleobury's induction talk had been made in a slow, even tempo as if she had been reciting a prayer in church, but now her voice became more incisive and calmly assertive. And her suggestions of relaxation involved larger and more complex muscle groups. When at last she was satisfied that her colleague's body was completely relaxed, Doctor Cleobury turned off the metronome and set about deepening Chen's trance through the use of fantasy.

'Tony,' she said. 'Tony, I want you to use your imagination now. I want you to picture yourself standing in an elevator. If you look up you can picture the floor counter. We're on the tenth floor right now, but in a moment I am going to operate the elevator and send you down to the ground. And with each floor we pass, the elevator will take you into a deeper sleep. Deeper with each count I make. Keep your eyes on the counter. I'm starting now . . .'

She began to count backwards from ten, and when she reached zero, and the ground floor of Chen's imagination, she told him to step out of the elevator and to remain there, 'in this deep, deep state.'

Chen's jaw was now resting on the upper part of his clavicle. At the same time there was a perceptible rigidity about his arms and torso, like a convict in the electric chair awaiting the switch to be thrown.

'You will remain comfortable in this deep, deeply relaxed state,' said Doctor Cleobury. 'I am now going to give you some simple instructions. I won't ask you to do anything you will not wish to do. Please nod your head so that I will know you understand what I am saying.'

Chen's head stiffened and then nodded.

'Lift your head, Tony, and open your eyes.'

As he obeyed her instruction, Doctor Cleobury stepped forward and, with a pencil torch, checked Chen's eyes for light sensitivity. He bore the light shining directly into his pupil without so much as blinking, and Doctor Cleobury nodded at Jake to turn on her discrecorder.

'It is towards the end of last year, Tony. November 22nd, to be precise. A patient testing VMN-negative has been sent in to see you for counselling. You're holding his computer card in your hands. The codename at the top right-hand corner of the file card is "Ludwig Wittgenstein". Tell me if you can see it.'

Chen breathed deeply and then nodded.

'I want to hear your voice, Tony. Speak to me.'

Some words emptied from Chen's slackened mouth. Jake understood none of them.

'English, Tony. We're speaking English now. Tell me if you can see the name.'

He frowned as his subconscious bent itself to Doctor Cleobury's suggestion. 'Yes,' he said. 'I can see it.'

'Now I want you to look at the man who is sitting opposite you. The man codenamed Wittgenstein. Do you see him?'

'Yes.'

'Do you see him clearly?'

'Clearly yes, I see him.'

Jake's heart leaped at the thought of what Chen's unconscious mind was looking at: the face of the killer himself. The possibility that she might obtain his description in this way might even make a subject for a future paper.

'Can you describe the man to us?'

Chen grunted.

'Tell us about Wittgenstein, Tony.'

Chen smiled. 'He is a very logical, passionate sort of man. Argumentative, but intelligent.'

'What about his physical appearance? Can you tell us something about that please?'

'To look at – ?' Chen's frown deepened. 'Medium to tall in height. Brown, wavy hair. Large, quick blue eyes. Thoughtful brow: I mean, his forehead constantly bends itself to thought. Sharply featured. The nose is a little hooked. And the mouth, a bit petulant, perhaps a bit effeminate, as if he looks in the mirror a great deal. Lean-looking, but not fit: it's not exercise but lack of food that keeps him slim. Intense . . .' He was silent for several seconds.

'Any distinguishing features?'

Chen shook his head slowly. 'Nothing, except maybe his voice. He speaks very properly. Without an accent. Like on the BBC.'

'What does he say to you, Tony? Does he tell you anything about himself?'

'He's angry. And scared he says.'

'They usually are,' Professor Gleitmann whispered to Jake.

'When I told him what the test meant, he asked me to explain how he could know this to be true. I said I could show him the PET scan we had taken of the inside of his head. He said that I might just as well show him the inside of a rhinoceros head, for all the difference it would make to him. Whatever I told him was merely a concept derived from experience and he couldn't accept it as a fact, only as an asserted proposition.' Chen's head began to nod again.

'Ask him if he gave any indication of his identity,' said Jake. 'What sort of job he does, where he drinks, that kind of thing.'

'Listen to me, Tony,' said Doctor Cleobury. 'Listen to me. Did Wittgenstein say anything about himself? Did he tell you what kind of job he does, where he lives?'

Chen shook his head. 'He said he didn't much care about himself, that's all.'

'Clothes,' prompted Jake. 'What was he wearing?'

'Tony, can you tell us what he's wearing?'

'A tweed sports jacket, white polo-necked sweater, brown corduroy trousers, sturdy sort of brown shoes which look expensive. A beige raincoat on his lap.'

'Age.'

'What age is he, Tony?'

'Late thirties, maybe.'

'Tony, I want you to tell me how you counselled him. Tell me about that, will you?'

'We made an appointment to discuss his future psycho-therapy. And some drugs. I gave him a course of oestrogen tablets, and some Valium.'

'All right, Tony. Let's move forward in time now. It's the day of the patient, codenamed Wittgenstein's first appointment. Tell me what happens.'

Chen shrugged. 'He doesn't show up, that's all. He never called to cancel. Just doesn't come.'

Doctor Cleobury looked at Jake. 'Is there anything more you would like to ask, Chief Inspector?'

'No,' she said, 'but when you're ending the trance I'd be grateful if you could tell Doctor Chen to remember everything he can of Wittgenstein's appearance. When he's fully conscious I'd like him to spend some time with one of our ComputaFit artists. Maybe we can work with something more tangible than just a verbal description.'

Jake switched off her discrecorder and dropped it into her bag. Doctor Cleobury started to count Chen out of hypnosis. Professor Gleitmann followed Jake to the door.

'I wonder if I might have a brief word with you in my office,' he said, holding the door open for her with one of his impossibly hairy hands. 'There's something I'd like you to see.'

They took the lift up to the top floor, and from one of his cherrywood bookshelves, Gleitmann removed a book which he opened and laid on the conference table in front of Jake. There was a photograph of a man. Jake glanced at it and then at Gleitmann.

'I don't know whether or not you noticed it,' he explained, nodding at the picture, 'but just about everything Doctor Chen said could equally apply to him, the real Ludwig Wittgenstein.'

'I don't quite follow you.'

'Well you see, Chief Inspector, the unconscious mind doesn't always distinguish things with any degree of precision. It is quite possible for Doctor Chen to have lied under hypnosis, albeit without culpability. I'm not at all certain that he did manage to distinguish between the man codenamed Wittgenstein by our Lombroso computer and the real one, the philosopher. It's quite possible that he may have merged them both together in his subconscious mind. For instance, take Chen's description of the patient's physical appearance: brown wavy hair, large blue eyes, petulant mouth, sharp features: all that could be said of the real Ludwig Wittgenstein.

'And do you remember that remark that the patient supposedly made about how nothing empirical is knowable, or words to that effect – how he would admit only to the existence of asserted propositions?' Gleitmann shrugged awkwardly. 'Well I don't remember much of what Wittgenstein actually wrote, but that sort of thing is pretty close to the man's general – *Weltanschaung*.'

'Yes, I see what you mean, Professor.'

'I'm sorry, Chief Inspector. It was a bold idea you had there, but the mind can play tricks on us.'

'What if Chen knows nothing about the real Wittgenstein? Wouldn't that make it more likely that his unconscious mind was speaking the truth?'

'It's a possibility. But Chen is an educated man, Chief Inspector. I can't see him not knowing something about Wittgenstein, can you? Good Lord, he read Psychology at Cambridge.'

Jake shrugged. 'So did I, Professor, and to be quite frank with you until a couple of days ago, you could have written what I knew about Wittgenstein on the back of a postage stamp.'

For a long time Jake had known the name merely as something of emblematic power, a name that was replete with intellectual symbolism, like the name of Einstein. Perhaps after all it was that Semitic suffix which helped to explain the exotic power of the name. But now that she had read Wittgenstein's shortest and most explosive book, the *Tractatus*, she had a better idea why he had been such an influential figure in philosophy. Quite apart from the enigmatic, almost hermetic quality of his writing, there was the subject of his investigation: how is language possible? It was something people, especially policemen, tended to take for granted, even though it provided the very stuff of man's inner life. Even more important than Wittgenstein's attempt to explain what language was capable of – or so it seemed to Jake – had been his attempt to explain what language was incapable of. This touched something deep within her soul, something that even bordered her own sexuality.

'Knowledge is a queer phenomenon,' said Jake. 'At least that's Wittgenstein's opinion.'

'Well I see you haven't wasted any time in filling in the gaps,' said Gleitmann.

'Filling in the gaps is my job,' said Jake. 'But there is one other possibility, of course. That this killer may actually resemble Wittgenstein in more than just a name spewed out by your computer. Suppose for one minute that he is indeed an intelligent, well-educated sort of man. Suppose for instance that he has read about Wittgenstein before, perhaps even been impressed by his thinking. Now isn't it possible that the shock of being tested VMN-negative might have triggered some kind of psychopathological disorder? A paranoid schizophrenic delusion, perhaps?'

Gleitmann rubbed his blue jaw thoughtfully. 'I suppose it might be possible. But as quick as that? I don't know.'

'Suppose he already had a diathesis, a predisposition

towards the illness. All that would then be required would be some kind of stress situation to transform the potentiality into an actuality. A stress situation such as being told that you were VMN-negative perhaps.'

'That might do it, I suppose.'

Jake smiled thinly at Gleitmann's reluctance to admit the possibility of what was to her increasingly obvious.

'Come on, Professor,' she said. 'You know damned well it would.'

When their meeting was over, Jake left the building. Outside the Institute, she found a yawn turning quickly into a stretch that demanded some kind of greater response than a brief flexing of neck and shoulder muscles. Exercise. Air: even the combusted air of Victoria. She decided not to take her car back to the Yard and having collected her gun from the glove compartment, she dismissed her driver and set off up Victoria Street.

Most Londoners, finding themselves in Jake's position, would soon have turned northwards in the direction of St James's Park. But the pull of the river was too strong for someone who had lived most of her life beside the river.

Even so, the view from Westminster Bridge was fraught with danger, there were so many beggars and petty thieves along the embankments, and the gun was a necessary precaution.

It was a sight which always managed to touch her soul, although the smog-laden air prevented the sun from lighting the saloon-bar boats, the glass tower-blocks, the satellite mushrooms, theatres and mosques. A feeling of calm overcame Jake as she watched the muddy brown Thames glide underneath her feet. She wondered if Doctor Cleobury's trance-through-relaxation technique might not have also worked a part of its spell on her.

Traffic was lighter than normal and she crossed from one side of the bridge to the other, stepping coolly over the supine form of a drunk sleeping in the gutter. Even the Houses of Parliament seemed to be asleep. She smiled as she tried to imagine the lies that were probably even now being told in that heart of democracy by the likes of Grace Miles.

This sense of calm refused to desert Jake despite the drunk waking up and, with an almost complete lack of consonants, demanding money of her. She reached into her bag and keeping one hand on the 30-shot automatic, she took out a five dollar bill with the other and gave it to him. The man stared dully at it for a moment, nodded, grumbled a reply, and then, thinking better of snatching the tall woman's shoulder bag, moved on, unaware of how close he had come to being shot.

Jake watched this majestic piece of work as he walked unsteadily along the pavement, towards the nearest off-licence, and felt nothing but contempt, for him and all men. She would as soon have blown his head off as rewarded his menacing demand for money.

It was the sight of the river, not the man, which had moved her.

I keep two notebooks. Particularly beautiful books, with smooth, creamy paper, a little yellowed by age, but of a kind that has not been manufactured for many years.

There is this one, containing my journal, which I call my Brown Book. And there is another, containing the details of those few individuals whom I have executed, or am planning to execute, which I call my Blue Book. I write with an old fountain pen. I'm not very used to it. Like most people I normally write something straight onto the computer, however I feel that that would be to remove me from the immediacy, the improvised character of these, my thoughts, which only a pen can translate.

Neither of these two books is particularly good, but they are about as good as I can make them. I dare say that they will only be finished when I am. In other words, their publication (about which I am having a few misgivings) will not be an event in my life.

Of course, it is not without the realms of possibility that, taken together, it should be the fate of these two humble volumes, in their poverty and in the darkness of this time, to bring illumination into one brain or another. But then, how things are in this world is a matter of complete indifference for what is higher.

Next to each other, these two books amount to a sort of a system. This is what is important for logic. Because the only necessity that exists is logical necessity. And the idea that there is some kind of natural explanation for everything, and that this natural law is something inviolable is, frankly, nonsense.

Turning to the Blue Book for a moment, you will see how, for each individual, a series of pictures serves to represent precisely how I will carry out his execution. (All right, I did depart from this in the case of Bertrand Russell, but that was a mistake; anyone can make a mistake.) These are simple, childlike drawings, such as might be made when completing an accident-claim form from a motor insurance company.

As a picture of a possible state of affairs, it's all logical enough. Of course it's not every picture that corresponds with reality in this way. You just have to take a walk around the Tate Gallery to appreciate that. In there are a great many pictures on view in which an arrangement of objects bears no relation to a state of affairs. This is the freedom of Art. It is what is sometimes called artistic licence, almost as if you had to write away to Swansea in order to get one.

As well as my Brown Book and my Blue Book which, taken together, represent my system, there is the approximate reality of my work.

To enter an approximate world you need the right equipment. My own RA machine and its body attachments represent the state of the art and cost me almost EC $50,000. The main part is just a box, about the size of a cereal packet which you attach to your computer. Then there is a full-face helmet that resembles something a motorcyclist might wear, and a rubberised exoskeleton suit that's more like what you see a frogman wearing. Inside the helmet, the visor acts as a projection screen, which is where you see the approximate world, and a loudspeaker over each ear lets you hear it. The suit is a flexible composite which enables you to touch and be touched by approximate things and approximate people. You switch on or off simply by lowering or raising the helmet's visor.

Originally I bought RA as therapy for my aggression, customising several of the existing program disks to my own specifications. When I felt more than normally hostile I would don the body attachments and plug myself in. Seconds later I would be in an approximate world, armed with a selection of lethal weapons enabling me to murder, maim and rape my way through a selection of highly realistic victims. But these days I find that I don't have to feel hostile to want to use this particular program, and I find that it keeps me on a fairly even keel.

Of course there are many other approximations of reality which one can explore. These other RAs include the erotic, the romantic, the fantasy, the comic, as well as the musical and even the intellectual. Many of these programs I have devised myself, and I look upon these pictures and sensations as a kind of art form, like cinema.

Of course RA is not without its drawbacks. Like any form of escapism such as drugs, or alcohol, it can become addictive for the weaker-minded individual. But that cannot be a problem for me.

It has been said, by the manufacturers of RA and other products like it, that what is real and what is unreal we must merely apprehend, for both are incapable of analysis. But this seems to me to be nothing more than the kind of tautology that typifies advertising.

The fact of the matter is that nothing empirical is knowable.

8

Jake took her place at the table between Gilmour and the man whom she had replaced in charge of the inquiry and who, heading up the Murder Squad, was nominally her boss: Commander Keith Challis. Adopting expressions of cool, calm, detached gravitas, they faced a roomful of journalists who were armed with cameras, boom microphones and discrecorders. As Gilmour opened the press conference, Jake recalled his last few words to her as they left his office on the fifteenth floor of New Scotland Yard, to take the lift down to the conference room.

'I hope you know what you're doing,' he had said gruffly. 'If this blows up in our faces, it'll be your head, not mine, that the Minister asks for. To my mind it looks as if she's giving you all the rope you need to hang yourself.'

'Yes, well I'm not ready to string myself up yet,' Jake had replied.

The introductions to the press over, Jake, as senior investigating officer, took charge of the police statement. A number of public relations seminars had helped her to develop presentational skills. She recognised the importance to the success of the conference of her own physical appearance and that morning had dressed with even greater care than was usual, choosing to wear a two-piece suit made of turquoise bouclé. She knew that it would be harder for the press to make a target of someone who didn't conform to the standard grey-flannel image of police authority. It wasn't her first experience of handling the press during a murder inquiry, but she treated it as if it was. There was no point in risking making the impression that she was in any way casual about things. She spoke clearly, carefully, watching both sides of the room like a presidential bodyguard, as if expecting that one of the journalists would throw something heavier than a loaded question. It was best to expect the unexpected.

'The police are now disposed to treat a number of random homicides of men, committed during the past few months, as the work of one individual. There are certain features of the killer's *modus operandi* which lead us to make this conclusion. While we are unable to supply details of the murderer's *modus operandi* for reasons of operational security, we can confirm, however, that all the victims were shot several times in the head, and at a fairly close range.

'I am sure that I don't have to explain to you all that, as is common with this kind of apparently motiveless crime, there is a paucity of facts as to the murderer's identity. At this stage of our inquiry, where there are hundreds, possibly thousands of remote possibilities to be checked, the investigative task is comparable to searching for the proverbial needle in a haystack. Consequently, an advisory team of experts, chaired by myself, has now been set up with the aim of studying all the murders using the resources of the European Criminal Intelligence Service, and in particular, the ECIS computer system. For those of you who are not familiar with this particular system, the integrated European Computerised Intelligence Service performs the task of the police intelligence officer, supplanting human judgment with pre-set computer programs. It is hoped that this will provide the analytical capacity needed to determine if there is, for want of a better term, a centre of gravity for all these killings.'

Jake nodded at a couple of uniformed police officers to hand out copies of the ComputaFit picture which the police artist had produced with the help of Tony Chen. She had accepted the possibility that his unconscious mind might have been lying, but without the picture there was very little that might have justified her calling a press conference.

'As a result of a description given to us by the killer's last victim, Oliver Mayhew, before he died, we are now able to issue an artist's impression of the killer. He is described as being aged about thirty-five or forty, of medium height, with wavy brown hair, blue eyes, sharp features and slightly built. When last seen, he was wearing a brown tweed jacket, white polo-neck sweater, brogue-type shoes, and carrying a beige raincoat.

'This is an extremely clever and ruthless, possibly psychotic individual with whom we are dealing, and who kills without discrimination or restraint. However, it would seem that it is only men who are at risk. So I would urge members of the public, especially men, to exercise greater vigilance when walking home alone at night.'

That ought to piss him off, Jake thought. She raised her voice above the slight murmur that had followed the issuing of the artist's impression.

'Let me take this opportunity to scotch the rumour that any of the killer's victims were selected by reason of a criminal record or their sexual persuasion. Or that any of them were murdered in response to an assault, an attempted robbery or a sexual proposition. There is absolutely no evidence to support the speculation that this killer is some kind of Hollywood-style vigilante. Nor is there any evidence that these killings are related to the criminal underworld. I cannot emphasise too strongly that these unfortunate victims were all, I repeat all, innocent men going about their lawful business when the killer struck. None of them had any reason to suppose that they had been selected by the killer. Moreover I am completely satisfied that none of them knew, or had ever met the killer before.'

'I would also like to quash the rumour that the murderer has already been in touch with the police. This is completely untrue. There has been no communication of any kind whatsoever. But if anyone believes that he has information which might be pertinent to this inquiry I would urge that person to come forward and make contact with the police immediately.

'Finally I want to address the killer. Whoever you are I urge you to give yourself up. I give you my word that you will be fairly treated and that I will do everything in my power to ensure that you receive the proper medical treatment. In saying this, I should like the record to state that my main concern is to prevent the taking of any more lives.'

Jake paused for a moment and glanced over her audience.

'Are there any questions?'

A dozen hands were raised in the air and Jake pointed at a face she half-recognised.

'Carol Clapham, ITN,' declared the woman. 'Chief Inspector, are you satisfied that robbery is not the motive behind these killings?'

'Perfectly satisfied. None of these men were robbed. As I recall, one man was found still in possession of a wallet containing over a hundred dollars. Next question.' She pointed to a man sitting in the front row.

'James McKay, *Evening Standard*. You mentioned hundreds, possibly thousands of remote possibilities to be checked. Would you care to say what any of them are?'

'No, I would not. Next.' She pointed again.

'Have any of the victims been mutilated in any way?' asked a third journalist.

'No comment.' Jake had no wish to provide any information for the copycat killers. 'Next.'

'Do you assume that the killer will strike again?'

'That would be a fair assumption, yes.'

She pointed a fifth time and then a sixth. Finally came the question she had been sure someone would eventually ask.

'John Joyce, the *Guardian*. Chief Inspector Jakowicz, would you care to comment on the rumour that these killings may be connected with the Lombroso Program currently being run by the Government's Brain Research Institute?'

Before Jake could answer, Detective Chief Superintendent Challis beat her to it.

'I think I can answer that question,' he said, glancing at Jake as if to reassure himself that she didn't mind him interrupting her. But she knew that this was just for appearance's sake: Challis really didn't care one way or the other whether his female junior minded or not.

'As the Chief Inspector indicated, there have been a number of rumours about these killings, linking them with everything from England's World Cup defeat to changes in the world's weather pattern.' He grinned, hideously. 'Let's just say that at this stage in our inquiry, we're not disposed to eliminate any hypothesis, no matter how fantastic.'

With that, Gilmour stood up and announced that the press conference was at an end. There were questions shouted at the retreating triumvirate, but these were ignored. And when they were outside, in the corridor behind the conference room, Gilmour breathed a sigh of relief.

'You fielded that one well, Keith,' he said.

'Thanks, sir,' said Challis. 'It was a bit of a googly, wasn't it? You just can't trust those fucking bastards on the *Guardian* to play a straight game.'

Gilmour nodded grimly. 'It's about time I had a word with the press office about them. Teach them a lesson. No press releases, that kind of thing. Keep 'em in purdah for a while, at least until they learn to toe the line like the rest of the reptiles.'

'Oh I don't know,' said Jake. 'You can't blame them for trying.'

Gilmour looked squarely at Jake, and, ignoring her opinion, complimented her on her own performance.

'You did well, young lady,' he said, patronising her as if he had been some kind of indulgent uncle.

Jake forced a smile over her clenched teeth.

'I hope you know what you're doing. If this blows up in our faces – ' For once he did not complete the prophecy. Instead, Gilmour pinched the bridge of his nose, and added, 'Let's just hope that this Wittgenstone bastard watches television.'

It was almost unthinkable that he would not, thought Jake as she drove home that night. Television was the great British god. True, she herself often came home and found that she had little energy left to do anything but stare into its unblinking eye. But it was for precisely this reason that Jake had located her own television set in an unusual position. Instead of being placed at an angle between two walls from where it could command the whole room like some kind of surveillance camera, Jake's set was placed in such a way as indicated someone who was not much inclined to watch it. The TV sat high up on a set of shelves, at right angles to the shortest wall and immediately opposite the door, which obliged anyone who wished to view the thing to stand. It wasn't that Jake disliked the newsreels of faraway wars, crime movies, or even the two-minute commercial segments that appeared every quarter of an hour. Even when Jake knew that there was nothing worth watching she still found television to be oddly compulsive. It was just that she tried to make her viewing sufficiently uncomfortable as to force her to do something else instead, like reading.

Here, too, her exacting job was having an adverse effect on her life, for as Jake's career progressed and kept her even later at the Yard, to the detriment of anything that might resemble a private life, she found that the effort required to read anything but trash was too great. Looking along her infrequently dusted shelves, Jake sometimes found it hard to believe that the books on them could belong to someone who had won an exhibition to Cambridge.

Many of her books were vulgarly-attired, improbably-plotted stories of parish pump murder investigated by wisecracking female private eyes or beery detective inspectors, whose lives were full of idiosyncratic hobbies, romantic dalliances, foreign adventure, smoothly-spoken villains, clever observations and satisfying denouements. Lives which seemed to Jake more richly various than her own. Jake's one consolation was that these stories were invariably written by people who clearly had little or no appreciation of the dull, unthinking, brutal ordinariness of real murder. It was an impression reinforced by the author mugshots which appeared on the dustjackets. These revealed the faces of rosy fresh young mothers, catty intellectuals in glasses, sleek well-dressed advertising types, dry-as-dust academics, prim dyspeptic maiden aunts, and also-ran psychos whose hard, dark, Boston Strangler stares reminded Jake of her father.

Now and then their ideas of foul murder made Jake laugh out loud. Mostly they made her want to get one of these authors down to the lab so that they could see a really foul murder in all its mouldy, messy and utterly wasteful horror.

Well of course I have considered the possibility that I am barking mad. When you've murdered nine men, you have to really. There are some people who consider that killing in cold blood, and in any great number, is ample proof of an abnormal psychology. But of course, that simply won't do. Not these days.

The policewoman on the Nicamvision said that I was possibly psychotic. Quite apart from the fact that modern psychiatrists have already abandoned the distinction between neurosis and psychosis, and dropped such outdated terms from the current official diagnostic catalogue of their profession, I don't think that I could ever reasonably be described as psychotic, in the sense that my thoughts and needs no longer meet the demands of reality. Even if one ignores the fact that the only reality one can be sure of is the Self, I would suggest that if anything, my thoughts and deeds pay rather too close attention to the demands of reality.

You want a psychotic? I'll show you a doozy. The Greek hero Ajax killing a flock of sheep he mistook for his Trojan enemies. Now there's a fucking psychotic. The trouble is that most of these junk-psychobabble words don't have much meaning. Schizophrenia is such a mouthful, for so little import. There's a West African tribe called the Yorubas who, to my mind, have a much better word for what Western shrinks would refer to as schizophrenia. They say that a person is 'were'. I think this might transpose rather well between the languages. To say that 'he is were' implies that someone no longer 'is', and operating in the present. What better word for indicating a split personality?

What Policewoman said made me laugh. 'I will do everything in my power to ensure that you receive the proper medical treatment.' Well that was sweet of her. Of course what she meant was that if I gave myself up, she would endeavour to make sure that I was diagnosed 'unfit to plead by reason of insanity', within the legal and, it is fair to say, entirely fallacious definition of insanity that is to be found in the English judiciary's McNaghten Rules. This would mean that I could not then be tried and, more importantly, it would mean that I could not be sentenced to punitive coma – most probably, irreversible coma. Good thinking, Chief Inspector. There's not much incentive to give yourself up to the police if you know there's only a hypodermic needle waiting for you.

And all that stuff about a rumour that I had been in contact with the police? Now I have kept every one of the press-cuttings to do with my work in the Blue Book. There's not one of them which suggests anything of the kind. This was pretty clever. The remark about a rumour that I had been in contact with the police was just the surface structure of what she was saying. If you look for the deep structure, what you would end up with would be a question: 'Why don't you communicate with me?'

At the same time, she keeps something in reserve in case I'm the shy type. She says 'fuck you' and slaps my face. She tells everyone about how butter wouldn't melt in the mouths of any of my victims. These were just innocents, she says, going about their lawful business. Nothing at all about them being VMN-negative. (And the way that Detective Chief Superintendent dealt with that rogue question – well, they don't want the Lombroso Program connected with these executions any more than I do. Their embarrassment would signal the end of my mission. Or at least make it bloody difficult. There's not one of my famous brothers who wouldn't be expecting me.) Now this is supposed to make me angry enough to get in contact with Policewoman in case the first tactic doesn't work.

The bit I enjoyed most was my description and that ComputaFit picture. I wonder how she managed to obtain it? There are only two possibilities: either Bertrand Russell did somehow manage to splutter out a few dying words (all the same, I can't see him working with a police artist), or that chink counsellor at the BRI managed to remember me. Still, the picture doesn't resemble me all that much. ComputaFits never do. You look at them and you say to yourself that if someone looking like that were walking around he would have been arrested many times over just for being so weird. But on the whole it wasn't a bad effort. The chink must have a good memory. Either that or they shot him full of something to make him remember.

Anyway, what is clear here is that Policewoman has issued a sort of challenge. What's the sign of someone accepting one? Must one adhere to a certain etiquette or convention? No matter. It's already quite obvious that she means it to be my move next. To accept the challenge or not. And clearly another killing must be made in accordance with some new rules which belong to the grammar of the word 'game'.

Yes, a game with Policewoman is a fine idea. My favourite game used to be Monopoly, but it is not what it was. The board itself is half as thick as it used to be. The Old Kent Road no longer even exists, thanks to the developers. Oxford Street has become the New Oxford Street Shopping Mall. Fleet Street is a wasteland. The green houses and red hotels once reassuringly solid and wooden are now hollow and plastic, and are supplied in half the quantity than of old. 'Chance' and 'Community Chest' cards have become hopelessly outdated. Free Parking. In London? That's a laugh. School Fees of $150. These days that would buy you a few textbooks. You win a beauty contest. This kind of thing was outlawed, several years ago. Doctor's Fee, $50. For what, a bottle of aspirin? And no-one gets out of jail free: you have to pay to stay in a decent one, and you have to pay to get out. And the rents.

No, things have changed since I was a boy.

But here, you know nothing about my childhood, do you? Then let me describe my first thought.

My first thought (in time it may also prove to be my last) was to cry out, no doubt stimulated by the hand of my deliverer and, in so doing, take my first breath of a strange new world. Of course we cannot talk about what went before and it's still too early to say what will happen after. But I think this is a reasonable assumption of what first occurred inside my VMN-deficient brain.

Since the moment I was plucked, head first, from out of eternity and dangled by my ankles in the cold light of what is temporal, I have spent some considerable time in attempting to think of what cannot be thought. The nearest that one may come to this is in the contemplation of the state of non-existence that exists prior to birth and after death. Believe me I have found it easier to bend my mind in trying to say what cannot be said.

I suppose you could say that my motive, such as I was ever possessed of one in this matter, was partly blasphemous, since my mission resembled the utterance of the Tetragrammaton – JHVH. I feel I must accept this since what is thinkable is possible too, in the sense that one cannot think of anything illogical: we could not honestly say what something that was illogical would look like.

No doubt there are some who would disagree with this, but the reality – such as reality exists in this poor world – is that it is as hard to think of something illogical as it would be to determine the precise ratio between the diameter and the circumference of a circle, and thus construct a circle of the same area as a given square. (A *piece of pie you might think, but speaking as one who has tried, it cannot be done.)*

Commonly the Final Solution of the Jewish Problem, as dreamt up by the Nazis, is considered to have been something unspeakable. But this is simply not so, and to say that language cannot represent the Holocaust is to misrepresent it as something not of this world. It is to suggest that it is a riddle, that the explanation for why it happened lies outside time and space, and that the ultimate responsibility for it does not belong to man. (These are the people who suggest that understanding implies condonation.) Yet it is the fact that the Holocaust is so very much of this world and therefore that it can indeed be said and is not something unspeakable, which makes it so terrible. (For it was a culture producing Mozart, Beethoven and Goethe which committed this crime. In the same way the Romans produced Horace and Pliny and yet still threw Christians to the lions. Great crimes are a corollary of great civilisations.)

The only limit to what can be said is the limit that separates sense from nonsense. (By this limitation it will be seen that the Holocaust makes perfect sense, although one condemns it.) And yet there persists this belief that that which may indeed be understood may also be unspeakable: that the sense of the world may be found inside the world.

But if there is any one value which does have value it must lie outside the whole sphere of what happens. The fact of the matter is that all propositions are of equal value and there are no such things as propositions of ethics. Ethics are transcendental and cannot be put into words. In short Ethics are impossible.

Why else should anyone choose to go against them? If it was possible for there to be some kind of moral proposition which forbade murder I would not deny it. But it is also impossible to speak about human will in so far as it is the subject of ethical attributes. And so I kill because there is no logical reason not to.

The truth of thoughts that are here communicated seems to me unassailable and definitive. I therefore believe myself to have found, on all essential points, the final solution of the problem. Die Endlösung.

... But here I've been killing time, when I should have been killing the next name on my list. And what a name it is. One of the shapers of the whole Western intellectual tradition: Socrates.

9

Jake's advisory team of experts was made up of Professor Waring, Doctor Cleobury, Detective Inspector Stanley, and Detective Sergeants Chung and Jones. Two days after the press conference they met in a room at New Scotland Yard to discuss the progress of the inquiry.

'This is the newspaper advertisement which the agency devised,' said Jake, drawing a PMT copy of the ad across the table in front of Waring and Cleobury. 'So far there's been only a limited response to this, or to my statement.'

Waring glanced down the list of VMN codenames and shook his head. 'I wonder what the public makes of this?'

'There have been one or two curious calls from the press,' Jake admitted. 'Which reminds me. I've been meaning to ask you, Professor. Where did the original list of codenames held by the computer come from?'

Waring shrugged. 'Do you know, Doctor Cleobury?'

She smiled. 'It was Doctor St Pierre's idea,' she explained. 'He was looking for some sort of list of names of people who he could be sure were dead — you know, for legal reasons. Anyway, he picked the current Penguin Classic catalogue, and fed it straight into the computer.'

'Penguin Classics?' repeated Jake. 'As in the paperback publishing company?'

'That's right. And when that list runs out, he's planning to use the names of all the characters who appear in the novels of Charles Dickens.'

Jake raised an eyebrow at that one. But the idea of catching the murderer of Edwin Drood was not without its own peculiar appeal.

'How is your effort with the Lombroso computer

coming along, Chief Inspector?' asked Waring. 'The electronic spike.'

Jake looked at Sergeant Chung. 'Perhaps you could tell us, Sergeant,' she said.

Chung straightened up in his chair. 'My hope that there might be some kind of an electronic spike has been pretty well fulfilled,' he explained. 'The computer decided to treat the erasure as accidental, although the basic memory is still in the process of reconstruction. However, the suspect's deletion of his own personal details could not be retrieved. Since then, as you may know, I've been working with our own police computer, and having created a fictional murder investigation, I've been using a series of names drawn by the computer at random from the list of telephone subscribers to create a list of hypothetical suspects, with the aim of generating a response from Lombroso.' Now he shrugged. 'But this sort of thing takes time. And not all of these VMNs are on the telephone.'

'How many so far?' asked Jake.

'Eight,' said Chung.

'Out of a possible 120,' said Waring.

'With the two who answered our advertisement, the six who replied to the letter they received from their counsellors, and the nine who are already dead, that makes a total of twenty-five,' said Jake. 'Less the VMNs who are already in prison, that still leaves seventy-five.'

'Seventy-four,' said Chung. 'We know that Wittgenstein deleted himself.'

'I wonder why there hasn't been a better response?' said Professor Waring.

'They're scared,' said Jake. 'Did you know that some of them think that they'll be rounded up, and quarantined. Maybe even worse. If I was in their position, I don't suppose I would be too anxious to come forward either.'

'Well, that's all nonsense,' said Waring. 'Stupid gossip, put about by irresponsible people.'

'Nevertheless, it's what some of them do believe,' insisted Jake.

Professor Waring nodded gloomily and stared at one of the papers in his file. It was clear he did not wish to discuss the matter any further. Which made Jake wonder if there might, after all, be some truth in the rumour. But she kept this uncertainty to herself. She recalled that Waring had been opposed to her ideas as to how the investigation should be handled. At the same time, she had a respect for his abilities as a forensic psychiatrist. He was the best in the country and there was no sense in further alienating Waring at this stage in her investigation. She could see that Waring was looking at the list of codenames which constituted Wittgenstein's nine victims. He read them slowly and in the chronological order of their murders.

'Darwin, Byron, Kant, Aquinas, Spinoza, Keats, Locke, Dickens and last, but not least, Bertrand Russell.' He looked up at the others seated round the table. With his prematurely white hair, half-moon glasses, undernourished, ascetic-looking features, and an Aran sweater of permanently-knit eyebrows, it wasn't difficult for him to appear thoughtful. 'I don't suppose there could be some kind of pattern there, could there?' he said vaguely.

'You mean some kind of intellectual pattern?' said Jake. 'Not according to the Computerised Intelligence System.'

'Computers have no imaginations,' Waring said contemptuously. 'How about we try for one minute to use our own brains to look for a pattern?'

Jake shrugged. 'Sure, why not.'

'Let's take Darwin for a moment,' he said. 'He was first. Well, who else would be? Origin of Species, you get the idea.'

Doctor Cleobury shook her head firmly. 'Except that this is the grandfather, not the son. It was Erasmus Darwin, not Charles, who was killed, Professor.'

'What's Erasmus Darwin written that could possibly merit inclusion as a Penguin Classic?' he said.

'He wrote some poems about plants,' said Jake.

Doctor Cleobury nodded, smiled pleasantly at Jake and then shifted on her largish bottom. Comfortable once more she checked the hem of her tight black skirt and then the edge of her permed blond hair. Jake thought she looked more like a barmaid than a psychiatrist.

'Surely what is more significant,' said Jake, 'is that five out of the nine were philosophers.'

'Six,' said Cleobury. 'If you want to count Erasmus Darwin's so-called Sensational School of Philosophy. Wait a minute – '

'What is it?' said Jake.

'Just that it was Erasmus Darwin who was one of the first thinkers to try and establish a physiological basis of mental phenomena – a medullary substance.' She shook her head and waited for everyone else to catch her up. 'Well, don't you see? That's precisely what Lombroso is all about.'

Jake nodded, uncertain that the discussion was leading anywhere.

'Highly apposite,' agreed Waring, warming to his original idea. 'But what could be the connection with Immanuel Kant?'

Jake caught Chung's eye. He shrugged disinterestedly. Detective Inspector Stanley was studying the contents of his tea cup as if searching for some clairvoyant indication as to a future line of inquiry. Detective Sergeant Jones, who was supposed to be making notes of the meeting, was yawning at his computer screen. Jake smiled as she noticed the obscene spelling he had given the name of Kant. Waring saw it too, and shook his head with vigorous self-reproach.

'Yes, of course,' he said. 'How stupid of me. His family came from Scotland and changed their name of Cant into Kant to suit the German pronunciation. Darwin took his degree of medicine at Edinburgh. Of course, it's not as strong a connection to Kant as Hume would have been, but still – '

Jake let the professor and Doctor Cleobury carry on in this rarefied vein for a while, establishing insignificant connections between the nine dead codenames, before finally drawing them back to her original remark.

'I suggest we try not to let ourselves get too carried away,' she said with a smile. 'I think what's important is that out of a list of 120 VMNs, twenty of these code-names are the names of philosophers. Not only do we know that the killer's own codename is that of a philo-sopher, but several of his victims have also had the names of philosophers. It strikes me that what we have here is a killer with a sense of humour. The idea of one philo-sopher killing others just tickles him.'

Waring considered this for a moment. 'But then why not choose all nine of them that way? Why just the five?'

'Or six,' added Doctor Cleobury. 'Don't forget Darwin.'

Jake shrugged. 'Possibly he may want to deny us the establishment of some kind of pattern.'

Waring sighed wearily. 'Then he's making a damn good job of it.'

Detective Sergeant Jones looked up from his screen. 'I wonder if he actually knows any philosophy?' he said.

Jake nodded. 'I've been asking myself the same ques-tion.'

The meeting meandered on through the remainder of the afternoon before Jake declared it over. At five, she went out to get some coffee. When she came back she found Chung waiting for her in her office. He looked uncharacteristically excited.

'What's up with you?' she said. 'Your premium bond come up?'

'Could be,' he said, grinning, and waving a piece of paper.

Jake sat down at her desk, exhausted, and removed

the lid from the Styrofoam cup. Meetings always made her feel as dull as carpet underlay.

'Let's hear it then.'

'A random name and telephone number just got a response from the Lombroso computer,' he explained. 'Bloke called John Martin Baberton. Anyway, at the same time, the police computer at Kidlington reveals that this Baberton fellow has got a criminal record for computer fraud and attempted murder.'

Jake looked up from her coffee. 'You're joking,' she said.

Chung glanced at the print-out he was clutching. 'And what about this? He's got a degree in Philosophy, and a history of psychiatric disorder.'

'He sounds too good to be true,' said Jake. 'Have you got the file there?'

'That's the funny thing. Records can't find the manual file. It seems to be missing. There's just his computer record.'

He handed Jake the print-out and watched her as she read it over. She lingered over Baberton's laser-jet-printed picture.

'These pictures aren't the best for identification purposes,' she said. 'But I can't help feeling that I've seen this man before. What's his VMN codename?'

'According to Lombroso, it's Socrates.'

'Another philosopher.'

'Address?'

'Two known. There's one on his Lombroso print-out, and another on the police file.'

'Which one matches his ID card number?'

'The police file.'

Jake read the warning from the Lombroso computer with interest. It was the first time she had come across one within the course of an investigation.

ATTENTION. THE SUBJECT YOU HAVE IDENTIFIED HAS BEEN TESTED VMN-NEGATIVE, SOMATOGENICALLY PREDISPOSED TO

Jake fed a length of hair into her mouth and sucked it thoughtfully.

'There's something strange here,' she said. 'We know that somebody with the codename Wittgenstein deleted himself from the original VMN database, right?'

'Right.'

'So who's this well-qualified bastard? You couldn't hope to pick a better suspect if you went down to central casting.'

There was a knock at the door and Detective Chief Superintendent Challis entered Jake's office.

In the early stages of the investigation, when he had been effectively supplanted by Jake, Challis had shown no inclination to become involved in the case again. But ever since the press conference, Challis had taken to appearing in Jake's office at all times of the day and asking her for progress reports. She wondered if his suddenly-reawakened interest in the case was spontaneous, or if someone higher up, perhaps someone in the Home Office, had requested that he keep an eye on things. Whatever the reason, she disliked his interference almost as much as she disliked Poison Challis himself. Challis was another old-style policeman, one who thought that women in the police force were best employed communicating bad news to the families of accident victims.

'Did I hear the word suspect, Jake?' he boomed, rubbing his hands.

For a moment Jake considered stalling him and then decided against it. He was the kind of senior officer who was apt to be unforgiving about being kept in the dark on something. So she told Chung to repeat what he had just told her, after which she added a note of caution.

'I'd like to keep this man under surveillance for a while,' she explained. 'It's just a precaution, only there's something strange about all this.'

Poison Challis sniffed. 'I'll tell you what's strange,' he said. 'It's this John Martin Baberton who's bloody strange. You heard it yourself. The man's a bloody psycho.'

'No, sir,' insisted Jake. 'What I mean is that this is all a little too – ' She shrugged. 'Too convenient.'

'What are you talking about?' Challis demanded. 'What do you mean, too convenient?'

Jake wondered if it was her imagination or whether she could smell drink on his breath.

'Haven't you got any faith in your own law-enforcement technology? Jesus Christ, woman, it's supposed to make things convenient. Not every result has to come from months of painstaking detective work. Not these days, anyway. Or is this just some of that bloody feminine intuition I hear you always banging on about?'

'No, sir,' said Jake patiently. 'I'd just like to wait a little, sir. I'd like to . . .'

But Challis was already on the pictophone. 'I want a tactical firearms squad ready immediately,' he barked at the startled man appearing on Jake's screen. 'What's the bloody address, Sergeant? Here, give me that piece of paper.'

Chung handed Challis the print-out and looked questioningly at Jake as Challis read out the address to the squad constable. Jake shrugged silently, but when Challis had finished speaking, she said to him, 'Sergeant Chung? For the record, I would like you to note that this course of action is being taken by Detective Chief Superintendent Challis against my advice. In my judgment – '

'To hell with your judgment,' snapped Challis. 'Who the hell do you think you are? I run the Murder Squad, not you. I'll say when we make an arrest and when we don't. You may know a lot about criminal psychology, Chief Inspector, but I know about law enforcement, and I can recognise a bloody collar when I see one. Now you can either be a part of this, or you can stay here and sulk. Which is it to be?'

Jake felt her eyes grow smaller. She thought of the set of tungsten electronic knuckles in her bag and wanted to hit him. She could barely conceal the sarcasm in her voice as she told Challis that she wouldn't miss it for the world.

But before she followed him out of the door, Jake called Gilmour's office.

The police car carrying Challis, Jake and Stanley left New Scotland Yard and headed north up Grosvenor Street, Park Lane and then the little Egypt that was the Edgware Road, before turning west towards the A40. The slip-road climbed and looped like a big dipper until they emerged into the main eight-lane carriageway, sandwiched precariously between two enormous water-tankers. It was almost eight o'clock but the Westway was still choked with homeward-bound traffic. Drivers in their two-door Honda micro-cars stared up at the light railway speeding by overhead, and almost envied the passengers aboard it but for the knowledge that they would certainly have been travelling in conditions that would have left an agoraphobic battery hen short of air. Jake shook her head pityingly. One of the few compensations about working the unsocial hours that her job required was that at the times she usually drove to and from the Yard, the roads were all but empty.

The big police BMW moved powerfully onto the toll-paying, speed-unlimited lane which, at the flat fee of $100 a day, was comparatively free of all but the fastest and most expensive German cars. They passed one set of high-rise flats and then another — airborne rabbit-hutches, the road so close to the smoke-grimed windows that Jake could almost see the irradiated lettuce on the plastic dinner plates.

In a few minutes they were at the White City, the two white concrete towers of the new European Television Centre towering over the landscape like a twin pack of toilet rolls, reminding Jake that however long the job kept her out, she wasn't likely to be missing anything good on the Nicamvision. Seconds later they were driving by H. M. Remand Prison, Wormwood Scrubs, recently expanded into what had been the old Hammersmith Hospital, and surrounded with a no-man's-land of searchlight and razor-wire.

At the Hangar Lane roundabout, they turned south towards Ealing and Jake quickly lost her bearings in a maze of quiet suburban roads that ran close to the Honda Corporation's golf course. At the end of one road, already blocked off by police, they met the flak-jacketed commander of the Tactical Firearms Squad.

'We've got the place surrounded, sir,' he said, indicating a large detached house set in about a quarter of an acre. 'My boys have just finished having a quick sniff around the place. Apparently there's a man's body lying in some long grass close to the tennis courts.

'Bingo,' Challis muttered, and glanced balefully at Jake.

'What did I tell you?' He nodded at the house. Behind drawn curtains there were lights burning.

'We haven't approached the place yet, sir,' said the TFS commander, whose name was Collingwood. 'But we've shoved a couple of mikes on the wall and it looks as if there's someone at home all right. Funny thing though. There's a man standing in the porch.'

'Doing what?'

'He's just standing there.'

'Didn't you bring nightsights?'

'Of course I did. But he's in shadow, I'm afraid.'

'Perhaps he's just stepped outside for a quiet smoke,'

suggested Detective Inspector Stanley. 'I do that myself sometimes. Perhaps he lives with a non-smoker.'

'Hang on a minute,' said the commander, and pressed his earpiece closer to his ear. 'One of my boys says he's got a gun. A machine pistol it looks like. Seems as if he might be waiting for us, sir.'

Challis nodded grimly. 'Probably using that body in the garden as some kind of bait. Gets one of us to walk up to the door to try and make an arrest and then opens fire.' Challis turned to Jake. 'What do you think about him now, eh? I suppose this bastard with the gun is there to stop the garden gnomes being nicked.'

'I'll admit I don't have an explanation,' said Jake. 'But I still think we ought to wait, sir.'

'For what?' sneered Challis, not expecting an answer. 'Can your men take a closer look, Commander?'

'No problem.'

'We could train some searchlights on the front of the place,' Jake suggested. 'Get a loudhailer.'

'And let him know we're here, so he can hole up in there? No way,' said Challis. 'I'm not going to risk a siege. The last thing we want on this is the press turning up.'

So, Jake thought, Challis was looking out for the interests of the Home Office after all.

Meanwhile the TFS commander had twisted a small microphone attached to his helmet round to his mouth and given the order.

For several minutes there was only the sound of what passed for silence in that part of London: traffic moving on the North Circular, a Nicamvision's stereo sound system turned up too loud, a dog exercising its owner's freedom to let it bark its head off, an ice-cream van insanely spewing out its signature tune "Oh What a Beautiful Morning", and the wind stirring the rhododendron trees.

Jake breathed uncomfortably, still unable to articulate precisely what was wrong with the whole situation. A long dark Mercedes drew up alongside the other police cars. Gilmour, wearing a dinner jacket, got out and extended an index finger in the direction of Challis. Whatever he said was almost immediately forgotten.

The sound of automatic gunfire is not at all distinctive, at least in a West London suburb. There, people are so unused to hearing the sound that it would almost always be attributed to a late or early fireworks party, no matter what the time of year, and ninety-nine times out of a hundred the sound would indeed turn out to be just that. But on this occasion, Jake, Stanley, Challis, Gilmour, and the TFS commander knew better. Instinctively they ducked and two of them, Challis and the commander, even reached for their weapons.

'What the hell's happening, Sergeant?' the commander yelled into his headset.

There was another, more protracted burst of gunfire and then silence again: traffic still moving in the distance, the Nicamvision still blaring, the dog barking more furiously than ever, and the wind in the trees. After a minute or two there were shouts from somewhere in the target's garden and the TFS commander, fingers pressed against his earpiece like some affected pop singer, stood up.

'All over,' he said breezily. 'The man in the house has been arrested.'

'Thank God for that,' said Gilmour.

'What about the gunman in the porch?' asked Jake.

'He opened fire and was shot,' explained the commander.

'Dead?' enquired Gilmour.

The commander frowned uncomfortably. 'In cases involving terrorists, a termination is the usual policy, sir. Unless there are instructions to the contrary.' He glanced awkwardly at Challis as if seeking confirmation that no such instruction had been given.

'And who ordered this operation?'

The commander's frown grew more profound as now he sensed that something was not quite right. He pointed at Challis. 'Him, sir. I mean, Detective Chief Superintendent Challis, sir.' He touched the earpiece again and turned round. Two members of his squad were frogmarching a handcuffed man towards them.

Gilmour stepped squarely in front of Challis as if he meant to kiss both his cheeks like a French general. But the congratulations he offered were bent double with sarcasm.

'Well done, Challis, well done,' he said grimly. 'You'll get a medal for this. I'll see that you do. And I'll be the one who pins it on your chest. With a fucking bayonet. If I'm not mistaken they've just managed to shoot one of our own people. An armed guard from Special Branch.'

Challis's jaw slackened. 'What? Well we didn't know, sir. I mean, who's he supposed to be guarding?'

'Him,' said Gilmour.

The two arresting TFS officers presented their charge, a fat, blowing, angry-looking figure with blood pouring from his nose and mouth, the result of a blow from the butt of a machine pistol. His fair hair was dishevelled and his shirt was torn, but there was no mistaking the corpulent figure of the Shadow Home Secretary, Tony Bedford, MP.

'You will understand that I couldn't prove this. Not exactly anyway. Some of it's nothing more than informed guesswork by Sergeant Chung and myself. And it will take a while to include all of this within the context of the official report – '

A day or so later, with Challis suspended pending an inquiry, the explanation for what had happened was supplied to Gilmour, Jake and Stanley by Inspector Cormack of the Computer Crime Unit, in Gilmour's office at the Yard.

'Just get on with it, Cormack,' Gilmour growled. 'And try to keep it simple.'

'Well, sir, it's like this,' explained Cormack.

'Wittgenstein must have hacked onto the police computer at Kidlington, possibly with the intention of leaving a message for the Chief Inspector here. But while he's there he decides to have a look around the system and discovers Sergeant Chung's random name and number program. He has an idea. He creates a police record in the name of the man he is planning to kill: a VMN-negative code-named Socrates, real name John Martin Baberton – the body that was found in Mr Bedford's garden. He gives Baberton the kind of background that is just perfect for us: an ideal suspect, and one that we might not be able to resist. And because he has a sense of humour he adds in one or two details, such as Mr Bedford's home address and Mr Bedford's picture.'

'That's some sense of humour, all right,' said Gilmour. 'But where did he get Bedford's address and picture? That's what I want to know.'

Cormack winced. 'It would seem from our own files, sir.'

'What?'

'Well you see sir, ECIS has a one-man, one-record database. It would seem that Mr Bedford has a small record. For civil disobedience during the protest marches against punitive coma a few years ago. He was arrested for obstructing a policeman in the execution of his duty.' Cormack shrugged apologetically. 'All Wittgenstein had to do was instruct our computer to copy some of Mr Bedford's details onto a file in the name of John Martin Baberton, sir. The dead man.'

'He's not the only one,' Gilmour said darkly.

'I'm sorry, sir?'

'Nothing. Then what did he do?'

'Well, after he killed his victim, and left him at the foot of Mr Bedford's garden – at least we assume that he did that first – Wittgenstein then had to activate Baberton's name as a VMN on the Lombroso Program. To do that he must simply have added Baberton's name and telephone number near the top of Chung's random program. If anyone had checked they would have seen that the address he used matched only the address on the Lombroso file and not the fake record held on the police computer which provided Mr Bedford's address, and said that the one on the Lombroso file was out of date. And of course, there was no manual file for a John Martin Baberton: another discrepancy. Also if Baberton had had a criminal record at the time of his being screened by the Lombroso people it would have been revealed on his identity card.'

Gilmour nodded solemnly. 'Why do you say that Wittgenstein must have hacked onto our computer with the intention of leaving a message for the Chief Inspector?'

'Well, in view of what happened, sir,' said Cormack. When Gilmour did not reply, he added: 'I heard that he left a disc, for Chief Inspector Jakowicz, in the dead man's mouth.'

'Who told you that, Inspector?'

'Detective Sergeant Chung, sir.'

'He had no business to do so. Things are quite bad enough with the press as it is. If they discover that the killer has made contact with us we'll never hear the end of it. So keep your mouth shut. Understand?'

'Yes, sir.'

'One more question and then you can go, Cormack. On the basis of what you have surmised about this unfortunate breach in our own data security, are you satisfied that the operation which ensued was precipitate?'

Cormack nodded. 'Wholly precipitate, sir.'

Gilmour smiled ghoulishly. 'Thank you, Inspector. That will be all.'

After Cormack had gone, they sat in silence for a few moments. Then Detective Inspector Stanley asked the APC what was going to happen to Challis. Gilmour drew one eloquent finger across his throat and shook his head.

'I've no choice,' he explained. 'There will have to be a formal inquiry of course, but in view of what Cormack has just told me, it's a foregone conclusion. Too bad. He was a good copper.'

Jake nodded, although she didn't agree with Gilmour's estimation of Challis's detective skills.

'This disc,' said Gilmour. 'Have you brought it?'

'I've had a copy made, sir,' said Jake. 'The original is still with the lab. They're subjecting it to every test that's known to science: fingerprints, voiceprint, accent analysis, background noise, atmospheric adhesion. There's nothing so far. We've traced the disc itself to one of a batch of Sony blank discs sold to an electrical retailer on the Tottenham Court Road. The owner sells ten boxes of the same brand every week.'

'And the dead man? What about him?'

'Six shots to the back of the head, as before. According to the lab report, he was killed in Bedford's garden. He was full of vodka and we believe that Wittgenstein met him, struck up an acquaintance with him, and then lured him to Bedford's address on the pretext that they would be having sex there. Baberton was homosexual. There's a well-known gay bar in Chiswick which Baberton used to frequent. We're still trying to find out if anyone saw Baberton on the evening he died, and if so, whether he was with anyone or not.'

'Keep me informed on that.' He nodded at the disc player on Jake's lap. 'All right. Let's hear it.'

Jake placed the coin-sized disc into the machine.

'The material is in two parts,' she explained. 'One on each side of the disc. The first half is a sort of crude axiomatic parody of Wittgenstein's most famous philosophical work, the *Tractatus*. The second half – well, I'll let you judge that for yourself, sir.' She pressed the button to start the disc.

'Like Moses and Aaron, his brother, I carry a walking stick. I carry it everywhere and in a way I think of it as like my penis, constantly stiff, engorged for love. But it also represents my conscience, for sometimes I mislay it.'

'Ten of my brothers have been killed. And I think of death a great deal. In fact, I've been thinking about it for years.'

'Death is the totality of Nothingness, the very opposite of what is in the world. It is determined by a combination of objects (things). The grave is a fine and lonely place but none I think do there embrace. It is only the boys of Chiswick who keep me logico-philosophicus.'

'What we cannot speak about we must, like the Angel of Death, pass over in silence.'

'We never talk. It is too dangerous to talk. The boys are rough and crude. Some of them are almost illiterate. There are no names, just the brutal, selfish enjoyment of another being as an object.'

'If I am to know an object, though I need not know its external properties, I must know all its internal properties.'

'I should go away, somewhere quiet where there is no temptation. Here I am not safe from the love that dare not speak its name.'

'Only facts can express a sense, a set of names cannot.'

'It is loneliness that drives me from my rooms. I have sunk to the bottom. The world of the happy man is different from that of the unhappy man.'

'At The Funfair in Chiswick . . .'

Jake hit the pause button.

'The gay bar in Chiswick, sir,' she said, 'it's called The Funfair.' She hit the button again.

'. . . there is a merry-go-round where all the young queers wait to be picked up. They sit on the horses and flirt outrageously with all the male spectators. There was a boy who gave me the eye as I watched him going round and round. They were all in a certain sense, one.'

'I asked him back to my room in Ealing. I gave him all the money I had. Money is not a problem for me. My relations, to whom I handed over the whole of my property, send me money when I need it. I object to the very idea of property.'

'Here, the shifting use of the word "object" corresponds to the shifting use of the words "property" and "relation".'

'I imagined us both lying together. It made quite a picture, although it was hard to distinguish one form from another. Pictorial form is the possibility that things are related to one another in the same way as the elements of the picture.'

'For one glorious moment I was able to transcend my very being. I did not belong to the world. Indeed, I was at the very limit of the world so that I was almost something metaphysical. Language and its limitations prevent me from saying more.'

'This remark provides the key to the problem, how much truth there is in solipsism.'

'I am revolted at my own debauched behaviour, my very intimacy with this young stranger an endorsement of my own loneliness. But how things are in the world is a matter of complete indifference for what is higher. God does not reveal himself in the world.'

'I am cast down into the deepest pit in hell. Reeking of

my own degraded thoughts and in my desperation to be away from the scene of this foul tableau, I take the boy into the garden to kill him. When he sees the gun, he appears to want to say something, then thinks better of it, and just laughs.'

'When the answer cannot be put into words, neither can the question be put into words.'

'And so my gun speaks for me, silently.'

'Jesus Christ,' Gilmour muttered after a few seconds had elapsed. And then: 'Is that it?'

'Side one,' said Jake, removing the disc and turning it over to play the other side of the killer's recording.

'Jesus Christ,' Gilmour repeated. 'You've got a right nutter there, and no mistake.' He looked at Detective Inspector Stanley to elicit support for this view.

'Sounds like it, sir,' agreed the other man.

'Has Professor Waring listened to that?'

'Yes, he has,' said Jake. 'He recommended that I speak to an expert. A professor of moral philosophy at Cambridge University.'

'Listening to that disc, it sounds to me as if a professor of psychiatry would be more bloody use to you. Eh, Stanley?'

The other officer smiled and shrugged vaguely.

'Sounds as if this fellow could be a queer after all,' said Gilmour.

'I don't particularly care for that word, sir,' she said. 'But since you mention it, he might indeed be homosexual. Killing his brothers, as he calls those other VMN-negatives, might be a way of sublimating a homosexual inclination. Or he could be trying to sell us a dummy. To get us to waste our time conducting our investigation among the gay community. As before, there was no evidence that the dead man had been interfered with sexually. None at all.

'As a matter of fact, Wittgenstein's own sexuality has often been debated, and while there are some biographers who have sought, rather sensationally, to suggest that he was an active, predatory homosexual, there is little or no evidence for that either.'

Gilmour smiled uncomfortably.

'Shall we listen to side two?' Jake asked, and switched on the machine.

'Greetings, Policewoman,' said the voice. 'Caught your show on television the other night. Thanks for the kind thought vis à vis my sanity and my pre-trial prospects. You need not worry. I have already given careful consideration to my own defence, in the unlikely but nevertheless logically possible event of my arrest.

'I am certain that I could satisfy the court's McNaghten Rules and maintain a successful plea of not guilty by reason of insanity. You should note that I would contend that it was the Lombroso test itself which disturbed the balance of my already precarious mind. At the same time I would almost certainly file a civil claim for damages on the basis of the duty of care owed to me and the reasonable foreseeability of my suffering some sort of nervous shock as a result of this scan. When this is all over and the Lombroso connection with these killings has been made public, I think you will find that many of the victims' families will also want to pursue some sort of joint claim against the Brain Research Institute. But that's another matter.'

The voice was cool and calm and entirely without an accent. As Tony Chen had described it, 'like someone on the BBC', except that it was almost too robotic. It had no modulation, no expression, no lilt; no idiosyncrasy of pronunciation that might indicate an area of origin.

Received pronunciation, as it was sometimes described. It made Jake shiver a bit as she listened to it once again.

'Your suggestion that my brothers are innocent was, as you must have supposed it would be, irritating to me. The fact is that I am providing the public with a valuable service. You see, these are all potentially dangerous men who cannot simply be left to their own devices. The logical extension of their identification is, as a bare minimum, containment. But since the advent of an official shoot-to-kill policy among law-enforcement agents, and the implementation of punitive coma as the new cornerstone of penal theory, the incarceration of violent criminals has been demonstrated to be of only secondary importance to an obsessively cost-conscious administration. As a consequence of this governmental example, I am moved to kill them myself, humanely and efficiently, and with the least possible inconvenience to society.'

Wittgenstein allowed himself a small chuckle.

'You know, instead of trying to hunt me down, you should be grateful to me, Policewoman. Just consider how many of my brothers might have turned into killers of women. Tomorrow's gynocidal maniacs. That's your bag, isn't it, Policewoman? Serial gynocide? At least that's what the papers say, and we always believe what we read there, don't we? Like poor Mr Mayhew's brave struggle for life in hospital?' He laughed again. 'Anyway, you just ask yourself how many more lives may have been saved as a result of the few that have already been sacrificed? Is this not simply a kind of utilitarianism?

'You challenged me to communicate with you, Policewoman. And I have now done so. Both semantically and syntactically you may find the message – or at least the first part of it – not much to your liking. No doubt you should have preferred it if I had seemed more obviously criminal. And if there had been a few clues to help you track me down. Sorry. I'll try harder the next time we play our little game. Expect a telephone call from me any day now, when I'll tell you where to find the next body.

And thanks. This is so much more fun. Frankly I was becoming rather bored just executing brothers one after the other, day in day out.

'Until then, I urge you to sharpen up your thinking and to consider carefully the grammar of what you will say to me. Remember, when eventually we communicate in a real sense you and I will be doing Philosophy. So be prepared. Yours bloodily, Ludwig Wittgenstein.'

Jake switched off the disc player.

'Well,' said Gilmour, 'I've never heard anything like that before.'

'It is quite unusual,' Jake admitted. 'However, the subject's sense of omnipotence, his feeling of invincibility is entirely typical in cases where a multiple killer has contacted police. It's something I'm familiar with, sir. Even Jack the Ripper was given to telling the police that he didn't think they were going to catch him. So to that extent at least he was actually conforming to type.'

Gilmour nodded approvingly. 'I'm sure you know what you're doing, Jake,' he said.

Although Jake knew she was correct in what she was saying, at the same time the killer's disembodied words had made her feel anything but confident within herself. She had recognised a certain logic in what he had said about the need to eliminate those other VMNs. Hadn't she said as much herself?

When Jake returned to her office she found Ed Crawshaw at her desk, writing out a note. As Jake came through the door he crushed it in his hand and stood up sheepishly.

'I know you're busy with this other thing,' he said, 'but I thought you'd like to know: we've a sort of lead in the Mary Woolnoth case.'

Jake closed the door, squeezed past Ed Crawshaw's

large frame and dumped herself in her chair. She felt the colour rise in her cheeks.

'So what am I – your bloody nanny?'

Crawshaw shifted uncomfortably from one foot to the other.

Jake sighed and closed her eyes.

'I'm sorry, Ed,' she said. 'It's this other thing, as you put it. It's got me worn out. Sit down.' She pointed to the chair on the other side of her desk.

He sat down and opened his mouth to speak, but Jake stopped him.

'No,' she said, 'don't say anything for a moment. Just let me try and clear my mind.'

Crawshaw nodded and, adjusting his belt, leaned back in the chair.

Jake opened her shoulder bag, took out a small hand-mirror and checked her make-up as if trying to render herself more human. Her eyes looked bloodshot and her hair was a mess. The ends were split like bamboo. She could hardly remember the last time she'd been to the hairdresser. At the same time, out of the corner of her eye she observed that Crawshaw was putting on weight. His grey suit fitted him rather too snugly, she thought. He had always been a big man but now she could see how he had the potential to become a fat one. It was an impression made easier by the red-haired Crawshaw's lardy complexion. He was spending too much time in the office and probably not eating properly: the wrong kind of food at the wrong time of day. It was easy to let yourself get out of shape when you were at the Yard. Jake counted herself fortunate that she wasn't much interested in food.

She found her lipstick and fixing her mind on the lipstick writing she had seen on Mary Woolnoth's dead stomach, she touched up the corners of her diamond-shaped mouth. Finally, as she studied the waxy red end of the lipstick she said, 'So what sort of a lead do we have, Ed?'

Crawshaw opened the manila file on his lap, drew out a sheet of yellow paper and floated it across the desktop to her.

'Detailed lab report on the dead girl's clothes. The collar of her jacket showed light traces of olive oil. Her mother says that Mary was always very careful with her clothes. She spent a lot of money on them, and had things regularly dry-cleaned. So the chances are it didn't come from her. The olive oil on the collar lapels would be consistent with the killer having grabbed hold of her. There was just a trace of the same olive oil on the clothes of one of the other victims too.'

Jake glanced over the sheet of paper.

' "Cold pressed olives from the Tuscany region of Italy",' she read, ' "producing extra virgin olive oil." Interesting. So we could be looking for – ?'

'– for a wop.' Crawshaw grinned. He shook his head to indicate that he was joking. 'For someone who eats pizza with his fingers. Or maybe someone who prepares it.'

'For that matter it might be anyone involved in food preparation,' said Jake. 'I think I've got some Italian olive oil in my own kitchen at home.'

And that was probably all she had, Jake told herself. The kitchen might have contained every modern convenience, but of food itself there was really very little. Somehow the late supermarket was never quite late enough.

She sent back the paper. 'Look, see if we can match this oil to a specific supplier.'

'That's not going to be easy,' said Crawshaw. 'This stuff's pretty common. I mean olive oil is olive oil, right?'

Jake smiled. 'I hear what you say, but do your best. By the way, how's the golden apple operation coming along? The one in the Mystery Bookshop.'

'No bites so far.'

'You might take a look at their stock,' she suggested.

'Maybe our greasy-fingered killer left a few prints on a book.'

Crawshaw nodded.

'Anything else?'

'Er no.' But Crawshaw stayed in the chair, shaking his head vaguely. 'Well, yes: some of the squad were wondering what's going to happen to Poison. I mean to Challis.'

'Challis is suspended on full pay, pending the result of an inquiry. That's all I can tell you, Ed.'

'On full pay, eh? Shame. A meat-hook would have been better. The word is that it was Poison's incompetence that got that copper killed.'

'That's for the inquiry to determine,' Jake said firmly.

'I guess so.' Crawshaw smacked his thighs and stood up. 'How's it going anyway? This other thing. Making any progress?'

'Some.'

'Need any help?'

'Thanks for the offer, Ed, but no. But what I need right now is a tame philosopher.'

My own feelings at the time of the death of Socrates were quite extraordinary. It never occurred to me to feel sorry for him, which you might have expected at the death of a brother. But he seemed quite happy, both in his manner and in what he said. He met his death obediently, without fear and with some nobility. I could not help reflecting that on his way to the other world he would be under the providence of God, and that when he arrived there, all would be well with him. So I felt no sadness or sense of remorse.

At the same time, however, I felt no satisfaction either. Before his death our conversation had taken the form of a philosophical discussion. Strange to describe, but I suppose I experienced a sense of pain and pleasure combined as my mind assimilated the fact that my brother was going to die, and that it was I who was going to kill him.

Largely our discussion centred around the topic of immortality, although I rather think that many of the views which he expressed to me were really Plato's. But that's another issue. At its most simple, we discussed whether it was a man's body or his soul which matters most. Considering where we were at the outset of this dialogue – a gay bar in Chiswick – it is strange to report that Socrates was of the opinion that it is the latter which must be cultivated at the expense of the former. If this seems an unduly ascetic position to take, this may have been due to the fact that I had spiked his Brandy Alexanders, not with hemlock, as you might have thought, but with ZZT, the so-called Obedience Drug much favoured among S & M devotees, and thus he may have been led to agree with me.

Nevertheless, his famous last words seem to me to be curiously ambiguous. Before I shot him, he asked me to offer a cock to the god of medicine. Perhaps there was some humorous homosexual double entendre to this remark. Or he may have been trying a little irony with regard to the Lombroso Program. At the same time, and this is the interpretation which I myself favour, he may also have been trying to indicate that death itself is a cure for life.

It is often assumed that death is the negation of life. But how can this be? Anyone who understands negation knows that two negations yield an affirmation. Can it therefore be said that 'this man is not alive' and that two such negations would equal an affirmation, ergo, life? Of course not.

You see how mysterious life really is. Life is no more the negation of death than death is the affirmation of life. Yet it is only death which can confirm that there has indeed been life as we know it. Death is not the opposite of anything. It is death, and nothing else besides. Schopenhauer writes of how a state of non-existence is really man's more natural condition, given that we spend so many billions of millennia in this fashion; and of how life itself is little more than an unnatural blip on the supra-millennial screen.

Aside from an approximately real experience, the nearest one ever comes to the full comprehension of death is the contemplation of the non-existence of that which itself gave life: the death of a parent.

It is curious how this Brown Book works both as a journal of my life and as an event in my life. And you who come after me – well, to you this may be a book like any other: but just as I have read a story and then myself am a participant in it, I hope that this will be true of this story and you.

Perhaps now you can see what it means to speak of

'living in the pages of a book'. This is because the human body is inessential for the occurrence of experience. Indeed, many of my most profound experiences have occurred within the pages of a book. Experiences which have affected my life. If we understand one sentence, even a sentence in a child's comic, it has a certain depth for us.

Have you ever caught yourself reading? You know, you're sitting in a chair engrossed in a good book, enjoying the story and the author's prose-style, and then suddenly, it's as if you have an out-of-the-body experience and you catch sight of yourself as you really are: not trading wisecracks with Philip Marlowe, or struggling with Moriarty atop the Reichenbach Falls, but as someone sitting alone in a room, with a book open on your lap. It can be quite shocking. Like a sudden jolting shot of phenothiazine to the schizophrenic. One minute he's battling international Communism and the next he's just a guy in a wet bed and a pair of dirty pyjamas.

It is this rare ability to step in or out of the picture which distinguishes reading. Perhaps Keats perceived as much when he wrote to his sister describing the pleasure he should take in being able to sit beside a window on Lake Geneva and spend all day reading, like the picture of someone reading. Like a picture of someone reading . . . that's a lovely revealing sentence. And quite typical of those Romantics, always trying to escape themselves. It conjures up such a powerful image of someone not only living but lost in the pages of a book, oblivious to the exterior physical world, to the hand which turns the page, even to the eye and visual field which conducts the printed information to the brain. Without a book I am chained to the earth. Reading I am Prometheus Unbound.

But perhaps our subject, namely my story, has stolen away from us while I have been theorising, like a shadow from an ascending bird. Perhaps you have found that the bird and its shadow are too far apart. I could make more *matter with less art, if that was what you really wanted. But must this Brown Book of mine become simply a catalogue of blood with every lethal detail painstakingly described so that you can witness the full horror of my work? Surely we can agree that this improvised bible of my endeavour should remain something detached, a sideshow inside the main show that is my dark heart. And after all it will be entirely your affair how you read it, day and night.*

Just remember this, however: thou read'st black where I read white.

10

Jake drove herself to Cambridge and enjoyed the two hours she took to get there. During the journey she listened to the Rachmaninoff second piano concerto on the disc player and resolved to buy the software to play the piece on her own piano at home. The melancholy product of the composer's own hypnotherapy, Jake had always believed that it was essential music for anyone who wished to gain a profounder understanding of depression.

Further on into her journey she stopped at a little tea-shop in Grantchester only to find that it had closed. So for a while she just sat in the car, allowed the windows to mist up, and smoked a cigarette thoughtfully while she listened to the opening moderato, with its famous eight chords, once again.

It felt strange, she thought, to be going back after all this time. Stranger than she would have believed was possible.

It was almost twelve by the time the wheels of Jake's BMW rolled down the ramp of Cambridge's short-term multi-storey car-park. She unfolded the sun-visor and, particular about her appearance as usual, checked her make-up in the vanity mirror.

When she exited onto Corn Exchange Street, her direction lay east, down Guildhall Place and across Market Hill, and it was only force of habit that carried her footsteps up Wheeler Street towards King's Parade, and the turrets and pinnacles of her old, eponymously named college's long roofed chapel.

Confronted with the magnesian white limestone of the place close up, memories of another person she had once been awoke in her like krakens. As usual, it was raining, but the rain felt good after the drought of London. A harsh wind blowing south off the nearby Fens cooled the old market town and she was not inclined to linger there. Instead she turned into the face of the wind and walked briskly away from her past, from the friends she had had, and from the acquaintances who there seemed friends.

Jake did her best to ignore the pink granite, techno-Gothic tower that was Yamaha College, now occupying the site of old Great St Mary's Church, which had been destroyed by fire at the turn of the century, and hurried on to Trinity Street.

Entering Trinity College by the Great Gate, she reported to the Porter's Lodge and informed a bowler-hatted Chinese, who reminded her of Charlie Chan, that she had an appointment with the college Master.

The man scrutinised his visitors' list, nodded curtly, picked up the telephone, buttoned the Master's number, and announced Jake's arrival in an accent that would have confounded Henry Higgins – a combination of Fenman, old Etonian, and camp Oriental.

'Sir,' he said, 'there be a lady to see you. Shall I escort her to your door?' He listened for a second or two and then nodded. 'Sure thing. Whatever you say, boss.'

Then he came round the desk, accompanied Jake out of the lodge and down a couple of steps, and pointed towards an ivy-clad building on the opposite side of the quadrangle.

'See that there building?' he asked.

Jake said that she did.

'The Master's housekeeper will greet you at the centre door,' he added. 'You got that, lady?'

Jake said that she had and the man went back inside his lodge.

The clock was striking its familiar bi-sexual note of twelve as Jake crossed the Great Court and, in spite of her determined negligence of sentiment, she found memories crowding in upon her: of the occasion when first she had tried to listen to her own male and female voice; of her early sexual experiences with an older Trinity woman called Faith; and of how, once, Faith had bent her head between Jake's naked thighs and tried, unsuccessfully, to bring her sister to orgasm within the time it took the loquacious clock to strike its dual note of twelve – forty-three seconds – while poor, simple schoolboys raced around the Great Court with self-conscious honour and importance.

She knocked at the Master's low, half-windowed door with its brightly polished letterbox. There was more evidence of smooth housekeeping within and the woman who answered the door had no sooner explained that the Master was just taking a telephone call and shown Jake into the sitting room than she was off polishing something else.

Jake walked over to the rear window and, stimulated by the sight of the Cam, allowed herself the recollection of a practical joke which some thug had played on Jake and her friend Faith as they had punted underneath a bridge near the back of Queen's. The thug had painted a football so that it looked like one of the bridge's stone pommels and with a tremendous show of effort, he had pushed the lethal-looking object into their boat. Thinking that they and their punt would be smashed to pieces, Jake and Faith leaped, as they imagined, for their lives, and were soaked. It was Faith, now Professor of English Literature at Glasgow University, who had seen the funny side. Faith always saw the funny side of everything, with one notable exception: when Jake, inspired by her friend's strident and family-estranging lesbianism, decided to tell her own father she herself was gay.

It was a piece of pure sadism made all the more satisfying for Jake, since by then she was as certain that it was not true as she was that her father was dying.

Banishing these and other memories, Jake turned away from the window and stood in front of the blazing coal fire. Having warmed herself, she surveyed the Master's books, some of them written by himself, and one of which Jake had read.

Although Sir Jameson Lang had been teaching Philosophy at Cambridge for over ten years, it was as the author of a series of highly successful detective novels that he was chiefly known to the public. Jake had read the first of these, a story in which the philosopher Plato, while on a visit to Sicily during the year 388 BC, turns detective in order to solve the murder of a courtier to King Dionysius of Syracuse. Jake recalled that in solving the crime (with the aid of Pythagorean mathematical principles) at the request of the King himself, Plato had managed unwittingly to offend this young tyrant who then proceeded to sell the philosopher/detective into slavery.

Just as well, Jake told herself, that the Metropolitan Police had trades union representation. As in Plato's day, there were few people who ever really welcome the Truth. The truth meant a trial and nobody, apart from the lawyers, ever welcomed that. Certainly not the murderer, and certainly not the murder victim's family who often regarded a criminal investigation as an unwarranted invasion of its privacy. It is said that justice must not only be done, but it must also be seen to be done. But Jake had her doubts. In her experience most people preferred that things be swept underneath the rug. No one cared much if an innocent man went to prison, or if a terrorist was shot dead while surrendering. No one thanked you for building a case against someone and then insisting on a show. As Jameson Lang had had Plato say to Dionysius, 'It is not every truth that sounds as sweet as birdsong, not every discovery that is welcomed among the occult, not every light that is approved from within the shadows.' Whatever you thought of his prose style, there was a lot in that, she thought.

The college Master made his appearance, apologising for the delay, only there had been a call from his copy editor querying a couple of points before his latest book went to press. Jake asked him if it was another Plato novel, and he said that it was. She added how much she had enjoyed the first. Sir Jameson Lang, a handsome man wearing a three-piece suit of Prince of Wales check, looked flattered. Fair-haired, blue-eyed, and with a shy, tight-looking mouth which gave the appearance of having suffered a small stroke, Lang appeared the quintessence of Englishness, although he was in fact Scottish.

'How kind of you to say so,' he drawled in the kind of voice which Jake felt might have suited some stuffy gentlemen's club, and offered her a sherry.

While he filled two glasses from a matching decanter, Jake glanced up at the painting above a mantelpiece that was heavily populated with porcelain figures. The scene in the painting was Arcadian in its setting and seemed vaguely allegorical in its meaning. Lang handed Jake her glass and bending down to the scuttle retrieved a couple of lumps of coal the size of small meteorites which he dropped onto the fire. Noticing Jake's interest in the painting he said, 'Veronese'. Then he ushered her to a seat and sat down in an armchair facing her. 'Belongs to the college.

'I was intrigued by your call, Chief Inspector,' he said, and sipped a little of his sherry. 'Both as a philosopher and as someone with a tremendous fascination for – the detective form.'

His eyes narrowed and for a second Jake wondered if he was making some reference to her own body.

'Now exactly how can I be of assistance to you?'

'There are a number of questions I was hoping you might be able to answer, Professor,' she said.

Lang's crooked smile widened slowly.

'Bertrand Russell once said that philosophy is made up of the questions we don't know how to answer.'

'I've never thought of myself as a philosopher,' she admitted.

'Oh, but you should, Chief Inspector. Think about it for a moment.'

Jake smiled. 'Why not just give me a short tutorial?'

Lang frowned, uncertain whether or not Jake was being sarcastic.

'No, really,' Jake said. 'I'm interested.'

Lang's mouth relaxed into a smile again. It was already clear to Jake that it was a subject he had devoted a great deal of thought to, and one which he was keen to discuss.

'Well then,' he began. 'Detection and philosophy both promote the idea that something can be known. The scene of our activity comes with clues which we must fit together in order to produce a true picture of reality. Both of us have, at the heart of our respective endeavour, a search for meaning, for a truth which has, for whatever reason, been concealed. A truth which exists behind appearances. We seek to penetrate appearances and we call that penetration, knowledge.

'Now whereas the commission of a crime is natural, the task of the detective, like that of the philosopher, is counter-natural, involving the critical analysis of various presuppositions and beliefs, and the questioning of certain assumptions and perceptions. For example, you will seek to test an alibi just as I will aim to test a proposition. It's the same thing, and it involves a quest for clarity. It doesn't matter how you describe it, there exists the common intention of wresting form away from the god of Muddle. Of course, sometimes this is not a popular thing to do or to have done to you. It makes most people feel insecure and quite often they resist what we do very strongly indeed.'

Lang sipped some more of his excellent sherry and laid his head back against the antimacassar on his chair.

'The work we do is often repetitive, going over familiar ground which one has already covered and breaking the stereotypical conclusions which may have been reached by others as well as by oneself. Indeed it is our Sisyphean fate often to be undoing what has already been done so as to grasp the nature of the problem more firmly.' He looked across at Jake. 'How am I doing so far?'

'Well,' said Jake.

He nodded. 'Despite Nietzsche's reservations about the dialectical method, that it is nothing more than a rhetorical play, our inquiry into truth, with its question and answer structure, has its origins in the Socratic form of dialogue. If confusion does arise it is because, to an inexperienced eye, it might seem that we are always looking for answers; but just as often, we are looking for the question. The real crux of what we both do is to attempt to see the anomaly in what appears familiar and then to formulate some really useful questions about it.

'In its purest form, ours is a narrowly intellectual activity, involving a dialogue with the past. And where we fail it is more often because of some false assumption or conceptual error in that cognitive, explanatory activity of ours.

'Of course, lack of proof is a recurrent problem with both of our activities. Much of our best work fails because we are unable to prove the validity of our thinking.'

Jake smiled. 'Yes. And yet it seems to me that I have one great advantage over what you do, Professor. I may occasionally lack proof for my theories. But I can always trick a suspect into confessing. And sometimes, worse than that.'

'Philosophers are not without their intellectual tricks,' said Lang. 'However, I take your point.'

'Now I see how you managed to make a detective out of Plato,' said Jake. 'And how it works as well as it does. I wonder what he would have thought about us.'

'Who, Plato?'

Jake nodded.

'Oh, I am sure that he would have approved of you, Chief Inspector. As an auxiliary guardian, in the service of the state, you are pretty much what he suggested.'

'Except that I'm a woman.'

'Plato was generally in favour of equality between the sexes,' said Lang. 'So I guess that it would have been all right, your being a woman. On the other hand, I don't think there can be any doubt that he would not have approved of me.'

'Oh? And why's that?'

'A philosopher and a novelist as well? Unthinkable. Plato was enormously hostile to art of any kind. That's what made writing a novel about him such fun.'

Lang stood up and fetched the sherry decanter.

'Top you up?' he asked.

Jake held out her glass.

'But look here, I'm diverting you, Chief Inspector. I'm sure you didn't come all this way for a philosophy tutorial.'

'Oh, but I did, Professor. But not on Plato. I'm interested in Wittgenstein.'

'Isn't everyone?' he said darkly, and sat down again. 'Well, of course you've come to the right place. No doubt you already know that Wittgenstein was a member of this college. So what do you want to know about him? That he was a genius, but that he was wrong? No, that's hardly fair. But this is too exciting, Chief Inspector. I'm as fond of reading conspiracy theories in the newspapers as the next man, but you're not going to tell me that he was murdered, are you? That sixty-odd years ago, someone bumped him off? You know, from everything I've read about him, he was rather an irritating, punctilious sort of fellow. An ideal candidate for murder.'

Jake smiled and shook her head. 'No, it's not quite that,' she said. 'But before I tell you, I must ask for your undertaking to treat this matter as confidential. There are people's lives at stake.'

'Then consider it given, on one condition. That you tell me about it over lunch.'

'Well, if you're sure it's no trouble.'

'No trouble at all. Mrs Hindley always makes too much, just in case I invite someone back.'

Jake thanked the professor and they adjourned to the dining room where Sir Jameson Lang's housekeeper served them with chicken broth, Spam fritters with baked beans, and then creamed rice with tinned mandarin oranges. While they ate, Jake told him what she knew: about the Lombroso Program, and of how someone, codenamed Wittgenstein, was eliminating all the other men who had tested VMN-negative. And then, over the coffee, she played him the disc.

Lang listened to the killer's voice with a look of rapt concentration. Occasionally he noted something down on a pad he had produced from his jacket pocket. And sometimes, frowning with what perhaps was horror, he shook his head slowly. When side one had finished, Jake played him side two. Lang sneered silently at some of the arguments, but when it too was finished he nodded emphatically.

'Fascinating,' he breathed. 'Quite fascinating. And you say that this disc was found in the mouth of his last victim: Socrates?'

'That's right.'

Lang pursed his lips. 'I suppose that could in itself be symbolic.' He gave a brief snort of astonishment. 'But the whole case is ripe with symbolism. Only you're not here to talk about that, are you? I presume you have questions which relate to this fellow's pretensions to being a philosopher himself. Perhaps even to the extent of believing that he is himself Wittgenstein. Am I right?'

'Yes,' Jake admitted. 'I can see the obvious parody of Wittgenstein's *Tractatus*. But concerning the content, I need your help.'

'All right then,' he said, and glanced down at the notes he had made. Then he got up from the table and opened a box of Havanas, which lay on the sideboard, and from which he took out a silver tube. 'But first I must have a cigar. I think more clearly when my lungs are clouded.'

Jake took out her own cigarettes, and poked one between her lips. Removing both cigar and its wafer-thin lining, Lang dipped the latter into the fire with which he lit first Jake and then himself. He puffed happily for several moments, walking round the creaking oak-floored room and, from time to time, glancing at his notebook. Finally he sat down once again, removed the Churchill from his mouth, sipped some of his coffee, and then nodded.

'First, he refers to his brother. Wittgenstein had brothers, one of whom killed himself. That might be significant.

'Then there is the relation between the covert, hidden aspect of what cannot be said to Wittgenstein's supposed homosexuality.' Lang shrugged. 'The theory that Wittgenstein was an active homosexual has been discounted by all but one of his biographers, an American.' He waved his hand dismissively. 'That he was homosexual is certainly possible. What is more likely is that he was simply asexual.

'Clearly, as you say Chief Inspector, he seems familiar with the style and structure of the *Tractatus*. Indeed, I should say that he knows it quite well.

'He recommends that you consider your grammar. Well, of course "Philosophical Grammar" was the substance of Wittgenstein's work between 1931 and 1934 and this was published posthumously, in the mid-1970s.

'It's interesting that he signs off as "yours bloodily". That's how Wittgenstein himself often signed off in his correspondence with friends and colleagues.'

Lang sucked some more at his cigar and then surveyed the darker brown end that had been in his mouth.

'Next, you mentioned the possibility that he might wish to concentrate on killing those other VMN-negative men whose codenames are the names of philosophers. I think you could be right, Chief Inspector. Wittgenstein himself believed that in the *Tractatus* he had found all the answers to the problems of philosophy. That he had done away with all that went before. For instance, he believed he had disproved most of what Bertrand Russell had written. So it's entirely characteristic that your killer should have eliminated him.'

Jake nodded and sucked hard at her cigarette. With no nicotine it was hard to find much satisfaction in anything other than the sensation of the smoke itself. Nevertheless, the sucking and blowing of smoke always helped her to concentrate.

'From what you've heard,' she said, 'do you think it's possible that he might have read Philosophy as a student?'

Lang smiled. 'Chief Inspector, you've no idea the kind of strange people who apply to read Philosophy. Especially here, at Cambridge. To paraphrase Keats, they are the kind of people who would clip an angel's wings. So, to answer your question, yes, it's possible. And if a young philosopher wanted a role model, then Wittgenstein would certainly be your man. His work has a turbo-charged quality, rather like Nietzsche's, and is always influential on students. That comparison with Nietzsche is useful because in the same way that he went mad, there's a madness that's also apparent in Wittgenstein's writings. Remember that crappy old saying about the thin dividing line between genius and madness? Well, all his life Wittgenstein, who was certainly aware of his great abilities, was also terrified that he might cross that imaginary line and lose his mind. I can well see how he might have an extraordinary appeal for a mentally unbalanced individual as much as for a logician.

'But it's also worth remembering that Wittgenstein came to regard the early work contained in the *Tractatus* as fundamentally mistaken. Perhaps you should consider the possibility that the killer might similarly be persuaded of the error of what he is doing. He promised to communicate with you, did he not? Yes indeed, he seemed to imply that you and he might have some sort of a dialogue. That might present you with a real opportunity to argue with him and, utilitarian considerations notwithstanding, maintain a logical position at odds with his own. If he's in any way sophisticated, he ought to respond to that challenge.'

Jake nodded thoughtfully.

'I don't suppose you might consider helping me out with that as well?' she asked.

'Frankly, I'd be delighted,' he said. 'I was rather hoping you would ask me. The idea of engaging a murderer in a philosophical dialogue is certainly an intriguing one. Contemporary philosophy in action, so to speak. But tell me, Chief Inspector, do you have any idea how he will make contact with you?'

Jake shook her head vaguely. 'However he does it, you can bet he'll be too clever for us to trace him. My guess is that he'll try and use a portable phone from a car he'll have stolen. If he called us while he was sitting in some multi-storey car-park in Central London it could take forever to find him.'

'Then hadn't we better give consideration to where you and I will be when he calls. If I'm to help you, then I ought to be at your side. And I regret that I am presently unable to leave Cambridge. At least for the next week or so, anyway.'

'I don't suppose that you have any video-conferencing facilities here?' she asked. 'A pictophone, maybe.'

The professor shook his head. 'No, we do not. Trinity finances are no longer what they were. It's the same for the whole university: thus we have monstrosities like Yamaha. Trinity has already been obliged to sell its unique wine cellar.'

'Would you be willing to have a pictophone installed here, Professor?' said Jake. 'I can have my people set up a permanent telecommunications link between us. That way, when the killer calls, you can participate in our conversation.'

Sir Jameson Lang shrugged. 'Just as long as I wouldn't have to do anything technical. Unlike Wittgenstein, who was rather good with his hands, I have no practical skills whatsoever.'

'All you'd have to do is press a button to open the conference.'

'Very well then. I'd be happy to.'

'Then I'll arrange it immediately. The sooner the equipment is installed, the better.'

It was time for Jake to leave.

'You can leave the disc with me, if you like,' Lang suggested. 'I'd like to listen to it again, if I may. There may be something that I missed. Incidentally, it might interest you to know that Wittgenstein had a real fascination for detective stories. The hardboiled, American variety. When you conduct your own investigations, Chief Inspector, it might be useful to remember that he himself placed little reliance on the so-called deductive science of Sherlock Holmes. He liked his detectives to be rather more intuitive. If one assumes that your killer is of the same frame of mind, trusting your own intuitions might ultimately prove to be very useful. To that end, I wonder if I could suggest something, while you're here.

'Perhaps' – he said hesitantly – 'perhaps, while you are here, you might like to take a look at Wittgenstein's old rooms.'

'I'd love to.'

'Yes, I think you'll find them interesting.' He glanced round his own quarters and smiled. 'They're not at all like this, of course. No, he was much more simple. As a professor he would have been entitled to have something rather grander. You know he came from one of the richest families in Austria, and reacted against everything that reminded him of that former privileged, luxurious existence. Even to the extent of having a brief fling with Communism. I shan't accompany you. I'll probably give you his whole biography if I do. No, I'll get someone to take you.'

The Master went to the telephone and called the Porter's Lodge. Then he wished Jake goodbye.

By the time Jake re-crossed Great Court, a man in a raincoat, not the Chinese, but another man, was standing on the steps of the Porter's Lodge to conduct Jake on her tour.

'Right then, miss,' he said, 'I believe the Master said it's K10 that you want to see.' He led the way back out the Great Gate and onto the street. 'That's in Whewell's Court,' he explained as they passed through another ancient doorway set in a wall beside the post office. 'So who was this bloke? The one who lived here?'

'Ludwig Wittgenstein,' she said. 'He was a great Cambridge philosopher.'

The porter nodded.

'Do you get many visitors wanting to see his old rooms?' she asked, wondering if the killer might have made some sort of similar pilgrimage.

'Well,' he replied. 'I've been here over ten years, and you're the first in my memory.'

They came to the foot of a small staircase, with red-ochre painted walls.

'It's at the top,' he said, going on ahead. 'Saw a philosopher on the telly once. Near enough a hundred years old, he was. And the bloke says to him: Having lived for so long, do you have advice for mankind? Anyway the philosopher laughed and said that he did have some advice. He says: "Yes. Don't ever help your own children." What about that, eh? "Don't ever help your children." What a mean old bugger, eh?' The porter laughed derisively. 'Philosophers eh? What do they know about real life, I ask you.'

Jake, who had received nothing but hindrance from her own father, admitted that there might be something in what he said.

The ascent to K10 came to an end before a plain black door above which was painted the name of the room's occupant, one C. Von Heissmeyer. Jake wondered if this could be an Austrian name, and if so, whether there was anything suspicious in that.

The porter knocked and waited. 'If the student's in, we'll need his permission,' he said, and knocked again. Then, there being no reply, he produced a set of keys and opened the door.

The rooms were simplicity itself, consisting of a kitchen, a sitting room and a bedroom. The orange sofa and armchair were as hard on the eye as the blue carpet underfoot. The single bed, with its plain, purple cover had been carefully made. The kitchen was neatly kept, with three dinner plates draining on the rack like the three computer disks in their box on the desk.

Jake went over to the triple-arched window and sat on the edge of the desk. In the courtyard below sat a greenish bronze figure of a man. In the distance were two devil's horns of the incongruous-looking Wolfson building. Her eye caught the reading list taped to the window pane, and then the matching pile of Penguin Classics.

It was strange how something so innocent, so commonplace as a pile of Penguin Classics could stir suspicion in her mind. This really was too absurd, she told herself. It smacked of something obsessive. But even though she knew it was ridiculous, Jake found herself paying close attention to the titles and their authors: *The Moonstone* by Wilkie Collins; *The Satanic Verses* by Salman Rushdie; *The Turn of the Screw* by Henry James; *Fear and Trembling* by Soren Kierkegaard; and *The Last Days of Socrates* by Plato. Pure coincidence, she told herself. The same was true of the row of books by Wittgenstein ranged along the mantelpiece and the framed photograph of him which hung above these. And weren't there many young people who liked to have a poster of a gun-toting Humphrey Bogart in their rooms: this one was from Howard Hawks's production of *The Big Sleep*. 'The violence screen's all-time rocker shocker,' said the blurb at the top of the poster. 'Bogy'n' Baby paired off for a hot time and the big thrill in cold, cold crime.'

Hadn't Professor Lang said something about how Wittgenstein had been interested in the American detective genre?

But what could have been more natural than that a student occupying Wittgenstein's old rooms in Trinity should also have been interested in him? And like him, like any young man, interested in the hardboiled detective?

By the same token, what could have been more natural in the present circumstances than that she herself should have been interested in anyone who might feel he had some kind of spiritual affinity with Wittgenstein?

Sir Jameson Lang had surely missed one of the most important differences between the philosopher and the detective. For the detective, nothing is ever truly itself and nothing more. A cigarette end was never just a cigarette end: it was also sometimes a sign, a clue, a piece in a puzzle awaiting connection with something else. There was more semiology than philosophy in that particular aspect of her work.

Only connect. To be able to really know something was only to know how things were connected. Like a psychoanalyst, it required connecting the past to the present and thereby obtaining some sort of cathartic resolution.

Of course there were times when connections eluded her, when she could connect 'nothing with nothing', when something could not be known.

And there it remained only to make things fit.

To fit. No detective much liked the verb. It smacked of corruption and of malpractice, of suppressing some connections and highlighting others. It was much too active. Too premeditated.

But life was hard, and Jake found herself taking a note of the student's name, just in case.

*This morning, after dreaming of my father, I woke up
with the word 'Shakespeare' on my lips.*

*The television clock was emitting a loud buzz which
continued on the same note for thirty seconds. At the
same time, the television turned itself on for the early
morning aerobics show. It was seven-fifteen, getting-up
time for office workers. I had worked the day before, a
Sunday, and although I had Monday off, I didn't like to
miss my physical jerks. So I wrenched my body out of
bed and seized a dirty singlet and a pair of shorts that
were lying across a chair.*

*The music started and, after a violent fit of coughing,
I took my position in front of the screen on which the
image of a youngish woman, scrawny but muscular, and
dressed in a virtually luminous green leotard and tights,
had already appeared. In time to the music, she started
to run on the spot, raising up each thigh in turn to her
chest.*

*'Come on now' – she grinned virtuously – 'let's stretch
those muscles and work those lungs. And one, and two,
and three and four . . . And one, and two, and three and
four . . .'*

I did my best to observe the pace she had set.

*'Remember, I'm watching you,' she joked. 'So no
cheating now. And one, and two . . .'*

*The rhythmic movements of the exercise began to jog
a few recollections of my dream. But it had been more
than just a simple dream. It was a real memory of early
childhood and my father, one of the first real memories
(as opposed to approximately real memories) I had had
in a long time. As I bounced mechanically up and down,*

I struggled to hang on to it for a while. It was extraordinarily difficult, and after a few more minutes the memory did not persist, fading like the image on a piece of photographic paper that has been treated with the wrong kind of chemical. No amount of bouncing seemed able to jog the memory back again.

'And relax,' said the instructor. 'Breathe in, breathe out, breathe in, breathe out.' Big smile. 'The weather next, after these messages.'

I collapsed onto the bedroom chair. But while physical exercises for the day may have been complete (I never bothered with the second session), there still remained my mental preparation. I always treat the first two-minute commercial break of the morning as the perfect opportunity for a therapeutic hate period. The fact is that I take violent exception to being patronised and find that the commercials help to bring out the very worst in me. So, for two whole minutes, I just shout and scream the vilest abuse at the various TV advertisers whose thirty-second messages fill the screen. Fortunately the apartments above and below my own are no longer occupied.

When all my little procedures for starting the day were complete, I showered, ate breakfast and went through the Sunday newspapers, looking for anything to do with my own story. As usual, there was something – you kill enough people, you get your story in the papers all the time. On this occasion it was a colour feature on the victims, with unnecessarily vivid close-ups of their gunshot heads and their dead bodies.

There were also some nice pictures of Policewoman, taken at her touching little press conference. These revealed a truly beautiful woman, a fact which until now had not been made clear to me, even on high-definition television. This is, I suppose, hardly surprising. Television, even high-definition television, does strange things to people. It makes their heads bigger, it makes them taller. In short, it makes them seem altogether different from how they really are in the world. That was also the case with Policewoman.

Clearly she is Jewish in origin. Her name would tell me as much. Her appearance confirms the matter. A dark-haired Sephardic beauty with cadmium-green eyes and cheekbones that were cut from purest marble (I was never much of a poet). Her chin is equally strong and helps to make her full mouth as stubborn as a salesman's optimism. Yet there is also just a hint of the coquette about the angle of her head and the purse of her crimson-lake lips – enough to soften the hard, questioning look in her eyes which might easily turn into contempt. A policewoman's face, albeit a distinguished one. Lady Disdain.

I imagine she must have been some kind of athlete when she was at school. It's difficult to tell from television and the photographs, but I think she must be tall. I expect she was captain of netball, and with those long, strong legs I'd also guess she might have become an efficient high-jumper. I dare say she wore her shorts a size too small and broke a few hearts.

She looks quite intimidating and it would not surprise me if there were a few unsatisfactory relationships with boys who found themselves unable to measure up to her advanced maturity. Doubtless they would have turned this fear of her powerful physicality against her in order to lend themselves comfort and protection. Did they call her names in mockery of her size, I wonder.

There was little information which the newspaper provided about Policewoman, except that she was thirty-seven, a graduate of Cambridge University, that she had served with the Met for thirteen years, and that she was an expert in the investigation of serial killings. It was fortunate that I had been able to access her file in the police computer which, in addition, revealed her name and address.

Almost idly I copied the magazine photographs of her onto the computer and, using the 3-dimensional imager, turned her this way and that, almost as if she had been a child's doll. But I soon grew bored of this and went to make myself a cup of Brio.

I was glancing through a pornographic magazine when it occurred to me that I could see Policewoman naked. Quickly I returned to the computer and copied a selection of photographs onto the program and started to assemble some photocomposites of her head and various naked female torsos.

I decided that her breasts should be neither too small, nor too large and that her nipples were probably as yet undarkened by a pregnancy. The pubic area presented a greater problem. First I found a pudenda with not enough hair and then one with too much. I was forced to find some more magazines. These were better and more explicit. When these were fed into the computer, she sat, wearing just a pair of white, self-supporting stockings, with her legs drawn up so that her knees almost hid her mouth, tugging at her immaculate labia with well-manicured fingers, and allowing me a midwife's view of her insides.

In another sequence of shots, I found a girl whose head position exactly matched those photographs I had of Policewoman, and who was depicted in the act of fellating a man, as well as in the act of full intercourse. When I had married this new material together with Policewoman I was able to see what little pleasure she might have taken in the heterosexual act. Of course, this had a great deal to do with her original facial expression which was that of someone appearing before a press conference as opposed to an erect penis. But all the same, intuitively I perceived more or less how it would be.

By way of contrast I found some shots of the same model engaged in lesbian acts. This sexual behaviour seemed to suit Policewoman's features rather better and I managed to comp an effective one of her guzzling on another girl's toffee-coloured clitoris.

With all this excitement under my belt, I simply had

to have sex with her, or an approximation of her anyway. So I copied the picture disk onto the RA machine and climbed into my exoskeleton. Then I unwrapped an RA condom and peeled it onto my erection before attaching the terminal to the suit. When all was ready I donned my helmet, plugged myself into the computer, and started to run through the pre-RA checks like a pilot about to test fly the old X-15. This was to avoid any accidents that might result from a sudden surge of approximate reality to the ears or, more importantly, the penis.

'Textures, on. Dynamics, on. Sound, on. Head track-ing, on. Body sensing, on. Phallus sensor, on.'

Then I dropped the visor-screen.

And there she was, standing before me in a pleasant forest glade, like Eve herself, without so much as a fig leaf to cover her nakedness. The image blurred a little as I stepped towards her and I made a small adjustment to the visor. Then I reached out and caressed her breast to test the glove, and felt her nipple harden as I touched her. Next, I slapped her face hard to test the sound quality, which was fine. Policewoman took the blow with a cry of pain, but no reproach. She just stood there, awaiting my next move, as programmed. I motioned her down onto her knees to check the RA condom and felt her approximate mouth envelop my penis. Everything was working perfectly. So long as the visor was down, the software would remain in operation, and approxi-mate reality would be nearly indistinguishable from the real thing. (Sometimes I think that I'm living a real life in an approximate way. Or should that be the other way round?) Better even. There are no laws in RA.

Then I fucked her, slowly, from behind, from the front, bent double like a suit carrier, legs splayed wider than a ballet-dancer's, in the mouth and up the ass . . .

Well, at least I am alive. As long as I can work and feel sensual, things cannot be too bad.

Of course this awakening of the sexual impulse vis à

vis Policewoman suffices to kill any love I might have had for her.

Unfortunately, the technology does not yet exist that would have enabled me to have recorded these events on film. So later on I had to make do with several photo-composites of the work I had done on the computer, and these I put into an envelope to send to Policewoman's home.

Having returned to reality, I read the rest of her file which included extracts of a speech she made to some European Community conference on law enforcement. She took her starting point to be George Orwell's The Decline of the English Murder (don't they all?), and argued the increase of the Hollywood-style murder, meaning the apparently motiveless serial killings of women which seem so fashionable these days. There's something in all of this (although I feel she missed the cultural importance of murder to our society).

I think that I will make a few notes for a paper on this. I could provide her with a few examples. But wouldn't her understanding have to be deeper than any examples I could give? Have I not got more than I could provide in any explanation? After all, can you really explain to another person what you yourself understand? Really she would have to guess what I intend. But still, I suppose it's worth a try.

If I could put it into words, fill in the gaps, add some light and shade, colour things in, she would surely be in the picture. I am not saying that it would make things easier for her. After all, the certainty of mathematics is not based on the reliability of ink and paper. But in the same way that people generally agree in their judgments of colour, perhaps we could arrive at some sort of under-standing.

I had started to tell you about how when I awoke this morning I had Shakespeare on my mind. I don't know much Shakespeare. At least, I can't quote very much. I've meant to do something about this, to brush up my

Shakespeare as it were. Brush up my Shakespeare? Let me tell you, on this particular morning, I had something rather more lethal than that in mind.

I boarded a train to follow him from his home close by Wandsworth Common, to Victoria Station. From there he walked down Victoria Street and, to my surprise, went into the Brain Research Institute. This was as near as I had been to the place since my fateful discovery. It had never occurred to me that anyone would actually take up the offer of counselling from the Lombroso Program's staff of psychotherapists.

I waited for him in the Chestnut Tree Café on the opposite side of the street where I had gone on the day of my own PET scan, and from where I had a clear view of the front door. I ordered a cup of tea and looked at my watch. It was three o'clock.

This was a preliminary surveillance. I didn't plan on actually killing him that afternoon. All the same, I had brought my gun along, in case a suitable opportunity presented itself. After all, this was my day off and it would be several days before I could operate like this again.

While I sipped one cup of tea and then another, I looked at my A-Z, trying to see which routes might best suit me were I to snatch an assassination attempt. A walk through St James's Park, perhaps. Or a stroll across Westminster Bridge. Those would do very well.

It was then that I caught sight of her coming out of the Institute: Policewoman. Taller than I had imagined, but then television does strange things to people. And of course now that she was wearing clothes, she seemed more formidable than the pliant, approximate reality of her I had been fucking earlier. I wondered what she would make of the photo-composites I had sent her and wished that I could have been a fly on the wall when she opened the envelope.

For a moment she stared across the street at the café, almost as if she had been looking straight at me. The door of her police BMW was open but she did not get into the car. Instead, her driver stepped out and they exchanged a few words. Then, to my horror, she started across the street, heading directly towards the café.

My first instinct was to make a run for it, but a second's reflection told me that it was unlikely she had anything but a cup of tea on her mind. So it appeared best to stay where I was, to sit it out, examining my A-Z, and pretend to be a German tourist if I was challenged. But at the same time I kept thinking of the ComputaFit picture that Policewoman had issued to the press and, as I waited for her to come through the café door, it now seemed a better likeness of me than ever before. I was glad I was wearing a hat.

I had sat near the door in order to be ready to follow quickly after Shakespeare, and I kept my eyes down as she passed by me on her way to the counter, so close that she could have touched me, and near enough for me to catch her scent in my nostrils and suck it down into my throat. I was not prepared for that. The smell, I mean. Smell is not something that RA has yet managed to simulate. The fact is that she smelt delicious, like some rare and expensive dessert-wine. I heard myself vacuum the air she walked in down my nasal passages as if she had been made of pure cocaine. It was obscene the way it happened, and for a brief moment I felt quite disgusted at myself. Now I started to feel myself colour at the memory of what I had done to an approximation of her body and hoped that she would not find it remarkable that a complete stranger should look so obviously embarrassed at his proximity to her. For several seconds I felt so conspicuous that I even asked myself if, in resisting arrest, I was prepared to shoot her. But then shooting things, real or approximately real, has become second nature to me and so I had no doubt that if I had to, I would.

I heard her ask the café proprietor for a coffee to take away and twenty Nicofree. The next sound I heard was her dropping her change on the linoleum floor. Instinctively I bent down and grabbed a few of the coins before they rolled out of the door. It was done in a split second, without any thought at all, a Pavlovian response to a commonplace occurrence. Something automatic, unthinking, and very stupid.

'Thank you,' said Policewoman, rising from the floor where she had found the rest of her change, and holding out her hand in front of me.

Our skins made brushing contact as I dropped the coins into her outstretched palm, an approximation of which had earlier cupped my balls as she sucked me.

'Do you need any assistance?' she asked.

'I'm sorry?'

She nodded at the A-Z open on the table in front of me.

I smiled with what I hoped looked like confidence. 'No, it's all right,' I stammered, 'I know where I'm going.'

Then she smiled, nodded once again, and walked out of the café.

When Policewoman was safely back across the street, I took out my handkerchief and mopped my face. For a moment I felt utterly exhausted, but almost immediately, seeing her car drive away, this gave way to a feeling of exhilaration and I found myself laughing out loud. The very next moment Shakespeare came out of the Institute and, still chuckling like a stream, I followed.

He returned to Victoria Station where I almost lost him in the crowd. But instead of boarding a train south back to Wandsworth Common, he took the Underground to Green Park and then walked east, along Piccadilly.

Shakespeare was an uncouth, greasy-looking fellow, tall, and swarthy like a Greek. So I was surprised when he paused in front of a bookshop and went inside. The strangest people seem to read books these days. One hardly expects a fellow like that to be literate. But he had no sooner entered the shop than he had left it again, crossed over onto the south side of Piccadilly and gone into St James's Church. Was he, I wondered, interested in architecture perhaps? This was, after all, one of Sir Christopher Wren's great designs. Or had he spotted his tail and was now cutting through the Jermyn Street exit in an effort to lose me? Leaving what instinct told me wasn't a decent-enough interval between us, I went after him.

Through the heavy glass doors separating the main part of the church from its vestibule I could see him sitting in a pew close to the altar. But for him, the place was empty.

I walked inside and occupied a pew only a few rows behind Shakespeare. His head was bowed and he seemed to be praying. Perfect for my purpose. No place, indeed, should murder sanctuarize. Steeling myself with the thought that Charles Darwin had considered Shakespeare so dull as to make him feel nauseous, I reached inside my coat to get my gun. But before my hand was even on the handle, he was up and out of his pew and walking towards the door and then stopping beside my pew and then grabbing both lapels of my coat and hauling me onto my feet. He was a big man and extricating my hand from inside my coat, I struggled to prise his two meat-porter's hands off me.

'What's your game, mate?' he demanded. 'You've been followin' me all afternoon. Haven't you? Haven't you?' With each repeated question he pushed his unshaven mug closer to mine, until I was close enough to taste the garlic on his breath. 'Ever since I left Wandsworth.' He nutted me gently on the bridge of my nose several times, as if indicating what was in store for me if I didn't answer him to his satisfaction.

'I'm a tourist,' I said weakly, pointing to the A-Z on the church pew as if to confirm my story.

His bristly face turned several shades of red on the way to becoming something darker.

'Shit,' he snarled. 'That's just shit, mate.'

'You've made a mistake,' I protested, still trying to reclaim my coat's lapels.

'No, you're the one who's made a mistake,' he said. 'Wandsworth Town, Victoria, Green Park, and now here. You tryin' to tell me that you lost your fuckin' coach, or something?' He nutted me again, only this time more deliberately. His head may have been deficient in the small matter of a ventro medial nucleus, but it lacked for nothing in solidity. 'Come on, you bastard, or I'll really give you a kiss. Why you followin' me?'

I really don't know what I would have told him. That I found him attractive perhaps? Who knows? But at that moment a couple of people carrying musical instruments came into the church, and my assailant, momentarily embarrassed, it seemed to me, unclamped his greasy paws from my coat. I needed no more articulate invitation to freedom and took to my heels.

'Bastard,' he yelled after me but, to my relief, he did not give chase. Even so, running out into Jermyn Street and down the hill to St James's Square, I did not stop until I reached Pall Mall.

When finally I recovered my breath and then my nerve I found myself laughing once again. That was always what was so interesting about Shakespeare, I said to myself. Right until the very last minute you never knew if it was going to end in comedy or tragedy.

Still keeping an eye out for him, I walked across Trafalgar Square and into the bar on the corner of Charing Cross Road where I ordered a beer and tried to think how best I could salvage something of the day.

While tailing Shakespeare I had been giving some thought to Policewoman and the promise I had made to contact her. Perhaps if I had been concentrating more on following Shakespeare . . . Now seemed to be as good a time as any to buy the equipment I needed to fulfil this undertaking. I already knew exactly what I wanted and where was the best place to get it. So I finished my *beer and, via the nearest twenty-four-hour bank where I picked up some cash, I caught a bus up Tottenham Court Road.*

TCR was much the same as always: dirty and disgusting, with rubbish strewn along the pavements from the piles of fastfood refuse sacks torn apart by the city's many rats. Some of these, bigger than cats, lay dead in the gutters, poisoned with their warfarin takeaways, their bodies flattened by the passing traffic and dried like biltong in the early spring sun. About the only thing that swept TCR was the wind blowing south from the Euston Road to Oxford Street.

Stepping smartly into the shop I was met with the usual sea of brown faces. What is it about Indians and Pakistanis that so attracts them to the retailing of electrical goods? It's the same the world over, from New York to Vienna. The Japs may have manufactured the equipment that now runs the world, but it's the Asians who sell it. Is it that the profit margins are just so good? Or is it that they find something sexy in the obvious consumerism of all those switches, knobs, dials, and flashing lights? Or perhaps it is electricity itself that they so admire: Islam has always had a fascination for power.

'Can I help you?'

'Yes,' I said. 'I'm looking for a portable phone.'

'Standard or video?'

'Neither,' I said, flatly. 'I want a sat-phone.'

The man rippled his sovereign-ringed fingers nervously and then smiled a combination of apology and amusement. 'These are illegal, sir,' he announced. 'We are not allowed to sell them.'

It was my turn to smile. I followed it with a hundred-dollar note.

'Cash,' I said. 'And you can swear you never saw me before.'

He told me to wait and went to fetch the shop manager, a tubby, bumptious little man with thick glasses and as many gold necklaces around his fat, bhaji-coloured neck as his minion had rings.

'The sort of phone you are requiring, sir, is not permitted,' he said, still holding my C-note. 'Please, what would happen to me if you were some fellow from the Home Office who was to catch me selling such a thing? I would be in court pretty damn quick and no mistake.' He glanced around the shop, which was empty of any other customers, and moved closer to me.

'What the hell are you wanting this kind of phone for anyway?' he asked in lower tones. 'If it's the avoidance of a telephone bill you are requiring then I can sell you a black box dialer. You can use this anywhere and pay nothing for your call whether it is Bombay you are telephoning or merely Birmingham. And much cheaper than a satellite phone too.'

'I'm going abroad,' I said. 'South America. Up the jungle, or what's left of it. I want to be able to phone home.'

The Indian shook his head ruefully. 'If this was me the last thing I should want to take would be a phone. What an opportunity you are having, to get away from the wife for a few weeks.' He laughed.

'Look,' I said calmly. 'I'm not Home Office. You can search me if you like. There's no need to worry. I'll give you a fair price, in cash.' I retrieved my C-note from his podgy fingers. 'Otherwise I can try somewhere else.' I shrugged and started towards the open door.

'Patience, sir,' he said. 'It is a virtue. I have just the equipment that you require. Only I must be careful. Come this way.'

He led me into the back of the shop which was stacked high with boxes of Nicam stereo televisions, discrecorders, portable karaoke players, and Reality Approximation equipment. Shifting several boxes out of the way, he said, 'We don't keep sat-phones in the front of the shop, for obvious reasons. You want a digital unit?'

I said that I thought I did.

He nodded and pulled out another box. 'Digital is best. I show you a good one. Only four thousand dollars.' He ripped open the box and tugged away at the ozone-friendly polystyrene packaging to reveal what looked like a small attaché case. For a moment he caressed it with his hand, before springing open the locks and folding the case open.

'Just like James Bond, eh?' He giggled, folding up a satellite dish that was about the size of a dinner plate. 'It works off the Injupitersat. One dedicated channel with a band-width that's five times the size of a normal portable phone. That gives you an extra-high-quality line. Focusing on the satellite is done automatically with the computer's own built-in compass, so you don't have to fuck about with books of astronomical tables or any shit like that. All you have to do is key the satellite's number, which you see on the handset, and then the normal international code plus whatever number it is that you want to call. Its one and only limitation is that you can't use it below ground level. In a house is fine, but don't expect to get through if you're sitting in some kind of basement.'

'I'll take it,' I said, and counted out forty-odd bills.

'You won't regret it,' he said. 'The CIA use this model, so it must be good.'

I looked at the country of origin. It had been made in Japan.

'Well that figures,' I said.

He folded the dish away, closed the case and held it out to me.

'Real pigskin too,' he said, stroking the case with his hand again. 'And it weighs less than two kilos. Anything else you would like?'

I handed him another couple of bills.

'Just your silence.'

11

Jake had not slept very well. Her T-shirt was wet with perspiration and her neck ached as if she had been standing on her head. She used the bathroom and then did a few gentle yoga exercises to try and move some blood up to her cortex. Ten minutes later, feeling slightly better, she put on her dressing gown and took the lift down to the ground floor where she collected the morning's post from her mailbox and carried it back upstairs to the top flat. She examined it without much interest: a couple of utility bills; and several pieces of junk mail trying to interest her in everything from a special mortgage so that she could live in Docklands, to sponsoring a Russian child. But as well as these other items, there was also a Jiffy bag which looked as though it might be interesting.

Back inside her flat Jake placed the parcel under the spectroscope on the hall table and while she waited for the electronic signal to tell her that it contained no explosives she searched the kitchen for something that might constitute breakfast. Finally she found just enough coffee to make a small espresso and a few bran biscuits on which she spread the remains of a jar of chocolate spread.

Back in the hall, the spectroscope sounded like a small air-conditioning system. It had been a routine piece of equipment for all senior police personnel since the early years of the new century, when the IRA had conducted a letter bomb campaign aimed at mainland police and their families. Mostly it had been a case of fingers and hands being blown off, but on one notorious occasion two children had been killed. Their deaths had been one of the factors which had persuaded the Government to introduce punitive coma.

When the all-clear signal sounded, Jake wiped her fingers clean of chocolate spread, tore the padded envelope open and then withdrew the contents. It was several seconds before she realised that the gynaecology spread for the benefit of the camera was putatively her own; and several more seconds before she stopped trying to account for how someone had been able to take such pictures without her knowledge and guessed that they were photo-composites. Instinctively she laid the pictures down and put on a pair of cellophane gloves before re-handling what might turn out to be forensic evidence.

Not that she would have cared for them ever to have been produced in court or held in some police file. Fakes or not, there was no escaping the fact that they were good fakes, of the kind that were appearing increasingly often in the tabloid newspapers.

Probably produced by a computer, she thought. The sort of thing that would entertain many of her male colleagues. The type of evidence some pervert might think to make copies of, for the general locker-room titillation of the lads at the Yard. Jake knew that there were many of her male colleagues who were jealous of her success and who might welcome the sight of photographs which would certainly embarrass her. Fakes or not, pictures which showed a chief inspector pushing a vibrator up her own vagina, and licking another woman's genitals, were nothing less than explosive.

She was surprised to discover that it was Wittgenstein who had sent them. She was sure it was he because there was a compliments slip on which he had typed 'yours bloodily'. He would surely have known that Jake's duty as a police officer would require her to have the photographs tested in the laboratory; and, as a corollary, that this would cause her acute embarrassment. Jake swore fluently for several seconds and for one brief moment she felt hatred for him. Somehow she had supposed he would be different. A fly buzzed on the window pane, and

hardly bothering to even look, Jake killed it without a
moment's hesitation.

Jake had the morning off, her first in several weeks.
She bought some groceries, failed to get into her local
hairdresser, and went to see Doctor Blackwell at her
clinic in Chelsea.

Her eyes closed, naked, standing to attention before
the doctor, Jake found her thoughts returning to the
photographs now in her shoulder bag. Her original irritation had given way to a curiosity that Wittgenstein
should have been sexually interested in her. This was
something unique in her experience as a detective. The
subject might almost have been worthy of a paper. She
wondered what she would have done if instead of Doctor
Blackwell, her therapeutic nude encounter had been with
Wittgenstein. She felt herself blush as she lay down on
the couch and waited for the Doctor to begin the session.

'Sleeping all right?'

'Not particularly . . .'

'Nightmares?'

'No.'

'Sleeping with anyone?'

'Not that I can remember.'

'Hostility to men?'

Jake swallowed. 'There was a tramp on Westminster
Bridge. He asked me for money, but I thought he was
going to try and rob me. I almost hoped he would, so
that I could have shot him.'

'You were carrying a gun?'

'I always carry a gun.'

'Have you ever used it?'

'Yes, but only in self-defence.'

'Ever killed anyone?'

'No.'

Doctor Blackwell's tone stiffened a little. 'You know,'

she said carefully, 'perhaps you should have shot this tramp you met.'

Jake sat up on one elbow. 'You're joking,' she said.

'Am I? This is Neo-Existential therapy, Jake, not something behavioural. We approach psychotherapy from the point of view that the major emotional sickness of our times is the inability to endow life with meaning. Don't you think it's just possible you might have worked something out of yourself if you had murdered him?'

Jake was shocked. 'But that's just it,' she said. 'It would have been murder.'

'You've said before that you'd like to have killed your own father, for the way he messed up your childhood.'

'But that was different.'

'Was it?'

'Yes.'

'If you had shot this tramp, perhaps in a way you could have killed your father. Exorcised his memory. Some worthless old man. What would it have mattered to anyone? And you a policewoman: who'd have questioned it?'

Jake frowned, angry now. 'No,' she said firmly. 'I don't believe that.'

Doctor Blackwell smiled. 'No,' she said. 'Nor do I. I just wanted to hear you say it.'

In the lab at the Yard, Jake handed over a plastic bag containing the photographs.

'Run some tests on these, would you?' she said to the technician, whose name was Maurice. 'Fingerprints, fibres, hairs, and anything else you can think of.'

Maurice nodded coolly and then slipped on some gloves. 'By the way,' he said, 'that disc you brought down? It was clean.'

Jake nodded uncomfortably.

'Now what we got here?' Maurice opened the bag and

took out the photographs. 'Be a couple of hours at least,' he said.

'All right,' said Jake, sitting down. 'But I'm staying here.'

Maurice frowned and was about to argue until he caught sight of the first picture.

'Those photographs aren't leaving my sight,' she said determinedly. 'Not for one second.'

Maurice shuffled through the rest of them and then grinned.

'Anyone ever tell you? You sure one photogenic lady.'

'Oh come on, Maurice,' said Jake. 'Those are fakes, photo-composites.'

'If you say so.' He nodded appreciatively. 'Nice though. Real nice.'

Jake resisted the temptation to punch him on his black jaw.

'There are ten of them,' she said. 'I want ten back. Have you got that?'

Maurice shrugged. 'If you say so.'

'Maurice, I'm saying so in capital letters as big as your stupid male libido. Right?'

'Right.' But the grin persisted.

Two hours later Maurice counted the pictures back into Jake's hand. 'Ten,' he said.

She dropped them quickly into her shoulder bag and quickly zipped it up. 'Find anything?'

Maurice stretched and rolled his head on his broad shoulders. 'I found it all really interesting,' he said, and then laughed as Jake thumped him on the chest. 'All right, all right, take it easy. No prints. Not a one. But I got an eyelash. Not yours. Not your natural colour. And some traces of semen.'

Jake's nose wrinkled with disgust. Men were like animals.

'Looks like your admirer got hisself all excited at his own handiwork. Well that's no surprise to me. I was beginning to get a little warm under the collar myself.

Anyway I've subjected his stuff to gel electrophoresis, and you're lucky – what we got was highly polymorphic.'

'You've got a DNA type?'

'Not quite. You're going to have to wait until I confirm it with the autoradiograph. But looks like, yes.'

'When you've got that we'll be able to match him with anyone we arrest, right?'

'Oh, for sure. Only there's not enough sample should any ambiguities arise on an appeal, or anything like that. I want you to understand that now. I've used all the semen there was to get the autoradiograph.'

'Thanks, Maurice. Thanks a lot. I won't forget this.'

He grinned again. 'Hell, I sure won't.'

Several hours later, Jake asked the three senior members of her investigating team to attend a meeting in her office. Sergeant Chung was the last to arrive and seated himself at a short way's distance from Detective Inspector Stanley and Detective Sergeant Jones. Jake sat on the edge of her desk. In her hand was a thin file supplied by the lab and containing the sheet of X-ray film used to produce Wittgenstein's autoradiograph.

'Gentlemen,' said Jake. 'I've called this meeting to inform you all of an important development.' She brandished the file in front of them. 'A DNA type.

'This morning I received some photographs. At least what purported to be photographs, of me, but were in fact photocomposites. Mr Wittgenstein had married the photographs of me which recently appeared in one of the weekend colour supplements with some pornographic pictures.'

'Do you think he was trying to blackmail you, ma'am?' asked Jones.

'No. I think he just meant to embarrass me. Well, he was only partly successful. The pictures are now in my safe and that's where they're going to stay for the time being. However, the lab has run some tests on them and found traces of semen. They ran a number of probes to see if they could determine some allele frequencies and found our killer's genotype. Gentlemen, the man we're looking for is most probably German, or of German parents.'

'Like the real Wittgenstein then,' said Jones.

'Actually, he was Austrian,' said Jake. 'But for the purposes of the genotype, they're more or less the same.'

Detective Inspector Stanley cleared his throat. 'Excuse me, ma'am,' he said. 'But aren't we forgetting something? The European Court has ruled that genetic population tests are inadmissible as evidence on the ground of their obvious racism.'

'We're hardly at the stage of preparing a case for the courts,' Jake said crisply. 'Right now we're trying to catch this bastard, not worry about his human fucking rights, Stanley. And if the database on allele frequencies within population structures speeds up the computer's matching the killer's DNA type to his identity card, then so be it. We'll bridge questions of what is and what is not inadmissible as evidence once we've got this maniac in a cage, right?'

Stanley shrugged back at her, and then nodded.

'Sergeant Chung,' said Jake. 'What is the current average time for matching?'

'How long is a piece of string? Well, as a rough rule of thumb, it takes the computer twenty-four hours to make a million comparisons. If you were to assume that the killer was in the last million of population, then seventy million comparisons, seventy days.' He shrugged. 'On the other hand, you could get lucky. He could turn up in the first million. There's no other way to do it. Not yet anyway.'

'Assuming he's got a genuine identity card,' said Jones. 'He might be one of those Russo-German refugees who came here illegally after the Russian Civil War.'

'Yes, he might,' said Jake. 'But let's try and be a little optimistic, eh?

'Sergeant Chung, how's that random accessing program with the Lombroso computer coming along?'

'Not bad. So far I've been able to get Lombroso to release about twenty names and addresses.'

'How many answers to the advertisement?'

'Ten,' said Stanley. 'One of them an imposter.'

'Any of those with philosophers' codenames?'

'No,' said Stanley, 'but we've got them all under surveillance anyway.'

'That still leaves fifty. How many of them are philosophers?'

Stanley opened his file and glanced down the list. 'Sixteen, ma'am.'

'Any luck with the gunsmiths?'

'Not a thing,' said Stanley. 'With his own gas cylinder he can make as much of his own ammunition as he wants. I think it's unlikely that we'll get any leads from that direction.'

'What about that student at Cambridge? Mr Heissmeyer – '

Stanley shook his head. 'The locals have got someone keeping an eye on him. But so far all he's done is spend his time on the river. And for what it's worth, ma'am, Mr Heissmeyer is an American, not an Austrian. Rowing scholarship, or something. Should get his blue this year.'

Jake shrugged and then turned to Jones. 'Jameson Lang's pictophone: is that installed yet?'

'Yes, ma'am. I spoke to the professor on it earlier today.'

'Call tracing. Where are we on that one? I want to be ready for this bastard when he phones.'

'I've organised a digital trace for any normal telecommunications traffic, and a keyword satellite monitor of the whole country. If our man uses the words "Lombroso" or "Wittgenstein" on a phone, the satellite should be able to tell us where the signal is coming from.'

'Discrecording facilities?'

'Automatic on all your lines, ma'am,' said Jones. 'Here,

at home, and on your portable.' He grinned. 'Best make sure you don't say anything rude about the Commissioner, eh? We wouldn't want you to get suspended like Mr Challis.'

Jake smiled at Jones, and wondered if he really meant what he had said.

Real meaning. There was never any doubt of what that amounted to with Mrs Grace Miles. She called towards the end of the day when Jake had started to think about going home. Jake noticed from the picture that the Minister herself was already at home. In the corner of the room she could see a baby crawling round Mrs Miles's red dispatch box.

'Gilmour tells me that you've got a genetic fingerprint. Is that right?'

'Yes. We're trying to find a match with an ID card.'

'Good. Someone's tabled a question about these killings in the House tomorrow. I want to be able to say that we expect to be making an arrest very shortly.'

'Shortly could be as long as seventy days, Minister,' said Jake. 'It might take the computer all of that to make the comparisons.'

Jake watched the Minister frown and then tug nervously at the string of pearls she wore round her neck. Jake wondered if they were real. She was dressed to go out. The sequin-covered dress was cut low to reveal what appeared to be a child's bare backside but was in fact the Minister's chest. She wore her long black hair pinned back from her but loose about her shoulders so that she looked like some kind of ancient Persian princess.

'Better to say something like "The police investigation is coming to a conclusion and they are confident of making an arrest before very long",' suggested Jake. 'Then if we make an arrest within the next few days it will seem as you knew more but weren't saying. That you were being tactically vague as opposed to being misleading. But to say that we will shortly be making an arrest seems rather wide of the mark, ma'am.'

Mrs Miles's slow nod accelerated as she saw the wisdom of Jake's advice. Even so she wasn't inclined to be grateful for it. Instead her face took on an irritated aspect.

'Yes, I expect you're right,' she said, and then added: 'Oh and by the way, what do you mean by making this loony an offer of medical help at your press conference? I'm afraid I was away in Brussels at the time, and I've only just read the transcript of what you said. I certainly don't recall anyone clearing that little idea with the Attorney General.'

'I wanted him to make contact with us,' said Jake. 'Maybe even to give himself up. There's not much percentage in that if all he has coming to him is a hypodermic needle and a long term of punitive coma. In my judgment – '

'In your judgment – ' Her tone was contemptuous. 'Need I remind you, Chief Inspector, that your job is to catch this maniac, not to determine whether or not he is to be regarded as fit to plead. Moreover, the theory of justice pursued by this Government, and for which we received an overwhelming mandate at the last election, is retributive. It is not reformative. No more does justice permit that individual offenders shall escape the full rigour of the law merely because of some alleged insanity. The public simply won't stand for it. They must be satisfied that a criminal has been punished. I would hope that when this man is caught he will be sentenced to an irreversible period of coma. At the very least he should undergo a minimum vegetative state of thirty years. But having said all that, my own feeling is that it would be better for everyone if he were not to be taken alive. I just hope that he's armed when you catch up with him, in which case you'll have little choice but to shoot him dead.'

Jake started to disagree but found herself, once again, cut short.

'That is standard practice, Chief Inspector: to shoot and kill all armed criminals. Or don't you read your own police policy documents?'

'Yes and I've written some of them too,' said Jake. 'All the same, we owe it to criminology to bring this man into custody. There's a great deal to be learnt from a subject like this in terms of forensic profiling.'

'Oh yes,' said Mrs Miles. 'That's your speciality, isn't it? Well Chief Inspector, the only thing the voters are interested in learning about this maniac is that he cries for his mother when they come to stick the needle in him. I hope I've made myself clear to you. Goodnight.'

The screen flashed and then went blank. After a couple of seconds, the machine asked Jake if she wished to save the automatic recording that had been made of her conversation with the Minister. Jake stabbed the 'yes' button angrily, sensing that it might be useful to keep a record of all her future conversations with a woman like Mrs Miles.

Jake swung around in her chair and stared at the blackened window in which her reflection was floating.

That was probably what it was like to be in a punitive coma, she decided. To be there and yet not there at all. A half-existence between life and death. Awful. She knew very well that Mrs Miles had not exaggerated about criminals facing an icy hypodermic full of limbo crying for their mothers. She herself had been obliged to attend the induction of several punitive coma states. As punishments went it was worse than a long term of imprisonment and almost worse than death itself. But this was what happened when society had become morally squeamish about capital punishment and when prisons had become too overcrowded and expensive to be practical for any but minor offenders.

Jake knew all the arguments in favour of PC. Coma was cheap compared with the cost of keeping a man in prison for ten or fifteen years. The advent of so-called intelligent beds, self-controlled pods operating, by means of individual computers, inexpensive heart/lung machines and intravenous feeding devices, as developed for the health-care sector, but hi-jacked by the prison system, meant that a convict could be kept in a year's coma for less than a tenth of the cost of an equivalent prison term. Coma removed the opportunities for engaging in further criminality that had been afforded by prison. Overnight, it destroyed criminal society and made expensive prison riots a thing of the past. And depending on the choice of chemical substance, coma was reversible with few deleterious physical or mental effects. There was even evidence from the United States, which had been the first country to introduce PC, that it was helping to deter violent, drug-related crime.

The arguments against PC were harder to maintain. To the objection that depriving a man of his consciousness was analogous to depriving him of life, the proponents of PC asserted that coma was more analogous to sleep, and that to be sentenced to a long period of sleep was, if anything, kinder than depriving a conscious man of an equivalent period of liberty, with all its attendant discomforts and indignities.

To the objection, heard in the United States Supreme Court and the European Court of Human Rights, that PC was a cruel and unusual punishment, it had been successfully argued that since the whole future of manned space-travel was dependent on deep-sleeping astronauts who had volunteered for their five-year missions to Mars and Venus, PC could not therefore be regarded as cruel.

The argument that in a subjective respect death concerns only consciousness did not survive the evidence of those convicts who had been returned from coma and reported their comatose dreams, which was itself confirmed by observations of electrical neuron activity in the brains of nearly all comatose convicts.

But a cold shiver ran down Jake's spine as she stared

into the void and tried to imagine it. She knew that she was ambiguous in her own attitude to PC. There were obvious advantages from the point of view of society in general. But from the viewpoint of the individual she could think of life as being of value only as a necessary condition of consciousness.

What had Wittgenstein said about it?

Jake retrieved her increasingly dog-eared copy of the *Tractatus* from her desk drawer, turned to the last few pages and read.

'Death is not an event in life: we do not live to experience death.'

That seemed logical enough. And this propositional form could easily be adapted to show that being unconscious was without question an event in life, and that it was perfectly feasible, with so much of the average human life being spent asleep, that people did live to experience the unconscious state as well. Hadn't Freud proved that consciousness was not a necessary condition of an interesting life?

Where then was meaning? Where in that impersonal black sky of frightful grandeur that was the universe was significance?

As Jake stared at her reflection, the depth of what lay beyond helped to bring herself into focus. A sense of other realities, of the trivialities of everyday life, of something different from the routine, all of these sensations gradually made themselves felt within her. To see yourself you had to look where you were not. To find meaning you had to have the will to turn away from yourself.

Was that why men like the one calling himself Wittgenstein killed? For a momentary flash of identity? For a few seconds of significance? To escape from a lifetime's lack of meaning?

Earlier that same day, Jake had felt a brief hatred for him. But now she found she could feel real pity.

I suppose you would like me to say something to the effect that I killed my victims when I heard the voices and that I believe that the voices came from God.

Naturally I've read of how other killers (although I hardly like to put myself in the same class as them) have tried this one on, and managed to have themselves adjudged insane, thereby escaping the needle. And I dare say you've been expecting me to claim something along these lines.

But the fact of the matter is this: we have you and I drunk up the sea. We have taken a sponge and wiped away the horizon. We have unchained the earth from the sun. And we are moving away now – away from all suns. We are perpetually falling backward, sideward, forward, in all directions. There is no up or down left. We are straying as through an infinite nothing. Do we not feel the breath of empty space? Has it not become colder? Is not the night coming inexorably upon us? Must not lanterns be lit in the morning? Do we not hear anything yet of the noise of the grave diggers who are burying God? Do we not smell anything yet of God's decomposition?

All right, I'll admit it. This is hardly an original thought. Not these days anyway. I can't claim this as my own. But you take my point. I mean, the contention that I killed when I heard the voices and that the voices came from God just won't do. I mean, it's hardly the claim of a sophisticated killer, now is it? It is too melodramatic, too theatrical for words. I mean, where's the imagination there, for God's sake?

Now if you were to suggest something along the lines of how I killed when I heard the voice and that I believed

*the voice was that of Friedrich Nietzsche, then at least
we'd be heading in the right direction. It sounds a bit
more original. And what's more, it's considerably nearer
to being true. Because each time I kill one of my brothers,
I am, of course, killing God.*

*But just a minute, I hear you say: if someone kills God
and God does not exist, then surely he's killing nothing
at all. It makes no sense to say 'I am killing something'
when the something does not exist. I can imagine a god
that is not there, in this forest, but not kill one that is
not there. And 'to imagine a god in this forest' means to
imagine a god is there. But to kill a god does not mean
that . . . But if someone says 'in order for me to be able
to imagine God he must after all exist in some sense',
the answer is: no, he does not have to exist in any sense.
Except one.*

*Where God does exist is in the mind of man. Ergo,
one kills a man, one kills God.*

*I know these things as thoughts. But my thoughts are
not my experiences. They are an echo and after-effect of
my experiences: as, when a train goes past my window,
my room trembles. I am sitting in the train, however,
and sometimes, I am the train itself. Intellect and passion,
thinking and feeling – really, they're all the same thing.*

*How fast has brother followed brother, from sunshine
to the sunless land.*

*On my next day off I drove round to the home of the
next brother on my list. I'm beginning to sound like
Adrian Messenger, I know. I don't mean this to sound
vengeful or vindictive as in some Jacobean tragedian's
play. No, it felt right, what I was doing, cold and pure
like crystal, but true. A sense of logical purpose had
infected my mind, which is where it started for all of us.
All in the mind. The mind of man – my haunt and the
main region of my song.*

After the farce with Shakespeare I decided to leave

the dramatists alone and, still trying to disobey my first inclination, which was to kill a philosopher, I chose a poet. Wordsworth – stupendous genius! Damned fool.

My preliminary surveillance had only just begun when I realised that I was not the only one watching over him. Parked outside Wordsworth's house (I thought I'd break the pattern again) was a scruffy grey van. For a while I paid it no attention as there was nobody in the driving seat. Imagine my surprise when the rear doors opened and two men got out to stretch their legs and smoke a cigarette. They didn't look much like policemen but then, these days, who does? And given that one of them was carrying a pair of binoculars I didn't suppose they could be from the Gas Board. The other one clinched it when I saw him unzip his anorak to reveal the flak jacket and machine pistol he was wearing underneath.

But what I failed to understand was how they neglected to observe me. Did they imagine that I wouldn't reconnoitre my target before going to work? Can they seriously have believed that I was just going to turn up on Wordsworth's doorstep and shoot him? Maybe they didn't much care whether Wordsworth was shot or not.

Perhaps, if I'd been there longer, they might have taken me into consideration as a possible suspect. As it was, I simply started up my van and drove slowly away, very much aware of how lucky I'd been. And of how I had underestimated the police. I would have to be more careful in future, I told myself. Especially since I was planning to use my satellite phone to contact Policewoman in the minutes leading up to my next brother's execution. It would hardly have looked professional to have been arrested in the middle of a philosophical dialogue.

I kept a careful eye on the rear-view video as I drove away, just in case I was followed. But the screen remained empty of traffic and even before I had reached the end of Wordsworth's road, I was scrolling down the list of brothers on my hand-held computer for the next target.

Fine, I thought, I always did like Wordsworth and was quite glad not to be his solitary reaper. Stop here or gently pass.

These many then shall die. Their names are pricked. But which one was to be next? Auden? Descartes? Hegel? Hemingway? Whitman?

Auden was certainly the closest, although I had a mind (in the sense of reality as a whole, or the Absolute) to kill Hegel out of pure idealism. Hemingway? Obsessed with death, and somehow too vulgar. Descartes? I had been saving him. All the same there was all the nonsense about deducing the existence of God as proof of the perceptible world. And in a way, he did start all of this. Yes, Descartes then. The father of modern philosophy. I would destroy him out of total scepticism. He shall not live. Look, with a spot I damn him.

I kill, therefore I am.

12

Jake sat alone in her office, her long, strong fingers steepled in front of her forehead as if she had been deep in prayer, or thought, or both.

Ed Crawshaw put his head round the door, cleared his throat, and, having gained Jake's attention raised both eyebrows by way of preface to a question.

'Yes, Ed.' She yawned. 'What is it?'

She rubbed her eyes which she assumed were sore from a lack of natural light and switched off her desk lamp. Was it the fluorine or the halogen bulbs that were supposed to cause blindness? Perhaps her life wouldn't seem quite so artificial if she had some flowers in the office.

'Got a minute, Chief?'

'Sure, take a chair.'

Crawshaw sat down.

'Remember the Italian olive oil we found on Mary Woolnoth's clothes?'

Jake said she did.

'Well it comes by the drum-load from Italy, to be bottled under licence here in the UK. Company called the Sacred Oil Company, based in Ruislip. Their bottled oil is then distributed all over the country by a company called Gillards. They're in Brent Cross. Gillards deliver the oil to a number of wholesalers in central London, including one in Brewer Street, Soho. The Soho delivery is always handled by the same driver, one John George Richards. Well it so happens that about eight years ago this Richards did two years under the needle for a sexual assault on a young woman. What's more, on the date of Mary Woolnoth's murder, he made a delivery to the wholesalers in Brewer Street.'

'That's interesting,' said Jake. 'I assume you want my autograph on an application to a magistrate for a search warrant.'

'That's right, ma'am,' said Crawshaw. 'If you wouldn't mind.' He handed Jake a paper. She read his document and then signed it quickly.

'Thanks, ma'am.' He stood up to leave.

'Oh, and, Ed? Let me know when you pick him up. I'd like an opportunity to talk to this guy myself.'

'Yes, ma'am.'

'Ed?'

'Ma'am?'

'Well done.'

Crawshaw had not been gone for very long when the switchboard rang to say that they had Wittgenstein on the line. Jake immediately hit the button on the pictophone link that had been patched into Sir Jameson Lang's rooms in Cambridge.

'It's him, Professor,' she announced to Lang's startled image. 'Wittgenstein. Are you ready?'

'Yes, I think so,' said Lang, and straightened his tie.

A message on Jake's computer screen told her that the call-trace procedure was already initiated. She told the switchboard to put Wittgenstein through.

'Chief Inspector?' he said smoothly.

'Yes. I'm glad you called.' She wished that they had been speaking on the pictophone and that she could see his face.

'Oh, I don't doubt it. Would you like me to give you a sound-level for your recording? Testing, testing, one-two-three. How's that?' He chuckled. 'You know, I really hope you are recording this. It could be historic. We've come a long way from messages chalked on walls near the scene of the crime. "The Jews are not the men that will be blamed for nothing".'

'Jack the Ripper,' said Jake, recognising the quotation.

'The message near the first victim. Now who was it? Catherine Eddowes?'

'Very good,' said the voice. 'I'm impressed, Chief Inspector. If it didn't sound so corny I should say you were a worthy opponent.' He paused. 'May I call you Jake? I feel I already know you quite well.'

'Be my guest. What do you want to talk about?'

'Oh no. This is your chat show, Jake. I'm here at your invitation. You're supposed to put me at my ease. Make me feel comfortable enough to reveal something interesting about myself: isn't that how it works? But I will say two things right away, Jake. One is to save you the trouble of trying to trace this call: I'm using a satellite phone. Ah, the wonders of modern science.

'And the other is that at some time during our little chat, I'll have to break off and kill someone. Who this is going to be will be a surprise, of course. I'm saving that until the end, when I will give you his codename. Don't let that worry you though. Just try and look at it from the point of view of my having to plug a new book or a record. We've got plenty of time until then. If my man sticks to his routine we should have at least twenty minutes.'

The voice sounded lighter and more flippant than on the disc. But Jake knew that Detective Sergeant Jones would already have wired the call through to the Yard's own forensic psychiatrist for a more accurate psychological evaluation. Even now there would be an acoustic engineer trying to isolate and identify any background noise. Jake lit a cigarette. To hell with the regulations, she thought. This was an emergency.

'I was hoping I could persuade you to give this up,' she said. 'Not to kill anyone else. There's been enough killing already.' She took a deep, fierce drag. 'Maybe even to give yourself up. You know, I'd like to help you if I can.'

'Did you like the photographs I sent you, Jake?' he said.

She realised that he was trying to provoke her, to see how far her willingness to help really went.

'They were very good,' she said evenly.

'You think so?' He made a little tutting, dissatisfied noise. 'I wasn't sure I got the lips of your vagina right. And your pubic hair. I couldn't work out if you were the bushy type or not. Whether the hair grows right along the edge of your labia or only as far the pubis. Well? How did I do?'

Jake felt herself colour. 'Come on,' she said. 'You know this call is being taped. Do you want to embarrass me in front of all my colleagues? Let's talk about something else.'

'What about your anus? Or maybe your nipples.'

'You know I think this is just an act,' she said. 'I don't think you're this kind of person at all. Listen, I've met some real sex perverts in my time, and you don't begin to come close. I think you're trying to impress me as being something you're not.'

Wittgenstein guffawed. 'All right,' he said.

Well that was interesting, she thought. You could contradict him without provoking him. It demonstrated that on one level at least she was speaking to a rational person anyway.

'Would it interest you then to know that I've been close enough to you to smell you Jake? What is that perfume you wear? Rapture, by Luther Levine.'

Jake gave a start. How could he know that?

'Some might find it rather cloying, but I like it. Fact is, there was something about it that gave me a hard-on. But then I'm much more influenced by smell than other people.'

'How did you know that: about my perfume? Have you been following me?'

'No,' he said. 'But we have met. Now then, what were we talking about? Ah yes, you were giving me some crap about wanting to help me.'

Jake struggled to keep her mind on the conversation.

But she was still badly rattled by his claim to have met her. When?

'Oh, but I do,' she said.

'Don't fool yourself, Jake.'

'Then at least let me try to persuade you not to murder another man. What would be the point of that?'

'Oh, but there is a point, Jake. While we may agree about the facts, that I am killing men, and that there exists a set of criteria for deciding upon the legality of my actions, regarding the validity of what I am doing, the criteria are less generally agreed. If we were to have a discussion about what I am doing or have done, first it would have to be concerned with how to describe that. It might necessitate an examination of the concept of right and wrong and morality in general. We could talk about whether my action can be demonstrated to be sufficiently against the interests of the community as to merit punishment; or whether it can be argued that these are in fact justifiable homicides.'

'But this is merely verbal – '

'You disappoint me, Jake,' he said. 'That might be a reasonable objection if no further consequences resulted from calling what I do illegal or legal, justifiable or unjustifiable. But of course it does matter when to say "illegal homicide" also means "to undergo punitive coma".'

'What you have done is quite clearly illegal. Murder is wrong by the standards of any decent society.'

'One would first require guidance as to how the words "murder" and "decent" are to be used. For instance, I can demonstrate very easily how any murderer should not be punished. Let us accept that the definition of a murderer is someone who has killed someone else, having intended to kill them, and in the full knowledge that neither society, nor indeed the victim, wished it. Thus, if Brown murders Green and serves a period of punitive coma, or imprisonment, after which he is returned to

225

normal society, he still remains a murderer. So you see it is not always true that a murderer should be punished.'

Jake looked at the pictophone screen and nodded at Jameson Lang. 'I'd like to introduce you to someone,' said Jake into the mouthpiece of the telephone. 'This is Sir Jameson Lang, Professor of Philosophy at Cambridge University. I hope you don't mind, but I've asked him to join in our discussion.'

'Frankly, Jake,' Wittgenstein said coolly, 'I'm a little surprised that you should cheat like this. Bringing a prompt – really it's a bit thick. But naturally I'm also flattered to be talking to the professor. I know his work well. The novels that is.' He sniggered. 'I can't think of any philosophical work he's ever done.'

'Hello,' said the professor, hesitantly. 'The example you were describing just now relies on improper philosophical grammar. Specifically your use of the word "should" punish. However, quite apart from the semantic issue here, the chief inspector is quite right: there is a universal standard which applies to the character of one's acts.'

'My turn to get semantic, Professor. It depends on what you mean by the word "universal". Speaking of the character of my acts, you mean only the character which they will seem to have from an ordinary point of view, under the ordinary conditions of inquiry, such as asking the ubiquitous man on the Clapham omnibus. Assuming there was still such a thing as the Clapham omnibus.

'But you see, Professor, I might have decided not to adopt his standard. I might have decided to adopt the standard of a South American headhunter, or an existential hero from a novel by Camus, or an anarchist maybe, perhaps even a right-wing vigilante, an extreme feminist, or a modern-day Maldoror. Could be I've decided to adopt all their standards put together. You see, their judgments as to the character of my acts have just as much right to be considered valid as some hollow, stuffed men from the dead, cactus land of Clapham. So you would have to deny that in themselves my acts have only one character, otherwise you would be guilty of bias.'

'But that is what society is all about,' said Lang. 'A bias towards a commonly held standard of what is right and wrong.'

'That does not give us the truth about my acts. Only the appearance of truth. For thousands of years, when a man took another man's property it was called theft. But for almost a century, in certain parts of the world this sort of thing was legitimised by the name of Marxism. Tomorrow's political philosophy might sanction murder, just as Marxism once sanctioned theft. You talk about the standard of a decent society, Professor Lang. But what kind of society is it that regards a President of the United States who orders the use of nuclear weapons to kill thousands of people as a great man, and another man who assassinates a single President as a criminal?'

'If you're referring to President Harry Truman,' said Lang, 'he acted to end the war. To save lives. Using the bomb was the only way to stop an even greater loss of life.'

'What I am doing is born of the same motive: to prevent an even greater loss of life.'

'But it's not your position to make such a choice. It sets a bad example in society.'

'You sound like a moral conservative, Professor.'

'Perhaps so. But naturally you must accept that in the eyes of the society you seem to say you reject, you must be caught and punished.'

'Must?' He laughed. 'No, I accept only the possibility.'

'You claim you're acting to save human life. Therefore you must surely accept that reverence for human life is the foundation of morality.'

'No, only worthwhile human life.'

'And what is the criterion of that?'

'In most cases, the subjective feeling that life continues to be worthwhile.'

'Well don't you think that the men you killed had the feeling that their lives continued to be worthwhile?'

'Very probably, they did.' His voice darkened a little as he added: 'But of course, they could have been wrong. Suppose Einstein had received some bad news about his wife and had lost the will to live. Would one not feel a certain obligation to remind him of how worthwhile a life his was? Would his own view of the worth of his own existence be the ultimate standard?'

'Yes, you're right there,' admitted Lang. 'One would feel such an obligation as you describe.'

'Then surely you must admit the possibility that there are some who might overestimate the worth of their own existences?'

'Logically I have to, I suppose. But I don't see how such a thing could easily be demonstrated.'

'Suppose that such a person was putting the lives of others at risk by clinging tenaciously to his own. Couldn't it be demonstrated then?'

'It might be.'

'Would you not feel justified in eliminating such a person?'

'It would depend on the circumstances,' said Lang. 'On how clearly evident was the risk to other people. I see what you're driving at, but I don't accept that yours is as clear cut a case as the one you're describing.'

'What criteria do you think would be acceptable in arriving at such a decision?'

'I suppose it would be an objective standard. An estimation of what the reasonable man would do in similar circumstances.'

'A subjective estimation of an objective standard?' Wittgenstein uttered a little chuckle. 'That sounds interesting. Don't you think that I might have tried to consider the case of my brother VMN-negatives objectively? And that I arrived at the conclusion that the risk to other people is demonstrable?'

'I quarrel with that demonstrability.'

'But, Professor, it was already demonstrable when I killed my first victim. From that moment on there was a clear and evident risk that others like me might do the same.'

'No, no, no,' Lang said irritatedly. 'You're trying to prove the cause from the effect. You're telling me that a murder you committed proves there was risk of others like you committing murder. I don't accept your use of the a posteriori argument.'

Wittgenstein chuckled. 'I'm afraid you'll have to, Professor, at least for the moment, anyway. It's time for me to go.'

'Please wait a minute,' said Jake.

'I can't, I'm sorry. We'll continue our little discussion another time. My next victim has turned up a little earlier than I had expected. Oh yes, I promised to give you his Lombroso-given name, didn't I? Well, it's René Descartes. And now I really must be about the eviction of a god from its machine.'

'Wait –' repeated Jake and the professor in unison. But Wittgenstein was gone.

'He wasn't bullshitting,' said Detective Sergeant Jones. 'We traced the call onto the Injupitersat, and from there to the London area. It's impossible to be more precise than that with a satellite phone.'

Jake shook her head with irritation. 'We should have figured he would use something like that.'

'Satellite phones are expensive, ma'am. Not to mention the fact that they're also illegal.'

'Yes. But that could also mean we might just be able to find out where he got hold of one. Supposing you wanted to buy a satellite phone, where would you go?'

Jones pursed his lips. 'Only one place to go for that kind of thing. Tottenham Court Road.' He shook his head. 'Be a bastard gettin' some of those blokes to talk, mind, if he did buy one there.'

'Yes, you'll have to guarantee them immunity against prosecution. You'd better let me sort that side of it out with the DPP's office.'

'By the way,' Jones said carefully. 'Was he right about your perfume, ma'am?'

'Oh yes,' said Jake. 'He was right. But I can't for the life of me think how I could have met him.'

'You sure they didn't mention your perfume in that magazine article?'

'Perfectly sure.'

'Perhaps he was just winding you up.'

'Yes. Perhaps.' Jake smiled thinly. Somehow she didn't think so.

'Want me to organise you a bodyguard? Just in case he does want to meet you.'

Jake thought for a moment. She didn't think one of her male colleagues would have asked for a bodyguard: not unless their families had been threatened. She shook her head.

'I don't think so. After all, he didn't actually threaten me. And anyway, I have my gun.'

This gets easier every time.

Descartes left the advertising agency in Charlotte Street where he worked and walked south towards the New Oxford Street shopping mall.

From St Giles' Circus to Bond Street, a glass canopy rose ten metres above the tree line, covering two storeys of shops, restaurants, foreign exchange tills, cinemas, building societies, exhibitions and market stalls selling every variety of trinket, craft and souvenir, and all to the apparently endless noise that was generated by the mall's many guitarists, jugglers, clowns and dancers, each of whom wore his or her determination to be entertaining like three stripes on a sleeve.

Descartes crossed from the mall's Rathbone Street entrance to the Soho Square exit, where a group of policemen, armed and armoured, lolled nonchalantly within spitting distance of their riot-vehicle, swinging their billy clubs and flirting with the prostitutes. Sidestepping one of the mall's patrolling sandwich-board automata (Eat at Jo's Sushi Bar/ Bath yourself brown, with Soldebain/ Only a cunt would drink a can of Canberra, said the small, fat robot), I followed him.

He was a hateful-looking figure, dressed in baggy, colourful clothes like one of the stupid clowns on the mall, his hair ludicrously short at the sides and long and sticking up on top, and carrying a clear plastic briefcase that allowed one an uninterrupted view of his newspaper, his cigarettes, his hand-held computer, his television and videotapes for the train-ride home. Probably he had just finished writing some crass piece of advertising copy for hamburgers, or a Protonic washing powder, or some brand of threadbare jeans. Yes, he looked like the style-conscious type to be writing a jeans commercial. Cogito ergo sum? I should bloody well think not, I said to myself as I left the mall. If you had one thought in your VMN-deficient head you wouldn't work for the hucksters.

He crossed the well-kept gardens of the square and then headed down Dean Street, pausing only to look in the window of a small bookshop, before ducking into a performing sex club.

For a short while I stood in front of the place, looking in the yellowish window at a collection of black-and-white photographs which depicted an unlikely sample of the girls who were supposed to be performing inside. It wasn't that they were too attractive to be exhibiting their naked bodies, merely that the pictures themselves looked so old, as if they had been taken ten or fifteen years before, when women still wore their hair that way, or had breasts that shape.

'Live sex show, just starting,' barked the florid-faced hippo seated behind the toughened glass of the box-office. 'Only twenty-five EC. The hardest show in London, sir.'

I counted five bills in front of him and retrieved a pink ticket from a roll the size of a dinner plate. The stairs creaked like falling timber as I stepped gingerly down into the bowels of the club. The girl on stage had just finished removing her knickers and was twirling them on the end of her finger, almost as if she had been trying to fan herself, because it was hot in there.

'Afternoon, mate,' she chirped, catching sight of me as I peered forward, looking for Descartes.

He wasn't difficult to spot, seated as close to the blanket-sized stage as possible, his hair a recognisably ridiculous silhouette against the bright spotlights.

I sat immediately behind him, although I don't suppose he would have noticed. He was much too busy watching the girl as she began to apply a large handful of Vaseline first to her backside, and then to the larger end of a champagne bottle. Surely not, I thought and found myself almost immediately contradicted as she squeezed the bottle inside herself until only the cork remained visible.

A thing is identical with itself. A useless proposition which nevertheless requires an effort of imagination. It is as if in imagination we put a thing such as a champagne bottle into its own shape and saw that it fitted. At the same time, we look at a thing and imagine that there was a blank left for it and that now it fits into it exactly. But this is something else entirely.

The obscenity of it was almost laughable. She drew the bottle inside herself and then pushed it out again. An inner process which stands in need of outward criteria. A human being defecating a champagne bottle.

René Descartes sat rigidly in his seat, not moving his head and, it seemed, hardly daring to breathe. Was this, I wondered, part of his basic quest for the self? Were his senses deceiving him now, concerning things which seemed hardly perceptible? Did he think that this was a dream in which he saw even less probable things than do those who are insane in their waking moments? Was he thinking that in reality he was at home, lying undressed in bed?

He could have been forgiven for thinking that this was some nightmare he was inhabiting. The woman grunted a little and then she giggled as she grasped the neck of the bottle and, with a horrible sucking noise, pulled it right out of her anus. It was like watching a patient, etherised upon a table, performing some surgery upon herself. The apparent impossibility of what she was doing and the sense of astonishment which I felt seemed to underline the dream-like aspect of the whole situation. To my surprise I found myself holding out my hand in front of me, as if to perceive it. What happens in sleep could not surely appear so clear, nor so distinct as this. But of course, Descartes knew that sleep deceives by the ingenuity of its illusions, that there are no certain

*indications by which we may clearly distinguish wakeful-
ness from sleep. From death, even.*

For a moment I was lost in astonishment. My astonishment could almost have persuaded me that I was indeed
dreaming. The bottle disappeared inside the woman
again. She squeezed it back a little and then vacuumed
it back once more.

A dream then. Even better. It was easier for us both
that way. I drew the gas-gun from my shoulder-holster
and reflected that I could hardly miss. All the same, if I
say 'The gun is aiming at point p on the back of Descartes's head', I'm not saying anything about where the
shot will hit. Giving the point at which it is aiming is a
geometrical means of assigning its direction. That this
is the means I use is certainly connected with certain
observations (projectile parabolas, etc.) but these observations don't enter into our present description of the
direction.

'Do it,' said the voice.

I froze with surprise. Who had spoken? Descartes?
Nietzsche? God?

'Yeah, go on, do it,' it said again.

The girl squealed, almost imperceptibly. I heard other
cries of wild encouragement.

'All right,' I said and lifted the gun barrel until it was
just a few centimetres from the back of his head.

The girl kneeling on the stage hauled the bottle out of
her ass and stood up to take a bow. Small explosions
of applause surrounded me as the audience showed its
appreciation. Everyone except Descartes. But I don't suppose anyone noticed. Holstering my gun again I made
my way upstairs to the light.

*Like him I dread awakening from this slumber. Just
in case the laborious wakefulness which would follow
the tranquillity of this repose should have to be spent not
in daylight, but in the excessive darkness of the difficulties
which have just been discussed.*

*

It's true, no one has interfered with my freedom. My life has drained it dry. A lot of fuss about nothing. This life had been given to me for nothing. And yet I would not change. I am as I was made. But I can still savour the failure of a life. After all, I have attained the age of reason.

But what kind of reason have I to assume that my gun will fire if my finger pulls the trigger? What kind of reason to believe that if I fired it at a brother's head it would blow his brains out? When I ask this, a hundred reasons present themselves, each drowning the voice of the others. 'But I have already done it myself innumerable times, and as often heard of others doing the same. Why only the other day there was an article in a magazine written by a former Mafia hitman who used to shoot his victims in the head while they were eating their soup.' (Well, at least I have the decency not to interfere with a man's lunch.)

Reason is first in Nature, created that Man may investigate and perceive, and it is to be distinguished from Sensibility and Understanding. Of course it has a very natural tendency to overreach itself, to overstep the limits of what may be experienced, and all inferences which would carry us across the slippery ground are fallacious and worthless.

And yet . . . the same mind that is capable of reason also produces monsters.

There is an engraving by gorgeous Goya in which various creatures of eternal night hover menacingly above the head of a sleeping man – perhaps Goya himself: certainly there are few artists who can rival his monstrous imaginings. These monsters in the engraving are, of course, symbolic. The real monster, as Hobbes tells us (and, for that matter, Freud), is Man himself – a savage, selfish, murderous brute. Society, says Hobbes, exists so that man may leave his brutish nature chained up at home, that he may aspire to something greater.

But if Man's original state is to be asocial and

destructively rapacious, then if he aspires to go beyond this state, does he grow nearer to God, or does he find himself growing further away?

For my own part I find the aspects of my character which are solitary, poor, nasty, brutish and short are far stronger than those civilising constraints which are imposed by society. I find that I understand, only too well, those who are at war against the world.

We all look to fathom the mind of a mass-murderer and to understand what makes him commit such heinous crimes.

Yet which of us can honestly say that in his Hobbesian heart of hearts, he does not already have the answer?

13

The man sat slumped in his seat, head on chest, arms dangling by his sides, a perfect caricature of a sleeping gorilla. The back of his neck looked painfully red, as if badly sunburned, but that was only encrusted blood.

Jake regarded the body carefully. It didn't look so bad. A dead man always looks tidier than a dead woman. Usually the clothes are left on, and there are no mutilations. Nothing missing like a breast or a nipple. No presents left inside the private parts. There were worse ways to get it than six times in the back of the head. This one reminded her of some photographs she had once seen of Mafia hits in Palermo. The neatness of the gang executions had surprised her. There was very little disruption to whichever business (usually a restaurant) was being operated on the premises. Just a few shots in the head and then out, leaving the victim to a pop-eyed contemplation of his shirt-front or his navel or his minestrone.

It was the same with this killer. Jake knew he must be a neat, fastidious sort of man. But she wondered if he took any pleasure in the actual act of killing. Or if, like a mob gunman, it was just something that had to be done, like filling in your tax-return, or going to the dentist. Business. Nothing personal. Just business.

She sat down in the seat behind the body, with Detective Inspector Stanley, who had been on the scene for rather longer, placing himself in the seat beside her. He didn't say anything. There wasn't any explanation needed to picture what had happened. Finally she nodded and said: 'Any witnesses?'

Stanley tugged his shirt collar down from his Adam's apple and flexed his neck before answering.

'Most of them buggered off the minute someone noticed that Mr Armfield, codenamed René Descartes, had been shot.' He laughed scornfully. 'Probably scared that their wives might find out that they'd even been in a dump like this.'

'What about the people who run this fleapit?'

'Well we've got the girl who was performing on stage at the time. And the owner, Mr Grubb. He was upstairs, on the cash desk. But they both say they don't remember seeing anything.'

Jake pointed at the stage. 'The girl would have been less than six metres from the killer when he fired. With those spotlights on she must have been able to see his face.'

'Apparently she had her back to the audience for the greater part of the act,' he explained uncomfortably. 'And also she was on all fours.'

'Doing what precisely?'

Stanley sighed and readjusted his shirt collar. 'I believe she was enjoying a bottle of champagne, ma'am,' he said, smiling thinly. '*Ab anam*.'

'I see,' Jake said with distaste. It never ceased to astonish her what men would find to entertain themselves.

'About how many men were watching this obscenity?'

'Grubb says he sold about ten or fifteen tickets in the two hours leading up to Armfield's death. We've already had the contents of his till sent down to the lab in case there are any prints.'

Jake pointed at the bloodstained back of the seat in front of her. 'Looks to me as if he might have been splashed a bit. There can't have been too many men walking out of here with blood on them.'

Stanley shrugged. 'Grubb says he can't remember.'

'Perhaps he just doesn't like policemen much. Any previous convictions?'

'A couple. Living off immoral earnings. Old stuff really.'

Jake glanced around at the cheap surroundings. 'Tell this Grubb that you're going to have a fire and safety officer go over this place. That he's going to look for broken fire alarms, blocked fire exits, that kind of thing. See if that doesn't jog his memory a bit. Then I want you to get some men to question everyone in this street. Building workers, traffic wardens, messengers, prostitutes, shop owners, everyone. I want to know if anyone remembers seeing a man with blood on him. Got that?'

'Ma'am.'

'Now, where's this girl who was on stage?'

'I told her to wait in the dressing room,' said Stanley. 'I thought you'd want to question her.' He pointed to the side of the stage. 'Through that curtain.'

Jake stood up and walked round in front of the seats. She stepped onto the stage and looking across the busy scenes-of-crime officers, tried to picture the scene as it might have appeared to anyone performing there. For Jake it was almost beyond imagination. The seating looked as if it had been removed from an old bus. There was a large hole in one of the flock-covered walls. Cheap linoleum covered the uneven floorboards of the small stage. From the toilets came the strong smell of disinfectant. It was hard to conceive of anyone choosing to come to this particular purgatory for entertainment. But come the men had, with direct eyes, to watch a woman's loss of being and general descent. Men, like rats in a cellar, waiting to feed upon a woman's corpse.

What must it be like? she asked herself. To stand there naked in front of a roomful of strangers. Worse than just naked: to perform, to display your body's functions, to become a living anatomy lesson for some amateur medical students. She wrapped her arms around herself and shuddered with disgust.

'Give us a show, ma'am,' someone called out. There were several guffaws.

Jake glanced back at her colleagues with cool distaste. They were all the same. 'Just get on with it,' she sneered.

The dressing room was hardly much more than a walk-in wardrobe, with a couple of clothes rails that were empty save for a couple of wire coat-hangers, and a wall mirror that made it seem bigger. Underneath a bare lightbulb was a girl about twenty years old, wearing nothing more than a red flannel dressing gown like the one Jake wore herself when she went to see Doctor Blackwell. Jake's unwilling witness sat on a greasy-looking futon, smoking a cigarette and muttering angrily.

'Who are you?' she snarled as Jake came through the door. 'What do you want?'

'I'm Chief Inspector Jakowicz.'

'Can I go now?' demanded the girl, like a petulant child.

'Hadn't you better get dressed first?'

The girl stubbed out her cigarette on the cover of an old magazine and jumped up from the futon.

'I'd like to ask you a few questions,' said Jake.

'I've already spoken to the other copper. I told him all I had to say.'

'Yes, well I don't much blame you for not telling him much,' said Jake. 'I can't say I'm all that fond of talking to him myself. Especially in a place like this. It's only a place like this that lets you see men as they really are.'

The girl snorted. 'That's for sure.' She shook her head in accession to Jake's request. 'Oh all right, ask away, if you want. But lock the door, will you? I don't want any of your mates walkin' in 'ere while I'm gettin' dressed and gettin' a free eyeful.'

Jake turned the key in the lock and leaned against the door.

'What's your name?' she asked, searching her bag for a cigarette.

'Clare,' said the girl, and slipped off her dressing gown.

Jake lit her Nicofree and regarded the girl's nakedness with an almost critical attention, as if she had been a painter or a sculptor. It was not a pretty face. It was perhaps not even handsome. Her nose was broken but not badly. The lips were too voluptuous and the teeth slightly protruding. Of intellect there was little sign, but you couldn't have mistaken the hard cunning that was visible in the face. Her skin was smooth and supple-looking. She seemed too young to be doing this kind of thing, but Jake left that unsaid at the risk of sounding patronising.

Clare rummaged in a tartan duffle-bag and found her underwear.

There was such a wanton libidinous aspect to the tough little face which seemed quite to overcome all its manifest imperfections. Jake could see now how she would be attractive to men.

'You saw it all, didn't you?' she said.

'You see everything in a dump like this,' said the girl and climbed into her pants.

'That's not what I meant.'

'No? What did you mean?'

'The dead man: ever see him before?'

'I said hello to him as he came down the stairs and sat down.'

'Would you recognise him again?'

She nodded and pulled up her skirt.

'So why did you tell my inspector that you didn't see anything? You know, you almost certainly saw the man who did it.'

Clare shrugged. 'I dunno. Scared, I guess. In this business, you can get into trouble if you talk to the police. People don't like people who talk to the law. You know.'

'Meaning Mr Grubb.'

'Yes. He can get a bit violent sometimes.'

'He hits you?'

'Sometimes, yeah. Never on the face, mind. And it's not just that. If he found out that I was telling you things now, he might assume I'd tell you something else another time. I might lose my job. Grubb says that there are plenty of Chinese who would do what I do, for half the money.'

'If I promise to sort it out with Grubb, will you take a look at some ComputaFit pictures and see if you can't help to improve them?'

Clare nodded again and pulled on a none too clean sweater.

'You promise you'll make it so that he won't take it out on me?'

'I promise. I'll have one of my men drive you down to the Yard.'

On her way back upstairs, Jake stopped for a moment and took a deep, unsteady breath. It made Jake angry to think of the men who came to this filthy cellar to see a girl, formulated, sprawling on a stage, pinned and wriggling on a floor. It made her angry to think of a girl like that making a commodity of herself for the profit of the man in the office upstairs. She felt her brow lower with distaste.

Jake searched in her shoulder bag for the set of electronic tungsten knuckles she kept there. The rubber grip meant that the user could hold them quite safely, but when the metal came into contact with the human body, they emitted an electric shock, thus enabling most female police officers to hit every bit as hard, if not harder, than their male colleagues. Good job too, thought Jake, with all the thugs they had to deal with, most of whom were prepared to belt a policewoman every bit as hard as they would a male officer.

Jake found Mr Grubb in his office with Detective Inspector Stanley seated on the corner of his desk. She disliked him almost instinctively. He was large and fat, but despite his expensive suit, his gold watch and his cigar, you could still see the grubby little schoolboy underneath the man. He was well-named.

'You the Chief Inspector?' snarled Grubb.

Jake kept the hand with the knuckles hidden for the time being.

'That's right,' she said breezily.

'Then tell your bit of prick to get off my back. It's no good him threatenin' me with fire and safety officers. I didn't see nuthin', all right?'

Jake looked at Stanley. 'Leave us alone for a minute,' she told him.

Stanley nodded uncertainly, and then stepped out of the room.

'I'm sorry, but what did you say you saw?'

Grubb grimaced at her. 'What are you? Deaf or something? I said, I didn't see nuthin'.' He laughed at her and set about re-lighting his cigar.

'If you did not see nothing,' Jake said, 'that means that you did see something.'

'Eh? What you talkin' about?'

'Don't you see? The two negatives cancel each other out. You know I'm glad you're going to help us because if you had said that you didn't see anything, I'd be worried that something might happen to you.'

'You threatenin' me, darlin'?' He spoke without even looking at her, as if in contempt of her.

'Yes,' said Jake flatly.

'I've done nuthin'. You can't scare me, luv.'

'No? I bet I could scare you, Mr Grubb. I bet I could have you begging for mercy.'

Grubb smiled. 'There's only one way that a girl like you could have me beggin' for mercy,' he said suggestively.

'Oh? And what's that?'

He laughed. 'Use your imagination, sweetheart.' Then he shook his head and, getting up from his desk, advanced towards Jake. 'You know, I do believe you're tryin' to get hard with me: is that right?' There was quiet menace in his voice.

Jake held her ground and nodded.

Grubb pushed his fat schoolboy's face closer to Jake's until she could smell the tobacco on his breath.

'Don't make me laugh. You don't – '

Jake thumbed the bezel on the grip of the knuckles and brought her fist up through a short arc. The knuckles emitted a low electronic hum as they accelerated through the air, but this was abruptly lost in Grubb's howl of pain and surprise as, with a small blue spark, her fist connected with his stomach. He doubled over, almost collapsing on top of her, but still finding himself able to flail at her with one fist. Jake neatly sidestepped the clumsy blow, and pulling the punch just a fraction, she caught Grubb on the side of the jaw. He collapsed onto the ground.

Jake stood over him, and grabbing him by the tie, she pulled his head clear of the floor and then let it drop a couple of times.

'How's your memory now?' she asked. 'Anything yet?'

'All right, all right,' Grubb moaned, rubbing his jaw. 'I did see him. No need to get violent.'

'Good,' said Jake. 'I'm glad you've decided to cooperate.' She twisted his tie tighter. 'I don't much like your business and I don't much like the crumbs like you who run it. It's lucky for you that I'm busy today, otherwise I'd ask some of the girls who work here about you. And if I found that you were the type who slaps them around, well that would really make me angry. Let's hope for your sake that I never have to come back here, eh?'

Jake yelled out for Stanley. He returned to the room and smiled when he saw Grubb lying on the floor at Jake's feet.

'Take this man down to the Yard, Stanley,' she said. 'Seems like he's remembered something after all. And the girl too.'

'Yes, ma'am.' Stanley helped a stunned-looking Grubb off the floor. 'What's the matter with you, then? Fall over, did you, sir? Come on, up you get.' Stanley nodded almost appreciatively at Jake and then led Grubb out of the office to the car.

Jake switched off the knuckles and dropped them back into her bag. Her high police rank sometimes left her on the slippery ice of intellectual detective work, constructing elaborate aetiological theories, with little or no friction underfoot. She enjoyed the almost academic conditions of her work. But it felt good to be back on rough ground again.

It was dark by the time Jake parked her BMW in the small car-park surrounding her apartment building. Before she got out of the door she put her head through the strap of her bag and adjusted it across her chest. Then she unzipped the bag and put her left hand inside, so that she had hold of the Beretta's neoprene grip even before she had pulled the door-handle. Now that he had her address she was more careful about her security. Was it possible that she might have even met Wittgenstein in her own building?

With this one thought in her mind Jake crossed the car-park and gained the front door without incident. The doorman glanced up from his evening paper. There was lipstick on his cheek.

'Evening, miss,' he said.

Jake released the big gun and zipped her bag.

'Good evening, Phil,' she said. Now she saw the head-line on the paper. Another man found murdered.

'This serial killer, miss: what makes someone do it?' said Phil. 'The wife says he must be gay or something, but none of these men who've been killed have been touched, right?'

Jake pressed the lift button and shook her head. 'None of them,' she said. 'That's right.'

'Myself, I reckon it's a woman who's got it in for men. Someone raped her when she was a kid maybe. You know the sort of thing.'

Jake said she did.

'I don't mind telling you, miss, I'm careful about how I go home now. I used to walk along the river, when the tide was out. But not now. No fear.'

'I wouldn't worry too much, if I were you,' said Jake.

At the same time she told herself she had no way of knowing if Phil might be a potential victim or not. All sorts of people were VMN-negative. Chung had told her that there was even someone in the Home Office who was rumoured to be VMN-negative. So why not her own doorman?

'Still it's wise to take a few precautions,' she added.

The lift arrived, but Jake remained where she was.

'Phil, you know that if you're a copper there are always a few weirdos who might want to get even with you.'

'I can imagine, miss.'

'If ever you saw someone hanging around here, some-one strange, you would tell me, wouldn't you? I mean you needn't worry about scaring me or anything. I should want to know.'

''Course I would, miss.'

'There hasn't been anyone hanging around, has there, Phil?'

'No, miss. Not that I've noticed.'

Jake smiled at him. 'Goodnight, Phil.'

'Goodnight, miss.'

Alone in her flat Jake made herself a cup of coffee and curled up in her favourite armchair to read. Normally she would have been reading a thriller, but for the past week she had been occupied with *Philosophical Investigations* by Ludwig Wittgenstein, in which the great philosopher had set out to correct the mistakes of his first book, the *Tractatus*.

In the book, Wittgenstein investigated the concepts of meaning; of understanding; of propositions; of logic; and of states of consciousness. It was a more difficult read and Jake found that she had to make a few notes in order to maintain her concentration; however, she considered that there was more in it for the detective than was to be found in the *Tractatus*. She wondered if she might not have some of the things she had noted down printed up, as slogans for the wall of her office in New Scotland Yard.

'Meaning is physiognomy.' Yes, she liked that. It referred to how a word has meaning, but all the same it seemed to speak of something vaguely forensic too. Jake also appreciated the implicit warning to those who would make a case based on the purely circumstantial that was contained in the thought that 'the most explicit evidence of intention is by itself insufficient evidence of intention'. And there was certainly a message for every detective in the answer to the question 'What is your aim in philosophy? To show the fly the way out of the fly bottle.' How often had she felt just like that fly?

Professor Jameson Lang had been right: there was so much common ground between the detective and the philosopher. More than she could ever have appreciated.

This growing interest in philosophy had, as its most important corollary, a sense of fascination for the man who had, indirectly at least, inspired it: the Lombroso killer. It was, she knew, not uncommon for multiples, spree-killers and lone gunmen trying to make a name for themselves by killing a public figure to arm themselves with some intellectual baggage as evidence of their being something better than a common criminal. Just as often it enabled their lawyers to try and shift the moral responsibility for their actions onto some hapless author, even to try and sue him if he was unfortunate enough still to be alive. Books do furnish a room, wrote Anthony Powell. Jake reflected that in these post-millenial days, books also furnished the well-educated life of many a mass-murderer.

Jerry Sherriff, the man who assassinated EC President, Pierre Delafons, had read him the whole of Eliot's *Waste Land* before blowing his head off. Spree-killer Greg Harrison was listening to a disc of John Betjeman's poetry when, armed with several hand-grenades, he ran amok through the streets of Slough, killing forty-one people.

The American multiple Lyndon Topham claimed that he had killed twenty-seven people out riding in various parts of Texas, because they were the Black Horsemen from Tolkien's *Lord of the Rings*. And Jake had lost count of the number of serial killers who claimed that their actions had been influenced by Nietzsche.

There was something different about this particular killer, however: Jake had feelings for him that detectives were not supposed to have about multiple murderers. Admiration was too strong a word for it. Rather it was that she felt fascinated by him. Her imagination had been roused by him. Through him she had come to learn certain things about the world. About herself.

Trying to understand him, trying to catch him was about the most stimulating thing Jake had ever done.

Jake slept for four hours and woke in the dark with a question gnawing at her memory like a dog's bone. Where the hell *had* he met her?

She rolled out of bed, pulled on her dressing-gown and went through to the kitchen where she put some ice and a slice of lime into a long glass, and poured herself some mineral water. She drank it greedily, like a small child after a nightmare. Then she sat down in front of her computer and switched it on.

If she could remember 'where' then she might also remember 'who'. She typed 'Where?' and waited for inspiration. When, after several minutes, none came she erased the word and thought again.

Another question en route to 'where'. When? When had he met her? As she typed 'When?' Jake was suddenly possessed of the certainty that he had already given her the answer. She felt a chill of excitement as she tried to recall what it was. Something small. Something in the very air around her. Something . . .

Her perfume. Rapture, by Luther Levine. He had complimented her on it.

Jake jumped up, grabbed her shoulder bag from off the back of the chair and emptied its contents onto the floor. Rapture had been a recent purchase. But when and where had she bought it? She sorted through the various till receipts and credit-card vouchers collected during the last few months thanking the slut in her who rarely ever tidied out her bag.

At last she found what she was looking for. Frankfurt Airport. That was where she had bought it. Until her trip to the European Law Enforcement Symposium, she had always worn Lolita, by Federico D'Atri. The purchase of the bottle of Rapture had been a spur of the moment thing. She had even scolded herself for buying it, imagining that she had succumbed to the sexy 48-sheet poster featuring a modern version of Fragonard's painting, *The Swing*. Since she felt guilty that she had fallen for the hype, it had been some time before she had actually worn Rapture. She remembered wearing Lolita at the press conference where she had issued a description of Wittgenstein. And it had been several days after that before she had actually finished the bottle of Lolita.

The first time she had worn Rapture – had been the day she had gone to see Sir Jameson Lang. Whoever Wittgenstein was, he had met her after that. He had made a mistake, she was sure of it.

Now if she could only recollect everyone she had met since her trip to Cambridge . . .

The problem with the RA equipment is that it does not merely convey an approximation of physical pleasure, such as the sexual act, it also conveys a close approximation of pain. Or, to put it another way, just as I am able to experience an approximation of killing someone, I am also able to experience an approximation of being killed myself. Hence, the machine needs careful handling.

This morning, when I awoke, it seemed to me that there was a rhinoceros standing in the room with me. The huge beast, two metres high at the shoulder, stood squarely at the bottom of my bed, scraping the carpet with its umbrella-stand feet and jerking its huge scimitar of a horn in my direction. It was so close that I could feel the animal's hot breath snorting from its nostrils onto my bare toes. I hardly dared to breathe, seeing that it had already turned most of the bedroom furniture into matchwood. I had the certain feeling that the slightest movement on my part would cause the rhino to charge.

My problem was this: if I was dreaming, then I could safely shake my head clear of the nightmare and jump out of bed; but if this was an approximation of reality, then, for reasons already described, I was in serious trouble. Even an approximate reality of a rhino's horn up my arse was not something I was eager to experience.

So I closed my eyes and tried to isolate my mind from my senses, asking myself some logical questions. Had I fallen asleep wearing the RA outfit? I certainly remembered putting it on, but not taking it off. I remembered using the erotic software, but there was no way that this would have included a rhinoceros. If I was in fact wearing the RA equipment, the only possibility was that having fallen asleep, there had been a power-cut and that when the power returned, the machine simply picked out a program at random.

On the other hand there existed the possibility that even these deliberations were part of my dream.

Naturally I recognised the program that the RA machine had chosen – or the one I was dreaming it had chosen. It was a short program based on an incident which had occurred in a Cambridge lecture theatre, when I had refused to accept, as Russell had insisted, that there was not a rhinoceros in the room with us.

The program had not been particularly useful as providing an experience of a real philosophical argument with a Cambridge don, for the simple reason that computers are excessively literal. The machine translated the sense of assertion involved as being something psychological, that existence could be a matter of simple will, and created a two-ton rhino. All I had really meant to say was that it is hard to regard the non-existence of a two-ton white rhinoceros when true, as a fact, in quite the same sense in which the existence of a rhinoceros would be a fact if it were true. Something of which I was now only too acutely aware.

I must have lain there for quite a while. And what happened was this: somehow I must have dozed off for a few minutes and when I awoke, the rhino was still there. This seemed to prove that I was not asleep, since it appeared unlikely that I could wake to the same dream twice and in quick succession. It seemed much more probable that I had, as feared, an approximation of reality. I was, after all, just going to have to bite the bullet, raise my visor-screen and accept what pain there would be in the few seconds before the other sensational parts of the program were able to turn themselves off.

This was easier said than done. And almost impossible to describe. Intense pain has that quality. Suffice to say that as soon as I moved my hand to raise the visor, the beast charged. Three or four seconds of an approximate sensation of being stamped and gored left me vomiting on the floor of my real bedroom. I had to call in sick and spent the rest of the morning in a hot bath trying to soak away some of my aches and pains.

But around lunchtime I felt well enough to do some reading. Perhaps the rhino shook me up more than I realised but re-reading some of my earlier notes, I could not avoid the conclusion that there were very many statements in the book with which I now disagree.

Indeed some of my ideas have changed so fundamentally that I wonder if I should go on with the Brown Book at all. In particular, my squeamishness with regard to the use of the word 'murder' now seems to me to have been mistaken. Morality had coloured my use of this word and I now think that a more perspicacious use of grammar will enable me to say what I want to say about various propositions.

I have been much too dogmatic. I think that I perceived something as if through a thick film and yet still wanted to try and elicit from it as much as possible. But I have resolved to let the earlier work stand, if only as a presentation of my old thoughts which, it cannot be denied, are nevertheless the basis of my new ones. Perhaps my old notes alongside my new notes will serve to present a kind of dialectic, not with the aim of arriving at a theory, but with the simple object of illustrating the ambiguities in language.

We can say that the word 'murder' has at least three different meanings; but it would be mistaken to assume that any theory can give the whole grammar of how we use the word, or try to accommodate within a single theory examples which do not seem to agree with it.

14

Jake stood alone in the room, watching the man on the other side of the lightly tinted glass. He too was alone. He sat motionless in a chair, too tired to seem nervous, staring at Jake and yet not seeing her. Seeing himself and yet hardly interested in a reflection he had become used to during the many hours of his interrogation. He smoked languidly, like a man who had been waiting for a flight long delayed.

She envied him the cigarette. On her side of the two-way mirror, all smoking, even a nicotine-free cigarette, was very strictly forbidden. The glow of a cigarette end was the one thing a suspect could see on the other side of the mirror in the interview room.

The door to the observation room opened and Crawshaw came in. He came over to the mirror and yawned.

'John George Richards,' he said. 'His story checks out, I'm afraid. He did make a delivery of olive oil to the shop in Brewer Street on the day Mary Woolnoth was murdered. But he made the delivery at around three-thirty, which was when Mary's body was first discovered. One hour before that he was making a delivery in Wimbledon. The time was recorded on the computer when it issued his delivery note. He couldn't possibly have driven all the way from Wimbledon, selected Mary, killed her, and then made the delivery in anything less than a couple of hours.

'Then there are the previous victims: Richards was away on holiday in Mallorca when Alison Bradshaw was killed; and he was in hospital having his wisdom teeth out on the day that Stella Forsythe was murdered. All of which puts him in the clear.'

'I suppose,' she said reluctantly. 'We had better let him go. Too bad. He was looking good.'

Crawshaw nodded wearily and turned to leave the room.

'Oh, and, Ed,' said Jake. 'Better put the surveillance team on that bookshop again.'

Back in her office Jake tried to bring her mind back to Wittgenstein. She re-read a transcript of their first dialogue, alongside a forensic psychiatrist's report which concluded, much as Jake herself had already concluded, that the subject was a highly organised non-social personality – an egocentric who disliked people generally; outwardly it was likely that he was capable of getting along with his fellow man but that he harboured resentment towards society as a whole.

Jake had smiled the previous evening when Sir Jameson Lang had telephoned her at home with his own reaction to this assessment: 'The way these psychiatrists describe him,' he had said, 'he sounds like a typical academic. With a personality assessment like that I should recommend that you conduct your investigation here, in college.'

The report concluded that on evidence other than the killings themselves, there was nothing to indicate insanity. The killer killed because he liked killing. He enjoyed the sensation of power that it gave him. He was playing God.

'That's something different,' Lang had remarked. 'Now, there you have the typical novelist.'

Jake had asked him how he proposed to handle a second dialogue, assuming that Wittgenstein rang again.

'Moral philosophical argument didn't seem to have much effect, did it?' Lang had said. 'Next time I thought I'd argue from a phenomenological point of view: scrutinise a few essences and meanings he might otherwise have taken for granted. You know, concentrate on the objective logical elements in thought. It's rather a useful way of investigating these extreme states of mind. Just the thing if he should turn out to be existentialist. Which wouldn't surprise me at all.'

But she was not long back at her desk when Wittgenstein did ring a second time; and as things transpired, there was to be no opportunity for Jameson Lang to argue with Wittgenstein.

Immediately he telephoned, Wittgenstein declared that in response to Jake's own lecture to the EC symposium on techniques of law enforcement and criminal investigation, he intended to deliver his own lecture, entitled 'The Perfect Murder' which he claimed he had recently given to the Society of Connoisseurs in Murder.

When Jake tried to open a conversation with him, Wittgenstein declared that they could either listen or he would ring off and kill someone straightaway. So, in the hope of preventing another murder, and in the vague expectation that they might learn something more of Wittgenstein himself, Jake reluctantly agreed.

In all, Wittgenstein spoke for almost eighteen minutes. He spoke as if there had indeed been an audience that was composed of anything but Scotland Yard detectives: as if there had just occurred some splendid dinner at the Guildhall and now, in front of five hundred guests wearing evening dress who comprised the Society of Connoisseurs in Murder, he, Wittgenstein, had risen from his place to give the keynote address.

After several minutes Jake glanced at her wristwatch. She didn't much care to be lectured by anyone, least of all a killer talking about the perfect murder. It crossed her mind to interrupt him, to challenge one or two of the statements Wittgenstein had made. But at the same time she did not want to risk angering him and provoking him to ring off. So she kept silent, fascinated with this protracted insight into the mind of a mass-murderer, occasionally glancing over at Stanley who, on catching her eye, would tap the side of his head meaningfully.

But when Wittgenstein announced that at the conclusion of his lecture, he would be committing another murder, Jake was finally moved to contradict him.

'No,' she said. 'I forbid you.'

The voice on the telephone uttered a short laugh. 'What's that you say?'

'I forbid you to kill anyone,' Jake repeated firmly.

There was a short silence. 'May I proceed with my lecture please?' said Wittgenstein. He sounded like some dry-as-dust old academic.

'Only if you promise that you will discuss this matter at the end of it,' said Jake.

'What matter is that?'

'What you said about killing another man. You promise to discuss it or I hang up right now. D'you hear?'

Another pause. 'Very well,' he sighed. 'May I continue now?'

'We'll discuss it?'

'I said so, didn't I?'

'Very well then. Continue.'

'Let me turn now to the murders themselves . . .'

'Be my guest,' said Jake.

But this time Wittgenstein ignored her.

Jake settled back in her chair and lit a cigarette. From time to time she glanced at the pictophone screen to see how Sir Jameson Lang was reacting to this bizarre example of public speaking in absentia. But the Cambridge philosopher and Master of Trinity College betrayed no signs of anything but fascination.

She reflected that he was probably thinking of how his own fictional detective creation, Plato, would have handled the situation. Better than she was doing, Jake didn't doubt. She admired and respected Lang, but all the same she found his interest in crime rather puzzling. She knew that he was hardly unique in this respect. The English fascination with the murder mystery was, as even now Wittgenstein was suggesting, more prevalent than ever. She had no explanation for this peculiar phenomenon other than the purely sociological: that it was the product of society's own decadence. Of that particular characteristic there was more than enough in Wittgenstein's twisted lecture and irritation began to give way to a certain astonishment the detective felt with regard to the perversity of a murderer's arguments.

Astonishment became absorption and after her first interruption she did not challenge him again. Later on, she thought she had been naïve to have trusted him to keep his word, for Wittgenstein had no sooner delivered the last phrases of his speech, which was to pass over a series of supposedly traditional toasts to a number of famous murderers, than he had rung off, leaving Jake to curse him for a liar.

But what was far worse than the feeling that she had been duped was the knowledge that somewhere he was almost certainly in the very act of committing his twelfth murder.

Later on that day, Jake was called to the City of London where, beside a public bar on Lower Thames Street, an as-yet unidentified male Caucasian's body had been found with six gunshots to the back of the head. There wasn't much to see beyond the simple confirmation that Wittgenstein had struck again and, leaving the scenes-of-crime officers to do their job, Jake returned to the Yard.

She found Detective Sergeant Jones and a tall, dark, unshaven man eating a bag of crisps waiting in her office. Both men stood up as Jake walked in and hung her coat on the hat stand.

'And who's this?' she enquired.

'This is Mr Parmenides,' explained Jones. 'I've taken a statement off him, but I think you'll find what he's got to say worth hearing yourself, ma'am.'

Jake sat down behind her desk and poured herself a glass of mineral water.

'I'm all ears,' she said wearily.

Jones prompted the man with a nod.

'A few days ago,' said the man, whose name and accent seemed to confirm that he was Greek, 'I think it was Monday . . . Anyway, I left home to go to work. This is at my cousin's restaurant in Piccadilly. I always start work at around six. But on my way I see this man is following me. I notice him for the first time on the train from Wandsworth, where I live, to Victoria. Then, later on, I see him again when I come out of the Brain Research Institute.'

Parmenides glanced uncertainly at Jones. 'You sure she all right to tell this?'

'Don't worry,' said Jones. 'The chief inspector won't tell anyone about you. You have my word.'

The Greek seemed reassured. 'OK. I believe. Well, Chief Inspector, the fact is that I am VMN-negative. You know about this thing I suppose.'

Jake nodded.

'I am going to the Institute once a week for counselling on how to deal with situations which may make me feel very violent, sometimes. Like football. And Turks. What will happen to me, I am not sure, but – ' He shrugged nervously.

'Please go on,' said Jake, more interested now.

'Well you see, this man comes after me. I take the underground from Victoria and he is there again when I come up in the Green Park. Then I am walking along Piccadilly, to my cousin's restaurant like I say, and I say to myself, "Why should this guy be following you, Kyriakos?" So I go into the church there, I – I don't remember the name – '

'It's St James's Church, ma'am,' said Jones.

'I know the one,' said Jake.

'Yes, that is it. And the man follows me inside. Now I am sure of him following me. He sits behind me, several seats behind. So after one or two minutes I am feeling very angry indeed at him. And so I get up and grab him round the throat and say "for why are you following me, you bastard?" ' Parmenides made an apologetic sort of gesture. 'You know, I have this fear that maybe he is something to do with the Lombroso Program. That maybe he is some kind of secret policeman.'

'Did he say anything?' said Jake.

'He say that he is a tourist. So I give him a good shake and say I don't believe. I say he will tell me for why he follows me or I will hurt him. Then what happens is that these two people come into the church and for one second I think they are with this man, and for another second I suddenly realise how I am behaving inside a church, of all places. I try to remember what my counsellor has told me about keeping my calm and holding my cool and so, I let him go and he runs off. Well after that, I think maybe he is just some sort of queer or something and maybe he just fancy me.'

Jake winced. 'And what persuaded you that he might be something else?'

'This man following me has left something behind him in the church and which I picked up. It is an *A-Z*, of London. And I am scared when I look at it later, in my cousin's restaurant, because the road where I live in Wandsworth – really, it is Balham – has been underlined, in the index at the back. With the number of my house. So have others too. Well, now it's yesterday, OK? And the fact is that I finally get up my courage to open this letter that my counsellor has given me. The one which the police have written, telling me please to make contact soon for my own safety. The reason I have not opened this before is that I am afraid that it is maybe some sort of deportation order – maybe even to quarantine people like me. Anyway I read what it say and then I remember the book and I think maybe the two are connected. And that maybe the man with the book is the one who has been shooting men in the head, and that these men are people like me. So, I come here today.'

'Did you bring the *A-Z*?'

Jones handed over a clear plastic bag containing the book.

Jake nodded. 'You certainly did the right thing, Mr Parmenides,' she told him. 'Do you mind telling me your VMN codename?'

The Greek grinned sheepishly. 'It is William Shakespeare,' he replied. 'What a great honour, yes?'

'Well sir, I think you've had a very fortunate escape,' said Jake. 'You were perfectly right. That man is the man we're looking for. The one who's killed all the other men. And he would almost certainly have murdered you too, had you not acted when you did. But I must ask you not to tell anyone else about this. You see, our only chance of catching him is by making sure we don't alarm him. If he suspects that any of his potential victims will be expecting him, then he'll go to ground and we might never get him. Do you see?'

Parmenides nodded. 'Sure thing. I understand. No problem, miss.'

'I'd like to ask you another favour, sir. I want you to go with Detective Sergeant Jones here and look at some computer-generated pictures we have of this man. See if you can't improve them. After all, you've had the best look at him of anyone so far.'

'Like on the telly. I know. Yes, OK.'

Jake nodded at Jones. 'And when Mr Parmenides has finished, Jones, have a car take him home. Then I want a guard watching him for twenty-four hours a day.' She smiled at the Greek.

'It's just a precaution,' she explained. 'I think you probably scared him off for good, but we can't afford to be too careful.'

The Greek got up. 'Thank you,' he said. 'Thank you very much.'

'No; thank you, Mr Parmenides.'

'All right, sir,' said Jones, ushering him through Jake's doorway. 'This way, please.'

'And, Sergeant . . .'

'Ma'am?'

'Do you know where Inspector Stanley is?'

'Not exactly, no, ma'am.'

'Find him, will you? Tell him to get himself in here.'

'Certainly. By the way, you'll find a list of all the addresses that have been underlined on your desk, ma'am. Do you want me to pass the *A-Z* on to the lab, for fingerprints?'

'It's all right. I'll do it. And, Jones? Well done.'

'Thank you, ma'am.'

When Jones and the Greek had gone, Jake read through the list of addresses he had typed out for her. A few of them she recognised as the homes of some of Wittgenstein's previous victims.

Ten minutes later a grumpy-looking Stanley presented himself in her office.

'Where have you been?'

Stanley looked aggrieved. 'In the canteen,' he said. 'I had hoped to be able to eat something today.'

'You can forget about dinner,' Jake said. 'You and I have got work to do.' She explained about Parmenides finding Wittgenstein's *A-Z*. 'Apart from the ones he's already hit, I want every one of these addresses put under round-the-clock surveillance. Don't inform the occupants. No sense in alarming them unnecessarily. But if Wittgenstein tries to kill inside London again, we'll have him.'

Jake allowed herself a small smile of satisfaction.

'Let's just pray he's not tired of working in London,' said Stanley.

Jake smiled. 'You know what they say about the man who's tired of London . . . ?'

The Perfect Murder

A lecture in memory of John Williams, before the Society of Connoisseurs in Murder, is traditionally an occasion to celebrate the fine art of murder, and I am honoured to have been asked to deliver it.

John Williams, one of the earliest British members of the modern aesthetic movement in murder, was a distinguished representative of those cultural values which are closest to my own heart. Like paintings or sculpture it is certain that murders too have their own peculiar differences and shades of merit, and when one examines the facts surrounding the two murders which John committed in December 1811, it should be clear to us all that he was indeed a great artist.

He was not trained as such; nor was he particularly aware of his gift. But I think he would have been the first to recognise that Art is never standing still: that what might be dismissed as foul murder today might be Art tomorrow. This principle is also mine. That one murder is better or worse than another in point of aesthetics is something I have based my whole philosophy of life upon.

As Thomas De Quincey, the previous occupant of this illustrious chair, said, in the first of his two Williams lectures: 'Murder . . . may be laid hold of by its moral handle (as it generally is in the pulpit and at the Old Bailey); and that, I confess, is its weak side; or it may also be treated aesthetically, as the Germans call it – that is, in relation to good taste.'

The moral issue is neatly disposed of by De Quincey. He argues that when a murder has not yet been done, when there exists merely an intent to commit murder, then it behoves us to treat it morally. But once a murder is over and done with, then, he says, what's the use of any more virtue? What indeed? But enough has been said about morality. Now comes the turn of taste and the fine arts.

I do not propose to spend too long referring back to De Quincey. But it would be wrong if I did not acknowledge my own personal debt to the thoughts which he expressed to this society as long ago as 1827, on the need to murder philosophers.

Would that Descartes had been killed, says Thomas. Hobbes was a fine subject for murder. Certainly one might have counted on Leibniz being murdered. Kant narrowly escaped being murdered. And, despite what is commonly held, De Quincey reveals not only that Spinoza met a violent and well-deserved end, but also that Bishop Berkeley murdered Père Malebranche by means of an argument which deranged his liver.

Today it is even more obvious just how much good can result from the murder of one dusty, arid, old philosopher. Both Marx and Freud were murdered by Jaspers. Bertrand Russell and G. E. Moore should have been murdered by Wittgenstein, as Ramsey certainly was. Heidegger died very properly at the hands of A. J. Ayer. It can be argued that Quine may indeed have murdered Strawson, however if he did, it could only have been with the assistance of Skinner. And Chomsky, well Chomsky may turn out to have killed nearly everyone he came into contact with.

That is another matter, however, and I shall say no more of it on this occasion. But before I come to the main subject of my lecture, which is 'The Perfect Murder', it is worth reminding my audience that such views as are expressed here are not likely to find favour with certain sections of the community. The gap which exists between the aesthetic ideals of this society and the dead letter of the law is dramatised, as I hope I may be excused for pointing out, by my absence. I must apologise for this. I did ask myself if I should take a risk and deliver my lecture in person. The answer was, more or less, 'What would be the chances of my being arrested and prevented from finishing my lecture?' With regret and out of respect to the memory of John Williams, I took the point.

It is for this reason that I am obliged to deliver this lecture via the Injupitersatellite now orbiting the earth. Perhaps then this event could be thought of as a form of extra-terrestrial communication: you, the inhabitants of the earth, receiving a message by mysterious processes from the stars. What could be more metaphysical?

Two hundred years ago, De Quincey described the seventeenth and eighteenth centuries as the Augustan Age of Murder — an age in which the fine art of murder flourished. A golden age of murder, so to speak. But what of our own age? Certainly the last hundred odd years have seen a greater quantity of murder than ever before. Has there also been an appreciable increase in the quality? Can we argue indeed that our times might have witnessed a renaissance in the art of murder?

Possibly. Let me begin by pointing out the huge influence that murder has had on all the other fine arts.

Cinema, now acknowledged as the dominant twentieth-century art form, has become a showcase for ingenious and well-choreographed murder, albeit fictional. Few of us bat an eyelid when we see a murder on the screen, no matter how realistic.

The crime novel and murder mystery have never been more popular than they are today. Art and photographic exhibitions routinely include depictions of murders and their victims. In the performing arts also, shows like *West Side Story*, *Sweeney Todd*, *The Phantom of the Opera*, *Jack!*, *Ian and Myra*, and *The Yorkshire Ripper* have all made music out of murderous subjects.

But it is not just Art that finds its single most important inspirational motif in Murder. The imitation or simulation of murder has become modern society's driving recreational force. An increasingly large number of

Reality Approximation video games actually provide the player with the impression that he is killing people, sometimes in their hundreds.

Elsewhere, television news-gathering services are regularly deployed to report on murders as they are detected and solved, following which their perpetrators become the stars of their own televised trials and punishment. Frequently it happens that their stories are turned into books which are then made into films. And thus real life fuels Art and the whole thing comes full circle again.

In this way we may see how fundamental murder actually is in our society. It is quite unthinkable that there should not be murder as that there should not be lying. And here lies its artistic importance. If murder has been an important source of artistic inspiration to the twentieth century, we can surely find instances where murder itself may be judged artistically.

That murder can exist within the concept of an artistic ideal is more generally accepted than might at first be realised. People discuss a concept of the perfect murder with much greater frequency than they ever do the perfect painting, or the perfect poem, or the perfect symphony. It might even be argued on this evidence alone that it is only the fine art of murder in which artistic perfection can be achieved at all.

Yet what is the substance of that perfection? Not merely that the murderer should get away with it, although that is undoubtedly important. Simply pushing a man off a cliff on a dark stormy night might well be hard to prove, but it hardly seems to fulfil the ideal that exists within the concept of the perfect murder. The perfect murder has, at its heart, a degree of difficulty in the problem of how to kill someone and get away with it; and also an ingenuity as to how this problem is solved and carried out.

Of course, it is these rare perfect murders which are the paradigm of artistry in homicide and it is ironic that while they continue to remain in a state of perfection –

that is, they are unsolved – the artistry must go unsung. It is only when they fall some way short of perfection that they may be celebrated at all.

Here is another argument for why murder must be considered as belonging to the finer arts. For almost every case of premeditated murder aims for that ideal of perfection. Murder allows for no compromise.

As I said earlier, the twentieth century has witnessed acts of murder on an unprecedented scale. Two world wars have served to devalue human life in general. Therefore it might seem unlikely that this last century should host a renaissance in the art of murder. Equally, there has been such a glut of assassinations in recent years that one might mistake quantity for quality. But there is little to be admired in the great majority of these murders, and most readers of the *News of the World* are satisfied with anything, provided it is bloody enough. Good taste, however, requires something more.

In searching for examples of murders which might distinguish this century from previous times, one must look around for some kind of yardstick as to how they may be judged. Here I think that one can do no better than to adopt De Quincey's own rough rule of thumb. Nerve is crucial, he tells us; and the degree of the murderer's audacity may be judged from the time and place of the murder. Thus, there is an art in killing a man on a busy street during broad daylight and remaining undetected. But most important of all, he argues, is the victim himself: he ought to be a good man, since only thus can the final artistic purpose of murder be demonstrated. This purpose is the same as that of tragedy which exists, in Aristotle's phrase, 'to cleanse the heart by means of pity and terror'. As De Quincey explains, how can there be any pity for one tiger who is destroyed by another tiger?

De Quincey shrinks from providing examples himself, as might be expected of a man whose familiarity with killing extended only as far as an attempt on the life of a tom cat.

On the other hand, I have no such scruples. It is true that I cannot claim to have killed any good men, whose deaths would arouse pity. The men I have killed would undoubtedly have killed many others. But still, you find your own murderous vocation where you can and my own personal tally of murders surpasses an attempt on a mere cat. I will, of course, be murdering in this fashion once again, at the conclusion of my lecture.

I think I may with some justification then, claim myself equal to the task of judging the artistic merit of other murders. But before I turn to an examination of various victims and their murderers, I must say just a few words about the means whereby murder is done.

The finest work of the nineteenth century, occurring so late in the century that it is tempting to regard them as belonging properly to the twentieth century are, without doubt the Whitechapel murders of 1888.

Nevertheless I am of the opinion that the nineteenth century's greatest artist was not equal to the best in that which followed. Jack the Ripper may have achieved the status of a legend, however I cannot consent to place him on the same level as Ramon Mercader – even his name sounds like murder – the man who assassinated Trotsky in 1940.

Trotsky, you will remember, had been expelled from the Soviet Communist Party following his defeat at the hands of Stalin for the Party leadership. Trotsky fled Russia and settled in Mexico City where he continued to oppose Stalin. None of these facts, however, would serve to make Trotsky's murder the work of art we judge it now. Our appreciation of this particular killing rests on one thing and one thing alone: Mercader's unique choice of murder weapon. For what Paganini was to the violin, so Mercader was to the ice-pick. An inspired selection and one with which Mercader carried our art to a point of colossal sublimity. Consider for a moment the sharp symbolism of his choice: a crude, proletarian tool so very much like the hammer and sickle that graphically represents the Bolshevik Revolution. Ice so common in Russia, and yet the privilege only of the wealthy in Mexico. It was almost as if Mercader was trying to remind Trotsky, living comfortably in Mexico City, of his own socialist origins. Then, reflect upon the physical area that was the subject of Mercader's assault, Trotsky's brain, the last repository of powerful opposition to Stalin. Acting through the person of Mercader, Stalin seems almost literally to be making the point to Trotsky that he will destroy all such counter-revolutionary thinking. The hard and unyielding tyrant's beak breaking upon the shell that contains the egg of opposition. Brilliant. Stalin rightly honoured this homicidal masterpiece by making Mercader a Hero of the Soviet Union. Can we do less than name Mercader as this century's greatest exponent of the fine art of murder?

But I feel there is one more murder of artistic merit which is worthy of mention, and that is the murder, in 1955, of David Blakely. He was the lover of Ruth Ellis who, having murdered him, was the last woman to be hanged for murder in England.

Blakely and Ellis had been lovers for two years. It was a turbulent, jealous relationship, with many infidelities on both sides. One night, Blakely left the Magnolia public house in Hampstead and found Ellis waiting for him with a revolver. She did not hesitate and shot Blakely several times at point-blank range. The artistic merit of this murder stems from a number of factors: the unfeminine choice of weapon, the unusual determination of the murderer herself and, of course (and most important of all), the singularity of the female artist. Just as it is difficult to find a female composer to rank alongside the likes of Mozart and Beethoven, or a female painter who stands as tall as Titian or Goya, so with the art of murder, there is a dearth of talent among the gentler sex.

Of course recent neurological research has revealed the

true reason for this absence of murderous instinct among women; and only time will tell if other aspects of creativity find similar explanation. But let us recognise a real contribution from a woman when one does occur and praise it accordingly.

You will recall that earlier on, I posed the question: Has the twentieth century witnessed a renaissance in the art of murder? Let me now answer this question.

There has been such a renaissance, but it is only one such as Walter Pater might have recognised in that I am describing a temperament, an inwardness of response that is in itself a new form of perception. This temperament declares the weightlessness of modern men and the precariousness of their prejudices. It recognises that all knowledge is merely provisional and that there is no essential truth save death itself. Anything is permissible which might reveal the soul of the artist, including murder.

This renaissance, this outbreak of the art of murder, identifies not the fruit of experience but, given its awful brevity, experience itself as an end. It breathes an atmosphere of absolute uncertainty, of continuous change, of new opinions, of a refusal to acquiesce in some facile orthodoxy. As Victor Hugo says, we are all under sentence of death, but with an indefinite reprieve. Therefore, with this particular renaissance, what we are seeing is an appetite for a quickened sense of life, a multiplied consciousness.

Writing in 1891, Oscar Wilde attributed the commonplace character of literature to the decay of lying as an art. More than a century later I feel I can celebrate a century's worth of literary and artistic excellence and attribute it to the renaissance of the murder as an art, a science, and a social pleasure.

And now, ladies and gentlemen, in conclusion, let me pass over the usual toasts to the Old Man of the Mountains, Charles the Hammer, the Jewish Sicarri, Burke and Hare, the Thugdom in all its branches, and give you my next victim, for I see that he is now abroad and so I must be about my business.

When Ocean Wharf, and other developments like it, was built, it seemed to herald a new lease of life for Docklands, an area which, at that time, had been in steep decline for over twenty years. It was but a temporary respite, but one bubble in the South Sea foam of bubbles that was the London property market of the late 1980s. Even before the last London brick had been laid, the final lick of paint applied to the mural of Churchill here, in the lobby of Winston Mansions, companies like the one which had built Ocean Wharf started to go bankrupt. And, as the years progressed and many of the other developments remained uncompleted, and the local council started to move more and more homeless families into flats which had once been on the market for hundreds of thousands of pounds, then dollars, buildings started to go unrepaired and prices tumbled even further.

The century came round a very sharp corner to find, once again, that Docklands was in steep decline. Indeed the decline seemed all the more dramatic because of all the money which had been spent trying to reclaim it for posterity, to no avail. As the first decade of the new millennium gave way to the second, there remained only a few isolated pockets of comparative affluence, like Ocean Wharf, in what was quickly becoming an urban nightmare of Orwellian proportions.

You might ask why, despite my wealth, I chose to come and live here, in what are virtually siege-like conditions: the architects who designed this development could never have foreseen that one day, Ocean Wharf would be surrounded by an electrified fence. Nor could they have ever envisaged that this would have been *necessitated by a local crime rate equivalent to that of New York's infamous South Bronx.*

Staring out of my seventh-floor window here in Winston Mansions, insulated from most sound and unfiltered air, it was hard to know what it was they had envisaged when first they constructed their models. Did they ever imagine shops and stores closed down for lack of business, looted of all their fittings, becoming the first outposts of whole shanty towns of anarchic youth? Could they ever have thought that their neat little parklands with their brightly painted benches and streetlamps would one day be wastelands of abandoned cars and fly tips? And those pieces of plastic, those human replicas which had seemed to happily people the balsa wood scale models — what would the architects have said if they had been told of the statistical probability that each one of them was engaged in the commission of a crime? It was well-named, this Isle of Dogs. 'Weialala leia Wallala leialala' went the police car's siren as it chased some lawless thugs across the unreal cityscape.

And yet it was for all these local attractions that I chose to come and live here. I had a vast amount of comfortable living space at my disposal, and at a very reasonable price too. Most important of all, I could indulge my taste for an outsider's existence, of living on the very edge of things, in the clean margin of a very dirty notebook. And yet still very handy for central London.

Sweet Thames, run softly till I end my song. Standing here, looking out across the river I found it easy to imagine myself singled out, alone. I have a temperamental hunger for solipsism. With me this is no intellectual posture, but a moral and mystical attitude, so strong that if I were to injure my leg it would lame my thoughts. For after all, knowing pain means being advised by some feature of our pain as to its whereabouts and being able to describe it. In the same way my kinesthetic sensations advise me of the movement and position of my limbs.

I let my index finger make an easy gathering movement

of small amplitude. I either hardly feel it, or don't feel it at all: but perhaps just a little, in the end of the finger, as a slight tension. Does this sensation advise me of the movement? For even without seeing I can describe the movement exactly. I must feel it, to know it – that seems certain. But knowing it only means being able to describe it.

Now if that same finger makes the same movement, but this time against the trigger of my gun, a slight pressure and metallic coldness against the flesh of my finger can advise me that it and the trigger are indeed moving. And watching the collapse of a man's body in front of me, his head machine-gunning the air with blood, enables me, even without watching my finger, to know that it has moved at least once.

But to know that it has moved six times is not a matter of keeping count: the gun is almost silent, as I have described earlier. The ears are nevertheless affected more strongly than by silence. I don't feel this in my ears, yet it has this effect. I know the number of the sounds because, after six, I move quickly in another direction.

15

'Absolutely not,' said Jake. She stared at Mark Woodford and Professor Waring with a mixture of surprise and contempt. 'No way. I'm sorry.'

'The Minister thought it was a good idea,' Woodford said smoothly.

Jake shook her head firmly. 'The Minister's not investigating this case. I am, and I think it stinks.'

The meeting took place several days after Mr Parmenides had come to the Yard with Wittgenstein's *A-Z*, in the Minister's rooms at the Home Office, overlooking St James's Park. Grace Miles was not present, as she was opening a new police station at her constituency in Birmingham.

Jake sat back in her chair and glanced uncomfortably around her. She wondered about the incongruity of the room's sleek, modern furniture, the cheap green china, and the pair of elephant tusks that were mounted on one of the beige-coloured walls. She thought this last item rather tasteless given that the elephant was now all but extinct, the few remaining kept in private zoos and safari parks. It was her favourite animal. She thought it ought to have been every policeman's favourite animal, on the basis that an elephant never forgets. And here were these bastards asking her to do just that. To forget all about catching Wittgenstein.

Mark Woodford sighed and avoiding Jake's eyes, inflated his lips thoughtfully. 'Normally we pretty much go along with the constitutional separation of powers,' he said, feigning some awkwardness. 'Legislative, executive . . .'

'Spare me the constitutional lecture,' said Jake. 'I know what they are.'

'All right then,' he said. 'But there are circumstances in which the legislative function might feel obliged to interfere in the workings of one of the other governmental functions.'

'I think what you're trying to say,' said Jake, 'is that you'll have me taken off the case. Is that it?'

'Yes,' said Waring.

'Go ahead and try,' said Jake. 'You know, I've always wanted to try my hand at journalism.'

Woodford smiled placatingly. 'There's no question of that surely, Chief Inspector.' He leaned across the table and folded his hands impatiently. 'Look, I don't understand what your objection is. Professor Waring's suggestion might solve all of our problems.'

'Everyone except Wittgenstein's.'

Woodford shrugged. 'I can't say I care much about his problems,' he said. 'The last victim, Hegel, makes it twelve people he's killed, for God's sake.'

'Maybe so,' said Jake. 'But he's still got some rights. There is still a proper way of doing things. And even if it could work, which I doubt, your way would just sweep it all under the rug. What is more, if it didn't work, he might break off contact with us altogether. Go underground for a while and then start this business all over again in about two years' time. Worse still, you'll end up making a legend out of this man, just like Jack the Ripper became a legend when he disappeared.'

'Look, just listen to the professor explain the idea to you himself,' Woodford insisted. 'Hear him out, please.'

Jake shrugged. 'Go ahead. But I can't see that it'll make much difference. Saint Francis could explain this to me and it would still smell like shit.'

Professor Waring glanced questioningly at Mark Woodford, who nodded at him as if to say that he ought to give it a try anyway. Woodford opened a file in front of him and started to turn the pages.

'From a reading of all the transcripts of your telephone conversations with Wittgenstein, and from everything we know about him, I have formed a very distinct impression of the kind of character we are dealing with.

'In many ways, he is like patients I have met before, in custody. My own clinical research has revealed that his type is commonly suicidal. His placing no value on the life of others, makes it probable that he places little value on his own.'

He cleared his throat as he approached what Jake knew to be the more delicate part of his thesis.

'In this particular case, I'm certain of it. And given the killer's identification with or delusion that he is Ludwig Wittgenstein, I see no reason why we may not turn his aggression against society towards himself. After all, one of Wittgenstein's brothers committed suicide and he himself had suicidal tendencies. I think that it is entirely feasible that Sir Jameson Lang might successfully maintain an argument for the killer to take his own life.'

Waring shook his head uncertainly.

'As to the moral-judicial issues that the chief inspector mentions, I think we must keep before us the very real danger to society of allowing him to remain unchecked. Naturally, as a doctor I have reservations about recommending this particular course of action. It might be argued that it runs counter to my own Hippocratic oath. But that oath is worth nothing if it allows an even greater loss of life. And really, Chief Inspector, don't you honestly think it would be better to kill yourself than to be sentenced to a lifetime's punitive coma? I know which option I would prefer.'

'That's rich,' Jake sneered at him, 'considering that you were on the Home Office Select Committee that recommended implementing coma as a viable punishment.'

Waring frowned and looked at Woodford. 'Perhaps the chief inspector is concerned that without an arrest at the end of her investigation, her career progress might be held up.'

'That has nothing to do with it,' she said quickly.

Woodford smiled thinly and helped himself to a rich tea biscuit. 'Look, I understand what it must be like for you,' he said. 'You've given everything to this case with a very definite end in mind. And now we come along and suggest a different sort of goal. Well, I can see how it would be very frustrating. Nobody expected you to be happy about it.'

'You're damned right I'm not happy about it. Look, you people can do what you like, but I still intend going after Wittgenstein in my own way.' To that end, Jake had already decided to say nothing of how Parmenides had brought her Wittgenstein's list of targets, and of how these were being kept under permanent watch.

Woodford shrugged. 'Well we certainly can't stop you doing your duty,' he said.

'And what about Sir Jameson Lang?' she asked. 'What does he have to say about your little scheme? He doesn't strike me as the type to go along with what you're proposing. Technically speaking, this is a conspiracy to commit an unlawful homicide.'

'That's a bit melodramatic, isn't it?' said Woodford.

'And as for Sir Jameson Lang,' said Waring, 'you leave him to us.' He turned to Woodford. 'I'll call him this afternoon.'

Jake stood up, pressing her chair away with the backs of her legs.

'Murder,' she said quietly. 'And don't kid yourselves that it's something else. Even Wittgenstein doesn't do that.'

The lift down from the top floor was a slow one and by the time Jake reached the ground, she had all but recovered her temper. A security woman searched her and then, glancing at a computer screen, checked to see that Jake had not left any unauthorised bags or packages behind her.

While she waited for her security clearance, Jake surveyed the many Russians and East Europeans waiting patiently in the lobby for whichever jobsworth Home Office clerk would interrogate them about their status. She knew that some of them would have been waiting there for several days in order to prove that they were in Britain legally. No one cared much for their comfort or their convenience. No one tried to make the whole process less indifferent than it already was. Small wonder, thought Jake, that people sometimes got violent.

When her clearance arrived, she walked out of the petrol-pump-shaped building onto Tothill Street, turning almost immediately right towards New Scotland Yard and the famous revolving cheese on a pole which had identified it in a hundred television series. The silver cheese caught the hot midday sun at regular intervals, flashing at her like a slow stroboscopic light. She wondered why that particular image seemed to be significant.

Back in her own office at the Yard, Jake called the lab.

'Maurice? Where are we on that autoradiograph?' she asked. 'Has the computer matched an identity card with the sample yet?'

'I wish you'd make up your mind,' he snarled back. 'You mean you want to start the DNA-matching program again?'

'What do you mean again?' she asked. 'Who told you to stop?'

'You did. I got a signed memo from you just yesterday. You told me to send you the graph too.'

'And did you?'

'You mean you haven't got it?'

Jake was beginning to smell a rat. 'Maurice. I'd like you to find that memo and then bring it to my office. Immediately.'

She waited several minutes and then he called back.

Even on the pictophone screen, she could see he looked worried.

'Is this some kind of joke?' he said. 'Because I've got better things to do, lady.'

'It's no joke,' Jake said. 'Well? Did you find the memo?'

'Funny thing,' he said. 'I've looked everywhere, and I can't locate it.'

'You say that the memo arrived on your computer screen yesterday, right?'

'Yes,' he said. 'I copied it onto my dayfile and made a hard copy to attach to the autoradiograph.'

'So what you're saying is that someone's been into your office and erased the record from your dayfile's memory.'

Maurice shrugged uncomfortably. 'Looks that way,' he said. 'But who would do a thing like that?'

'I've a pretty shrewd idea,' said Jake.

'Maybe I should report this.'

Jake thought for a moment. While she couldn't see Woodford or Waring snooping around the lab and erasing files from a technician's PC, she had the feeling that they were behind it. No doubt there were others who were prepared to carry out their orders: police officers who did not wish to see the Lombroso Program and, as a corollary, the Government's much-vaunted law and order platform irreparably damaged. As it certainly would be when the true facts became known of how Wittgenstein had exploited the very system that had been designed to control him.

No doubt these same people would have preferred that Wittgenstein be dealt with rather more discreetly than an arrest and trial allowed. It was bad enough that Woodford and Waring were intent on having Wittgenstein remove himself from the equation. But it seemed infinitely worse that there should be policemen who were willing to obstruct evidence in order that they should be given sufficient time in which to carry out this intention. What was clear was that if she wished to continue with her investigation, then she would have to move more subtly than any inquiry into missing evidence would permit.

'No, Maurice,' she said. 'Leave it with me for the moment, will you?'

He looked relieved. Gratitude made him more respectful. 'Yes, certainly Chief Inspector. Anything you say. I've more than enough work to do anyway, without answering a lot of questions.'

Jake ended their conversation with a push of a button. It seemed that she could no longer rely on catching Wittgenstein through the genetic fingerprint on his identity card. But nor could she simply sit back and hope that one of the police teams watching the various London addresses which he had marked in his A-Z would get lucky. She reminded herself that being a detective meant that one was never satisfied with what one already had: that the process of enquiry was, of necessity, a continuing one. Quite simply it was a matter of reassessing something because there was absolutely no logical reason to do so.

She turned to face her own computer screen and called up all her own case notes to check that nothing was missing. There wasn't a great deal on the file, but everything she remembered was still there. Having accessed her notes, she decided to re-read them and so, page by page, Jake went through the file, hoping that some new line of enquiry might occur to her now. There was something in her mind of what Sir Jameson Lang had said about the real Wittgenstein's preference for the more intuitive detective. Perhaps she herself could be more intuitive now. She knew from previous cases how, when an investigation was over, you could look back through the notes and see something you ought to have known was significant – something that had been there all along, just waiting to be noticed. She hit the 'page-down' button. Something so small she might have ignored it. Something she might have misunderstood, concerning the use of words perhaps. To some extent a detective's job was a grammatical one. To shed light on a problem by clearing misunderstandings and ambiguities away, not to mention lies. She felt almost as if she were directing herself not towards phenomena but, as one might say, to the possibilities of phenomena.

Jake smiled to herself. She was beginning to sound like Sir Jameson Lang. Well maybe he was right. Maybe a detective was a kind of philosopher and her criminal investigation was, in reality, a philosophical investigation. Perhaps it had been that all along.

She needed a cigarette but found that she had run out. She had meant to buy another packet on her way back from the Home Office, only Woodford and Waring's callous little suggestion had put it out of her mind. Cursing them both, Jake grabbed her bag and went outside again.

The roar of the traffic on Victoria Street robbed Jake momentarily of her bearings. It was force of habit that turned her to the right, towards her usual source of supply for smokes and good coffee, the Chestnut Tree Café.

In front of the Brain Research Institute, her arms folded against the draft from a passing water-tanker, Jake crossed the road. But as she made for the café's open door she found her footsteps slowing.

On the pavement, near to his monstrous black beetle of a machine, sat a motorcycle messenger, drinking from a large Styrofoam cup of steaming tea. Jake paused as she recollected that her Gynocide Squad was still trying to catch the motorcycle messenger who had murdered several office receptionists. But it was not this which had attracted her attention. It was what this grimy-faced youth was balancing on his leather-trousered knees. An A-Z London street atlas.

'Yeah?' said the youth, frowning as he noticed Jake's attention. 'What?' He looked himself over as if checking that he had not caught fire.

'Do you need any assistance?' Jake said, half to herself.

'I'm sorry?'

Then she had nodded at the man's *A-Z*.

'No, it's all right,' said the messenger, his tone and expression making it clear that he thought Jake was probably mad. 'I er . . . know where I'm going. All right?'

Jake went into the café and bought the cigarettes. But her thoughts were somewhere else. She had suddenly realised that this was where Wittgenstein had met her. Here, in the Chestnut Tree Café. She had dropped her change and he had helped her to pick it up. No wonder he had been able to recognise her perfume. She had been so close to him. Their hands had actually touched.

Breathless with excitement, Jake sat down at the table where he had been sitting, lit one of her cigarettes and then glanced through the window. From here he would have had a perfect view of anyone going in or out of the Institute. He might even have come in here after his own Lombroso test.

Wittgenstein's face lay half-melted across the hard edge of her mind's eye, Jake thought, like one of the soft watches in Salvador Dali's painting *The Persistence of Memory*. She roped her brain tightly onto the rack and tried to stretch out a full and accurate account of what she remembered.

When she could think no more she walked quickly back to the Yard. Seated behind her desk again she called up the ComputaFit pictures of Wittgenstein on the screen of her terminal and compared her own mental image of the man in the café with the ones which had been constructed by Clare and Grubb after the murder of Descartes in Soho. Then she looked at the ComputaFit obtained from Doctor Chen, Wittgenstein's psychotherapist at the Institute, through hypnosis.

Of the three pictures, the one that most matched her own memory was Chen's. So much for Professor Gleitmann's opinion that Chen's unconscious mind had lied.

She wondered if she had devoted enough time to Chen. He was after all, the only person who had spoken at length to the killer. There could be no question that his hypnosis had been handled expertly. But had enough account been taken of the language barrier? Chen spoke excellent English, but was it his first language? Was it English that his subconscious mind used, or Chinese? Might that not make a difference to his answers to her questions? Questions which, directed to his subconscious, were also directed towards the essence of language. Might not those questions see in the essence only something that already lay open to view and that became surveyable by a rearrangement? But what about what lay beneath the surface of his answers? Was there something that lay within, which could be seen when you looked into it and which further analysis might dig out?

Perhaps that was why the stroboscopic light effect on the silver cheese outside the Yard had seemed significant.

Jake called the Brain Research Institute and asked to speak to Doctor Chen. She asked him if he minded being hypnotised once again, only this time she wanted to question him and for him to answer in Chinese.

'What you're saying' – Chen grinned – 'is that you think there's something wrong with the way I speak English.'

Jake smiled back at him and shook her head.

'Not at all. Look,' she said, 'you learned English, right?'

He nodded.

'But you grew up speaking Chinese?'

'Yes.'

'These are very different languages.'

'Only on the surface,' he said. 'Man is a syntactical animal, surely. And all languages share the same deep structure. The genetic universal grammar, as it were. The blueprint for language that's in every newborn baby's mind. It's the merest accident that I grew up speaking Chinese rather than English.'

'Agreed,' said Jake. 'However my enquiry here relates

to linguistic use. And that's a factual question. I need to know how form and function interact. I have to try and understand your intentions. For instance, how what you say relates to the reality you have perceived.'

They were in Chen's office at the Institute. Jake was accompanied by Sergeant Chung who was setting up the stroboscopic light on Chen's desk.

'I want to speak to your unconscious in your natural language,' she added. 'The translation will be done by Sergeant Chung at a conscious level.'

Chen shrugged. 'All right,' he said. 'I'll give it a try, if you think it will help.' He smiled inquisitively. 'Are you planning to try and induce the trance yourself?'

'Yes,' said Jake. 'I have a master's in Psychology. Rest assured, I've done this before. But we'll forgo the use of an intravenous substance this time. I don't much like them, and of course you'll be able to return to what you were doing, almost as soon as we've finished here.'

Chen nodded and settled back in his armchair as Jake switched on the light.

There is a popular misconception that good hypnotic subjects tend to be weak-willed acquiescent individuals who are given to submissive behaviour. But it is entirely the opposite state of affairs which is true: the more intelligent make the more susceptible hypnotic subjects, having a greater capacity for concentration than weaker-minded people. Chen was an easy subject and highly absorptive which, as Jake was aware, indicated a developed imagination.

When she was satisfied that she had induced the hypnotic trance, she explained that she wanted to ask him some questions in Chinese and that he would hear another voice next. She told him that he should answer in Chinese and that he should now nod if he understood.

Chen nodded slowly, and then they began.

'Would you please ask him if he remembers the patient codenamed Wittgenstein,' Jake instructed Chung.

Chung translated the question into his own language.

Jake thought that Chinese, with its high and low sounds existing so close together, sounded like someone trying to tune an old radio. Listening to the pair of them jabbering away, Jake found it hard to accept that Chinese could have anything in common with English, even at the deep, genetically preprogrammed level.

'Ask him if he can remember some of the things Wittgenstein said.'

Maybe she was wasting her time. Here she was, trying to investigate how language represents reality and yet she had given no consideration to the question of how anything manages to represent anything. It was not something they taught you at the Hendon Police Training College. Not something that anyone taught, except maybe people like Sir Jameson Lang. And just how far should any criminal investigation go? Had she not already gone a lot further than she was supposed to?

'Ask him to describe Wittgenstein once again,' she told Chung. 'Let's see if we didn't miss something.'

Once again Chung translated her question, frowning fiercely as he spoke. What was there about the Chinese language, Jake wondered, that seemed to make people irritated while they were speaking it? Chen sighed and then drooled slightly while he thought of his answer. He spoke hesitantly, adding one word to another and then another, almost at random.

'Brown raincoat,' Chung repeated. 'Brown shoes, good ones. Brown tweed jacket, with leather bits on the elbows. He doesn't know what you call them. A special word. Not badges. Like badges.'

'Patches?' said Jake.

'Maybe, yes.' Chung craned his head forwards so as not to miss the rest of Chen's speech.

'White shirt. No, not a shirt. Like a pullover, but not like a pullover. A pullover with a polo neck. But not made of wool. Made of the same material as a shirt.' Chung shrugged. 'A white polo neck anyway.'

Chung's words seemed to touch something deep within Jake's own memory.

It was curious that Wittgenstein had mentioned her perfume, because a sense of smell – something clinical and antiseptic – was what she remembered most about him now.

'Yat,' she said, 'ask Doctor Chen if it's the same kind of white polo neck that a dentist might wear.'

Chung translated and then, hearing Chen's reply, nodded.

'Yes, he could have been a dentist.'

Jake shook her head.

She had offered to help Wittgenstein and he had smiled at her with what he might have thought looked like confidence. But what Jake had seen had been teeth that were scaled and yellow – teeth that were badly in need of dental work.

'No,' she said thoughtfully. 'I don't think he's a dentist. His teeth aren't good enough. I've never ever seen a dentist with bad teeth.

'Yat, you remember you said that the only way the killer could have broken into the Lombroso system would have been if he was using a computer that was already on the EC Data Network?'

'Sure.'

'Ask Doctor Chen if he thinks that Wittgenstein might be a male nurse or some other kind of hospital auxiliary staff?'

Chung put the question and Chen replied that he thought he probably was.

'Just like the real Wittgenstein,' said Jake. 'He worked in a hospital for a while, during the Second World War. It was one of the reasons that enabled him to avoid being imprisoned as an enemy alien.'

Chung shook his head. 'That's the trouble with you British,' he said. 'It was the same with the boat people back in Hong Kong. You always locking people up who couldn't possibly do you any bloody harm.'

Jake brought Chen out of the trance.

'Find anything useful in there?' he said pleasantly.

Jake explained her hunch about Wittgenstein working at a hospital.

'Pleased to hear it,' he said, and then stood up and stretched.

'Well,' said Jake, looking at her watch. 'I think we've taken up enough of your time, Doctor Chen. I'm grateful.' It was probably too late to find anyone still working at the Ministry of Health.

'No problem,' he said again. 'Next time see if you can't help me to stop smoking.'

Jake and Chung returned to the office they used when they were at the Institute, where Jake called the Ministry. She found herself connected with a picture of an impossibly fit and healthy looking girl in a leotard, and an incongruously brusque male voice on an answering-machine which informed her that the Ministry was closed until nine o'clock the following morning.

'Well I guess that's it until tomorrow,' said Jake. 'Thanks a lot for your help, Yat. I really think that was useful.'

'Don't mention it,' he said. 'Translation makes a nice change from computers.'

They walked back to the Yard.

'Your train goes from Paddington, doesn't it?' said Jake. 'Can I offer you a lift?'

'Thanks,' he said. 'But only on one condition. That you let me take you to the best Chinese restaurant in Soho first. It's owned by a cousin of mine.'

Jake grinned. 'All right. It's a deal. But won't your wife be waiting for you?'

Chung smiled back. 'Her mother's staying with us at the moment. She thinks her daughter should not have married a man from Hong Kong.'

'It's because she's narrow-minded,' Jake offered.

'No.' Chung laughed. 'It's because she's never eaten at my cousin's restaurant.'

My brain hurts. Really, it does.

But is it any wonder? Is it any wonder when there are over 30,000 different kinds of protein swilling around in there? Is it any wonder it hurts when you consider that one gram of brain tissue uses up more energy in keeping you conscious than a gram of muscle uses to lift a barbell? When you consider that your brain consumes about a quarter of all the calories you use in a day?

But before you calorie-conscious people start getting excited and reaching for your philosophy textbooks, let me quickly add that bending your brain to understanding something like Maurice Merleau-Ponty's The Phenomenology of Perception *uses no more calories than having a dump, or picking your nose. Unfortunately for fatties, the fact is most of the calories get used in just keeping the old head-set humming, otherwise G. E. Moore might unwittingly have been responsible for the world's first Cambridge diet.*

Even so it seems to me that my own Gulliver must have been putting in a lot of overtime lately. Sustained thought on the subject of Murder during the last few months must have been using that little bit more energy. Thus the skull-fracturing headache.

The problem is that brain cells are determinedly social. They will insist on speaking to their neighbours – up to 100,000 of them at any one time. And with all the mental sensation that is the inevitable corollary of mass-murder, the electrical firing that's been going on inside the central coconut must look like the sky above El Alamein.

If only the brain wasn't such an efficient little bastard – just 2 per cent of body weight, as a matter of fact. In my case that's about 1.7 kilograms. It will insist on making hundreds of back-up copies of thoughts – even the thoughts one had hoped one had forgotten – storing them in all sorts of different neuronal nooks and cranial crannies. It is like a prudent man going abroad who, having considered the possibility of being robbed, separates his cash and spreads it throughout his luggage and person. This is why when one part of the brain is physically destroyed, for example that part dealing with the recognition of colour, there's another part of the brain which can manage it just as well.

Try as I might to prevent it, my more murderous brain cells just love talking to the others, poisoning them with their logical pictures of the facts in an attempt to win them round to their cause.

This brings me no small discomfort. Insomnia being the worst torment. Sometimes I lie awake the greater part of the night, watching them at work. It's easy enough to spot when something's happening. All thought becomes an image, and the soul becomes a body. Thought actually manifests itself in little hot spots that are the colour of blood. Recently there's been a lot more of this colour than normal and the other night, the inside of my dome resembled one of those volcanic lava flows that sometimes spew out of Mount Etna and engulf a couple of local villages.

The chief area of neuronal discussion seems to be that I should move on from killing my brothers and start on the human race in general. A sort of business expansion scheme. This seems to me to be a lamentable trend and one which worries me considerably. I had hoped that I could keep things in check a bit, but of course lacking a VMN, ultimately this may not be possible. It may be that in time I shall be forced to close down the company altogether.

16

They drove to Soho and ended up parking as far away as St James's Square. Chung apologised for the distance to his cousin's restaurant.

'I don't mind walking a bit,' said Jake. 'Frankly, I could use the exercise.'

'Me too,' he agreed. 'Although I do manage to work out a bit at home. I've got a heavy punch bag hanging from the ceiling in the garage. I give that a good kicking in the morning. Lately I've been imagining that it's my mother-in-law.'

'They walked up the short hill that led onto Jermyn Street and turned east towards Regent Street and Piccadilly Circus.

Opposite Simpson's, Jake paused in front of red brick office building and nodded at the smoked glass door.

'A girl was murdered in there,' she said. 'Just a month or two ago. It's hard to believe, isn't it?' She glanced up and down the street. 'It all seems so peaceful, so civilised, so very . . .' Her eyes alighted on the black wall of St James's Church.

'What is it?' asked Chung.

Jake shook her head vaguely. 'Nothing,' she said, but started to retrace her steps in the direction of the church's curiously theatre-like door. 'At least, I don't think it's anything.'

In front of the church, which seemed hardly like a church at all with its bulletin board of visiting speakers, Jake considered the matter syllogistically, as two separate premises. She could not see how the conclusion she had in mind might logically follow these. But even as she told herself that such an invalid conversion would of course lead to an invalid judgment, she remained convinced of the possibility that the thing might be tested empirically. The question was: how?

Seeing her momentarily absorbed like this, Chung remained silent, even when he was obliged to follow her as she walked through the church, out into the stone-flagged courtyard on the other side, and across Piccadilly. She led him up Sackville Street and stopped outside the Mystery Bookshop which, even at that time of the evening, was busy with browsing customers. He noticed that she was smiling a little now and when finally she spoke again, there was a quiet look of triumph in her face.

'Crime is common,' she said. 'Logic is rare.'

'Are you going to tell me what's going on?' he demanded. 'Or shall I just call you an ambulance?'

'It is upon the logic rather than upon the crime that you should dwell.' She pointed not to the Mystery Bookshop, which Chung felt might have better suited her cryptic remark, but to the doner-kebab restaurant next door. A man was writing some prices onto the inside of the window with what looked like a piece of red crayon. The name above the door was Parmenides.

'Would you mind very much if we ate Greek rather than Chinese?' she said.

'Not at all. So long as you tell me what the hell you're up to.'

'Certainly, but let's get off the street. He mustn't see us yet.' She led him into the doorway of a nearby tailor's shop. 'The man in the restaurant window is called Kyriakos Parmenides,' she explained. 'But his Lombroso-given name is William Shakespeare.'

'He's VMN-negative?'

Jake nodded. 'A few weeks ago, Wittgenstein followed him to St James's Church, back there, where he planned to shoot him. But Parmenides scared him off and while he was making his escape, Wittgenstein left behind his A-Z of London. This contained the addresses of all his potential victims who lived here.

'Parmenides found it lying in a church pew where Wittgenstein had been sitting. Well then, after a while, he realised the significance of the book, and like a good citizen handed it into the police.

'But consider this, Yat: Parmenides works next door to a bookshop from where, one hour before she was horribly murdered, Mary Woolnoth bought a paperback novel. When Wittgenstein attempted to shoot Parmenides, he was sitting in a church that's not twenty metres from the office where Mary's naked body was found. The killer wrote on her body with a red lipstick. And he was left-handed.'

Jake leaned out of the doorway and nodded at the restaurant window.

'And there he is, also left-handed, writing a menu on his windowpane with what looks like a piece of red lipstick.'

Chung nodded. 'I see what you mean,' he said.

'Jessie Weston, the girl he killed before Mary Woolnoth, was also a murder mystery novel fan. I can't prove it yet, but I wouldn't mind betting that she also bought a book in that shop. Which is where he saw her. I wouldn't mind betting that all the murdered girls came down this street at some time or another prior to their deaths.'

'It's an interesting hypothesis,' agreed Chung. 'But it all sounds a bit circumstantial.'

'If I'm right, it should be easy enough to push him out into the open.'

'What have you got in mind?'

'Are you carrying a gun?'

'Of course. I'm a copper, aren't I?'

'All right, here's what I want you to do. Go in there and order something to eat. I'll follow you in a couple of minutes. But when I do, act like you'd never seen me before.'

Chung crossed the road and went inside the restaurant.

Jake walked towards the Mystery Bookshop.

A free-standing display card in the window announced that four leading crime writers were in-store to sign copies of their latest novels. As she came through the door, Jake glanced briefly at the names and then the matching men and women who were seated at a long table behind large stacks of their new books. She recognised none of them. Each author stared hopefully at Jake as she swept by their table. Only she wasn't planning to buy anything. She wasn't even going to so much as look at a book.

Jake smiled at the idea of these four self-important crime writers sitting there like a panel of television pundits, forgotten by the general public and largely ignored by the shop's other customers, while next door a real-life multiple killer was about to be provoked into betraying himself.

She found what she was looking for in front of those few shelves which were a temporary home to post-modernist crime novels.

The woman was a tall, strong-looking brunette, wearing a tight denim shirt and skirt. Jake's eyes caught the curve of her bare breast between the pearl buttons. Bright red lipstick gave her a cheap, tarty appearance.

'Recognise me?' Jake asked in lowered tones.

The WPC glanced at Jake uncertainly, glanced outside and then nodded.

'What's your name?'

'WPC 548 Edwards,' said the woman.

'Where's your surveillance team, Edwards?'

'They're outside, ma'am, in a blue van.'

'Are you wearing a wire?'

The WPC nodded.

'Good. So everyone can hear me now. This is Chief Inspector Jakowicz speaking. I've reason to believe that the man we're looking for, the Lipstick Killer, works in the kebab restaurant next door.'

WPC Edwards frowned. 'That figures, ma'am,' she said quietly. 'I was in there the other day, buying a cup of coffee, and one of those fellows behind the counter gave me the weirdest look.'

'Have you a red lipstick on you?'

The WPC nodded, rummaged in her shoulder bag and then handed it over.

'WPC Edwards and myself are going next door now,' Jake explained to her hidden audience. 'There's a Detective Sergeant Chung who's already in there. Your orders are these: be ready for him outside if he tries to make a bolt for it.'

'What are you planning to do, ma'am?'

'You'll see.'

Jake led the way past the table of unsigned books and their self-pitying authors, and out of the shop. She paused as she caught sight of the blue surveillance van and, as if on cue, the passenger's window slid down to reveal the face of Detective Inspector Ed Crawshaw. He made a thumbs-up sign. Jake nodded back at him and, followed by the WPC, turned into the kebab restaurant.

It was the smell of olive oil she noticed first. Then Chung seated quietly in a corner, studiously chewing his way through a large and well-stuffed pitta-bread.

Parmenides's hospitable smile faded a little when he recognised that one of the two customers standing in front of his stainless-steel counter was Jake. On a shelf behind him stood a large bottle of the Sacred Oil Company's extra-virgin olive oil.

'Hello, Chief Inspector,' he said nervously. 'What can I do for you?' He glanced at WPC Edwards, swallowed hard, and added: 'Have you caught this fellow yet? The one who followed me?'

'Not yet, no,' said Jake. She tilted her head sideways, towards the WPC. 'Actually I just met an old friend of mine, in the bookshop next door, and we thought we'd come in here for a coffee.'

Parmenides seemed to relax a little. He pointed at one of the Formica tables ranged along the mirrored wall.

'Please,' he said. 'I'll bring them over. Cappuccino? Espresso?'

'Two cappuccinos, I think,' said Jake.

The Greek bowed slightly and set about the operation of the machine.

The two women seated themselves on opposite sides of a table. Jake paid no attention to Chung. Instead she picked up a copy of the *Evening Standard* which had been left on a chair, and laid it on the table. As soon as he had turned his back to the tables Jake produced the lipstick and wrote the name 'MARY' in large red capital letters onto the cream-coloured table top. She then covered this with the newspaper.

After a couple of minutes the Greek came over bearing the two coffee cups. Smiling he bent forward to lay them down and at the same time Jake pulled away the newspaper to reveal Mary's name.

Belshazzar could not have looked more shocked. Parmenides's face drained of colour. First his jaw dropped, then the two coffees. He turned and ran towards the door, snatching a long knife from off the counter top as he went, with Jake, WPC Edwards and Chung in close pursuit.

Outside in the street Jake drew her weapon and shouted after him to surrender. He kept on running, and seeing his way impeded by two more men waving guns and badges, he raised the knife.

Jake stopped still, steadied her arm and aimed low. She saw Crawshaw and the other officer move smartly away from her line of fire. She felt the cold first pressure of the trigger, caught her breath for a millisecond, and then squeezed.

He catapulted forward onto the pavement, clutching at an instantly bloody thigh. Crawshaw moved in quickly to kick the knife away. Not that it mattered. Even before Jake had got to Parmenides where he lay on the pavement, even before she saw the wound, she knew that the bullet had severed the man's femoral artery – the sheer quantity of blood told her that much.

Underneath the stubble the Greek's face was deathly pale. He did not look as if he was in pain, rather that he had been somehow anaesthetised. His eyes focused briefly on Jake, flickered, closed and then opened again. For just a moment he seemed to smile at her. It was a smile she had seen once before, when her father was dying of a brain tumour. A smile, replete with silent contempt.

Crawshaw tore off his scarf and using his truncheon as a capstan made a quick tourniquet round the wounded thigh. He did his best to stem the flow of blood, but the wound was too severe and the man was dead even before WPC Edwards had finished radioing for an ambulance.

Jake walked to the unmarked police van where, according to the regulations, she calmly handed Chung her automatic. 'For the inquiry,' she explained.

Chung nodded and put the gun into his pocket.

'I only meant to wound him,' she heard herself say. 'He had the knife. I thought he meant to use it when he saw the other two officers.'

'You done right,' he said. 'You warned him and then aimed low. That's what you're supposed to do. It's just too bad you hit him there. A centimetre either way and right now he'd be sitting on the pavement and calling you all sorts of fucking names.'

Jake sat on the edge of the van and considered her reaction to having killed a man. She thought she ought to have felt worse about it, despite the fact that Parmenides had murdered six women. That was awkward too. A confession might have made things just that little bit more convenient. As it was, she realised that she would now have to hope that the scenes-of-crime officers would find evidence that would help to convince a coroner's court that her action had been justified.

By now the street, suddenly cordoned off at both ends, was full of policemen helping to bolt the stable door. Jake wondered how it was they had contrived to be on the scene quite so quickly. Then she remembered that Vine Street station was only round the corner. That would be where she would have to go now to make her statement.

'You all right?' said Chung anxiously.

Jake looked at him, frowning with puzzlement.

'Me? I'm fine.'

It was almost twelve by the time she arrived back home from Vine Street. Everything in the flat seemed cold and lonely, but the central heating was soon working and she was glad that she would not have to explain what she had done to anyone else. The pictophone rang a couple of times, but she ignored it. Instead she turned on the television and poured out a large glass of whisky to try and divert her thoughts.

She ought to have known that the midnight television news would cover the shooting. But there was no reason for her to have suspected that the coverage would be quite so brutal and voyeuristic. She was aware that programmes shown after midnight were not obliged to conform to any broadcasting guidelines. This meant that late-night television was comprised mostly of pornographic films. Jake had no idea that the same freedom extended to news broadcasts.

The crew had arrived on the scene in Sackville Street less than fifteen minutes after Jake had left it. Dealing with the incident chronologically, they filmed first the kebab restaurant and then the pavement along which Parmenides had run. Next they filmed his knife, followed by a gun: not Jake's Beretta automatic which had accompanied her to Vine Street, but another identical weapon as shown by one of the many other policemen. Last of all the hand-held camera moved down the street to where the Greek lay dead in a kidney-shaped swimming pool of blood: it focused in close on his bare thigh, the bloody tourniquet that Crawshaw had made, and the coin-sized hole from the .45-calibre bullet. Last, and most shocking of all, the television reporter lifted the dead man's head by the hair the better to show his lifeless features to the camera.

The commentary was no less sensational than the pictures.

'This criminal filth,' snarled the reporter, shaking Parmenides by the hair, 'was almost certainly responsible for the brutal murders of six young women.' He bent forward to shout into the bloodstained ear.

'You were scum,' he yelled. 'A filthy animal. Being shot like this was too easy for you, you shit. You should have been made to suffer, just like those women you murdered, you cunt. I hope that they give the police officer who plugged you the George medal for killing you. And if, somehow, your greasy spirit can still hear me, we all hope that you burn in hell, you scum. For what you did, you should have been – '

Jake found the remote control and turned it off. Then she drained her glass. What she had seen left her feeling sickened. Somehow she had had to see it on television for it to sink in that she had killed a man.

After a minute or so she began to be aware of an empty feeling in the pit of her stomach and her hands started to shake. Then her skin started turning hot and cold. Absurdly she found herself recalling details from her university first-year psychology notes about the way in which her own brain's hypothalamus, like a tiny temperature gauge, would be trying to control her body's autonomic nervous response to what had happened; and about René Descartes's notion of human beings as reflex machines. It was strange how one thing put you in mind of another.

That smile she had seen on Parmenides's face. Her father's sardonic smile. She was quite shaken by the memory of it.

Tears welled in her eyes and when she walked to the

bathroom her legs felt unsteady beneath her. She was retching before she was even halfway through the door.

Nobody understands me.

Certainly a lot of people think they do. The other day I was in the Mystery Bookshop and I stopped in front of this bookcase and it was full of studies in the psychology of multiple murderers, or serial killers as they are also sometimes known. Yes, I mean full. There must have been at least fifty different titles. I browsed through a few of them. But not one seemed to me to have properly listened to the words of the supernatural songs they each claimed to have understood so well.

Mostly these books on why people become multiple killers boil down to two separate theories.

There is the old-fashioned Marxist theory that interprets the multiple's behaviour as the product of historical materialism: society's original victim metamorphosing into society's oppressor. And then there is the more modern, but essentially Nietzschean view that the multiple has an intense desire not to reject but to belong to society – a society in which fame is the touchstone to success and where murder is merely the short cut to its achievement.

Neither one of these vulgar interpretations of violent criminality seems particularly satisfactory. Perhaps I can explain it better.

In "The Adventure of the Copper Beeches" Sherlock Holmes explains his 'art' of detection as 'an impersonal thing – a thing beyond myself'.

So it is also with the art of murder.

'Crime is common. Logic is rare,' he informs Dr Watson. 'Therefore it is upon the logic rather than upon the crime you should dwell.'

Yes indeed ladies and gentlemen, logic. Logic, where nothing is accidental. Logic, which deals with every possibility and where all possibilities are its facts.

The logic of murder is a darker knowledge that follows the diligent study of an intellectual hatred. Now unlike love, hate's a passion in my control, and a sort of broom to clear the soul. Once set free it shows how man at one time walked on earth before Christian love began, and how a man might walk when all such things are past. How hatred of God may bring the soul nearer my God, to thee.

17

Jake thought it might have been the Scotch. She awoke late and found that she had enjoyed her soundest sleep in years. And she felt better than she could have imagined possible. Better than perhaps she had a right to. As if she had been purged of something. True, she had thrown up, but now she was more ravenously hungry than something as epistemological as the voice of conscience would have allowed. It was not just a complete absence of guilt for what had happened: after all she had not meant to do anything but wing Parmenides. It was something else altogether. A feeling as if a great weight had been lifted from her, that it was time to put certain things behind her and start again.

For once Jake had something in the fridge. She made herself a lavish breakfast of fresh orange juice, Greek yoghurt, bananas, strawberries, seedless grapes, toast and honey, and some strong coffee, and wolfed it all down.

She knew it was wrong to think that some kind of account had been settled, but that was how it felt. And try as she might, Jake could not experience a sense of revulsion at the notion that somehow Doctor Blackwell had been right after all. That the horror she had experienced at having shot and killed a man had dislodged something that had been stuck like a fishbone inside of her. There were no easy explanations for what had happened but, for perhaps the first time in her adult life, Jake felt at peace with herself.

When she arrived at the Yard the first visitor to her office, Ed Crawshaw, managed to restore Jake's faith in herself even further.

'I tried to call you last night,' he explained. 'Where were you?'

She shrugged. 'I didn't feel like speaking to anyone.'

Crawshaw nodded. 'I was at the Greek's flat all night, in Balham,' he explained. 'I thought you might feel better about what happened if you could have seen what we found there.'

'What did you find there?' she said quietly.

He paused for a moment and took a deep breath. 'Hell,' he said, finally, and then shook his head. 'Unspeakable.'

'Then just tell me that I shot the right man, Ed.'

'No doubt about it. Parmenides was the Lipstick Killer all right. We found some tapes he made: sort of a diary I guess. Pretty sick stuff, most of it. Apparently he came here and met you, right? And he was VMN-negative?'

Jake nodded.

'And this Lombroso killer tried to top him as well?'

'That's right.'

'Yes, well it seems as if Parmenides thought that almost becoming the victim of another multiple killer himself endowed him with a kind of immunity. He decided that acting as any normal citizen would have acted in the circumstances and coming here with the Lombroso killer's A-Z was the best way of demonstrating that he was just that: a normal citizen – just in case anyone wondered any different. Least that's what was in his diary, anyway.'

'I guessed it might be something like that,' said Jake.

Crawshaw shrugged. 'Who knows? Maybe he also reasoned that by coming here and, within the course of the Lombroso inquiry, confessing that he was VMN-negative, it might also have nullified the effect of his mental state becoming known to us within the context of our inquiry into the Lipstick killings.'

Jake frowned. 'Well, I met him and I'm not sure he would have been capable of the kind of sophisticated thinking you're suggesting, Ed. I think I prefer your first explanation.'

Crawshaw nodded. 'Yeah. Yeah, you're probably right.' He smiled and moved towards the door. 'Incidentally,' he said. 'It was the bookshop where he was selecting them. In his flat we found hundreds of murder-mysteries. The funny thing was that he never seemed to read any of them. Most of the books were still in their paperbags.'

He nodded with an air of tired satisfaction.

'I think it's time you went home and got some sleep,' said Jake.

Crawshaw yawned. 'I guess you're right.'

'And, Ed?'

'Ma'am?'

'Thanks.'

Later that same morning, after receiving a congratulatory call from Gilmour, Jake tried the Ministry of Health again.

For several minutes she was shunted from one bureaucrat to another like a delivery of horse manure. Finally she was permitted to explain her request to a civil servant called Mrs Porter, whose double chin and smoker's cough seemed to Jake a poor advertisement where matters of the nation's health were concerned. Mrs Porter was not enthusiastic about Jake's request.

'Let's get this straight,' she wheezed. 'You want someone in this department to check the personnel records of all male nursing and auxiliary medical staff in London and the South East, to see if among them, there are any men who are German, or of Germanic origin. Is that right?'

Jake confirmed that it was.

'Are you quite sure that you can't be a little more specific, Chief Inspector?'

Jake offered that if she could have been more specific she would very likely have been halfway to making an arrest. 'All I've got is a suspect's racial genotype and the probability that he's employed in some kind of nursing or auxiliary work.'

'I don't mean to sound unhelpful,' said Mrs Porter, 'it's just that since we became part of Federal Europe, there are quite a few Germans working in British hospitals. It would help if we could try and narrow down that sample. If you could give me the name of a few regional health authorities, something.'

'I can't, I'm sorry. Couldn't you use your computer to do the checking?'

Mrs Porter's voice took on a weary tone. 'Yes, well I wasn't planning to try and do it manually,' she said. 'Look here, what I mean to say is, I'll do my best for you. All right?'

'Thank you. I appreciate it.'

'But these things do take time to set up. Much longer than they take to carry out.'

Didn't it always? reflected Jake. There could be little question that the male obsession with mathematics had helped to make the world a more dangerous place. But had the technology which it had inspired actually made things any easier? Jake had her doubts.

'How long?'

'A couple of days.'

It was depressing, Jake thought bitterly, but managed to fix a smile to her face all the same.

'Any earlier than that would be great,' she said. 'But a couple of days would be fine.' There was no point in trying to bully the woman. No point at all. Unless she wanted to end up with nothing.

She was beginning to wonder how much her own reliance on male technology was affecting her ability to reason as a woman. Jake liked the idea of feminine intuition a lot more than she liked the phrase with all its implied patronisation. She preferred a more scientific approach to account for sex difference in cognitive ability. But there was no doubt in her mind that it was something like feminine intuition which was now required in this particular case. A change in attitude and approach of the kind that she had lectured the conference in Frankfurt about.

Men had a tendency to complicate matters, to look for problems before they looked for solutions. They were obsessed with their own importance and, it seemed to Jake, they did their best to guard this with unnecessary obfuscation.

Women were more straightforward, less romantic in their thinking. What was needed now was a simpler thought process than all the computers and laser-tracking technology seemed to allow.

It seemed impossible to dig the hole deeper, but perhaps she could dig the same hole in a different place.

The hospital where I work is only a short way south of the River Thames and close to the wreck of HMS Belfast, bombed by the IRA just over a decade ago. On the other side of the river is the Tower of London, and although it continues to receive many visitors every year, I have yet to see it myself, although I have worked in the lab as a pharmacy technician for several years. Perhaps one day I shall take a chance and walk across Tower Bridge and visit it, but there always seems to be something else more important to do.

Not that many people feel inclined to spend much time near the river these days. The large number of illegal immigrants living in boats on the river has made the area near the hospital as dangerous as it is insalubrious. In high summer the stink of untreated sewerage dumped straight into the Thames is almost overpowering. At night the area is such as Dickens might have described, containing a whole underworld of robbers, prostitutes, drug-dealers, sharps, scavengers, beggars, pickpockets and pimps. Of the police there is little evidence, except at the hospital where the protection of nursing staff from their own patients necessitates the presence of a large contingent of armed constables.

On one occasion, the dispensary itself was subjected to a well-organised raid when several men armed with sawn-off shotguns held us up and stole every drug we had, killing a dispensary porter who offered them resistance. You can still see the bloodstain on the dispensary floor where he fell. When two of the robbers were caught, it was this hospital which supplied the drugs to Wapping New Prison (formerly the offices of The Times newspaper), where their sentences were carried out. And it was me who prepared the two insulin injections which sent them into irreversible punitive coma. (Insulin is no longer used: the ticket being one way only. Today the penal system employs other substances, like TLG, or HL8, the effects of which can be reversed, although sentences of irreversible PC are frequently handed out. Especially for convicted murderers.)

It says something about the state of a modern hospital that it supplies drugs to prisons to put men into comas. This place used to be the most famous teaching hospital in the world. I once saw a film, made over fifty years ago, which was all about the humorous carefree lives of the nurses and medical students who were at this place. How quaint it all seemed then, and how very English. Of course the major changes are that this is no longer a teaching hospital, no longer part of something called the National Health Service, no longer surrounded by grass and trees. A high fence now encloses the hospital, and medical students now learn their medicine in Edinburgh – the one university hospital still to receive a direct grant of money from the Government – or somewhere abroad. Anyone who was a medical student here in 1953, when that film was made, and who saw the hospital now, probably wouldn't even recognise it as a hospital at all.

Still, the work is satisfying enough, in an unimaginative sort of way: preparing ointments, capsules, suppositories and medicines. Most of it is cheap substitute stuff for more expensive drugs which are manufactured in Germany or Switzerland. I wouldn't touch any of it myself. If I'm sick I attend a private clinic where they can get all the proper drugs. Mind you, I have to pay for it and so it's just as well that I don't have to manage on a pharmacy technician's miserable allowance. Fortunately my parents left me a substantial income from a trust fund. The fact is, I needn't work at all, however it is real work among real people and when I am doing it I don't have to think about anything else. Dealing with drugs and medicines requires that one be very precise and this exactness in what I do is the most pleasing part of it. Everything is what it is and not another thing. And of course there's always the added attraction of an armful of something decent.

I'm not at all unusual in this. Most of the people I work with are involved in some kind of substance abuse. There are even one or two of them supplementing their meagre incomes by manufacturing methadone at home which they then sell to the local Chinese.

Not that I can imagine why they want to bother with methadone when the junk-city contains plentiful supplies of good opium, which is about the only thing – apart from feeling-up the occasional cagegirl – to get me down there. A couple of afternoons a week you'll find me aboard a particular junk moored close to Bermondsey Wall, smoking ten or fifteen pipes. Just like Dorian Gray. On average, I have about thirty or forty a week. This is not at all excessive. There are men I know, and not just Chinese, who smoke maybe two or three hundred pipes a week.

The best thing about opium is what it does to time. Or to be more precise, what it does to the way one judges time. After a couple of pipes you have the impression that you might have been on the boat for a day at least. You ask yourself 'What time can it be?' Then you pause for a moment, perhaps imagining some vast clock-face, before stating a time. The idea is accompanied by a feeling of great conviction, inasmuch as you say a time to yourself with perfect assurance and without feeling any doubt whatsoever. If you were to ask me the reason for this feeling of conviction I would have none. I could not explain it any more than I could describe the aroma of coffee.

So then, sometimes I will say to myself, 'I am sure that several hours must have passed, and that it must be at least ten or eleven o'clock at night.' But when I consult my watch and I see the correct time I realise that perhaps *as little as ten or fifteen minutes have actually elapsed. That a quarter of an hour has become half a day. In this way it can be seen how time is little more than an aspect of human will.*

It's at times like these, when I'm wondering about the riddle of life in space and time, that I think the solution lies outside time and space altogether. Outside my own life itself perhaps. It's true, suicide is a very old solution to a very old problem, but perhaps ultimately it is the only solution. What is certain is that it is the final solution.

18

The next day, Jake called Sir Jameson Lang to discover whether or not he intended to cooperate with Professor Waring's plan.

'I rather expected you'd be calling,' he said. 'Waring said you were opposed to his idea. But you see, I've really no choice but to do as they ask. Trinity is no longer as rich as it was. In fact, college finances are pretty tight. The University has been pursuing the Government for a rather lucrative grant. I don't think it would be too pleased if I put the Government's nose out of joint at this precise moment in time. You know, I'm not even sure if I should be talking to you, Chief Inspector. They warned me that you might try and dissuade me.' He looked awkward and embarrassed on Jake's pictophone screen.

'Are you telling me that they threatened to withdraw this grant?'

'That's about the size of it, yes. And I don't mind telling you, I wish I'd never set eyes on any of you people. The whole business has me worried sick. My academic reputation won't be worth a damn if any of this ever gets out.'

'Is that all you care about? What about due process? What about this man's life? Think about that for a moment. You're talking about persuading another human being to take his own life. Exactly where does that fit into moral philosophy, Professor?'

'You're right to regard it that way, as it happens,' he said. 'This is almost certainly one situation where moral philosophy can make a practical contribution to the solution of an actual moral dilemma. I've thought about this a great deal and I think society will be served if I can persuade this maniac to kill himself instead of other people.'

'Sounds to me as if you'd rather rely on utilitarianism than on your own intuition, Professor,' Jake replied. 'Your own gut-feel.'

'It's no good basing a moral approach on intuition. No good at all. Different people have different intuitions.'

'But surely you don't reject the idea of intuition altogether?'

'Not for a moment, no. I'm in favour of intuitions. But which ones? We have to judge intuitions, to see which is the best one to have. And the best way of doing so is through a higher level of critical moral thinking.'

'And how's that to be done?'

'We have to do our moral thinking in the world as it is,' he argued. 'But at the same time we are constrained by the logic of concepts. Facts are observed. Values are chosen. The intuitions we ought to cultivate are those which have the highest acceptance utility. Now I can't see many people, apart from you, Chief Inspector, who would argue with trying, for the greater good, to persuade a man who has already killed a dozen innocent people to do away with himself. It seems to me that you are arguing from a rigidly legalistic principle. But you're not looking at the facts of the matter. Look at the facts first, then decide what principles you should adopt.'

'So why does my intuition tell me that what you're planning to do makes you feel uncomfortable, Professor?' she asked him. 'Is it that you prefer to contemplate these moral dilemmas from the comfort of your rooms in Trinity College perhaps? Utilitarianism is a rather sharp sword for a philosopher to have to wield.'

'Oh it's not that I'm squeamish,' Lang declared. 'Only that I doubt that philosophical argument is entirely equal to the task. In my opinion they would be better advised in having a forensic psychiatrist to talk to this fellow. However, Professor Waring disagrees. He believes that

Wittgenstein would prefer to talk to me: that he finds it intellectually flattering to cross swords with a Cambridge professor of philosophy. Waring says that philosophy is what this whole thing is about.'

That much seemed certain, Jake thought.

She turned away from the empty pictophone screen and banged her desk with frustration. Somehow she knew that Waring's plan might well work and that unless she thought of something, and quickly, Wittgenstein's collar was going to slip through her fingers. Perhaps his own as well.

Later that same morning, Jake's thoughts returned to this picture she had of things slipping through fingers. Somehow it brought to mind Wittgenstein's *A-Z* again, and a teasing game she had sometimes played at school.

She called Detective Inspector Stanley and asked him to bring Wittgenstein's *A-Z* to her office immediately.

It had been a simple childish sort of joke which involved grabbing a novel by D. H. Lawrence, or some other moral iconoclast, from the briefcase of a friend and, with the aim of embarrassing her, trying to determine if the book was at all inclined, by the implication of an excessively frequent consultation, to fall open at one of the more lurid pages. As if to confirm her theory now, Jake drew open the desk drawer and took out her own copy of London's *A-Z*. She balanced the book by its perfect bound spine on the palm of her hand and allowed it to fall apart into two sections, at the pages covering that area of south-west London where New Scotland Yard is located.

Stanley arrived carrying the *A-Z* in a plastic evidence bag as if it was a goldfish he had won at the funfair.

Jake flung her own copy aside and grabbed the bag from out of Stanley's outstretched fist. His jaw dropped as she tore off the special warning label that had been stapled on to it.

'This is such a simple idea that I can't imagine why I didn't think of it before,' said Jake, and took hold of the book.

'What are you doing?' hissed Stanley. 'That's evidence. You can't handle that. There are fingerprints on it — you'll spoil them.'

'Shut up,' said Jake and repeated the simple manoeuvre. The book parted itself slowly and then lay open on her palm like an exhausted bird. Jake uttered a yell of satisfaction.

'Just like *Lady Chatterley's Lover*,' she said. 'It opens first where it's most been read.'

She scanned the two facing pages of streets, underground stations, parklands, dual carriageways, fire stations, and hospitals, closely, as if she had been reading from the Book of Life.

'Pages seventy-eight to seventy-nine,' she murmured. 'From Waterloo Station as far east as Rotherhithe; Tower Bridge down to Peckham Road. Let's see now. There are one — two — three — four hospitals in this area. And one of them is Guy's.' She stated this last fact as if it had been what the thunder said.

Stanley corrected his shirt collar. 'I'm sorry I don't quite see the significance,' he said.

'Don't you?' said Jake, turning to her pictophone screen and keying out Mrs Porter's number at the Ministry of Health. 'Guy's Hospital was where the real Wittgenstein worked, during the war. In the pharmacy.'

'That's a hell of a hunch you're playing.'

'Have you got a better one?'

Stanley shook his head.

When Jake found Mrs Porter, she asked her to check for a German or a man of Germanic origin who might be working at Guy's.

'My goodness, you have narrowed it down,' said Mrs Porter. 'Right then. No problem at all. Just give me a couple of minutes.' She turned away from the pictophone camera and devoted her attention to her computer.

Jake waited with patient expectation, like someone having her Tarot read by a famous clairvoyant. Stanley looked on, vaguely disapproving. Finally, Mrs Porter looked back at the camera.

'At Guy's Hospital there are three male persons of the racial type you've designated,' she said, with all the natural sententiousness of her profession. 'A Mister Hesse and a Mister Deussen, but both of them are surgeons. And then there is a Mister Esterhazy, who works in the hospital pharmacy.'

'He sounds interesting,' said Jake. 'Can you send me all there is on him?'

'Well really I should get the Chief Secretary's permission . . .'

'Mrs Porter,' said Jake. 'I can't tell you too much, but people's lives are at stake here.'

'Then I can't very well refuse,' said Mrs Porter. 'It's not much, but I'll send you what's in the file.'

'Is there a photograph?'

'No, I'm afraid not.'

'Damn,' said Jake. 'A handwriting sample, perhaps?'

'Er yes, a small one.'

'Then send that as well, if you would, please. And thanks, Mrs Porter. You've been a great help.'

Jake gave Mrs Porter her computer's data communication number and then watched as the information started to arrive on her screen.

'Right,' she said to Stanley. 'Let's make a MAP.'

Jake moved the Ministry of Health's data onto one half of the computer screen while on the other she called up an investigative menu. From the twenty available files she selected the one titled 'Criminal Information Database'. The computer gurgled for several seconds and then provided Jake with another list. Finding 'Multiple Homicides' featured as File Number 15, Jake typed that number and waited. The system was hopelessly antiquated with a response time that could infuriate all but the most patient of people: sometimes Jake found herself waiting as long as thirty seconds for the computer to find a specific information file. Once again the computer gurgled and once again a series of further choices appeared before her eyes. Finally Jake managed to key into the Multiple Analysis Program.

As developed by her former employers, the European Bureau of Investigation, the MAP was the very latest expert guidance system for assessing a suspect's personality as a possible multiple killer. From a worldwide database of some 5,000 multiple killers, compiled over a period of fifteen years, the MAP included up to 300 common characteristics of known multiple offenders.

The detective fed information about a suspect into the computer. Then the MAP awarded a certain number of possible points for each item of information that tallied with known multiple behaviour. For instance, the MAP awarded maximum points if the suspect was white, since it happened that most multiple killers were white. Blacks could only obtain a maximum number of points in this respect if the victim was elderly and white: this was because the existing database showed that murders of elderly whites were most commonly committed by blacks. When all the information available to the detective had been fed into the computer, the MAP counted up the number of points and offered the detective a statistical probability that the suspect was indeed a multiple killer. Even then there was nothing automatic about what resulted from the program's assessment. The sole responsibility for if and how the results were used remained the detective's. For Jake it was the one computerised system of investigative analysis that she actively enjoyed using.

Stanley stood over her shoulder as Jake started to key in the information using the Ministry's personnel file on Esterhazy as a reference. When it came to the suspect's religion Jake was surprised to see that Esterhazy had described himself as a Manichean.

'What the hell's a Manichean?' Stanley growled.

'Manichean? It's not really a religion at all,' Jake explained. 'More a kind of viewpoint that considers Satan to be co-eternal with God. Equal sides of the same coin, so to speak. St Augustine was a Manichean for a while, until he thought better of it. Eventually it was denounced as a heresy.'

She glanced at the record of Esterhazy's distinguishing marks. 'Excellent,' she murmured. 'This guy has three tattoos.'

The EBI held that tattoos were one of the most common physical similarities among multiple killers. Examination of the bodies of 300 multiple killers, dead or alive, had revealed that almost 70 per cent of them were marked in this way. It was generally held by forensic psychiatrists that self-mutilation was often an early indicator of criminally aggressive behaviour. The greater the percentage of body area covered with tattoos, the greater number of points the MAP would allocate to the suspect.

She glanced over at the laser-printer as it sprang into swift action.

'Is that the handwriting sample they're sending?' she asked Stanley.

Stanley leaned over the machine and inspected the printout. Then he tore it off the main sheet and handed it to Jake.

She opened her desk drawer and took out a magnifying glass which she passed over the handwriting as if she had been looking for a fingerprint. Graphology had been a major part of her training with the European Bureau of Investigation.

'Look at this,' she murmured. 'The handwriting is hardly joined up at all. It's mostly capital letters. Small ones too.'

Stanley bent over her to take another look.

'Neat though,' he observed.

'Too neat,' said Jake. 'This is someone who's really straining to keep things under control. It's almost like he could explode at any minute. I wonder when this was written.'

'Maybe when he joined the hospital,' Stanley suggested.

Jake typed a description of Esterhazy's handwriting onto the program.

'Other distinguishing characteristics?' She picked up the glass and was silent for a minute while she searched again. Finally she handed Stanley the glass.

'Take a look at the way he writes his letter "W",' she said, pointing them out on the copy. 'Here, and here.'

'It's more like a letter "V",' said Stanley. 'With a stroke in the middle. Like a pen nib.'

'But don't you think it's actually rather vaginal?'

Stanley looked again.

'Now you come to mention it,' he said. 'Yes, you're right, I think.'

Jake typed her description and then pondered her own graphologist's analysis.

'You know, that might just indicate a possible Oedipus complex.'

'The bloke who fucked his mother, right?'

'Yes, Stanley,' she said coolly, 'the bloke who fucked his mother, Jocasta. More pertinently, he also murdered his own father, Laius, King of Thebes.'

'So what does that mean?'

'It means that our friend here may be paranoid. He may resent paternal and, therefore, all male authority. Believe me,' she added, 'I know what I'm talking about. That's one thing Esterhazy and I have in common.' She smiled to herself, and glanced sideways at Stanley but his crumpled face registered no sign of surprise. She almost thought there ought to have been a fanfare of trumpets.

'That sounds criminal enough,' said Stanley. 'Where does this bastard live?'

Jake glanced up at the side of the computer screen still containing the details of Esterhazy's personnel file. She

318

hit the keyboard to send the cursor in search of this information.

'Nurses' home, at Guy's Hospital,' she said.

'The nurses' home?' Stanley sounded shocked.

'I imagine it's the male nurses' home,' Jake said patiently.

'Whatever it means, he sounds like a bit of an outsider to me,' said Stanley. 'Leastways someone who's not much at home in this world.'

'You could be right,' said Jake. 'But let's see what the program says, shall we?'

She finished typing in the rest of the information and glanced over the result.

SUBJECT:	Paul Joseph Esterhazy
Age	35
Racial Type	White Caucasian
CHILDHOOD:	
Siblings	None
Brought up by 2 Parents	
Brought up by 1 Parent	Yes
Brought up by Foster Parents	
Brought up in Care	
Juvenile Record	None
ADULT LIFE:	
Dropped out of School	No
Dropped out of Further	
Education	Yes
Criminal Record	No
Marital Status	Single
Sexual Preference	Heterosexual
Religious or Other Belief	Manichean
Credit Rating	Positive
PHYSICAL:	
Height	1.72m
Weight	59kg
Eyes	Blue

Hair	Brown
HIV	Negative
Tattoos	3
Recent Psychiatric History	Unknown
Recent Medical History	Suffers from insomnia
Previous Sexually Transmitted Disease	Yes/ Gonorrhoea
Drug Abuse	Yes

EMPLOYMENT:

Describe	Pharmacy technician
Shift work	Yes
Overachiever	No
Underachiever	Yes
Length of Employment	5 years
Employer's Assessment	Highly intelligent, very reliable, private, quiet, possibly introverted, keeps himself to himself.

HANDWRITING SAMPLE:

Appearance	Meticulous, capital letters.
Distinguishing Characteristics	Something vaginal about the letter W [♥].
Analysis	Possible Oedipus complex: might indicate paranoia; subject may have resentment of paternal, and hence all male, authority. This might occasion criminality.

VICTIM(S) AND MODUS OPERANDI:

Sex of Victim(s)	Male
Racial Type	White
Age of Victim(s)	Various
Choice of Weapon	Gas gun
Mutilation	Negative
Anthropophagy	Negative
Souvenirs	Unknown

Sexual Abuse	Negative
Hour of Day	Various
Day of Month	Various
Geographical Factors	Mainly in London area

When she was satisfied that there was nothing more she could usefully add, Jake instructed the program to calculate the degree of probability. The machine gurgled, emptied half of the screen, flashed several colours and was silent for almost a minute. Finally a number arrived on screen.

'56.6 per cent probable,' said Jake.

'Not much better than an even chance,' said Stanley.

Jake grunted. Accessing the original MAP once again, she asked to review the existing 300 characteristics of the database. This took several minutes to read through.

'You know,' said Jake finally. 'There's nothing here about transportation. What's a multiple's most common mode of transport?'

'Truck,' said Stanley, hardly hesitating. 'Small van, or an estate car.'

'Right,' said Jake. She cleared the screen and accessed the main menu. This time she selected the National Vehicle Licensing File to check if a vehicle was registered to Esterhazy. After a short pause the computer returned with the information.

'Bullseye,' said Jake. 'He owns a blue Toyota Tardis van, registration Gold Victor Bravo 7–8–3–7 Romeo. Now if we assume that the van is worth another three points, that takes us to almost 60 per cent.'

'That's a bit more like it,' agreed Stanley.

Jake started typing again.

'One more thing,' she said. 'That racial marker we had from the killer's DNA . . .'

'A German. So?'

'So Esterhazy isn't an English name.'

'It isn't?'

Jake fed Esterhazy's name and identity card number into the computer.

'It's Hungarian or Austrian, I think. Let's see what his birth certificate says, shall we?'

A copy of the document flashed up on the screen.

'Parents born in Leipzig,' said Jake. She looked at Stanley triumphantly. 'I'd say that about clinches it.'

Five minutes after Jake finished the Multiple Analysis Program, Detective Sergeant Jones came into her office. He was holding a compact disc and looked angry.

'Yes?' said Jake. 'What is it?'

'It was orders,' he said. 'From Gilmour. I didn't have any choice.'

Jake guessed what he was talking about. 'Wittgenstein called, didn't he?'

Jones took a deep breath. 'About half an hour ago. Gilmour said you weren't to speak to him.' He glanced awkwardly at his shoes. 'He told me to leave it to Professor Lang to handle the conversation.'

Jake nodded numbly. 'With what result?'

'I brought the recording,' said Jones and handed her the disc. 'I'm sorry, ma'am.'

Jake smiled bitterly. 'It's not your fault. Did he say that he was planning to kill another one?'

'No, I don't think so.'

'What about Lang's little suggestion? Do you think that it had its desired effect?'

Jones shrugged. 'Hard to say, ma'am.'

'All right. Get onto Airborne Surveillance. See if they can find a blue Toyota Tardis van, registration Golf Victor Bravo 7–8–3–7 Romeo.'

Detective Sergeant Jones leaned on Jake's desk and made a note of the number.

'Come on, Stanley,' said Jake, heading out through the office door. 'We'll listen to the recording in the car.'

'Where are you going?' Jones shouted after them.

'Hospital,' said Jake. 'To get my fucking head examined. Maybe they can tell me why I bother coming here.'

'That's all we need,' Jake screamed as the car twisted loudly onto Victoria Street. 'This madman to go and top himself just as we're in sight of arresting him. I could kill those stupid bastards in the Home Office.

'Better put the siren on,' she told her driver. 'We need to make tracks.'

Jake switched on the disc player and inserted the recording.

'I'm afraid you'll have to settle with having me today,' Jake heard Lang tell Wittgenstein, much as if he had been apologising to a student for another don's absence from a tutorial. 'Chief Inspector Jakowicz is unable to come to the phone right now.'

'The lying piece of shit,' said Jake. 'So much for moral philosophy.'

'I hope she isn't sick,' said Wittgenstein. 'I hope she isn't upset because of what happened the last time. I had promised to talk, after my lecture. To discuss things.'

'No, no,' insisted Lang. 'It's nothing like that.'

'Well, something more important, no doubt,' he replied, sounding rather piqued. 'I dare say we can get along without Chief Inspector Jakowicz, just this once.'

Immediately she heard Wittgenstein's voice she realised that he sounded different: lacking confidence, tired, depressed even. And as their conversation progressed he allowed the professor to take the conversational initiative, to lead the argument. He seemed hardly sure why he had bothered to call at all. He spoke quietly, in dull monotones, with long, ponderous silences. Jake realised how vulnerable he might actually be to whatever phenomenological interrogation Lang had planned for him.

'Man is a temporal being,' said Lang.

'Yes,' said Wittgenstein dully.

'A self-creating being who chooses his own fate, wouldn't you say so?'

'Oh, I agree.'

'And being conscious, through one's own will of one's own temporality, then the only real certainty about the future is . . .'

'. . . is death,' added Wittgenstein.

Jake held on to the door handle as the car swerved through traffic.

'To live well,' she heard Lang say, 'to really live life to the full, you have to live in the hard light of that fact.'

'Absolutely, yes,' said Wittgenstein. 'That is both one's nature and one's ultimate fate.'

'The more so in your case.'

'How so?'

'Well,' said Lang, 'it seems to me that by killing all these other men who, like you, tested VMN-negative, you are merely postponing your real desire to take your own life.'

'There may be something in what you say.'

Jake punched the back of her driver's headrest.

'Can't we go any faster?' she yelled. Out of the corner of her eye she saw Stanley nervously lift his Adam's apple clear of his shirt collar as the car gave a lurch of speed forward. The driver, who was used to angry demands from the back seat that he should go faster, betrayed no emotion on his lean moustachioed face. He fed the steering wheel through his strong hands as calmly and expertly as if he had been making a perfect circle of pizza dough. In front of the car, the traffic widened like an opening zipper. Speeding past Waterloo Station and round the three-storey-high shanty town of hardboard and corrugated iron, they almost hit a vagrant who was standing motionless in the middle of the road like a traffic bollard. They missed him by only a few centimetres.

'Stupid bastard,' Stanley muttered, twisting around in his seat to look through the rear window at the quickly shrinking figure. 'Someone ought to move all these people.'

'I think I'm right in saying, Professor Wittgenstein,' said Lang, 'that suicide has been rather common in your family. Not to mention the fact that your own adolescent hero, Otto Weininger, took his own life.'

'You're right, of course. My brother Rudolf killed himself. It was a merely theatrical gesture. Weininger's death was altogether something else. It was an ethical acceptance of an intellectually predisposed fate. A noble thing.'

'As I recall, there were many Viennese men who were moved to kill themselves in imitation of Weininger. But you did not. Was it simply that you did not dare to kill yourself? That you did not have the courage?'

Wittgenstein uttered a long, deep snort of amusement. 'You're very good, Professor. I see your game. Well perhaps you'd call it a game. It certainly isn't a perfect game. It has . . . impurities. I compliment you. Well then I shall also call it a game. Existential Leaps, perhaps. But only because I am dazzled by your ideal.' He spoke languorously, as if savouring the full implication of Sir Jameson Lang's design. 'It is quite admirable.'

'I am glad that you think so,' said Lang, apparently undisturbed by Wittgenstein's complete understanding of what he was trying to achieve. 'If I may add one more thing, however . . .'

'I should insist on it.'

'I'd be correct in assuming that you believe in God?'

'Yes, you would be correct.'

'Therefore, you have the perspective for suicide. The God relationship and the Self. That's very important. I mean, any atheist can commit suicide. They have no sense of spirit. The point about suicide, that it is a crime against God Himself, altogether escapes the atheist. Well, what I'm trying to say is this: all this time I imagine you've been thinking that in killing these other men you were killing God.'

'That's fair I suppose.'

'I won't ask you why. I'm not interested why. But I'm sure you have your reasons. Whatever they are, I respect them. I feel quite sure you must have given the matter a great deal of thought. But look here, if you really want to wave two fingers in the face of God, then you've been missing the point. That's not the way to do it. To flee from existence itself is the most critical sin, the ultimate rebellion against the Creator. What is required of you is intensified defiance, the heightening of despair.

'The last time we spoke you described yourself as an artist. I don't doubt it. Only as such, yours is a common dilemma: the sin of living life in the imaginative as opposed to the real world, of Art instead of Being. Naturally God plays the crucial role in your heightened sense of despair. In your secret torment, God is your only hope, and yet you love the torment and will not abandon it. Somehow you are aware that what you must do is let go of your torment and take it upon yourself in faith, and that you cannot do. So your defiance of God intensifies and you kill others to prove it. But, as I say, real defiance is shown most of all by killing oneself.'

Wittgenstein sighed. 'Perhaps you're right,' he said wearily. 'What you say about the artist's existence feels true.'

'How do you feel about killing yourself?'

There was a long silence.

The car left Southwark Street and sped along Southwark Bridge Road into Borough. St Thomas Street. Guy's Hospital. The security guards on the gate lifted the barrier and stepped quickly back as the car roared past.

'Does it make you feel afraid?'

Jake cursed Lang loudly.

'Do you believe in eternal life?'

'Eternal life,' Wittgenstein whispered, 'belongs to those who live in the present.'

Jake heard him smile as he added:

'Is some riddle solved by me surviving for ever? Is not this eternal life itself as much of a riddle as our present life? When the answer cannot be put into words, neither can the question. Well then. The riddle does not exist. And the solution of the problem of life is seen in the vanishing of the problem.' Then he rang off.

Jake buttoned down the electric window and leaned out of the car to address the gate-keeper.

'Where's the nurses' home?' she asked.

'Nurses' home? You're a bit out-of-date, aren't you? That closed two years ago.'

'Drive on,' said Jake. 'We'll try inside the butcher's shop.'

The car accelerated forward and came to a screeching halt at the hospital's front steps. Jake sprang out of the car and raced up to the front door where, startled by the speed of her arrival, two police guards met her with pointed guns. She waved her ID in front of their bovine faces and demanded to be taken to the hospital administrator.

The first policeman took off his cap and scratched his head. 'Don't have one, ma'am,' he said.

'The manager then,' she said. 'The director. Whoever's in charge.'

Both men continued to look puzzled.

'Who is in charge?' the first policeman said to his colleague. 'I dunno.'

'Ask her,' suggested the other, and pointed to a nurse.

'We want the person in charge,' the first policeman said to the nurse. 'The one that runs the place.'

The nurse smiled unpleasantly, as if she had been about to provide some very nasty medicine.

'Make your mind up please,' she said. 'Which is it to be? The person in charge, or the person who runs the place? They're not the same.'

Jake resisted the temptation to draw her weapon and press it to the nurse's forehead.

'We want someone who knows about the personnel who work here,' she said patiently.

'Well why didn't you say? You don't want the person

who runs the place. You want a personnel director. But which one? Student, surgical, nursing, administrative, technical or . . .'

'Technical,' yelled Jake. 'I want a pharmacy technician.'

'All the way down that corridor, then second corridor on your right, fourth door on the left,' said the nurse and walked quickly away.

Jake turned to look for Detective Inspector Stanley and found him leaning against one of the graffitied walls, already looking decidedly greenish. Hardly disguising her contempt, Jake said: 'Oh yes, I was forgetting about your stomach, wasn't I. You'd better wait outside.'

Stanley nodded weakly and staggered out of the doors.

'I'll come with you ma'am,' said one of the policemen. 'It's best I do, to be quite frank. You never know who's hanging around in this place. There are some very dodgy types who walk in and out of these doors, I can tell you. It's not like the Metropolitan Police Clinic at Hendon.'

'All right,' said Jake. 'Come on then.'

They walked briskly down the foul-smelling corridor the nurse had directed them to. Further away from the entrance hall, they started to find that the corridor was lined with patients lying on the floor, some of whom got up from their dirty mattresses to beg for a few dollars towards their hospital bills. The guard thrust them all roughly aside.

The technical personnel director's office was opposite what looked like a bank vault, but was in fact the hospital dispensary. Another two armed guards stood on either side of a barred window in a steel-plated door. The door to the personnel director's office was made of reinforced glass. Jake's guard pressed the bell and lifted his mug towards the video camera scanning the both of them.

'Visitor for the TPD,' he said.

The door buzzed and sprang open.

The technical personnel director's office was small and barely furnished. The telephones looked like they'd been there since the hospital was built. The computer was a cheap Strad such as the poorest student might have owned. A half-eaten hamburger lay on the desk. On the television were some girls doing aerobics in costumes that were a couple of sizes too small. From the prurient camera-angles it didn't look like the kind of aerobics that the viewer was meant to join in with.

Jake confronted a Welshman wearing a pinstripe suit and a zip-up cardigan who smelt heavily of sweat and fried food. She handed him her identity card.

'I'm Chief Inspector Jakowicz,' she said. 'I was hoping to find one of your employees, Paul Esterhazy, at the nurses' home, however I understand from the gate-keeper that it has closed. Is Mr Esterhazy currently in the building?'

'It's his day off,' said the director, examining Jake's identity card with considerable interest. 'Murder Squad, eh? Is Paul in trouble or something.'

'It is very urgent that I speak to him, sir,' said Jake. 'Do you have his present home address?'

'He only lived in the men's hostel very briefly,' said the director. 'Temporary like. Just while he found himself somewhere permanent to live.'

'Well then if you could just oblige me by telling me where that is.'

The man's piggy eyes narrowed. 'Paul wouldn't harm a fly, you know. I've known him for years. Gentle as a lamb, he is.'

Jake, who wished she had a dollar for every time she'd heard that, said that she merely wanted Esterhazy in order that he could help her with her enquiries.

'But that's always what you people say when you arrest someone. Are you going to arrest Paul? Because if you are, I'll have to speak to the hospital lawyer before I can give you his address.'

Jake sighed and asked why.

The man smiled a patronising sort of smile. 'Believe me, Chief Inspector,' he said, 'there's not much that we do in this hospital that we don't speak to the lawyer first of all. If you only knew the number of malpractice suits we have to deal with here.'

'Look,' Jake hissed back at him. 'I'm not one of your damned patients, and I'm in a hurry, so if you wouldn't mind . . .'

The director tut-tutted and shook his head. 'Well, put the case that I did give you Paul Esterhazy's address, which I'm not saying I do have, mind. And put the case that you went there to arrest him. Put the case that while you were there arresting him you, or one of your men, shot Esterhazy. Put the case that prevented by law from suing the police, he or his family might well decide to sue the hospital instead, for releasing confidential information to you.'

Jake nodded grimly. 'Very well then. You give me no choice. Put the case that you give me Paul Esterhazy's address this minute, or I shall be obliged to arrest you.'

'On what charge?'

'Double parking. Sex with a minor. Drunk and disorderly. Come on, will you? What charge do you think? I'm a police officer trying to do my duty, and you're obstructing me. So what's it to be? Postal code or caution?'

'Look, I'm not refusing to give you his address, see? I'm only saying that I should call the hospital lawyer first of all.'

'I've no time for that,' snapped Jake. 'The address now, if you please.'

The director turned to face his computer screen, his face wrinkled with displeasure. He tapped the keyboard several times, then stood up and went over to the tiny printer which was already in action. Finally he tore off a sheet of paper and handed it to Jake.

'Thank you,' she said crisply.

'Now perhaps you'll tell me a little more of what this is all about.'

But Jake was already walking out. 'If you leave your

TV on for long enough, you'll find out,' she yelled out from the corridor.

Outside again, Jake found Stanley and her driver waiting patiently for her beside the BMW.

'Docklands,' she said, as she came down the steps and jumped into the back of the car. 'Ocean Wharf as fast as you can.'

Stanley was opening and then closing the car boot.

'Come on,' she shouted. 'Let's go.'

He got in beside her and she saw that he was cradling a pump-action shotgun.

'Just in case,' he said, patting the weapon like a favourite pet. 'That's a pretty tough area.'

The car leaped forwards, heading east again, Druid Street and the Jamaica Road along to the Rotherhithe Tunnel, under the Thames where the air was cool and fetid. Then the sun again as the car emerged onto Limehouse Road in the shadow of the Docklands Light Railway overhead.

Turning south onto West Ferry Road, they caught sight of the Isle of Dogs, and then the car was immediately enveloped in a swirl of gritty dust blowing like a mini-typhoon off one of the area's many abandoned building sites. Rotting nineteenth-century houses, their sides shored up with baulks of timber, their roofs patched with corrugated iron gave onto modern tower blocks that stuck out of the dusty, rubble-strewn landscape like giant cacti. A helicopter skimmed around the pyramidical roof of Canary Wharf, hovering like a bluebottle: it was a unit of Airborne Surveillance on permanent attachment to protect what was left of what once had been the pride of the Docklands development from the depredations of the sordid colonies of wooden shanty-housing which, at a short distance away, surrounded it.

Canary Wharf Tower was startlingly different from any other object in sight. It was an enormous structure of sunburnt steel and glass soaring up, floor after empty floor, 300 metres into the air, and visible from as far away as Battersea. From the backseat of Jake's BMW it was just possible to read, picked out on its electronic advertising hoarding of white neon lights, in elegant green lettering, the rotating slogans of the only three companies which had offices there:

GOLDSTEIN LIFE ASSURANCE. BECAUSE YOU MIGHT NOT LIVE TO REGRET IT.

THE YAMURA 22-CARAT GOLD COMPACT DISC. 8 OUT OF 10 JAPS SAY THEY PREFER IT.

ROYAL MARSDEN ONCOLOGICAL INSURANCE. A LUMP SUM, JUST WHEN YOU NEED IT MOST.

Keeping pace with the toy railway as if they had been following some drug dealer who was aboard it and making a desperate attempt to escape the police, they had Canary Wharf, Heron Quays and South Quay on their left, the whole business area of the Docks on the other side of a maze of barbed wire and surveillance cameras. Even the streets leading up to its outer barriers were patrolled by private security guards in black uniforms with jointed truncheons.

The car turned down one of these side streets where a small gang of youths had collected in front of a bonfire and were engaged in teasing a stray dog, and as if in confirmation of the area's tough reputation, a rock bounced off the BMW's toughened windshield, and Stanley worked the magazine of the riot gun expectantly.

'Relax,' said Jake, as the car pulled up to the fortress of razor-wire that was the Ocean Wharf compound. But she herself felt anything but that. The security guards waved them through, and in the car-park, beyond the entry gate, stood a blue Toyota Tardis van. They checked the registration.

'Looks like our man's at home,' Jake said as she caught sight of it. If Wittgenstein was indeed contemplating suicide by now, thanks to Sir Jameson Lang's persuasion, then being a pedestrian in Docklands would have been a good way of doing it.

There were four apartment blocks in Ocean Wharf and Jake consulted her printout to see which one was home to Wittgenstein.

'Winston Mansions,' she said as they climbed out of the car. 'Seventh floor. Let's hope we're not too late.'

Stanley looked up at the height of building. 'Let's hope the lift is working,' he added.

Inside the glass doors of Winston Mansions a fruity voice was describing a commercial for a brand of dog food that promised to produce less dog waste than any other brand. The voice came from a television screen behind the doorman's desk. When the doorman saw Jake and Stanley he turned the volume down, and the voice sank somewhat, though the words were still distinguishable. People rarely ever turned a television off completely.

'Is Paul Esterhazy at home?' said Jake, flashing her ID in front of the doorman's face, although there was no need. He had already seen the police car.

'Went up about thirty minutes ago,' said the doorman. His eyes stayed on the screen. 'Want me to call him?'

'Metaslim. Increase your metabolic rate. The only effective way to help you lose weight,' said the television.

'No,' said Jake, going towards the lift. 'We'll announce ourselves.'

Stanley pressed a button to summon the lift.

'S'not working,' said the doorman. 'Company that's supposed to service it went bankrupt.'

Jake glanced around the lobby. 'The stairs,' she said. 'Where are they?'

The doorman pointed at a brightly lit corridor behind him. At the end of it was a grey steel door. Jake started towards it.

'Save you a journey,' the doorman added. 'Supposing you was planning to go up to the seventh floor. Mr Esterhazy's the only tenant on that level. So he keeps the fire doors locked from the inside, for security, when I'm not around. S'made of steel, just like that door in front of you, miss. You might bang on it all day and he wouldn't hear you.'

All through this explanation the doorman's eyes never strayed from the television screen. He was like some small animal hypnotically fascinated by the movements of a snake.

'Want me to call him now?'

Jake smiled politely and nodded with slow patience.

The doorman buttoned a number on the internal pictophone and then turned back towards the TV.

'Usually takes a while for him to pick it up,' he explained.

A minute passed with no answer.

'Are you sure he's in?' Stanley frowned.

'Only one way up, only one way down. Unless he jumped of course.'

'Perhaps you were distracted,' offered Stanley. 'By the TV.'

The doorman looked scornfully at the policeman. 'Nothing worth watching,' he said. 'No, he's up there all right. In trouble then, is he?'

But it was Esterhazy who answered first.

'Yes, Joe, I'm here. What do you want? I'm a bit busy right now.'

'Not me,' said the doorman. 'The police.'

Jake recognised the voice immediately. It was Wittgenstein all right. There was no mistaking that voice. She pushed the doorman gently aside and looked into the pictophone.

He sat with his head tilted slightly to one side. Looking like an excrescence of thought, the curly hair grew wildly towards the same side as the angle of his head. The thin face was almost completely expressionless, but as Jake studied it more closely she saw something sulky and slightly petulant about it. It was the eyes that held Jake. They stared out from the deep shadowy hollows of his face as if from behind a masque, like the eyes of some nocturnal animal. She was reminded of photographs she had seen of survivors of the Nazi concentration camps.

'It's me,' she said. 'Chief Inspector Jakowicz.'

Esterhazy smiled broadly.

'My dear Chief Inspector,' he said smoothly. 'Is this a social call or are you here on business?'

Jake's heart was in her mouth. She had him. There was no way he could get away from her now. In a way she was almost sorry.

'I'm here to arrest you.'

'Well, what a relief. I thought you were going to try and bore me into killing myself, like your Professor Lang.' He laughed. 'The very idea of it: ridiculous.'

'No, nothing like that,' she said.

'You know, I've been expecting you,' he said. 'By which I mean I believed that you would come, though your coming did not occupy my thoughts. I don't mean that I was eagerly awaiting you, Chief Inspector. What I mean here is that I should have been surprised if you hadn't come at all.'

Out of the corner of her eye Jake caught sight of Stanley, his lips pursed in a silent whistle and his forefinger revolving suggestively next to his forehead.

'Well, I'm here now. Can I come up and talk to you?'

'But we're already talking, aren't we?'

'In person.'

'I am, in person. If I were not I should already be dead.'

'I wish to talk to you about a number of murders,' Jake said stiffly. It was the cop coming out in her and she flinched as she heard herself. She added, more gently, 'Don't you think it would be better – ' But it was too late.

'This despotic demand of yours,' he said. 'This wish . . . Curious that you should have used that word, with its expectation of non-satisfaction. I wonder, what is your prototype of non-satisfaction? Strange, isn't it?

That a wish seems already to know what would satisfy it, even when that thing is not there at all. Even when it could not possibly exist.'

Jake tried to hang on to the conversation. 'It seemed simple enough when I said it.'

Esterhazy tutted fussily. 'You of all people should know that wishes are a veil between us and the thing wished for. It's a problem for you, I know, to speak to someone like me with something as crude as ordinary language.'

'We seem to be getting into a dead end here,' said Jake.

'Easy, isn't it? In philosophy. In life. But you're right, a dead end is exactly what this is, for both of us. For your philosophical investigation and for mine.'

He smiled, sadly it seemed to Jake.

'I agree. So why don't you stop wasting time and let me come up and we can sort it all out?'

'I'm afraid I cannot permit that. You see I have no intention of being "sorted out" as you put it. That would mean spending the next thirty years of my life in a punitive coma. Now that really would be a waste of time.'

'You know there's no way out of here,' said Jake.

'Oh but there is,' said Esterhazy. 'By the time you manage to break in here, I shall be squaring the circle, so to speak.'

Stanley frowned. 'What's he mean?' He looked belligerently at the doorman. 'You sure there's no way out?'

Jake said to Stanley, 'He means Infinity. He's going to kill himself after all.'

'Oh not because of any argument deployed by that fool Jameson Lang,' said Esterhazy.

'So why?'

'As I said, I have no intention of wasting time in a coma. As soon as you arrived here, I realised the game was over. You're the reason I have to kill myself, Jake. You're the reason.'

'Please,' she said, 'don't do it.'

'You mustn't blame yourself, Jake. It was always part of my plans.'

Covering the microphone with her hand, Jake asked the doorman if there was a way onto the roof.

'Don't try and stop me,' said Esterhazy.

'I can't let you go like this,' said Jake. 'Aren't you afraid?'

The doorman handed Stanley a set of keys.

'I'm touched,' said Esterhazy. 'Really I am.'

'Don't think I'm climbing all the way up there with you,' said the doorman.

'But, Jake, you don't understand. Feeling the world as a limited whole – now that is something to be afraid of.'

The screen went blank. Jake turned to the doorman.

'These apartment buildings usually have some kind of window cleaner's hoist on the roof. Is there one up there?'

'Sure,' he said. 'But it's never been used these past twelve months. The cleaning contractor went bust at the same time as the lift company. I don't know that I'd want to trust my life to it.'

But Jake was already through the door to the stairs, followed closely by Stanley.

He said nothing until they were standing on the roof, recovering their breath.

'Look, ma'am,' he wheezed. 'Why don't we leave it to the TFS? Let them handle it, eh?' He helped Jake to manoeuvre the hoist out over the edge of the roof.

'What? And let them shoot him dead? No, I want this collar. I want a proper trial. Besides, by the time they get here he may well have topped himself.'

She climbed into the hoist and inspected the controls which required two operators standing at opposite ends. Stanley peered nervously over the edge.

'Best for him, best for us, eh? Save us the bother.'

'You sound like one of those bastards at the Home Office,' she said. 'Look, are you getting in or not? I can't operate this thing by myself.'

'But it's ten storeys,' pleaded Stanley. He shook his

head grimly and climbed aboard. 'I don't know why I'm doing this. The bloke's a nutter.' He took hold of the control handle and nodded to Jake at the other end of the platform. 'What do I care if he tops himself or not?'

The hoist jerked and then dropped half a metre.

'Slowly,' yelled Jake.

'What the fuck happens when we get to his window? Suppose he doesn't decide to top himself? Suppose he decides to kill us first? What then?' Stanley drew his gun as he spoke. Jake was already holding hers. The hoist was moving smoothly now.

'When we get to the seventh floor, we'll shoot the windows out,' said Jake. 'Then climb inside.'

'Jesus,' muttered Stanley, and trembled visibly.

Jake looked up at the distance they had covered. The sun had lent a huge fireball to the smoked windows of the top two floors. For a moment Jake had the thought that she and Stanley were both disposal experts working to defuse some huge nuclear device which had exploded in their faces. A blast of wind cooled her face and shook the hoist under their feet. Stanley groaned. They reached the seventh floor. She blinked and tried to focus through the brightened window and when at last she saw him it was like seeing an X-ray photograph develop in front of her eyes.

There is nothing that cannot be solved by murder, money, or suicide. I've killed an apostolic number. And I've got plenty of money. Which only leaves option three. No problem.

If, as Malraux says, 'death changes life into destiny', then suicide makes destiny subject to personal choice. In life's great bridge game it's the last card you can play.

Naturally enough, suicide affects the total perception of a life in a way that no other death can ever do. Fatal car accidents, air-crashes, cot-deaths, executions, even murders are as nothing when you take a long look at the sui side of life. If eternity changes us into what we really are, then suicide is the ultimate moving force for that change.

Take Mr and Mrs Suicide, Vincent and Sylvia: what would their reputations have been had they not killed themselves? Both were completely unknown at the time of their deaths. But after that dread act, not only does their work become famous, but also a certain poignancy attaches to it. They achieve the status of artistic martyrdom. Their works become icons.

No such delusions on my part need detain us here. Nor is my self-slaughter referable to my recently concluded philosophical dialogue with Professor Sir Jameson Lang. His arguments, strongly reminiscent of something Kierkegaard once wrote, were already familiar to me. Indeed I hold his truths to be self-evident.

The fact is that it was already in my mind to kill myself and it might just as well be done now as later on. Especially as my mind is clear and equal to the task of

the great philosophical discourse with the terrible name-
less one which will follow the big sleep.

How then, am I to tell you of the circumstances of my
death?

Do you wish to be told plainly that I returned home
and hanged myself? Even if it were true, it would not be
much of an end to my life's story. To say only what is
true is as dull as it is to say nothing except what can
be said, that is, something that has nothing to do with
philosophy. Although this method is the only strictly
correct one, I suspect it may not be satisfying to you.
Naturally you require something more, something metaphysical perhaps. I am sorry to have to disappoint you.
No doubt you would have preferred some story of the
way I killed myself, and what happened immediately
after my death. Some story which might serve as an
explanation for everything that has gone before.

But my stories only serve as explanations in the following way: anyone who understands these stories eventually
recognises them as nonsensical when he has used them
as steps to climb up beyond them. Just as, in a few
minutes, I will use some steps to climb up and put my
head in a noose. Like me, you must also, so to speak,
throw away the ladder after you have climbed up it. You
must transcend the story as a mere proposition, and then
you will see the world aright.

I regret that circumstances prevent me from saying any
more than this, however what we cannot speak about
we must pass over in silence.

19

The switchblade was still open in her hand, the blade a razor-sharp, silver thumbnail protruding from her clenched fist. She held it by her side, at an arm's length, like one of the Sharks or the Jets in *West Side Story*, ready for the rumble. Only the rumble was over. Even now the two ambulancewomen were manoeuvring the man's body on to the trolley. They strapped him down as if he might have preferred to get off and walk. Not much chance of that, Jake thought. Not with a crushed windpipe.

Pleased with the way the knife had performed she lifted it up to inspect it more closely. She had bought it on an impulse, while holidaying in Italy the previous year. Just something to put in her shoulder bag and make her feel a bit safer, when she wasn't carrying her gun. She was almost surprised that she should have used it in the particular way she had.

The two ambulancewomen lifted the top of the trolley clear of the wheels and then steered the man by remote control, out into the corridor outside the apartment and towards the lift door, like a toy she had once had as a child. Not a toy for a girl, her father had said. Better than a toy for a girl, Jake thought.

Downstairs, in the lobby, the doorman did what he was supposed to do and held the door open while they steered the man out into the car-park. The trolley collided with the back of the ambulance rather too vigorously, it seemed, and automatically engaged the electronic lift. This picked him off the tarmac like a binful of garbage and drew him inside the long body of a vehicle that was covered with advertisements for Lucozade and

Elastoplast. At the very second the door closed beside him, the blue laser light on top of the roof started to flash in all directions like random bolts of lightning.

The two ambulancewomen regarded Jake and, more especially, the knife that was still in her hand, with some uncertainty. One was about to say something but then her colleague caught her eye and shook her head as if to indicate that it was probably best if they didn't ask any questions. Their job was just to collect their fare and take him to hospital. Nothing more. But the woman holding the knife spoke to them.

'Where are you taking him?' she said. 'Which hospital?'

One of the ambulancewomen shrugged and held up the man's identity card.

'Depends on his ID,' she said. 'I haven't stuck it into the computer yet. As soon as we do, his bar code'll tell us where he's registered, and that's where we'll take him.' So saying, the woman holding the card climbed into the driver's seat.

Jake pointed out two men sitting in a nearby police car.

'See those cops?' she said to the second woman.

'I see them.'

'They'll be following you. So try not to lose them.'

'Sure, anything you say, lady.'

Jake watched them drive away, Stanley following in the police car, two sirens whistling like sex-mad construction workers. When they were out of sight she went back inside the door of Winston Mansions and up to the seventh floor where a motorcycle cop, who had arrived on the scene at the same time as the ambulance, was already restraining those other residents of the building who were curious to see what had happened. The door to Esterhazy's flat stood open. Jake walked into the apartment, picking her way carefully across the pile of shattered glass that had been one of the windows, and surveyed the scene.

The apartment was simply, even starkly furnished, with none of the sensational features that might have delighted some tabloid newspaper intent on depicting the mind of a serial killer as an aspect of interior decoration. There were no heads parboiled in pots still hot on the cooker, no torture chamber, no paintings or photographs of dead bodies, no collections of women's underwear, no human skin hanging on a tailor's dummy awaiting a needle and thread, no glass case with guns and knives displayed like so many insects and spiders. There was only one picture – a portrait of Sir Winston Churchill which, matching the mural in the lobby downstairs, Jake suspected had been there since the time Winston Mansions was built. Esterhazy's own peculiar gun was still in its shoulder-holster, which hung from the back of a chair.

It was true that Jake found the colour scheme in Ester-hazy's apartment was not to her own taste: a royal blue carpet, black woodwork, and yellow walls. Blue and yellow were classic opponent-process colours, mutually antagonistic to each other as neural sensory experiences, but that was hardly an indication of homicidal mania. The plain fact was that Esterhazy's apartment seemed to provide no more obvious insight as to what had turned him into a mass-murderer than might have been obtained from the leaves in his tea cup, or a selection of Tarot cards. How ordinary it all seemed, and then all the more extraordinary, because of the nature of the man who lived there.

It was not the first time that Jake had encountered this phenomenon. She was quite used to the idea that mass-murderers could live what were outwardly quite ordinary lives. It was the thoughts in their heads that you had to worry about, not the pictures on their walls or the tro-phies in the display cabinets. Real evil, she knew, did not always adorn its home with black velvet curtains and human skulls for ashtrays. The most unusual thing in the whole place was the severed end of the rope tied round one of the beams, from which Esterhazy had tried to hang himself, and the fallen stepladder he had used to climb up to the noose, and which he had then kicked away: the ladder which, no more than a minute or two afterwards, she herself had used to climb up and cut him down. It was Jake who had given Esterhazy the kiss of life. The taste of him still lingered on her lips. It was strange, perhaps because of what he was, something dangerous, something alien to her, but somehow she had almost enjoyed breathing the life back into him, as if he had been some drowned sailor, or Don Juan washed up on her island.

And for what had she saved him? It was as well, she reflected, that she was not a sentimental person, because she well knew what it was to which she had delivered him. Jake lit a cigarette and smoked it, irritated with herself now, for there is nothing of so infinite vexation as one's own thoughts. She tried to tell herself that what happened to Wittgenstein, to Esterhazy, was not her affair. She had done her duty, according to the law, and in spite of the very best endeavours of nearly everyone around her.

It would be up to others now, the lawyers, the judges, the psychotherapists, and probably the politicians, what became of him. Perhaps he would succeed in a not-guilty plea by reason of insanity. She remembered having once said something about making sure that he got medical help, so she would make sure that a forensic psychiatrist other than Professor Waring was able to examine him. Perhaps the fact that there had been several articles in the various medical and psychiatric journals to the effect that, based on his writings alone, the real Wittgenstein might have suffered from some sort of bipolar-affective disorder (what was once called manic-depressive psychosis), would count for something in helping to sustain a plea of insanity.

The truth was that having done her duty Jake's sincerest hope was not that she could help the Crown Prosecution Service to build a water-tight case against

Esterhazy, but that he might end up with something better than an ice-cold needle in his vein. This was a strange sensation for her. Normally she didn't much care one way or the other what happened to the men she arrested. But then Esterhazy was hardly like any other man she had ever known.

That was what she hoped. But in Jake's heart she knew it would be different. In her heart she had always known it would be different.

She sat down at Esterhazy's desk to wait for the scenes-of-crime officers. She noted all the computer equipment, and then the black-rubberised Reality Approximation Outfit which lay on a special leather recliner like a discarded shadow. If he had been into that kind of shit, she said to herself, then there was no knowing what might be in Esterhazy's mind. There were some people who said that protracted use of RA was every bit as dangerous as LSD. Then she noticed two notebooks on the desk, one brown and one blue, and curious about what was in them she opened the brown book.

Six Months Later

A crowd had gathered outside the front gate of Wandsworth Prison. It was early evening and its number continued to be swollen by people who were on their way home from work. The mood was quiet but even so, a small squad of riot-police was in attendance.

Jake arrived early, having misjudged the time needed to get through the evening traffic. She parked her car in a nearby garden centre and, to fill in time, bought some geraniums for her window box. As she waited for the assistant to debit her cash card, it crossed Jake's mind that she could buy some flowers for Esterhazy, that he might welcome some colour in the last few hours of his conscious life. She glanced about her and, seeing nothing that wasn't rooted in soil, asked the assistant if they had any flowers. He sniggered and pointed out to the yard where there were hundreds of plants flowering.

'What do you think they are?' he sneered.

'No, I want cut flowers.'

The man's sneer grew deeper. 'This is a garden centre,' he said. 'Gardens grow, know what I mean? You want cut flowers I suggest you walk down to the cemetery on Magdalen Road. You'll get cut flowers there, although speaking for myself, I can't imagine anyone wanting to cut something down as was already growing.'

'Spare me the botany lecture,' said Jake, and selected a well-bloomed hyacinth, one of the new red variety, from a box nearby.

'You don't want to take that one,' said the assistant. 'That one's in full flower. Be finished in a day or so. Best have one that's still budding.'

Jake shook her head. Another day would be too late for Esterhazy. 'No, this one will do just fine.'

'Please yourself,' said the man.

Having placed the geraniums in the boot of her car, she walked on towards the prison gate. She thought it was probably safer to leave her car where it was, than in front of the prison. Just in case anyone decided to slash her tyres on the off-chance that the car belonged to a member of the prison staff. The sun had set but she kept her sunglasses on, to stop anyone recognising her. Esterhazy's trial, and her own role in his capture, had been well reported on television. But the crowd paid Jake little attention as she walked up to the gate, deceived by the red flower she held in her hands. There weren't many police or Home Office officials arriving at HMP Wandsworth who brought flowers with them. She had presented her ID and was through the door in the gate before any of the demonstrators were aware that it had opened and closed.

'You here to see the jab?' enquired the warder still holding Jake's identity card in his gloved fingers.

She said that she was and the warder picked up a computer.

'Just a mo', while I check you off on the guest-list,' he said. He grinned to himself as his forefinger held down one of the keys. The computer clicked like a geiger-counter as it scrolled down a long list of names. 'We wouldn't want any gate-crashers, would we? Yes, you're all right, ma'am.' He glanced uncertainly at the potted plant.

Jake wondered if he was thinking of inspecting it for drugs or something.

'Is that for him?' he said.

'Yes. All right?'

The warder shrugged. 'Under the circumstances, I s'pose so. I'll get one of my men to walk you down to the new wing.'

'Don't bother. I know my way.'

'Fair enough,' said the warder and returned to reading the previous day's edition of the *News of the World*. On the front page was a photograph of a rather bemused-looking Esterhazy, underneath a headline which read, 'PSYCHO KILLER GETS THE HOT MILK TOMORROW'.

Jake grimaced and walked quickly away.

Wandsworth's Punitive Coma Wing was of recent construction. It had even won an award from the Institute of European Architects. Built of red brick, like the Victorian walls which surrounded it, the PC wing was a large dome resembling an observatory from the outside, and a library from the inside. Reinforced-concrete ribs supported a ceiling of many windows which from beneath looked like the huge eye of God. Around the interior circumference were what seemed to be large filing drawers, many of which, like a mortuary, contained the comatose bodies of convicts.

The PC wing was colder than the outside air, being partly refrigerated, and, dressed in a light linen summer-suit, Jake was soon shivering. She quickened her step as she crossed the main floor underneath the eye of the dome, heading towards the holding cells.

The sight of one open drawer, slightly larger than a coffin, interrupted her step. Curious, she stopped to examine it more closely. The bottom of the drawer was upholstered in soft black calf leather, which was the only concession made to the prevention of pressure sores. A number of tubes and catheters, which would be attached to the convict's body, protruded from the drawer's sides. On the front of the cabinet was a small flat screen on which the body functions could be read and a card key lock to prevent anyone from interfering with the drawer's occupant. Jake's shiver progressed as far as her jaws, and rubbing her bare arms she quickly carried on her way.

In an antechamber close to where Esterhazy was spending his last few conscious hours, a small group of people had assembled. Most of them were faces she recognised from the Home Office and the Brain Research Institute: Mark Woodford, Professor Waring, and Mrs Grace Miles. For the first time, television cameras were also there to cover the event, having successfully petitioned the High Court that if print journalists were allowed to witness such events, then why not other media as well?

Jake stopped to see how ITN was covering the event and was all the more interested when she saw that the programme was being presented by Anna Kreisler. She herself had been the object of serial killer David Boysfield's obsession; and this was the case which Jake had made the subject of her lecture to the EC Symposium on law and order when first she had been requested to command the Wittgenstein investigation. It all seemed like a very long time ago to her now.

Anna Kreisler, elegantly suited in Chanel, with the slightly plastic good looks and perky air of a model airhostess, was responding to questions posed on air by an unseen studio anchorman. It was an indication of the importance that ITN were attaching to coverage of the punishment that Kreisler was there in person and not behind her usual desk in the studio.

'What's the atmosphere like there in Wandsworth Gaol, Anna?'

'Well, as you can imagine, Peter, it's very tense here. A sizeable crowd has gathered outside the walls of Wandsworth Gaol to protest against Paul Esterhazy's punishment, and although the police are in attendance, they're not expecting any trouble. This kind of thing differs very much from what used to happen with capital punishment because, unlike then, now there is no expectation of a last minute reprieve. Telephone calls from the Home Secretary commuting a sentence to life imprisonment are a thing of the past, because of course there is no such thing as life imprisonment. I spoke to the prison governor a little earlier and he told me that Paul Esterhazy ate a light dinner at around five o'clock and that he refused the opportunity to speak to a priest. Since then I understand that he's spending his last few hours watching television.'

'So he might even be watching this broadcast. Anna, we still don't know much about Esterhazy's motives for these dreadful crimes: at the trial it was suggested that the balance of Esterhazy's mind may have been affected by protracted use of reality approximation programs. Has there been any word from Esterhazy himself as to what made him into a mass-murderer? Any indication of remorse?'

'No indications of remorse whatsoever, Peter. Of course, we now know that the background for these murders was the Lombroso Program and that, like Esterhazy himself, many of his victims had been given the names of famous philosophers in order to protect their identities. Esterhazy was himself an undergraduate at Oxford University until he was sent down for drug abuse, and some commentators have suggested that this may have brought about a resentment of intellectuals in general, and philosophers in particular. It's also a bizarre coincidence, but like the real Ludwig Wittgenstein whose name Esterhazy was given, he himself came from a rich Austro-Germanic family, and spent some time working in the pharmacy at Guy's Hospital. This was one of the factors which was alleged to have contributed to Esterhazy's failed defence of not guilty by reason of insanity.'

'Anna, you've spoken to lots of people who have met Esterhazy. What kind of a man is he?'

'By all accounts, a highly intelligent one, Peter. Well read, well educated, skilled with computers. He was popular at work too. Many of the people who knew him at Guy's said he was a nice man, well-mannered, the studious type who wouldn't have harmed a fly. But at the same time it seems he was a rather solitary, lonely figure. We know how he became estranged from his parents many years ago, and so far there has been no sign that they have any wish to re-enter his life at this late stage in the day. Records also prove that Esterhazy was married for a while, but his wife divorced him and has since changed her name. All attempts to trace her have so far proved fruitless.'

'So in many ways, even now he's in custody awaiting punishment, Esterhazy remains something of a mystery?'

'Very much so, Peter. What's frustrating a lot of people is that carrying out this punishment today might mean we never discover any more about him. But it's only fair to say that Esterhazy may be something of a mystery even to himself. There have been occasions, especially during the trial, when he seemed unable to distinguish between reality and an approximation of reality, as I think you mentioned earlier. For that reason there are lots of people who believe that the proper place for Paul Esterhazy is not in a PC drawer, but in a hospital for the criminally insane.'

'You mentioned the Government's Lombroso Program, Anna: where do you think this leaves that and other controversial aspects of the Government's law and order policy?'

'Critics of the current policy, most notably the opposition spokesman on Law and Order, Tony Bedford MP, have argued that the Lombroso Program constitutes an invasion of human rights and should be scrapped. But I think that's unlikely to happen, Peter, since the European Court has already ruled that since the accent of the Program is on care and counselling people who have an innate capacity to develop an aggressive disorder, the Program does not constitute a violation of human rights. Nevertheless radical changes will have to be made, not least to the Program's security, and it's being said that heads will have to roll. But until the results of the public inquiry, we won't know how the system's security was breached and exactly who will be held accountable. And of course until that result, the Program itself remains in suspension.

'I'm now joined by the Minister for Law and Order, Mrs Grace Miles. Mrs Miles, how do you answer the critics of punitive coma who say that it is a cruel and unusual punishment and has no place in a civilised society such as ours?'

Mrs Miles smiled, almost painfully.

'First of all, Miss Kreisler, let me correct an earlier remark that was made about the Lombroso Program. The Lombroso Program is not just this Government's policy. It is part of the policy of the European Community, as enacted by all the member nations in the European Parliament. It just happens to have been introduced in this country first of all.

'Now to your questions about punitive coma, I would say this: the European Court has ruled that it is neither cruel, nor unusual. This kind of punishment has existed in the United States for a number of years and has many proven advantages, which I don't propose to discuss now. This hardly seems like the most appropriate time. However I will say this about its detractors. What surprises me about them is that their arguments are the same arguments that these same people used to use against the return of hanging. I myself was, and am against capital punishment. But everyone felt that in certain cases, such as this one, some punishment tougher than imprisonment was required. I think PC does that job very well indeed. And the best argument of all for PC as the law's ultimate sanction is that, where mistakes are made – and let's face it, any system is fallible – a sentence can be reversed. I would only add to that that there is clearly no room for doubt in this particular case.

'Moreover, I for one welcome the presence of cameras here today. The public has a right to know about the punishments meted out in its name and at the taxpayer's expense. Just as long as the faces of those participating in the execution of the sentence can be obscured. I look on this kind of broadcasting as performing a valuable public service.'

Jake could stand no more of someone as manipulative as Mrs Miles defending the freedom of the press, and walked slowly away from the cameras. She was surprised to find Mark Woodford come after her. She hadn't seen him since the day when he and Waring had tried to persuade her to let Sir Jameson Lang try and talk Wittgenstein into killing himself.

'Haven't had a chance to speak to you,' he said. 'But well done, you know. For catching this poor fellow. No hard feelings?'

Jake shook her head. 'I was just doing my job.'

'That's right. We were all acting for what we thought was the best, weren't we? By the way, congratulations about your promotion. I hear you're heading up the Murder Squad, now.'

'It's just temporary,' said Jake. 'Until they can get someone to replace Challis.'

Woodford lowered his voice. 'Oh I wouldn't be surprised if you ended up doing the job permanently,' he said. 'The Minister likes your style.'

Jake glanced back at Mrs Miles who was still talking to Anna Kreisler.

'I can't say I care much for hers.' She shook her head. 'I can't say I care for my own very much either. Not when I see a circus like this.' Jake was walking towards the chief warder.

'Well just remember this: it was you who found the star act.'

'Like I said, Woodford, I just did my duty.'

'You heard that Doctor St Pierre resigned?'

Jake said she hadn't.

'Oh yes. It's not public yet. But someone's head had to roll for what happened. And St Pierre was the obvious candidate, I'm afraid. There's a new security chap on it now. He's going to change the whole system procedure, before the Program is implemented throughout the European Community, so there shouldn't be any more problems of unauthorised entry. And when the thing is up and working it really will make your job a lot easier.'

Jake smiled sardonically. 'I wonder,' she said. 'Well, if you'll excuse me.'

She went over to the chief warder and asked if she could see Esterhazy alone for a few minutes.

The warder looked at the flower and then at Jake. 'What's the plant for?' he asked suspiciously.

'It's for Esterhazy,' she explained. 'Something beautiful for him to see and smell before he's PC'd.'

'Against the regulations probably. But under the circumstances, I suppose it'll be all right. This way, if you please.'

Jake found Esterhazy watching television in his cell, under the watchful eyes of two warders. His hands manacled in front of him he was sitting on the edge of a chair, engrossed in the BBC's outside broadcast coverage of his own punishment. When he saw Jake he turned and smiled.

'Ah, the hyacinth girl,' he said. 'You know I shall miss

colour most of all. It's my experience that one only ever dreams in black and white.'

Esterhazy was older and more distinguished than Jake remembered from the trial. Lofty even. Like someone who was easily tired by the mundane thoughts of his fellow men. She was struck by his physical resemblance to the real Wittgenstein. Only he was more athletic – vigorous even – than she might have imagined. And there was about him an air of electric intelligence such as Doctor Frankenstein might have set his sights upon in creating his famous creature. He spoke in an exaggerated sort of way, like a character from some Victorian melodrama. His restless eyes became fixed for a few seconds on the flower in Jake's hands. She said nothing. He rose from his chair, took the pot out of her trembling hands and laid it on the table beside the television set.

'How kind of you to bring me a red flower,' he said. Nostrils flaring he pushed his whole muzzle into the bloom and closed his eyes.

Jake heard him breathe deeply through his nose, savouring the sweet scent of the flower. He repeated this behaviour several times before his eyes opened again. He glanced at Jake and she saw mischief run down his face like a bead of sweat.

'If I had asked you to bring me a red flower, would you have looked up the colour red in a table of colours and then brought a flower of the colour that you found in that table?'

Jake shook her head. 'No.'

'But when it is a question of choosing or mixing a particular shade of red, we do sometimes make use of a sample or table, do we not?'

'Yes, we do sometimes,' she agreed.

'Well,' said Esterhazy, returning his slightly-hooked nose to the flower, 'this is how memory and association may be said to work, within the context of a language game.'

'You're still playing games, even now?'

'Why not?' He pouted and pointed to the television screen. 'When I myself am to be made the subject of what might be conceived as a game, albeit a concept with rather blurred edges. Oh yes, I know what you're thinking. You're asking if a blurred concept is a concept at all. Is an indistinct photograph a picture of a person at all? Is a man who is neither wholly dead nor wholly alive still a man?'

'I don't know,' said Jake. 'Perhaps.'

He grinned. 'Then again, perhaps not. It seems to me that I shall be more like this plant. Hair and fingernails pruned from time to time. Watered and weeded. Periodically checked for signs of infestation. But largely shorn of relevance other than the purely symbolic.'

'You killed people.'

He shrugged quickly. 'I envy them.' His grin widened. 'I owe you my life, I suppose. But tell me, what were you saving me for?'

'There are rules in my game too,' Jake said. 'It isn't a proper game if there is some vagueness in the rules. You, of all people, should realise that.'

He sighed and nodded. 'Yes, you're right I suppose.' His smile returned. 'You know, you've done me a real favour, bringing me this little hyacinth. I've been racking my brain for a strapline of less than 150 characters, to put on my drawer's computer screen. One of the condemned man's last little privileges. Too generous. The gentlemen here have been reading me some of the other convicts' lines in the hope that I might be able to decide what I wanted.' He groaned and rolled his eyes. 'Of course, most of them are impossibly sentimental. The average criminal has a rather vulgar turn of phrase, especially when it relates to how he wishes to be remembered. But you have inspired me with this flower of yours. Thank you.'

'What words are you going to have?'

'Surprise,' he said. 'Read my drawer in a couple of hours.'

'I'm sorry about . . . all this. Really I am.'

He shook his head dismissively. 'Will you do me a service?'

'If I can.'

'I understand that it is permitted to visit someone who is in a coma. Gardeners say that if you talk to a plant then it will thrive. Would you come and talk to me now and again?'

Jake shrugged. 'What shall I say?'

'Name things. Talk about them. Refer to them in talk. As if there were only one thing called "talking about a thing". Speak to me as if you were a little girl talking to her doll. You owe me that much for keeping me alive. Will you do this?'

'I never much liked dolls,' said Jake. 'But I'll make an exception in your case.'

He seemed relieved by this assurance.

Finally she asked him why he had done it. What was it that had motivated him to kill all those men?

The bright eyes rolled heavenwards. His accent suddenly turned American.

'My motivation?' He smiled laconically. 'Well gee, it was all based on my inner emotional experience I guess, discovered through the medium of improvisation.' He shook his head. 'Motivation . . . You make me sound like Lee Strasberg, for God's sake. People always ask a killer that question, Jake. "Say, Cody, what made you do it? What made you go and kill all those women?" They must get so tired of being asked that question, and not finding much of an answer. Embarrassing for them. They ruin their lives and don't even have a good explanation for it. So after a while, they try and think of some kind of explanation, just to get people off their backs. And what do they say, these killers? "I had visions of Christ and all his angels telling me to do it." Or, "The voice of Allah spoke to me and told me to kill the infidels". But you know, this kind of explanation goes right back to man's beginnings and was first employed by Abraham.

"God told me to kill my son, Isaac, and I was going to do it." How lucky for Abraham that he heard His voice again, and stopped short of murder.

'Today, when we accept that a killer believes what he says to be true, that religious defence strikes as being evidence of his insanity. And if we think he's bogus and that he's lying about having heard a voice, then we go ahead and jab him. But whichever one applies, this kind of explanation for committing such appalling crimes remains generally comprehensible to us. It's not particularly original, but we can readily accept that there would surely have to be some extraordinary explanation to do something as heinous as kill your mother and your father and your own puppy dog. In a sense, it's the only explanation which people can understand.' Esterhazy smiled to himself and looked distant for a moment.

'But if you want an explanation that's better suited to these modern times, Jake, I'll give you one. If the absence of logic is what characterises faith, then the opposite also holds true. Where one has faith in nothing, then there is only logic that's left to answer to. So just as another man might have claimed that God made him kill twelve men in cold blood, I'm saying that it was not the voice of God which made me do it, but the voice of Logic. I heard the voice of Logic and his ministers of Reason and I had this compulsion to kill.' He smiled wryly. 'It's a different kind of madness, that's all.

'But you've read the notebooks, haven't you?' He shrugged eloquently. 'What do you think? You're the detective. This was your investigation. You caught me. You must have the answers. It's you who have restored the moral order to a world that was temporarily upset by my crimes. How very Shakespearean of you, Jake. Perhaps it's me who should be asking you questions. Well, what do you think, Chief Inspector?'

Jake shrugged. 'Any restoration such as you describe would be an illusion, in my opinion,' she said. 'You ought to know all about illusion, Paul. Look at you, spending half your life with that Reality Approximation machine. Even now you might believe that you're still wearing your RA suit and helmet. If I have an explanation at all, it's that you can no longer distinguish between what is real and what is unreal. But that doesn't make you so very different from a lot of other people. Nobody cares much for reality anymore. Maybe they never did. Is that what you would call a moral order? If you ask me, there's not much balance around anywhere. And this – this investigation was just a holding action. Until the next time.'

They didn't say much more after that. For a few moments she sat in silence and let him hold her hand. She tried to remember the last time she had held a man's hand. Her father had tried to hold her hand as he lay dying in hospital and she had pulled away. Things were different now. She had stopped hating. It was time to be compassionate. To care. Maybe even to love.

Jake left him alone during the few minutes which remained. She would have left the prison if she could. She had no stomach for what was to follow. But the provisions of Homicide (Punishment of Murderers) Act 2005 required that, as senior investigating officer, she be present when the sentence was carried out.

Watched by almost twenty people, to say nothing of the millions watching on television, Esterhazy met his punishment as bravely as was possible, considering that he was already strapped down onto a hospital trolley when the coma technician produced the hypodermic. There was an audible gasp among two or three of the spectators as the needle caught the light from the glass ceiling like an upturned sword. Esterhazy turned his head away from the television camera and waited in silence. The technician swabbed his neck with a piece of cotton wool and the air was filled with the scent of something antiseptic.

The prison clock was still striking midnight as the

needle entered his jugular vein and the plunger was depressed. Coma was almost instantaneous.

Next the body was wheeled into the main storage hall, and under the huge eye, it was transferred to the waiting drawer. Electric wires and pipes were attached to Esterhazy's naked torso, and when everything was in place and working to the coma technician's satisfaction, the drawer was pushed smoothly shut.

Jake waited until the television cameras had gone before moving in closer to read what the technician was typing on the screen: Esterhazy's epitaph. She recognised it as some lines from *The Waste Land*, the ones which followed the hyacinth girl.

> Your arms full, and your hair wet, I could not
> Speak, and my eyes failed, I was neither
> Living nor dead, and I knew nothing,
> Looking into the heart of light, the silence.
> *Oed' und leer das Meer*.

Jake wiped the tear from her eye, collected the hyacinth, and went out into the sunshine.

What can I tell you about what it was like, lying in that drawer one lifetime, and then gone somewhere else, I don't know where? How can I describe it to you?

The picture is something like this. Though the ether is filled with vibrations the world is dark. But one day man opens his seeing eye, and there is light.